COMPLICATED CREATURES

Part One

in the
COMPLICATED CREATURES SERIES

A Novel

ALEXI LAWLESS

VIVRANT
PRESS

PART ONE

PERFER ET OBDURA; DOLOR HIC IBI
PRODERIT OLIM

—Ovid

"Be patient and tough; someday this pain will be useful to you."

PROLOGUE

July—Present Day
Central Jakarta, Indonesia

DERRICK MARKHAM PAUSED at the sweeping expanse of windows overlooking the city. The late afternoon sun burnished the massive construction site below, workers crawling over steel beams and raised earth like arthropods. Derrick imagined his nearly finished skyscraper resembling a hot orange spire rising out of the dense Jakartan cityscape.

"What a beautiful day to close a deal," he murmured, smoothing his tie into place. Today, he didn't want one distracting stitch out of place. He reminded himself that this afternoon's meeting should go off without a hitch. All that hard work, preparation, and negotiation was finally going to culminate in a crisp, satisfying finish.

A brisk knock sounded at his office door before it opened. Turning, he saw his attorney and lead negotiator slip through, carrying a sheaf of papers in a portfolio. Derrick liked the sleek, polished look of her in an elegantly feminine three-piece suit. Samantha was a beauty, certainly, but only a fool would be taken in by her looks. In the time they'd worked together to finalize this deal, he'd become acutely aware that her appearance only distracted from the acuity of her mind. Her eyes gave her away. That cool, obsidian gaze took in everything.

She stopped near him, glancing over his appearance, her brief assessment resulting in a pleased smile. "You look dapper, Derrick. The chairman will appreciate your choice in tie color."

"China red. Not too obvious, you think?" He fiddled momentarily with his cufflinks.

"No, he'll appreciate the nod," she said. "Here are the contracts with the adjustments you agreed on last week." She flipped open the portfolio. "Note the chops for your signature are here. Make sure the insignia faces down, like so." Taking out the marble chop, she showed him deftly which side to press first. "Chow may ask for a clause adjustment on the payment terms, but don't waver. His modus operandi suggests he'll test your mettle by playing hard ball in the eleventh hour to see what competitive offers you may have."

Derrick thought on that a moment. "How do you know that will be his approach?"

Her mouth curved slightly. "Rumor has it."

Derrick tutted while he moved toward his desk to pick up his mobile phone. He'd worked with her long enough to know anything she told him would be founded in far more than mere rumor. Samantha was nothing if not thorough. He appreciated having a partner-in-crime who could help anticipate the chess moves while he focused on finishing the construction of the skyscraper. Derrick could already taste the finish with the conclusion of today's deal, and he felt the impatience to get started flitting at the edge of his concentration. He could hardly wait to board the jet home later tonight. It had been nearly two months since he'd seen his family. He turned on his phone, glancing at the picture of his son on the screen.

"Don't worry." Sam spoke up beside him, snapping the folio shut. "You'll be back in California for your son's baseball game by this time tomorrow."

Derrick smiled at the thought. "I was thinking I'd take him to the game in the T-Bird. Let him show off a little to his friends afterward."

"My guess is all little boys like to be driven around town by their dads after they win their little league trophy," she smiled, laughing softly.

"That they do," Derrick agreed, enjoying the image in his mind's eye. He could almost feel the dry California sun on his skin, so different from the stifling humidity he'd gotten so used to in Indonesia. "And where will you be this time tomorrow?" he asked.

"Sitting by the beach in Bali, God willing."

"Good plan." Derrick briefly imagined that svelte figure of hers in a bikini.

Sam moved toward the door, refocusing him. "Ready to do this?"

Derrick nodded, slipping the phone into his pocket, his mind shifting to the meeting. He watched Sam touch the earpiece under her dark hair, murmuring to an unseen listener that they were heading toward the conference room. His bodyguard, Carey Nelson, stepped out in front of him as they left the office. Carey had the build of a lineman, easily over six-foot-five, with solid, broadly packed muscle. He had an agility of movement and speed that belied his size. They'd worked out together often enough over the past few weeks that Derrick knew Carey was swift, his movements spare and efficient.

They took a short walk down the hall toward an impressive conference room with stunning floor-to-ceiling views of downtown Jakarta and a massive, highly-polished table that could easily seat at least thirty people. The typically unrelenting sun was just beginning to wane into a late afternoon haze, casting a pleasant glow over wood-paneled walls. The Chow Yun group was already gathered at the conference table, his own team also in place, making small talk. After a round of obligatory handshakes, Derrick settled into the chair at the opposite end of the table from their leader, Edward Chow.

"First, let me say how thrilled I am that we are so close to completion on the construction of the Fortune Tower," Derrick began, his voice confident. "This skyscraper will be home to the new Southeast Asian headquarters for Chow Yun Industries and Markham International. I'd like to personally thank Mr. Edward Chow for his vision in the completion of this project—"

A sudden, resounding boom rocked the room as glass shattered. Derrick felt his neck squeezed as a hand jerked him back and forced him to the floor. He turned, disoriented, trying to fend off an attack when he saw Carey pushing him further under the conference table. He felt two strong arms hook under his armpits and drag him backward. There was a cacophony of sound, discordant edges blurred by the gusts of wind rattling through the blown-open window and muting shocked screams.

We're forty stories up, Derrick thought, dazed. He could hear glass crunching, the crack of more gun shots, shouts, people scrambling.

A voice sounded close to his ear, "I need you to crawl low with me, Derrick. I'm going to get you out of here, but you listen to me. Don't deviate."

He blinked as Sam let go of his arms to jerk out of her suit jacket. She slid backwards and turned to her side, pulling a 9mm from her back, the holster hidden beneath her dark vest. She thumbed off the safety as chaos exploded around them.

"Derrick, can you handle a gun?" she asked calmly, reaching down her leg to pull another from a holster strapped to her ankle.

"Jesus Chr—" Derrick found a small revolver thrust into his hand.

"We crawl quick and low now. You follow me close. Carey's on your six."

"Carey's on my…" Derrick wondered distantly how she could talk to him in her work voice as if they were still standing in his office.

Are we still in my office? Am I imagining this?

He opened his mouth to speak, but no sound came out. In shock, he registered the hysterical screams and the jolting staccato of high-powered rifle rounds hitting the walls amidst the rush of wind pummeling through the once-pristine conference room.

"Derrick. Derrick, open your eyes and follow me." He heard Sam speak to him, her voice calm but urgent. He blinked open his eyes. She stared at him hard before flipping fluidly and belly crawling under the table, knocking a chair out of the way as she neared the entrance to the conference room. There was a flurry of commotion around them, men shouting in Mandarin, Indonesian and English. He couldn't make sense of it; couldn't process anything outside of survival.

Sam touched her earpiece. "Where's the shooter, Talon?"

Another crack sounded, and he saw one of Chow's men go down, blood flowing from his mouth as he grasped the side of his chest. Derrick stopped, fixated on the dying man's face only a handful of feet from his own, his eyes vacant.

Sam turned around. "Carey, can you knock the table over and block the door while I get Derrick out?"

"You got it," Carey replied, maneuvering deftly.

Another crack sounded, then panic as Chow's men dragged someone back. Pools of smeared blood drenched the ivory travertine floor. Derrick blinked, staring at the man who'd been shot.

"Chow. *Oh my God*, is that Chow?"

"Derrick!"

He watched the blood pooling, transfixed, the color shocking and vivid against the pale limestone.

"*Derrick!*" Samantha grabbed him, smacking his face hard, jolting him from his daze. "Look at me, Derrick. Focus. We're getting you out." Carey overturned the conference table with a crash, giving them a barricade. "One of my men is locating the shooter. Another is flying a chopper to this tower right now. Keep it together, Derrick. You stick close to me, and this time tomorrow you're in California."

Derrick nodded, his throat working as he swallowed back panic. He looked down at the gun she'd put in his hand. An eerie calm settled over him.

"The sniper still has the door," Carey told her.

Derrick heard another crack, watching with widened eyes as another man from Chow's group slumped to the ground during a bid to get to the conference room entrance. He couldn't tell if Chow was still alive or if anyone on his own team had been hit. People were crouching behind the table with them, some shocked silent, others crying or shouting into mobile phones. His hand squeezed around the reassuring weight of the gun she'd put in his hand.

Sam pressed her earpiece again. "Talon, status!" she barked over the noise and chaos.

It could have been minutes; it could have been seconds. He saw Sam nod to Carey, felt Carey grab his shoulder, urging him forward toward the door. He wondered minutely if he was crawling toward his death. He found himself praying, his whispered psalm disembodied and distant, as if it were someone else speaking it.

And yea, though I walk through the valley of shadow and death…

"Almost there." Samantha stopped mid-crouch, her head cocked as if she were listening for something.

Her head came up.

She and Carey looked at each other at the same moment.

Suddenly, Carey picked him up by the neck and the back of his suit jacket, flinging him across the open space not blocked by the conference table. His shoulder slammed into the wall from the force of Carey's throw. Dazed, Derrick winced as he glanced around the hallway, trying to sit up. He couldn't believe they'd walked down this wide, wood-paneled hall so casually only minutes ago, thinking of nothing but closing this deal and heading home. How self-assured he'd felt. How cocky. *What a fucking joke.*

He saw a couple of Chow's men managed to drag him into the hall-way, cradling his body in their arms, shaking, petting the older man anxiously. Chow was covered in blood but appeared to be alive, barely conscious as he muttered something unintelligible, a rivulet of blood trailing from his mouth. Sam crouched near him, speaking to his men urgently in Mandarin as she hastily looked over his wounds. One of them answered her as she asked questions, pointing down the hall toward the bank of stainless steel elevators.

"What is she saying? What's happening? Is Chow okay?" Derrick struggled to ask as Carey helped him up and began pushing him past the group.

"She's asking where Chow's head of security is. More of his men are on their way. They're coming up from the parking garage," Carey answered, pushing him down the hall toward the stairwell.

"What about my team?" Derrick sputtered, trying to glance back over his shoulder.

"One of our men just shot the sniper. A secondary team is seeing to the people left in the conference room, and they'll get everyone to safety. Our job is to get you out," Carey answered calmly, urging Derrick up the steps.

Sam burst into the stairwell behind them, lithely bounding past Carey and Derrick. "Chow's passed out," she shouted over her shoulder. "Looks like he took one to the chest and another in the arm, but he's alive."

Carey hustled him up the metal stairs. As Sam pushed open the door to the rooftop helipad, Derrick felt the *whump whump whump* of helicopter blades slicing through the thick humidity of the late afternoon heat. A dark Sikorsky landed, the wind whipping at his hair and clothes. Derrick watched a man jump out to swing open one of the back doors. Sam and Carey hustled him to the chopper, bodily lifting him in. She pushed him into the seat, snapping a harness around him while Carey crawled in, shutting the door behind his broad frame. The chopper lifted off before the door was even closed. Sam glanced down at the skyscraper they were sweeping away from in a wide arc, hawk-eyed, watching for any signs of trouble. Carey settled in beside him.

Distantly, Derrick realized he was still clutching the handgun Sam had handed him in the conference room. He stared down at his hand, aware the last fifteen minutes of his life was the closest brush with imminent death he had ever experienced. He saw Sam's hand cover his own. Mute, he looked up into her alert dark eyes, watching him as she carefully withdrew the gun from his hand. Derrick realized belatedly his hands were shaking.

"What just happened?" he managed to croak out.

Sam holstered the gun on her ankle, smoothing her suit leg over it as if she were adjusting a trouser sock. Derrick blinked, feeling more disconcerted as the chopper veered heavily, the skyline tilting.

"Not your typical day at the office, Derrick?" Sam asked, her mouth arranged into a consoling smile.

Derrick's hands shook harder. He tried and failed to quell the burst of emotion rioting through his body as he grasped the situation.

"What *the fuck* just happened?" he shouted suddenly, anxiety crawling up his throat as the shock and adrenaline wore off. His hands clenched into tight fists as he fought for control.

"Calm down, Derrick," she told him. "You're all right." Sam slipped her hand over his with a pat of comfort. "The worst is over."

"What—" Derrick took a deep breath as his voice broke. "What was that—" His throat worked. He tried vainly to swallow.

Sam smiled gently, squeezing his hand again before letting go. "That was an assassination attempt on Mr. Chow. And possibly you, since the sniper didn't stop after he hit Chow. I don't have an immediate update on Chow's status, but I believe he's still alive." She produced a small bottle of water, handing it to him. Derrick gulped it down gratefully.

"We have three confirmed dead, all Chow's men," she continued. "Your team is rattled, but only Garrison took a shot to the shoulder."

"Second chopper just landed," Carey spoke up, his finger at his earpiece. He looked at Derrick. "We're medevac'ing Garrison and Chow to the hospital. Garrison will get patched up. Shot went clean through. Nothing vital hit."

"Nothing vital...?" Derrick mumbled, closing his eyes. He felt achy and exhausted. "Who would want to kill me or Chow?"

"He's made a lot of enemies since leaving Shanghai. A lot of bad land deals. He's got some unresolved karma," he heard Sam answer, her voice wry. "I doubt you were a target, but we'll know more as soon as we identify the sniper and figure out who he was working for."

"Jesus," Derrick muttered, opening his eyes. He glanced out the window toward the sun setting on the horizon. "Did you know this would happen today?" he asked.

"No, Derrick." Samantha shook her head. "Chow was a risky partner from the get-go, and we knew the odds of something going down while you were in the same room seemed higher. We'll be able to illuminate you and your Board with the details here by the time you're stateside."

"Stateside?" Derrick blinked.

"We're flying you out to the jet now," Samantha confirmed. "Like I said, by this time tomorrow, you'll be back home in California." Sam touched her earpiece briefly, listening. "My men found the sniper's spotter and backup trying to slip out of the building," she informed him after a moment. "We'll interrogate him after we get you on the flight."

Derrick glanced up. "I thought you were just a negotiator. Where the hell did you learn how to do that?"

Sam glanced at him. "Which part?"

"Don't bullshit me," Derrick snapped, realizing distantly his sudden fury was misplaced. But he couldn't seem to stop himself, his words erupting from him. "An hour ago you were drafting fucking *contracts* for chrissakes! Now you've got a 9mm under your suit and you're interrogating would-be assassins. Who the hell are you?"

Derrick saw a brief flash of her teeth as she grinned. "I'm still Sam,

Derrick. The only difference between me and typical corporate counsel is that I don't just push around paper." She leaned forward, extending her hand. "Formerly Lieutenant Commander Samantha Wyatt of the United States Navy. Now it's just Esquire," she smiled reassuringly. "Pleasure protecting you today, Mr. Markham."

Derrick shook that slender, manicured hand, still feeling dazed and confused. "You saved my ass," he breathed.

"Well, I sure as hell wasn't gonna leave you there," she teased, her eyes gentling.

Derrick nodded before he sat back, allowing his head to fall against the headrest as his eyes closed. "I was almost shot today, and now I find out my general counsel can kill people with her thumbs," he muttered, trying to calm down.

"True story," Carey grunted next to him.

Derrick's head whipped around. "Seriously?"

Carey shrugged.

"I was *kidding*. You were kidding, right?" Derrick asked, looking back at Sam.

Her dark eyes lit with amusement, as she tried to suppress a smile. "I find weapons more effective, but I can use my thumbs in a pinch," she replied, leaning back to examine her silky dress shirt. She noticed blood on one of the cuffs, cursing. "Damn. I love this shirt," she muttered.

Derrick looked to Carey again. "I thought you were the one in the military."

Carey snorted. "I followed her. This one makes GI Jane look like a Cabbage Patch doll." He smirked, watching Sam roll up the sleeves of her blouse.

"You said you were going to interrogate the sniper's backup?" Derrick asked. "The spotter?"

Sam nodded. "I'll find out as much as I can and let you know more."

"Are you turning him in? To the Jakarta police?"

Carey laughed softly beside him. "Derrick, I doubt he's Indonesian, based on the physical descriptions our men have given us. These assassins were highly trained marksmen. It's a friggin' miracle Chow didn't die in that conference room. My guess is they're wanted for crimes in other countries. Jakarta police will be the least of their worries, trust me."

Sam nodded in agreement. "Like I said, we'll let you know more when we know more. You have my word on that."

Derrick remained silent for the rest of the short flight. When the chopper landed near a private jet on a quiet airstrip, he exhaled a relieved breath. A man in fatigues approached the chopper as it landed. Before he opened the door, Derrick gripped Sam's arm.

"Samantha, thank you. Seriously," he told her, releasing a shaky breath. "You saved my life."

She smiled, patting his hand gently. "You're welcome, Derrick. Now giddy up. Your jet is waiting."

"I can never repay you—"

"Sure you can," she replied. "Invoice is in the mail." The door to the helicopter opened. "You'll be home in no time, Derrick. Enjoy your family."

With that, Sam hopped out before Carey escorted him toward the waiting jet. Derrick glanced back one last time as he reached the stairs to the aircraft. The sun had set, the darkening skyline ablaze in cinnabar and orange. Jakarta looked like it was on fire in the distance. Derrick realized again how much had happened since he'd stood at his windows, looking down at it all, oblivious of the sudden impact in the minutes to come.

"I could have died," he murmured to himself.

"But you didn't," Carey replied from beside him.

"I had no idea she was capable of that." Derrick shook his head, wiping an unsteady hand down his face. "But thank Christ for it," he murmured as he paused at the steps of the waiting jet. Derrick's eyes found her again. Samantha leaned against the Sikorsky, conferring with the man in fatigues, hand tucked into her trouser pocket, poise relaxed.

"She's impressive, that one."

Carey laughed softly behind him. "You don't know the half, Mr. Markham. You don't even know the half."

CHAPTER 1

Early August—Present day

Jack Roman's office in the Loop, Chicago

JACK

"WE'VE GOT A buyer I like for the penthouse duplex."

Jack looked up from his paperwork, surprised. "Must be good for you to bring it up when you know I don't have any intention of selling it," he replied.

Mitchell Gartner, Jack's long-time friend and business partner, ignored his comment as he sat down across from Jack. He flicked open a file on his lap. "S. Wyatt. Senior partner with Lennox Chase. Looking for a fifteen percent discount with a cash offer. Background checks out. I think you'd like this neighbor." Mitch's eyes were bright. Jack knew that look was either from a done deal or trouble to-be-had.

Jack Roman sat back, steepling his fingers as he regarded Mitch. The building he owned and lived in was an exquisitely renovated neoclassical brick building with Beaux-Arts architecture. The Whitney was a legendary landmark in downtown Chicago, just off of Michigan Avenue, with lush views of Grant Park and the windswept waters of Lake Michigan. The penthouse level was over ten thousand square feet, featuring two duplex penthouses with wide limestone terraces and breathtaking views of the city, park, and water. The penthouses shared an entertainment area with a large pool that separated the two spaces. Jack had resolutely kept the second penthouse unoccupied since the renovation was completed nearly two years ago, though not for a lack of interested parties.

"You know I want Jaime in there," Jack said, his voice flat.

Mitch slipped the file in front of Jack. "I know, but he doesn't want to leave the house in Oak Park. It's a better place for Maddie to grow up in anyway. A real neighborhood with other kids, and she can ride her bike."

"I want to talk to him again about it," Jack answered, glancing at the closed file.

"Okay, but it's a good offer. I know you want your brother in there, but if he says no, I think it's an ideal situation."

"A fifteen percent discount is pretty steep, even for a cash offer," Jack commented drily, looking for more reasons to block the deal. "And don't think for a minute I don't recognize that look in your eye. What're you up to?"

Mitch shrugged. "What's not to like? Comes from money, excellent reputation, obviously good with business, and we could use this cash in hand to pick up that lot in the South Loop before word even gets out."

"And?" Jack prompted, head tilting ever so slightly.

"And you should see the picture of Wyatt," Mitch grinned.

Jack couldn't help the smirk from rising. *Canary. Meet your cat,* he thought. Mitch was what you could call a switch hitter. Mitch enjoyed his fair share of lovely women, but the certain allure of a good-looking man could turn his head from time to time. Mitch had excellent taste. Couldn't fault him on that. Jack had no doubt this S. Wyatt would be a looker if Mitch's eye had that glint.

"I'm sure," Jack responded. "I need to catch a flight to Washington tonight. I want to talk to Jaime first. If I decide to go through with it, it's a five percent discount, they can't sublet, and they can only resell in five years on my terms."

Mitch let out a low whistle. "Hardball, huh? You know the price we set was outrageous from the get-go. This offer is more than fair."

"I know it. I just want to set the terms early on that we're playing by my rules. Set an early precedent for neighborly conduct if it gets that far," Jack replied. He fingered the paperwork sitting in front of him, already shifting his attention to the plots and land developments he was considering.

"You may have met your match with this one," Mitch said after a moment, refusing to drop the subject.

"Oh?" Jack's dark brows popped up. "And why's that?"

"Wyatt's recent promotion to Senior Partner at Lennox Chase is based on performance under, shall we say, high-pressure situations. Don't think this one will be someone you can steamroll."

"I thought Lennox Chase was an insurance company," Jack replied, his brows rising. "What kind of high-pressure situations do insurance companies have? Too many claimants all at once?"

"Wyatt leads a division called 'Human Asset Protection.' That's fancy terminology for kidnap, ransom, and assassination attempts on executives and government officials, that sort of thing. Basically a private protection agency for big-wigs situated within an insurance company."

Jack felt mildly intrigued at the prospect of having a James Bondish-type neighbor. He had to admit it had been a while since he'd found anything outside of work interesting. Having a neighbor whose idea of a Monday staff meeting involved fielding ransom demands was probably the most excitement he'd seen in months.

"I had lunch with Michael Lennox at the Union Club the other day," Mitch continued. "The numbers aren't public, but the Human Asset Protection division is Lennox's bread and butter these days," Mitch told him. "Lennox Chase is now one of the top three businesses that provide this sort of service in the world, whereas five years ago, they were just underwriters."

Jack wasn't surprised Mitch had managed to ferret this information out over lunchtime drinks. Mitch traded in confidences like Jack gathered favors. Everyone had their own currency.

"All the more reason Wyatt shouldn't get a discount," he replied. "I'll talk to Jaime tonight and let you know if he's a definite no. You can handle the interview and the negotiations if I decide to pull the trigger."

"I'll wait for your word," Mitch acquiesced.

"Good." Jack glanced down at the watch. "Let's switch gears. I need to head out in an hour. Let's work through the latest on construction updates."

August—A week later

North Gallery District, Chicago

SAMANTHA

THE SIXTEEN RESTAURANT, inside the Trump Tower and Hotel, arguably boasted the most stunning panoramic views of lakefront Chicago. The warm afternoon sun hit the Chicago River and Lake Michigan at that perfect angle, making the water shimmer like crystal-cut glass in the distance. As Sam followed the hostess through the restaurant, her attention shifted from the quarter arc, three-story vistas to the man waiting for her in the bar.

Mitchell Gartner had the lean, androgynous look of a dandy from a bygone era. His dark golden hair was pushed back from his face in an attractive wave. Vintage Oliver Peoples perched on an elegant nose. She pegged him to be in his early-to-mid-thirties, around her age. Spotting her approach, Mr. Gartner stood, a smile curving his mouth as he reached out to shake her hand. She admired the impeccable summer-weight suit and custom Oxford shirt.

"Ms. Wyatt, great to meet you in person," he smiled, moving to pull out her seat.

"Likewise. And please, call me Sam," she answered, settling in the chair. She gave him a moment to check her out unobstructed as she placed her drinks order with the waiter who'd appeared at her side.

As she turned back to him, she noted the appreciative look in his eyes. She hoped that boded well for her bid.

"So, Mr. Gartner," she began. "I'm glad you reviewed my offer. Are we drinking to celebrate or are we drinking to negotiate? I hope it's the former." Sam smiled. "I don't usually get to kick back and enjoy a view like this with a cocktail on a weekday afternoon."

He laughed a little, a pleasant sound. "Well, I suspect it'll be a little bit of both. And please, if you allow me to call you Sam, please call me

Mitch. It's only fair." His eyes were warm.

A charm offensive. She liked it.

"I have a strong feeling you probably don't play fair, Mitch," she teased. "Especially if you want to negotiate on a cash deal while plying me with what I'm sure will be some powerful cocktails."

Mitch laughed at that. "Who says I don't simply want to enjoy the company of a lovely woman after a long day?"

"I'll admit I was wondering about that," she replied. "Our offices are a stone's throw from each other, and yet you invite me to drinks at a neutral location with a breathtaking backdrop—nice choice, by the way," she said, admiring the view. "I'm guessing you like me for the penthouse."

"I do," he admitted.

"But there's a catch."

"There is." Mitch inclined his head. "Your offer is good," he continued after a moment. "But we're in no hurry to fill the space."

"Oh, I know." Sam smiled. "That penthouse has been vacant since you completed your renovation a couple years ago."

Mitch shrugged, his face belying nothing. "Finding the right kind of person to share that gorgeous space is top of mind for the owner."

"You mean Jack Roman."

Mitch smiled.

"And may I ask what defines the 'right kind of person,' Mitch? Other than the willingness to put their long-term money where their mouth is. So to speak."

"Well, there is that," Mitch replied. "Jack enjoys a great deal of privacy. He's had that space to himself for quite a while now. He's...understandably picky about who he'll be sharing it with. You understand."

"So this is an interview," she surmised.

"Interview isn't the word I'd choose," Mitch replied casually. "Consider it a get-to-know. And I'll admit a personal curiosity. You have such an interesting background."

"Don't we all?"

"Ah, but yours more so than others." He smiled, eyes amused behind his glasses.

The waiter returned to their table holding a long-stemmed martini glass, the tiny chips of ice swirling through a perfectly-executed martini.

Sam hummed her appreciation as she sipped her drink. Crisp and delicious. "Fair enough. What would you like to know before you try to gouge me, Mitch?" she asked affably.

"Gouge you?" Mitch chuckled. "I pity the man who tries to gouge you. Besides, I'm completely curious from what little I know. Truly."

"What would you like to know?"

He touched the condensation on his glass as he watched her. "First, how did you get into…ah…insurance?"

"What do you mean?" Sam asked, amused. "I take it I don't come across as your typical adjuster?"

Mitch grinned in response, shrugging.

"I'm willing to bet you have a nice little file on me, Mitch," she guessed, considering him. "I'm also willing to guess you're looking for the color behind the facts?"

Mitch nodded, sipping his drink.

"Well, alright," she agreed. "But let's make this fair. If you get to interview me—"

"You mean ask you questions in a friendly effort to get to know you," he corrected with a grin.

"Right. What you said," she grinned back. "Then I get to ask you questions too. Turnabout's fair play and all that jazz."

"But I'm not trying to buy something from you."

"No, but you are trying to take something from me, Mitch," she replied easily. "My money. And the skinny on my…shall we call it *unusual* backstory. A little give-for-get never hurt," she reminded him, her face pleasant.

Mitch considered her for a moment. "You have a deal. Ladies first," he gestured.

"I'd like to know how a good Indiana farm boy becomes one of the sharpest bookies in Northwestern University history."

Mitch nearly choked on his drink. "How did you find that out?"

"I worked in military intelligence for years, Mitch. I have a feeling you and I have information-gathering in common," Sam replied, sipping her martini.

Mitch coughed behind his hand. "You were a Navy officer, I recall."

"Yup. Joined up young. A family legacy, though I'm sure you know that."

"Still, that's rare. Why did you join?"

Sam smiled, turning to admire the lake. "I liked it. Not the discipline, mind you." She slanted him a look. "But the physicality of it. The problem-solving required in…shall we say 'tense' situations."

"A woman who enjoys danger."

"No." She shook her head. "I'm no hell-raiser. I just enjoy the discernment and decision-making that comes with having to be on your toes all the time. Wins are that much sweeter when you know the severity of the consequences." Sam took a pleasant swallow of her drink before turning back to him. "Now back to my earlier question, Mitch. How does a kid who grew up in corn fields get into running an underground betting and gambling ring in one of the most prestigious colleges in the Midwest?"

"So you know I was a farm boy," he replied, his smile a little self-deprecating. "And you were kind enough not to point out I was a *poor* farm boy. I went to Northwestern on scholarship. But it was pricey, and I had expensive taste, even back then," he chuckled.

"I noticed. Nice watch."

He glanced at his Hublot, his dimple showing. "So, among my scholarship deals with the school was sports. I was pretty good back then. The Big Ten Conference that Northwestern competes in—well, let's call it a small world. It's easy to figure out who's who—"

"I think I see where this is going."

Mitch nodded, eyes twinkling now. "…Including who was hung over from the night before. Whose girlfriend left him for another player. Who was getting cortisone shots. That sort of thing. I started taking bets sophomore year."

"And by the time you were a senior, you were running the house on sports and running a tidy little gambling operation out of your fraternity," Sam concluded.

Mitch grinned. "That part was actually Jack's idea. He was a card shark from the get-go. Grew up playing poker with Chicago politicians. Nobody stood a chance against him."

"And between your head for running books and his contacts—"

"Let's just say we figured out early on we'd make good business partners."

"And because of his connections…no chance of getting caught," she said, brows raised. "That may be the best undergrad job *ever*," she marveled.

"Beats slinging coffee," he shrugged. "Now is it my turn to ask the questions?"

"Sure." She smiled.

"I couldn't find much on your military career. I know that you worked in counter intelligence and that you specialized in interrogation."

Sam tilted her head. "I'm surprised you found out that much."

"Why interrogation?"

Sam shrugged, nonchalant. "I'd always been decent at languages, but that propensity combined with the nature of being a woman made for a good interrogator, I guess."

Mitch looked puzzled. "The nature of being a woman? How do you figure?"

"Come on now, Mitch," she teased. "You look like you know your fair share of ladies. And though you may be too gentlemanly to say it, you know we like to ask complicated questions with no-win scenarios. Consider it a genetic predisposition."

Mitch laughed heartily. "Finally a woman who admits it! I always wondered how I could never win an argument and never figure out what I did wrong at the same time."

"Well, don't go telling trade secrets of the fairer sex," Sam smiled. "It's a delicate art that takes years to refine."

"Let me guess. That's why you decided to become an attorney," Mitch said, tucking his hand under his chin, rapt.

"I believe you're trying to take my turn again, Mitch," she chided.

"By all means…" He gestured casually. "Ask away."

"Why has Jack kept the penthouse empty for so long? The real reason."

Mitch considered her, swirling his drink. She wasn't sure he'd tell her, but she figured she had nothing to lose by asking.

"Jack has a younger brother, Jaime," Mitch finally answered. "His wife died tragically a couple years ago, as we were finishing the renovations on the Whitney."

"I'm sorry to hear that." Sam inclined her head.

"Thank you," Mitch acknowledged. "Cassie was a lovely girl. Jack has always been close to his brother. He was hoping Jaime would agree to move in once the shock had passed."

"That makes a good deal of sense."

Mitch nodded. "So you see why Jack's been remiss in filling the space quickly."

"But Jaime doesn't want it," she deduced.

"I'm not certain," he answered smoothly.

Too smoothly, she thought. If he'd had two years to make a move and hadn't, the place was hers to lose.

"To your continued success in seeing opportunities on the playing field and closing good deals," she toasted.

"And to your intelligence-gathering and interrogation of unsuspecting men on sunny afternoons," he smiled in return.

"Only a fool would consider you unsuspecting, Mitch."

"So how does one go from being a Naval interrogator to an attorney?" Mitch asked after a moment.

"It was at my commanding officer's recommendation, actually," she admitted. "He thought I'd make a fine JAG. When I decided not to go that route, he suggested law school."

"I'm not familiar with a Jag if it doesn't involve four wheels," Mitch responded.

That made her chuckle. "Sorry—bad habit. Everything gets cut down into acronyms, particularly in the military. It stands for Judge Advocate General. It's the legal arm of the Navy."

"And that wasn't for you?"

Sam shrugged. "Honestly, by the time I got the recommendation, I felt like I'd learned what I needed to learn from serving. I'd done a couple tours already, and I knew it was time to switch careers."

"I can't condone your choice of the University of Chicago for law school as a Northwestern grad," Mitch teased.

"Well, I hope that's the only black mark against me in that file of yours," she replied.

"So far," Mitch grinned.

"I'd better redeem myself pretty quickly then and point out we have another thing in common," she replied.

Mitch's brow popped up. "Oh?"

"We both appreciate Marc Chagall."

Mitch blinked in surprise. "How did you know I like Chagall?"

"I'm in insurance, Mitch. Lennox Chase insured the *The Concert* before you bought the piece. I especially like that you had it installed at the Whitney."

"It's the foyer separating the penthouses," he murmured. "But then, you already knew that."

Sam smiled.

"You do your homework," he commented.

"So do you."

"But there's still something I don't know," Mitch responded, shifting forward.

Sam's brow lifted in question.

"You join up with Gage Pearson directly after graduating. Their one and only new associate that year. Yet you only stay for two years? And you leave mergers and acquisitions at one of the top law firms in the country for…insurance?"

"You sound incredulous, Mitch."

"I am incredulous, Sam."

She laughed softly. "It makes sense, believe me."

"Not from where I'm sitting, it doesn't."

"I enjoyed the negotiations," she admitted. "But all those hours trapped in conference rooms, breathing recycled air, counting hours like sand…" Sam shook her head. "I couldn't go from high-stakes operations to just stacking chips in the back. Wasn't my scene."

"Fair enough," he commented. "But how did you fall in with Lennox Chase? I didn't know they were even in the security business."

"They weren't," she replied. "They insured high-value individuals for things like accidental death, but the kidnap and ransom business has become a much bigger issue in the past fifteen years, particularly in politically unstable countries where the multinational corporations Lennox insures like to operate."

"So you decided to change the game."

Sam savored her martini, nodding. She considered the start of her business. The thrill of starting something from the ground up.

"A close friend of mine had a private protection firm for businessmen and politicians," she continued. "I'd occasionally accompany clients who leveraged his services on business trips. The first time I was asked to sign a K&R agreement—I saw the opportunity to fill a niche and expand his services."

"You had all the ingredients," Mitch surmised.

Sam nodded. "I had the business negotiations, the language skills, and the connections. My partner brought the security know-how and all the ex-military resources business people were willing to pay top dollar for. We help facilitate deals, negotiations, and transfers, whatever makes the process smoother in less-than-ideal situations."

Mitch's gaze sharpened. "And Lennox Chase was already a significant underwriter for companies that would require these types of services."

"Exactly." Sam smiled. "Immediate clientele. And easy to package."

"That's pretty damn brilliant," Mitch murmured.

"Isn't it?" she smiled, sipping her drink. "So now that we have a mutual admiration society going, let's get down to brass tacks. Do I get the penthouse, Mitch?"

He considered her for a moment, ignoring the question. "That's a very different path from a Texan debutante," he observed.

"Yeah, well… I never did like white dresses much."

Mitch laughed softly, regarding her.

"My daddy always said if you can't find peace out in the pasture, you've got a lifetime of looking for trouble ahead of you," she admitted ruefully.

"And will you be trouble?" Mitch asked.

"I guess that depends on how much you're going to try to charge me for that penthouse." She smiled.

"Why do you want it?" he asked instead. "You're wealthy. You could live anywhere you like, and yet you want the Whitney. Why?"

Sam shrugged. "Why wouldn't I? It's a stunning building. Your renovation and attention to detail is bar-none. I like the idea of living in a building with such a gorgeous history. And between us," she confided, "I used to walk past it nearly every day when I was going to law school and thought to myself, *That's it. I want to live in that grand old dame,*' and that was years before you renovated it."

Mitch considered her, his gaze assessing. "We'll give you a five percent discount on your cash offer," he said after a moment. "You have to guarantee not to sell within five years, and we'd need to sign off on any sale. It would be your residence and yours alone. No subletting or people we aren't aware of living there."

"Ten percent, and I'll better your offer by agreeing not to sell for at least seven years," she countered blithely. "This isn't a *pied-à-terre*, Mitch. It'd be my haven. The place I recharge and relax. Of course I wouldn't sublet or have randoms in there. I'm not hosting the *Real Housewives of North Shore.*"

Mitch's smile was assuaging. "Jack values his privacy."

"A sentiment we share."

"Seven percent," he answered softly, eyeing her through his tortoise shell rims.

"I'm giving you more than what you asked for on the other clauses, Mitch," Sam tutted. "It's not compromise if it doesn't sting just a little bit on both sides, now is it?"

Mitch looked bemused. "I hate to see you not get the penthouse, but we both know Jack doesn't need to discount the space at all," he responded. "Besides, I was never much for sting."

Sam finished what was left of her drink. "Well," she sighed. "I hate to walk away from the Whitney, but I have to say, I don't think Jack Roman would find a better neighbor than a woman who travels seventy-five percent of the time and has a penchant for sleeping off jet lag the few times she is home."

"The glamorous life of an international jet-setter."

"It's terrible, isn't it? I swear I'm not complaining." She smiled ruefully. "I will also say that you and I both know that you priced that penthouse higher than market value from the get-go, so my offer isn't so much a discount as it is leveling the playing field."

"You pointed out yourself—I'm an ex-bookie. Level playing fields aren't my interest."

"A good reason I won't ever invite you to poker night," she laughed, standing. He stood alongside her, ever the gentleman as he helped her with her chair.

Sam hid a smile as she picked up her handbag. First rule in negotiations. Always be able to walk away. Second rule, dangle something delicious in your wake.

"Tell you what," she began. "I'll give you a bead on the next Chagall that becomes available before word's out, and we'll call it a deal. Sleep on it and get back to me," she told him, shaking his hand.

Mitch smiled, his eyes bright. "Does this mean I also get an invitation to poker night?"

Sam shook her head, laughing. "You'll have to earn it."

"That would be a pleasure," he murmured, releasing her hand. "I enjoyed meeting you, Sam."

"The feeling's mutual, Mitch. You know where to find me when you come to your senses."

They exchanged warm smiles.

Sam had a feeling she'd be hearing from him within the week.

August—Later that night
Washington, D.C.

JACK

"WYATT CAME UP on the years of sale but is holding out for ten percent on the cash deal."

Jack frowned for a moment, listening to Mitch on the other line.

"Why would I agree to that?"

"Because I'm pretty sure this is your dream neighbor. Never home. Seven years before sale, will stick to agreed parameters, and may actually be the most ideal candidate we've seen in two years," Mitch answered. "For a variety of reasons."

Jack rubbed the bridge of his nose. It had been a long day of politicking and glad-handing, and he could feel a headache gathering strength. "Why are you pushing this so hard, Mitch?"

He heard Mitch sigh. "One, the money."

"We don't need the money."

"Of course not. Neither does Mark Cuban, but that doesn't prevent him from accumulating cash any more than it should us."

Jack stood in the study of his parents' Georgetown home, the place they spent the majority of their time while Senate was in session. He walked to the wall of shelves, running a finger over his mother's legal journals and law books. "Another reason then?"

"You're in a stasis, Jack. If you don't want someone else up there in that crystal castle of yours, you need to convert the whole thing to one penthouse. When you move on to the next thing, we'll make a killing selling it to some professional athlete or a daytime TV mogul."

"Who says I'm moving?"

"That's why I said stasis, Jack," Mitch replied. "Look, I wouldn't recommend this if I didn't think it was a great situation. Wyatt's eager to move. We could close fast and move on the South Loop property in conjunction. Just consider it."

Jack paused at the edge of the study's desk. "Any other reasons?"

Mitch laughed into the phone. "Again, you should see Wyatt."

"Do I need to meet this person?"

"It's your call, but I think you'd go for this either way."

Jack sighed, rubbing the bridge of his nose again. "Dad wants me to stay the weekend. Go duck hunting. Go ahead and close this. I trust your judgment, and I want the South Loop lot tied up before anyone knows it's coming up."

"Duck hunting," Mitch snorted. "That's just his excuse to sit outside and smoke cigars all weekend. I never understood the wisdom in drinking bourbon and wielding a shotgun."

Jack chuckled. "I think he imagines the ducks are the house speaker sometimes. It's his way of letting loose some steam."

"Don't say I didn't tell you so if you come back one of these days with an ass full of buckshot and a bad hangover," Mitch commented.

"Buddy, if I came home with an ass full of buckshot, I think a hangover would be the least of my worries," Jack replied, wry.

"I'll have to talk to Wyatt about cutting you some good rates on personal liability insurance."

"You do that. See you in a week or so, Mitch," he signed off, sighing as he closed his eyes. He heard his mother walk into the study, carrying a glass of wine.

"You look tired, Gianni," she commented, calling him by his nickname as she sat on the couch. "How much have you slept this week?"

Jack shrugged as he sat beside her, slanting her a smile. He'd struggled with insomnia most of his life. He needed about four hours a night to function, though it wasn't unheard of for him to get by on a handful of hours on a stressful week.

"I slept a little on the flight here. I'm okay, Ma—"

She smacked his shoulder. "Don't lie to your mother."

"Wouldn't dream of it," he replied with a fond look. "You always catch me anyway."

"True. How was your day?"

"Good. Productive. Had a few meetings. Lunch with Dad on the Hill. I just got off the phone with Mitch. I have a buyer for the penthouse."

His mother sipped her wine, considering him. "You should sell it."

Jack fiddled with his phone for a moment before looking up at her. "I want to talk to Jaime again."

"No, Gianni," she countered, her mouth hardening into the expression she got whenever her position had been decided. She'd changed out of the suit she wore under her judge's robes, but she looked no less formidable in a button-down and dress slacks. "You need to respect his choice. He and Maddie are fine where they are."

"He should be closer to me," Jack replied, facing her. "And it's closer to his office to be downtown. I can help take care of Maddie. It makes more sense."

"You can't decide for him, Gianni," his mother responded, her tone softening as she patted his arm. "I know you want to protect him, but he's doing better. He and Maddie are fine. You need to sell the penthouse if you have a good buyer. Keeping it open sends him the wrong message."

"It doesn't."

"It does. It tells him you don't think he's okay. It tells him you don't believe in him."

Jack sighed, closing his eyes again, his head dropping back on the sofa. "You know I don't think that."

"I know you love him. I know you want everything to be okay. He's seeing his way back. We have to give him space," she told him, straightening his collar.

"So says the Italian mother," he replied, opening his eyes to smirk at her.

"Sell the penthouse," she ordered gently. "He'll be secretly relieved."

"How do you know that?"

"I know everything," she answered sagely.

Jack laughed, picking up her hand and kissing it. "You don't, but if God had a *consigliere,* you'd be it."

She chuckled. "How long will you be in town?"

"Through the weekend. Dad wants to go hunting."

His mother rolled her eyes. "Poor ducks."

"Poor ducks? Poor me," Jack replied in mock annoyance. "I'm the one that will have to sit in the swamp with him for hours on end."

"You're a good son," she commented. "Now tell me about this actress you're dating."

"God, *Maaa...*" Jack groaned.

"What? I'm allowed to ask questions about my son's love life."

"No. No, you're not," he argued. "Leave it alone. She's just someone I'm dating. It's nothing serious."

"Nothing serious? I've seen you two all over newspapers and magazines this summer. It *looks* serious," she sniffed.

"Well, it's not," Jack replied.

"It's funny. I have a thirty-six year old son who won't get serious about anyone and a twenty-seven year old son who couldn't wait to get married out of college." His mother rolled her eyes.

"Be thankful for that, at least."

"You just haven't met her yet, Gianni. You'll know when you do. You'll fall like a ton of bricks. Just like your dad when he met me," she predicted, a knowing expression on her face.

Now it was Jack's turn to roll his eyes. "Dad didn't fall like a ton of bricks, Ma. You told him to get his shit together and put a ring on it or you'd marry Uncle Tony instead."

His mother smiled serenely. "Same difference."

"That phrase doesn't even make sense."

"Sure it does," she responded. "You'll know exactly when to give up the fight. I look forward to seeing it happen."

Jack rested his cheek on his hand as he smiled at her. "I love you, Ma. Even if you're the bossiest, most stubborn woman I know."

"I love you too, Gianni. Even though you're an overprotective big brother and you humor your father too much with this ridiculous hunting business. Now come help me make dinner."

CHAPTER 2

September

The Whitney, Chicago

J A C K

"YOU FUCKING SEX god. Get your ass back to bed. I'm not done with you yet," Rebecca called out sleepily.

Jack smirked as he slipped into his swim trunks. Rebecca was all talk. She'd be passed out within the next five minutes. It was already three in the morning. He'd been fucking her for hours. She'd come so many times, it was amazing she hadn't fallen into a coma yet. He padded into the adjoining bathroom suite, looking for a towel.

Unfortunately, he was still wired, and he was meeting Mitch for a run early. He ran a hand through his hair, sighing. *Goddamn insomnia.* No matter. A few dozen laps and he'd be fine. He preferred to burn off that internal disquiet, plug into the source physically, and drain it dry. If he was lucky, he'd be able to batten down afterward for a couple hours.

As he stepped out of the bathroom, tossing a towel over his shoulder, he caught sight of Rebecca, naked and passed out, just as he'd predicted. She looked gorgeous, sex rumpled and exhausted, her strawberry blonde hair tangled across the pillow. Jack pulled the sheet over her creamy skin. He could kiss that skin for hours. He *had* kissed that skin for hours. During the summer they'd been dating, he'd had her just about every way and on every surface he could get her on. It would be a shame to see her go when she finished filming in Chicago.

Jack switched off the lights on his way out. As he got to his landing, he glanced through the windows overlooking the terrace and out into the darkness of Grant Park beyond. He thought he could see the muted reflection of backlit water against the walls. Frowning, he trotted down his stairs to the leaded glass doors, wondering who would have turned on the pool lights this time of night.

The top floor of the Whitney boasted a rectangular pool and outdoor space separating the two penthouses. He'd had the pool fully restored to its former glory with Italian marble mosaics in lilting Art Nouveau patterns, cleverly hiding the muted lighting installed along the pool's ledges. Jack stopped in surprise as he watched a slim figure cutting through the water in graceful, arcing butterfly strokes. He could tell the figure was a woman, but he couldn't tell who it was from the darkened area he stood observing.

Wyatt had recently moved in, but he'd yet to meet his enigmatic neighbor. He knew he wasn't married from the application and background file he'd glanced at briefly when Mitch had first approached him with the offer. Perhaps this woman was his girlfriend?

A girlfriend who does laps like an Olympic athlete at three o'clock in the morning?

The polite thing to do would be to leave the woman in peace, returning after she'd left, but he was too intrigued to be polite. He watched her slice through the water, catching the edge and flipping fluidly, dark hair flowing behind her as she raced underwater, popping back up for another lap.

It was another ten minutes before she finally slowed, walking up the pool steps, wringing out her hair. Jack took a breath in, an unexpected riff of awareness spiking down his back. The mystery woman was a stunner. Athletic and lean, the reflections from the pool danced on her skin as she reached for a towel. He could see her features clearly enough now to see she had high cheekbones, dark, almond-shaped eyes, and a lush mouth. She wasn't conventionally beautiful, but she was striking. She was also incredibly difficult to stop staring at. Jack swallowed as she concentrated on patting herself dry in a simple black suit that did more for her figure than she probably intended, given the seriousness of her swim.

Clearing his throat, Jack stepped from the shadows on his side of the terrace. She turned to him with an alert look. One glance and she smiled before slipping into a bathrobe lying on a chaise. She walked over to him with no hesitancy, face still smiling as if she knew him while she extended her hand.

"Hi there, neighbor. Fancy seeing you here in the middle of the night. I hope I didn't wake you." She spoke with a surprising familiarity, her voice husky like she'd singed her vocal chords with a swallow of whisky. Her grasp was firm, a contrast of soft skin and slightly calloused fingers.

"No, not at all," Jack immediately responded. "I was up. Didn't want to interrupt your laps. Thought you might be training for a medal," he smiled, releasing her hand. So this had to be his neighbor's girlfriend. *Lucky guy.*

She chuckled softly. "Nah, nothing that serious. I'm just jet-lagged out of my mind. Thought I'd work off the extra energy, try to get some sleep before the sun rose."

"Good plan. I was hoping to do the same."

"The water's perfect." She smiled at him, drying her hair with a towel as she continued looking at him with a disconcerting familiarity. "Like slipping in a bath," she murmured, her voice sexy as hell. It was a distinctive rasp, sensual, and warm all at once.

Jack fought to tamp down the attraction, recalling Rebecca upstairs, trying to imagine what his new neighbor might think of him lusting after his girlfriend. She was still watching him, like she was waiting for him to say something.

"Have we met before?" Jack asked, trying to make out more of her face in the muted light.

She chuckled softly, shaking her head. "I'm gonna blame that tired old line on the lateness of the hour," she teased. "But no, we haven't met. I just got here, so there hasn't been a chance as yet. It's nice to finally see you in person, though."

She turned to move toward the large doors leading to their shared foyer and elevator banks. "Photos don't do you justice," he thought he heard her say.

"Are you a friend of Wyatt's?" Jack asked after her.

She smiled over her shoulder at him.

"I am Wyatt," she replied. "It was nice to meet you, Jack," she said, disappearing through her terrace doors, leaving Jack standing by the pool. Stunned.

September—The next morning

Mitch's Loft in the West Loop, Chicago

JACK

"S. WYATT IS a woman," Jack accused, leaning against Mitch's door-frame as his friend swung it open.

"Why yes, Jack," Mitch answered, his brows raised. "I found that rather obvious the first time I met her too," Mitch responded, sipping his coffee. "Want some?" he asked as Jack sauntered into his loft.

"No, thanks. You led me to believe she was a man." Jack accused.

Mitch looked up at him. "Uh, nope. Can't remember doing that."

"You only ever used her first initial or her last name. You never said he or she, but the way you talked about her made her sound like a man," Jack responded, wondering why for the life of him he felt so put out.

Mitch shook his head. "All her early bids came under her letterhead, S. Wyatt," he paused to think. "She works in a male-dominated industry. It's not surprising you jumped to the wrong conclusion with those data points. But her details are listed in the file under the final sale. Including her full name and a snapshot we got from her background check. Clearly you didn't read it."

"I skimmed."

"Oh, you *skimmed*." Mitch rolled his eyes. "Right. You signed off on the deal over a month ago. Hell, we rushed closing so you wouldn't change your mind last minute. Why are you so damn irritated all the sudden?"

Jack looked up to exposed rafters of the loft, not entirely sure why he felt alternately irritated and hot-under-the-collar, like someone had pulled one over on him—a rare, unwelcome feeling. He hadn't gotten a wink of sleep all night, swimming with ferocity after Samantha had disappeared before falling into bed, only to toss and turn, thinking about a woman who was not the one in bed next to him. He was so preoccupied with Samantha that he'd turned Rebecca down for a morning quickie, opting instead to confront Mitch with what had clearly been his own oversight. *What was his problem? And why the hell did it matter?*

"I want the file back," Jack told him flatly.

Mitch sat down, stretching his legs in front of him. "What do you suddenly want to know? You could have cared less when we were going through the negotiation outside of the basics. What happened?"

"I ran into her swimming laps like it was her job at 3:00 a.m. It was…" *Incredibly hot, irrationally distracting,* "…disconcerting."

Mitch smiled, standing up. "It's unsurprising, considering her background. You'd know that if you did more than *skim*."

Jack's brows popped up. "I thought you said she was in insurance. What else does this woman do?"

"Technically, she's an attorney. But before that, she was a Lieutenant Commander in the Navy," Mitch replied, tucking his ID and key into his running shorts.

"The United States Navy?"

"No, the maritime branch of the Irish Defence Forces. *Yes*, the US Navy. Jesus, Jack," Mitch smirked. "You really didn't get any sleep, did you?"

"You're not going to tell me she was a SEAL, are you?"

"No, nothing that serious." Mitch replied, nonplussed. "She was an interrogator."

"Wait, *what*?" Jack's eyes widened. "Nothing serious!? Did she torture people? Water board them?"

"I'm sure she didn't," Mitch answered, sarcastic. "She probably just asked questions nicely, batting those gorgeous eyelashes. Are you crazy?" Mitch smacked the back of Jack's head as he led the way out of his loft. "Our investigator couldn't find anything from her naval career outside of the basic facts, so let's just say you shouldn't piss her off. I'll fill you in on what she told me if you're buying breakfast."

Jack was floored. His new neighbor made James Bond look like an alcoholic slacker. "Why do I feel like you've been holding out on me?"

"I distinctly recall telling you Wyatt was something to see," Mitch remarked, taking off toward the Loop. "Twice!" he shouted over his shoulder.

Jack snorted as he followed, quickly catching up. "We both know that goes two ways."

Mitch set a fast pace as they headed down Randolph Street. "Are you suggesting that I would put an unfit neighbor into that penthouse? Male or female?"

Jack's dark brow quirked in reply.

"Okay, now I'm offended by that on two fronts," Mitch shook his head, exasperated. "First, I would never play a practical joke on you that had literally multiple years' worth of implications. I'm not that committed to humiliating or irritating you. Secondly, I have impeccable taste," Mitch sniffed. "You know it, I know it, and your mother has confirmed it. Sam Wyatt will be the best thing that happened to you in a while. Mark my words."

"How do you figure?" Jack panted, already feeling the effects of last night's sleeplessness.

"She's smart, rich, ridiculously attractive, and I'm willing to bet she'll be able to outfox you. I can't remember the last time you had a challenge like that," Mitch stated, pausing for traffic.

Jack took the moment to glare at him. "You mean to tell me you sold the penthouse to *set me up*?"

Mitch shrugged. "If it happens, it happens. If not, you got one hell of a neighbor." He took off again.

"And did you stop to think about what would happen if I dated and dumped her, Mitch?"

Mitch barked out a laugh. "Oh Jack, I did think about what would happen if she dated and dumped you. I figured you could console yourself on Rebecca's magnificent cleavage."

"You're an asshole," Jack puffed out as Mitch turned up the heat again, sprinting out ahead of him. He was a good match for Mitch on a normal day, but on no sleep, he was getting his shit kicked in. Jack pushed, feeling the burn in his legs as he caught back up. They were running too fast to talk at this point. Jack tried and failed to ratchet up his irritation to outright anger. Mitch was right. The situation with Samantha was far more intriguing than irritating any day of the week. Not that he'd admit that now. Or ever.

They ran fast for five miles before adding sprinting intervals along the lake. Jack was an exhausted, sweaty mess by the time they reached the diner they usually refueled at. Mitch eyed him, laughing silently.

"Shut up," Jack muttered before he could say anything. "Seriously. I haven't gotten any sleep in two nights. I don't want to hear it."

Mitch's expression immediately altered. Jack ignored him as he placed his usual order before getting up to wash his hands and rinse off his face in the restroom. When he returned, he was relieved to see a hot cup of coffee and a tall glass of water waiting for him.

"What's going on?" Mitch asked as Jack downed the water. "You were doing really well for a bit and then, sometime in August, it started getting bad again."

Jack shrugged, putting some cream into his coffee. "It's fine. I'm fine. Don't read into it."

Mitch's brows shot up. "Don't read into it? I'm the closest thing you have to a sponsor. Not to mention the fact that I'm your best friend. So let me ask again: What's going on?"

Jack sighed, realizing he wasn't going to get out of it. Mitch was a dog with a bone. Truth was, even he didn't really understand his recent vicissitude. He'd just felt so restless recently, his mind constantly working, his body on hyper-overdrive, particularly when he lay down. There were periods like this, a drawn-out build up when the insomnia would get so bad that he'd be awake for days, just waiting for one massive crash.

"Are you tempted?" Mitch asked, peering at him over rim of his coffee cup.

Jack shook his head. "You know I'd call you before I did that."

"So you are. *Dammit.*" Mitch shook his head before leaning forward. "Do you have anything in the house? Does Rebecca use anything?"

"No, Mitch. You know I wouldn't let her stay over if she did. I don't need that kind of temptation." Jack sighed, running a frustrated hand through his hair. "It's nothing I can explain. I've just been—I don't know. Bored, I guess. Restless."

"I will have a drug-sniffing dog over there faster than you can say 'K-9 unit' if you're lying to me."

Jack rolled his eyes. "Four years dope-free. Want to see my chip?" He flipped Mitch a middle finger.

"Now, boys, put your birdies down or you'll get no breakfast," their usual waitress scolded, dropping a plate of eggs, bacon, and fruit in front of each of them.

"Sorry, Frieda. Jack has deplorable manners. I can't take him anywhere," Mitch complained, tucking into his eggs.

"Excuse my rudeness, Frieda," Jack apologized to the older woman, giving her his best smile. "I was just trying to explain to Mitch that I already have a mother and she's a lot smarter, nicer, and more attractive than he is."

Frieda rolled her eyes. "Enjoy your breakfast, boys. You both need showers."

Jack and Mitch blinked at each other before laughing, settling into their food.

September—Friday afternoon

The Whitney, Chicago

SAMANTHA

PHOTOS REALLY DID not do that man justice. Not by a long shot.

Sam groaned in the interior of her car as she caught sight of Jack Roman getting out of his Aston Martin in the bay next to hers. She should have known he drove the sexy-as-sin car she'd admired the few times she'd seen it parked in the garage. What did she think he'd be rolling around in—a station wagon?

Sam watched Jack unfold himself gracefully from the car, all easy masculinity in a GQ suit and an optic white shirt. He ran a hand through dark, well-cut hair before reaching in to pick up a briefcase, unbuttoning his collar. He looked like a walking, talking billboard for deliciously irresponsible behavior and a treasure trove of regrettable decisions.

Sam's instant attraction to him made her face color. As he heard her approach, she schooled her face into an easy-going smile, casually waving as she parked and turned off her car.

Don't wait. Please don't wait, she chanted internally, feeling worse for wear. She'd spent nearly the entire day in debriefs and meetings, still suffering tremendous jet-lag and operating on only a couple hours of sleep. She was a little delirious from exhaustion, literally counting the moments until she was in the bath, sipping a red, and tumbling into bed for what she was hoping would be several hours of continuous, dreamless sleep.

Literally the last thing she wanted to do was make nice and force herself to avoid eye-groping her new neighbor. Especially a neighbor who made her aggravatingly aware of how insanely attractive he was and who was probably perfectly aware of his effect on anyone in a five-mile radius. And because it was exactly what she did not want, Jack waited, leaning against his car and whistling softly as she got out. She briefly considered whether the whistle was for her or the car.

"Nice 'vette," he smiled.

The car. Of course. She felt oddly relieved and disappointed at the same time.

Jack sauntered around to the driver's side, admiring the vintage '62 Corvette. "And in the original Rally Red. I'm impressed."

"A car enthusiast." She smiled. "Thanks for noticing," she replied, locking the door.

"I didn't properly introduce myself last night. I'm Jack Roman," he told her in a deep-pitched baritone.

Sam noticed his eyes were a striking silver as he smiled down at her. One glance at the way he looked at her, and Sam knew exactly what he was. *A lethal habit,* she thought. *The accelerator on a race car. A halo jump on a crystal clear day. The best possible rush with the worst possible consequences.*

She'd have to steer clear of this one. The last thing she needed was a headlong crash into the reality of what men with his looks and his reputation really were. She needed a fling with a charming, seductive, unapologetic tom cat about as much as she needed a hole in the head.

Sam shook his hand, the study of friendly indifference. "You look a little less startled and a little more dressed," she teased. "Samantha

Wyatt. Most people call me Sam."

"Thus the initial confusion," Jack replied laughingly, his light eyes studying her as he squeezed her hand gently. "Mitch had given me the distinct impression that you were a man, Samantha."

"Funny," she responded quizzically, noting his use of her full name. "Mitch and I met before the sale. Figured he'd share that tidbit with you."

"I was traveling. We didn't get into the specifics."

"Hope it's not a problem." She shrugged, turning toward the elevator. "Course this means you'll need to get used to all my cocktail parties and idle, gossiping girlfriends."

Jack walked alongside her, shortening his gait. As he reached past her to key in the code to the penthouse floor, she caught a whiff of his subtle cologne. *Incredible.* Sam struggled not to take a deep breath in as he turned back to her.

"Cocktail parties, huh? Sounds like you're going to throw some ragers." His silver eyes were mesmerizing.

"I'm jerking your chain," she replied, stepping into the elevator. "My idea of a rager right now is a glass of wine and a bath before I face plant into bed." Sam closed her eyes for a minute, leaning her head back against the elevator wall. She felt a slight sway as the hours of feeling dead tired layered up and hit her.

"Whoa," Jack murmured, putting a steadying hand on her shoulder.

"Sorry. More tired than I thought," Sam muttered. The warmth of his hand seeped right through her jacket. She liked it. Too much. Sam pulled away a fraction of an inch.

"Don't sweat it," he commented, dropping his hand as he leaned against the mahogany elevator wall, giving her space. "I know the feeling. You go for so many days and then it all hits you like a freight train. Where'd you come from?"

"Moscow."

"Yeah, that'll do it," he replied, watching her as she straightened, putting a little distance between them.

The doors opened to the foyer separating their apartments. Sam smiled as she caught sight of the painting hanging in the center. Jack followed her gaze.

"One of Mitchell's selections. You a fan?"

Sam shrugged. "I am now. I think the only reason he got on board with me taking the penthouse was a guarantee that I'd get him the inside track on the next pieces that pop up."

"I'm sure that wasn't the *only* reason," Jack laughed. "It was good to finally meet you. Have a deep sleep," he grinned, turning right toward his door while she swung left. They were separated by a long hallway of Italian white marble. Two ornate black doors faced each other like chess pieces. Queen and King.

"You know…" Jack started.

She paused, her brow raised in question as she looked at him over her shoulder.

"You should try to stay awake as long as possible so you don't wake up in the middle of the night," he continued. A small smile tugged his lips to the side; his hand rested on his open door. "Perhaps another swim would help?"

Now Sam had been schooled in the art of non-reaction over the years. She'd considered it a professional necessity. She wasn't just good at hiding what she was thinking, she was even better at pretending. And she was pretending not to be wildly attracted to this striking man sporting startling silver eyes and a surplus of sex appeal.

She paused, glancing out at the floor-to-ceiling windows lining the hall. They overlooked the pool, shimmering gently as the sun set over Chicago. The idea of a swim was appealing. Very much so. She looked back at Jack. He was smiling, waiting for an answer, his hand still on his door. One foot in, one foot out.

"I'd hate for you to have to fish out my drowned body from the pool, Jack," she replied after a significant moment. Sam opened her door. "Bad form for a new neighbor, don't you think?" She smiled once more before slipping inside, breathing a sigh of relief as she shut her door.

She didn't see Jack's light eyes shift towards contemplation as he closed the door to his own apartment.

He'd heard that sigh.

CHAPTER 3

September—Saturday night

The Whitney, Chicago

SAMANTHA

STARTLED AWAKE, SAM blinked, momentarily unsure of where she was. Her phone vibrated again somewhere under her pillows. She fished around, glancing at the screen as she answered.

"Are you on fire?"

"Uh... No?"

"Are you in jail?"

"Not this time."

"Are you in the hospital?"

"You wish."

"Then why are you calling me when you know I'm sleeping? Do you want to get *put* into the hospital?"

Carey chuckled. "You're so damn ungrateful. I'm calling to get your hibernated ass up. You've been conked out all day, and we both know how you get when you oversleep. When was the last time you ate?"

Sam glanced at her watch, trying to recall. Shit, she'd been out for nearly twenty hours. On cue, her stomach rumbled.

"Whoa, even I heard that. Jump in the shower, and I'll be there in thirty. I'm cooking."

Thirty minutes later, on the dot, Carey was at her door in jeans and a t-shirt, his baby blues warm as he grinned down at her.

"Bear, you're a bastard for waking me up but a saint for making me dinner," she told him, her voice full of affection.

"Sammy girl," he answered, shifting a canvas bag of groceries to one arm as picked her up with the other. He gave her a noisy kiss on the cheek as she ruffled his short blonde hair.

Sam was slapping him back playfully when Jack's door opened. He stepped out behind a gorgeous redhead, both dressed to the nines, ready for a night on the town. The redhead's face teased Sam's memory, but she couldn't place it. They paused mid-conversation, taking Sam and Carey in. Sam noted the redhead's appreciative glance at Carey. Jack's eyes narrowed as his gaze flickered over them.

Sam dropped down neatly, waving to him. "Hey, Jack."

"Samantha," Jack nodded in acknowledgement. "Who's your friend?" he asked, shifting his gaze.

"Carey Nelson," Carey responded, stepping forward to introduce himself.

"Jack Roman," Jack returned smoothly. They met midway down the hall, clasping hands and leaving Sam and the redhead to watch while they engaged in some kind of man handshake/staring contest.

Sam stepped around Carey, wondering at his sudden protectiveness. She extended her hand to the redhead, introducing herself. "Hi, I'm Sam Wyatt, Jack's neighbor."

"Rebecca Holland." The redhead smiled in return. "I didn't know you had a neighbor?" Rebecca said to Jack, her brow cocked.

"It's recent," Jack answered before turning back to Sam. "You two staying in?" He glanced over her again, his light eyes cataloging her cut-offs and bare legs, the faded NAVY t-shirt.

"I'm making her dinner," Carey replied, tucking an arm around her and squeezing her gently to his side. "She's liable to chew someone's arm off if she doesn't eat soon," Carey teased, winking down at her.

"Uh-oh. Sounds like me on a juice cleanse," Rebecca laughed. She leaned forward to hit the elevator button. "We'd better get a move on, or I'll be chewing your arm off, baby," she told Jack, her tone just a touch lascivious.

Jack nodded, still watching them.

"You two have a good time," Carey called out, drawing Sam back toward her door.

She waved as she closed the door behind them, then turned and punched his arm hard. "What was that?" she asked.

Unfazed, Carey kicked off his shoes and padded into her kitchen, setting the groceries on the counter. "That was your neighbor checking you out with his girlfriend, a world-famous actress, *right there* under his nose," he replied, pulling out vegetables and a crock pot from the bag.

Sam's brow creased. "He was not, you troglodyte."

"He was," Carey rebutted. "Blind, deaf, mute men in Egypt noticed, Sammy girl. And stop calling me a caveman," he huffed. "I'm your best friend. It's my job to watch out for you."

Sam shook her head though she smiled in spite of herself. "You know better than anyone I can take care of myself, Bear. But thanks for the overprotective-brother act. I already know all about Jack Roman. I'd have to be wearing a crash helmet to get that reckless."

"Rebecca Holland's smoking hot though. *Damn*," Carey murmured appreciatively.

"I knew she looked familiar. You said she's an actress?"

"Yeah. Pretty good one. She did that television show about surviving a plane crash on that island? She's doing movies now. Supposed to be in town filming."

Sam chewed on that one while she helped wash the vegetables.

"What are you making me?" she asked as he moved around, pulling out cooking utensils.

"Been cooking my world-famous chili since this morning," he grinned, putting the pot over one of her Viking burners.

"You mean your mama's world-famous chili recipe you stole," she teased.

Carey looked affronted. "Go turn on some music I can cook to, and let me work my magic."

A short time later while they listened to some good Texas blues and chatted about everything and nothing, Carey pulled the lid off the pot of chili and leaned over it, breathing in a sigh of pleasure. He stirred, lifting a spoon out to savor his work.

"Taste," he told her, holding the spoon toward her. Sam stopped chopping, leaning forward to take a sip. He pulled back a little. "Careful.

It's hot."

She licked her lips, thinking. "More cayenne. Maybe one more garlic."

Carey nodded, adding both ingredients. They moved around each other fluidly, used to each other's shape and presence from growing up together.

Carey opened her subzero, poking his head inside. "Cold Shiner Bock, thank God," he muttered, pulling two bottles out and popping the caps off on the marble counter.

"That's Italian marble, asshole. Not a can opener," she chastised, accepting the beer he handed her as he grinned unapologetically.

"Sammy girl, this slab of rock's been around for longer than you and me, and it'll be around a lot longer. It can take being functional," he teased, clinking his bottleneck against hers before taking a long draw. "So," he said after a moment. "You gonna tell me what's been on your mind?"

Sam frowned. "What are you talking about?"

"You've been off the past couple months. Since Jakarta at least. I've been waiting for you to tell me why. Now I think you should just spit it out."

Sam thought about that, sipping her beer. "Business has doubled in the past two years," she started, turning around to chop tomatoes. "We've come so far, but there's a lot more I want to accomplish. I just wonder if we're too close sometimes—too caught up in the day-to-day of being on the ground. The European office is fine with those ex-British SAS guys we put in a year ago. You and I have been all over Asia recently, but I wonder if—"

Carey leaned back against the counter, following her train of thought. "You want to focus on expanding the business. You think the guys are ready to step up and take over the day-to-day?"

"They can be." She turned to look at him. "We can't sustain this, much less grow it more if you and I are always on the ground. I guess Jakarta just brought it all home. For one thing, we need to steer the ship, and for another, we're getting too damn old to be dragging people out of hot zones. We can't be caught up in the wrangling on the front lines all the time. It's exhausting trying to do both."

Carey snorted, flexing his bicep. "Speak for yourself."

She laughed, tossing a dish towel at his head. He caught it easily, flinging it onto his shoulder.

Sam took a drink of her beer before continuing. "We're not kids anymore, Bear. Our field days are getting limited, and you and I need to be strategizing how to get to the next place with the business. I want to overtake Leviathan. I want to become number one. You know the guys better than anyone. What do you think?"

Carey tilted his head, considering her for a moment. "Talon is ready to step up and lead the security and strike teams. He did well in Jakarta. I've had him running smaller security ops without me, and he's killing it, but Rush needs a little more time on your side of the table. He's too tactically focused. He needs help pulling up and seeing the bigger picture." Carey put a lid over the pot and took another pull of beer. "Chili needs just a little more time. Let's sit."

Carey followed Sam to the sofa, one of the few pieces of furniture she'd already picked for the place. Carey jokingly called it "man-sized," a huge dove colored sectional that was so wide he could easily lay down on it from nearly any direction. He sprawled across it lazily, taking a moment to glance around.

"You need a television," he muttered.

"Eh," she shrugged, tucking her feet under her. "There's too much crap on these days, and it's not like I have the time."

"You stream CNN, BBC, and Al-Jazeera twenty-four seven at the office."

Sam rolled her eyes. "That's the office. This is my oasis. No news, no advertising, no BS."

"No sports," Carey grumbled.

Sam laughed. "You've got your own house for that. You want to come over and hang out, you have to actually talk to me. No zoning out on the tube or getting caught up on your phone. You're right in one sense though." She glanced around. "I need to hire a decorator." Sam loved the open space, the massive leaded windows, and the walls she'd had painted in soft colors. It felt warm but empty, like she'd never unpacked, though no boxes were in sight.

She'd lived sparingly the past few years. She didn't have a lot of knickknacks and personal effects outside of an old photo of her dad with his arm around her little brother, sitting on the fireplace mantle. Ryland must have been about eight at the time, hanging onto one of the wooden fences at the ranch, hair mussed from the wind or dad's hand. She glanced away before Carey caught her looking at it.

"I'm buying you a TV for your housewarming gift," Carey grumbled.

"Is that a gift for you or a gift for me?" she asked.

"Both."

Sam chuckled before distracting him with their earlier conversation. "I was thinking of sending Rush to London to shadow McCall," she said. "Put some polish on that Southern boy charm."

Carey chuckled. "I can't think of a better method to set him in his ways."

"Why's that?"

He smiled, shaking his head. "Sammy, I think Ian McCall is a brilliant ex-SAS counter-terrorism expert with impeccable breeding and a fancy Oxford degree, but he has a massive stick up his ass. He won't get a good ole boy like Rush, and he'll try to change him instead of playing up his strengths. Rush will dig in and get stubborn. Or worse, he'll start to doubt whether he can do it."

Sam thought about that. "Well, who then?"

Carey brows shot up. "Isn't it obvious? You."

Now it was Sam's turn to shoot her brows up. "I don't know about that."

"You don't know, or you don't like the idea of letting someone besides me that close to you?" Carey asked, hitting the nail on the head.

Sam sipped her beer, taking a moment to think through her reply. She'd worked in teams for years. But truth be told, she'd always been more of a loner. The only person who worked with her day-in and day-out and knew her well was Carey. But she'd worked with Evan Rush for a while, trusted him, knew him to produce results, follow orders. He had an easy-going, amenable way about him that made people feel instantly at ease.

"I can feel the cogs in your brain turning," Carey chuckled. "You're overthinking. He's a natural. He'll be able to leverage anything you teach him quickly. He's a talker and a charmer. You're a talker and a charmer. You're both good at building alliances. People think you want the best for them. Win-win scenarios."

Carey was right. She knew he was right.

"Fair enough, Bear. He'll be with me, and Talon will shadow you, so he can see how we interact. We assess in a couple months and then send them out solo."

Carey's smile was broad. "We can go on vacation. How'll that be?"

Sam laughed. "Jesus, I thought I'd kill someone after Jakarta screwed up my Bali plans. Anything without a phone and involving a beach will be welcome. You?"

"Texas," he replied easily. "Waking up early with Dad. Drinking coffee on the porch. Riding out with the boys. Lord, I can smell that tall grass now."

"You always want to go home," she remarked, smiling at the dreamy look on his face.

"And you never want to come back," Carey sighed, taking another sip of beer. "You should, you know. Pops misses you. He says he only gets to hear your voice when you talk about the ranch. Come back with me for Thanksgiving."

"You just want me to help with the steers—and you know I can't commit to anything until we see where business is at," she answered, her tone nonchalant though her heart squeezed a little.

Carey made a scoffing sound. "You know I'm just as invested in seeing our work succeed. That doesn't mean you can't make time for family, Sammy girl."

The oven timer went off. Saved by the bell. She got up to check on the cornbread, dipping a toothpick into the center to test it.

"Just like mama taught you," Carey grinned, sidling up with the butter.

Sam slathered the browned top with the salted butter, thinking about how she used to help his mother out when she was a kid, her little brother Ryland and Carey rough-housing and carrying on in the yard.

"How is Aunt Hannah?" she asked quietly, cutting the cornbread as Carey pulled down plates and bowls.

"She's good. Asks after you all the time. Wants to know if you're dating. She just finished remodeling the kitchen."

Sam nodded, feeling the unwelcome and powerful press of emotion thinking about home—the ranch she'd grown up on. She hadn't been back in over a dozen years, since she'd buried her father and Ryland right next to her mother and her granddaddy, the only other family she'd had. After it had happened, she'd left partial ownership and management of the ranch in Grant Nelson's capable hands, asking him and his wife to move into the main house permanently. He'd been the foreman at her father's ranch for as long as she could remember. Aunt Hannah had basically been her mother after her own had died giving birth to Ryland. Though Sam promised regularly she'd return, time had made a liar out of her.

"I know you still get sad, Sammy," Carey spoke up from behind her. "But staying away from home isn't gonna help you heal, baby girl." She felt his broad hand at her shoulder.

Sam closed her eyes, leaning on the counter. "I can't just yet, Bear," she admitted quietly. "I'm not ready," she said, slipping a hand over his.

"You'll never be ready," he murmured, broad fingers tangling with hers. "You can't get ready for heartbreak. You just have to let it hurt, Sammy. Besides," he said, dropping a kiss to her head. "It won't be as bad as you think it'll be. You've forgotten how beautiful it is. The smell of the fields. The heat of the sun on your face."

"You mean the smell of manure and the sweat from wrangling cows and fixing fences all day," she amended, her tone dry.

"Well, yeah," he chuckled. "That too."

They set the table, Sam carrying over the cornbread and greens, Carey ladling bowls of hot chili. When they sat down to eat, Carey held up his beer to toast, blue eyes twinkling. "Here's to lying, cheating, stealing, and drinking…"

Sam smiled at their old toast. "If you're going to lie—"

"Lie for a friend."

"If you're going to cheat—"

"Cheat death!"

"If you're going to steal…?" she smiled, leaning toward him.

"Steal a heart," Carey sighed, clutching his chest dramatically.

"And if you're going to drink—" Sam clinked the bottleneck of her beer against his.

"Drink with me."

CHAPTER 4

September—Friday night, a week later

The Whitney, Chicago

JACK

JACK KNEW THAT when a woman got a man a gift, she expected to see him using it. Unfortunately, he was due to pick up Rebecca in a few short minutes, and he couldn't remember exactly what she'd given him.

"It wasn't a tie," Jack muttered to himself, perusing his walk-in closet. Rebecca had given him something on his birthday, a few weeks ago now, and that present had been followed by series of mind-blowing orgasms. Maybe that was why he couldn't recall her more conservative gift. He tried to remember what the box she'd slid toward him had looked like. It was small. Too small for a tie. *Was it a tie pin?* No. *She wasn't watching reruns of Mad Men again, was she?*

She'd gone through a brief retro period at the beginning of the summer, wearing vintage dresses with gloves and Ray-Bans. Bright red lipstick like Marilyn Monroe. The press had loved it, already covering her night and day since she'd come to Chicago. He'd been a little relieved when she'd gotten onto a new trend. The red lipstick was pretty to look at but a bitch to wash off his face and body.

Jack opened the drawer holding his watches. *No, she didn't get me a watch.* That he probably would have recalled. He caught a glimpse of a black, alligator skin box tucked in the corner.

"Cuff links!" he crowed, picking up engraved cuff links with onyx frames, relieved it was something he could wear this evening. She'd mentioned a few days ago that she hadn't seen him wear his gift, and he'd heard the pique in her tone.

Sliding on the cuff links, he shrugged into his dinner jacket and headed toward the foyer, grabbing his wallet, phone, and keys. As he swung open the door, he glanced down at his watch to make sure he still had plenty of time to pick Rebecca up before they hit his black tie gala at the Art Institute of Chicago.

"Well, don't you look like a tall, cool drink of water?"

Samantha's trademark rasp immediately snapped Jack to attention. He looked up to see her waiting for the elevator, a vision in a cobalt blue Grecian gown. Her hair was pinned up in an intricate set of artistic twists. He was momentarily, uncharacteristically caught off guard as he took her in.

The elevator dinged softly, and Sam's brow arched, a soft challenge and a question all at once. Her lips twitched in humor. Jack realized belatedly he'd been gaping.

"A lovely compliment from a lovely woman. The best kind," he replied, feeling a little bemused as he followed her into the elevator. The heady scent of orange blossoms and jasmine wafted gently behind her. Jack nearly closed his eyes, his senses saturated. "You look magnificent, Samantha," he said sincerely. Her look tonight was so complete, so perfect. A goddess. He wondered briefly how many other men wanted to worship at her altar as he reached for the elevator button.

"First floor, please, and thank you, Jack," she murmured, a little smile still playing at her lips. "You look like you're about to spend the night gambling away at the baccarat tables in Monte Carlo," she commented.

Jack smiled at the compliment, wondering who she was going out with tonight. Looking like that, it had to be someone special. He felt his temples tighten thinking about it.

He leaned back casually against the elevator wall. "Well, it'll be an expensive night, but not at the tables, sadly. Mitch and I are hosting the Cure for Cancer fundraiser at the Art Institute tonight."

Sam's teeth flashed as a genuine smile popped to the surface. "I should have guessed! Great choice. Did Mitch have anything to do with it?"

"One guess," Jack replied, slanting her a look.

"I should've known," she laughed. "Can't fault that man's taste."

"Are you headed to the gala, by any chance?"

The elevator doors slid open.

"Maybe I'll see you there." Samantha smiled as she stepped out, the faint drift of her perfume filling his senses again.

September—A few hours later

Art Institute of Chicago

JACK

"THERE'S MICHAEL SUTHERLAND. He just lost a ludicrous sum of money on a mining gambit in Australia. He might be willing to sell his Lincoln Park commercial properties to stay solvent," Mitch murmured.

Jack glanced around the Contemporary Arts wing, noting with satisfaction that anyone who had a name in Chicago—or who wanted to become a name in Chicago—was in attendance. He caught the eye of Mr. Sutherland, nodding in acknowledgement while he accepted a club soda and lime from the bartender. "Well, that's interesting. When did you find this out?"

"Poker game last night at the Casino Club," Mitch murmured. "He was notably absent. I did some digging," he continued, sipping his champagne. "Good to see he's still up for a little charity this year."

Every fall, Jack and Mitch hosted one of the biggest social events of the year. The Roman Foundation Charity Gala raised millions for cancer research at the University of Chicago Medicine. This year, he and Mitch chose to host the event at the Art Institute, taking advantage of the gorgeous Contemporary and Asian art collections, the dramatically lit gardens, and God willing, the pocket books of the influential and well-to-do attendees. Crowds of impressively-dressed people milled about, sipping champagne and pretending to discuss the art and cancer research while they really dished on each other: who was wearing what, who was divorcing whom—and in his and Mitch's case, who would be ripe for short sales and takeovers.

They'd spent the better part of the last hour working the room, shaking hands and thanking patrons, asking after people and making polite chit-chat. Once Rebecca had disappeared to the ladies' room, Mitch started filling Jack in on the juicier tidbits on the Who's Who in attendance.

"Look into the building he owns in River North too. I've had my eye on that one for the past year," Jack murmured, casually waving to an acquaintance across the room.

"Any particular reason why?" Mitch asked, hiding his surprise behind his champagne glass.

"Because that land is right next to the Chicago River and Merchandise Mart, and I think it's high time we opened a new luxury apartment building that makes the Trump building look like its kid sister. Don't you agree?"

Mitch laughed, delighted. "A buy-one-get-one-seriously-discounted? Evil. I like it."

"We're just helping a good man who's down," Jack shrugged. "Set the wheels in motion. I want to move on this before anyone else realizes what the hell he's gotten himself into."

"Will do." Mitch nodded before glancing over Jack's shoulder. "Rebecca—have I told you how breathtaking you look tonight?"

"You did, but I never mind hearing a nice compliment twice," she flirted.

Jack turned, immediately switching gears as he slid an arm around Rebecca's waist. He pressed a kiss against her temple.

"He's right, beautiful. Love the dress. I'll especially love slipping it off of you later," Jack murmured into her ear, his hand drifting low to the exposed back of her daring white gown.

"And that's my cue to leave," Mitch commented, amused. "Have fun, kids. Jack, try not to traumatize our more conservative donors while you grope your girlfriend. Rebecca," he nodded, "always a pleasure."

"Likewise," she replied, wiggling her fingers at him as he sauntered off. "I have some plans for you tonight, baby," she whispered, sliding a hand down his shirt.

"Oh?" Jack asked, his brows rising. "And what would those be?"

"I'm going to tie you to that bed of yours and tease your—"

Jack's attention snapped to the entrance of the gallery the moment Samantha strolled in, turning heads as she greeted a group of people she knew. She was escorted by a different man than the one he'd met last week. This one was medium height and well-built, with light brown hair and the dark tan of someone who spent a fair amount of time outdoors. She looped her hand in his arm casually, smiling as they passed the flashing cameras of the press group covering the party.

"...and then I'm going to—" Rebecca continued whispering in his ear, unaware that she'd already lost his attention. Jack nodded distractedly, turning away from Samantha and her mystery date, wondering why he was so damn taken by her, and why he was so annoyingly irritated she was with yet another guy. *It's none of your damned business*, he reminded himself.

Jack was saved from his mounting discomfort by a colleague of his father's, coming over to congratulate him on the success of the evening. Years of training as a politician's son and a businessman kept him smiling, and he stopped on occasion to shake hands, pose for photos, and make small talk, occasionally touching the silky skin at the small of Rebecca's back. She looked every inch the movie star tonight, and donors and fans alike had kept them both busy until it was time to sit down for the gala dinner.

They'd hired a popular Saturday Night Live comedian and Second City alum to emcee the night's festivities. The talent was jocular and lively, seamlessly transitioning from stand-up comedy to the evening's auction, which included vignettes from cancer survivors and family members. Jack gave a short speech of thanks on behalf of the Roman Foundation, unerringly pinpointing Samantha amidst dozens of tables. His gaze narrowed as he noticed Samantha sitting between Mitch and her date. Mitch whispered into her ear while she sat with a small, secretive smile on her mouth, nodding as if they were sharing a private joke. Jack shook off the momentary distraction, directing a winning smile out into the crowd as he asked donors to be particularly generous that evening. When he sat down, he glanced at Samantha again, only to have her catch his stare. She raised her champagne glass in silent salute. He returned the gesture in kind, wondering again why he found her so utterly diverting.

"Darling, I'll be gone for just a moment." Rebecca excused herself after dinner, waving to the emcee. "I haven't seen him since I did SNL a couple years ago."

"Take your time," Jack murmured, nodding absently as he continued chatting with a couple of long-time donors at the table.

Jack's brother, Jaime, appeared by his side, handing him a fresh glass of club soda. Though Jaime was nearly ten years younger, they looked closer in age. Jaime was a lankier version of Jack, lean from years of cycling and residual grief—though you'd never know it the way he turned the charm on. Jaime turned to acknowledge the couple Jack had been speaking with.

"Mrs. Allen, you're looking especially stunning tonight. Mr. Allen, you're lucky I'm an honorable man, or I'd steal this lady right out from under you," Jaime joked, patting the older man on the shoulder. Mr. and Mrs. Allen were probably old enough to be their grandparents, but Jaime was incorrigible and Mrs. Allen clearly loved the banter, evidenced by the blush in her cheeks. Her husband chortled, shaking hands with Jaime enthusiastically.

"How's your business doing, Jaime?" Mr. Allen asked, pumping his arm.

"On fire since the IPO, thanks for asking," Jaime replied. "Now would anyone mind if I borrowed my brother? I need to catch up with him. It's been weeks!"

"We talked two days ago," Jack muttered as Jaime led them out of the banquet and out toward the garden.

"You looked like you needed saving," Jaime replied. "And you seem distracted. What's up?" he asked as he sipped his champagne, pausing next to an Anish Kapoor sculpture. An orchestra sat at one end of the garden, playing a Cole Porter standard. Couples swayed languidly, talking and laughing, enjoying the warm autumn breeze.

"We should take the boat out before the wind turns too chilly," Jack commented, thinking about the Bermuda-rigged ketch he and Jaime shared.

"Maddie would like that," Jaime nodded. "We didn't use it enough this summer."

"How's next Friday?"

"It's good, but you still haven't answered my question."

Jack sighed, shrugging as he spotted Samantha on the edge of the dance floor, talking to the man she came with. Though the guy smiled easily and often enough, Jack could sense he was uncomfortable when he tucked a finger in his collar, tugging his bow tie as he leaned in to say something in Samantha's ear. She laughed, smiling up at him. Jack emptied his glass, setting it on the tray of a passing waiter.

"Now I get it," Jaime remarked, following Jack's gaze. He looked over Samantha quizzically. "I don't remember her. Is she an ex?"

"Who's an ex?" Mitch asked, coming to stand beside them.

"That super-fox in the blue dress," Jaime answered, sipping his champagne.

Mitch's eyes spotted Samantha immediately. "Ah, the gorgeous and lethal Samantha Wyatt," he murmured appreciatively. "She took the penthouse," he added for Jaime's benefit.

"The penthouse?" Jaime glanced up at Jack in surprise. "As in you have a neighbor now and you won't be hounding me to move in every other week—*that* penthouse?"

"The very same," Mitch confirmed when Jack just rolled his eyes. "Samantha's here with the other partners from Lennox Chase. They have a couple tables tonight. She gave me a check for the Foundation with six zeroes. Swear to God, nothing is sexier than a beautiful woman tucking a huge sum of money into your pocket," he sighed, hand patting his breast pocket. "Well, except if she'd been naked of course, but honestly, that's just been the best part of my night."

As if she could sense they were talking about her, Samantha looked up, catching Jack's eye again. She inclined her head in acknowledgment.

Jaime glanced from Samantha to Jack, then back to Samantha. He suddenly left them, making a beeline toward her.

"…and ladies and gentleman, he's off!" Mitch chuckled. "He's either gonna get her for you or get her for himself," he joked over his shoulder, trailing Jaime toward Samantha and her date.

Jack considered turning back inside and finding Rebecca but thought better of it. It was inevitable he and Samantha would speak again tonight. And the sooner he spoke with her, the sooner he could get over whatever this strange aggravation was. He had no claim on her. Had no idea if she was half as attracted to him as he was to her. And to top it off, he was here with someone else.

What am I thinking? Jack fumed. *And why the hell does she get under my skin so much?*

"I had to meet the woman who finally convinced my brother to sell the penthouse next to him. I thought he'd never give that up," Jaime declared as he pulled up to her. "I'm Jaime Roman. What a pleasure to meet you," he told her as he kissed her hand with flourish.

Samantha watched him, amused. "Sam Wyatt, and it's a pleasure to meet you as well. I'm a huge fan of your mobile locater app."

"Don't I know it," her date interjected with a thick Southern drawl. "There's no hiding from her, even during lunch," he joked amiably. "Evan Rush," he introduced himself, shaking Jaime's hand.

"Wives everywhere love me for that app, and husbands everywhere would like to spike my head over a spit." Jaime laughed as he shook Evan's hand.

"As do teenagers, lazy coworkers, and parolees, I'm sure," Mitch interjected, moving forward to brush Sam's cheek in a social kiss. "Sam, I said it earlier, but you look astonishingly beautiful tonight. Like Pallas Athena, worshiped by thousands of supplicants before going to war in your honor," Mitch told her, stepping back to admire her dress.

"I already gave you the check, Mitch," Sam replied, her eyes glinting with humor. "No need to blow smoke up my ass."

Mitch threw back his head as he laughed, drawing the attention of the people around them. Rebecca must have heard as well, appearing by Jack's side, eyes curious, smile bright.

"What have I missed?" she asked, glancing around the group.

Mitch made introductions. Jack noted Samantha's expression remained pleasantly neutral while others gushed over Rebecca's recent work. Rebecca preened, enjoying the spotlight. Though Jack knew he shouldn't, he couldn't seem to help thinking that Rebecca, famous for her looks and talent, didn't hold a candle to Samantha's relaxed self-possession. She was utterly confident, moving easily among Chicago's power players, charming but desultory, sensual without being overt. Beautiful, certainly, but not reliant on her looks. Jack detached himself from Rebecca's arm.

"Samantha, a word?" he asked, slicing through the conversation.

Jaime and Mitch glanced between the two before smoothly redirecting the conversation and engaging a suddenly uneasy Rebecca. Evan glanced at Samantha, a question in his eyes. She nodded at him as Jack stepped toward her, gently directing her toward the outdoor bar.

"May I get you something besides champagne?" Jack offered.

"A bourbon would be nice," she murmured.

Jack placed the order, requesting another club soda for himself.

"You don't drink?" Samantha asked, clearly surprised.

Jack shrugged easily. "Occasionally. But it's not my poison."

"And what is your poison?"

He eyed her dress.

Samantha laughed, a husky, sexy sound. "So your reputation is earned."

"Which one is that?"

"The one about you being a wily, unapologetic, womanizing rake."

"That's a mouthful."

"Oh, Jack," Sam smiled, her eyes dancing. "I think that's what you're about to be on the receiving end of if your date's death stare is any indication."

Jack glanced at Rebecca. *If looks could kill.* He smiled reassuringly at her before turning back to Samantha as he leaned against the bar.

"I understand you wrote a big check," he said to Samantha, allowing his gaze to wander over the romantically lit dance floor.

"I wrote you two big checks. You'll have to be more specific."

"The one for the Foundation tonight," he clarified. "Thank you."

"My pleasure," Samantha replied, accepting the bourbon from the bartender. "Your Foundation is impeccably run and organized. I like the transparency you provide on funding allocation. It's obvious you have people who know how to run a business managing it."

Jack tipped his head in acknowledgement. "Thank you. It's a cause that's near and dear to my family's heart."

"You've lost someone to cancer?"

"Hasn't everybody?"

Samantha remained silent, watching him. Jack couldn't tell if he'd offended her or if she was just waiting for him to answer. "My Uncle Gianni and two of my grandparents," he admitted quietly, surprised at his own candor.

"I'm sorry to hear that," she said softly. "Were you close?"

Jack took a breath. "I don't remember my grandparents well, but I loved my Uncle Gianni. He was my father's youngest brother. I look a lot like him."

"And was he also an unapologetic rake?" she teased gently after a pause, lightening the mood.

"You forgot wily."

"How could I?" Samantha laughed. "That's the best part."

Jack laughed with her. "Yeah. He did all right with the ladies," he conceded.

"Like uncle, like nephew."

"Pretty sure that's not how the saying goes." He grinned at her.

Samantha waved her hand airily. "Po-tay-to, po-tah-to."

"And how about the other check?" he asked. "Are you happy you wrote it?"

Samantha's mouth curved into a small, secret smile. Jack had the sudden notion he'd like to make her smile like that often.

"I've been living out of a suitcase in one form or another since college. Believe it or not, waking up in a place I recognize is a relatively new development," she confided.

Jack's brows rose. "Congratulations. I hope you love living there as much as I have."

Samantha nodded. "I'm certain I will."

"And will you have a housewarming?"

"Perhaps." She shrugged.

"And will you invite me?" he asked, tipping his face toward her as her scent teased him.

"I think you'll have to make sure you get permission first," she murmured. "Your two o'clock," she told him, finishing her drink.

"Baby—what are you up to?" Rebecca sidled up to him, draping herself against his chest.

"Just thanking Samantha for her donation," he answered, slipping his hand around her waist, gently urging her back. Rebecca's eyes narrowed.

"Happy to help," Samantha responded with a pleasant expression. "Please excuse me. I see a client I'd like to say hello to," she told them, returning to Evan and guiding him toward another group of people at the edge of the gardens.

"You two looked cozy," Rebecca purred, her fingers sliding up Jack's dress shirt. Jack grasped her wrists gently.

"You sound jealous," he remarked, turning away. "Glenlivet 18. Rocks," he said to the bartender.

"You're drinking?" Rebecca asked, surprised.

"I figure it's a reward for a successful evening," Jack shrugged. "More champagne?" he offered.

Rebecca shook her head, crossing her arms.

"Were you really talking about donations?" Rebecca asked as the bartender handed him his whisky. He took a sip, savoring the dram. Jack leveled a knowing smile at her. "You *are* jealous."

"And if I am?" Rebecca shrugged a creamy shoulder. "You've been watching her like a hawk all night. Should I be worried?"

"Rebecca..." Jack cajoled. "I'm here with you tonight. And you look amazing," he told her, trailing a finger down her arm. He took another sip of his drink before setting it down. "Come on. Let's dance." He drew her out to the dance floor, pulling her close.

The orchestra was playing a bluesy version of "Moondance," and Jack guided them along smoothly, his thumb circling the small of her back. She shivered delicately, and he smiled against her temple, his eyes tracking back to Samantha at the edge of the garden.

"You know the filming is wrapping soon," Rebecca murmured against his shoulder.

Evan was saying something in Samantha's ear. She laughed at whatever he said, nodding. Jack's hand tightened on Rebecca's.

"I know we haven't talked about me leaving..."

Jaime joined Evan and Samantha, handing her a glass of champagne. She didn't drink, but she smiled her thanks.

"...I'd like to continue seeing you. I was thinking maybe you could come out to see me in California. Visit me on set."

Jaime was showing them something on his phone. Jack wondered if it was pictures of Maddie, but his fingers were moving too quickly, like he was working an app. Sam leaned in, clearly interested in whatever he was showing her.

"What do you think?"

Jack blinked down, refocusing. "Sure, baby. That'd be nice."

Rebecca's mouth compressed into a thin red line.

Not the right answer? Jack tracked back over the conversation, wondering what trip wire he'd hit.

"What *is* this to you?" she whispered harshly, turning her head away as they circled the floor.

He frowned, drawing her chin up. "Hey."

Rebecca jerked her face out of his grasp, stepping back. "I'm still here, and you're already planning your next score," she whispered furiously, eyes hurt. Rebecca glanced around quickly, unwilling to cause a scene. She turned to leave.

"Rebecca, stop," Jack told her, pulling her back against him. "You're overreacting," he said into her ear before he turned her to face him again. "What's going on?" he asked, looking into her eyes.

"Isn't it obvious?" she asked quietly.

"Apparently not." He pulled her back into his arms as the orchestra began playing a Sinatra number. The group of people dancing around them parted as he drew her toward the center of the floor.

"I'm falling for you, Jack," Rebecca admitted, her cheek resting against his lapel. "I don't want this to end when we're done filming in Chicago."

Jack said nothing, leading her gently along the dance floor as he tucked their hands against his chest. Rebecca's eyes welled, and she blinked furiously, holding her emotion back. Jack pressed a warm kiss to her forehead, gliding her through the steps.

"Let's just enjoy this dance, Rebecca. You look so beautiful to-night..."

"What's going to happen to us, Jack?"

"Baby, let's just focus on what's happening between us now. Hmmm?" He dipped her low, kissing away her troubled expression.

HOURS LATER, WHEN Jack took Rebecca to her hotel, she slid her hand into the waistband of his dress slacks and pulled him forward, whispering how badly she wanted him. How she needed him.

And so he gave himself to her. Harder and rougher than usual, yanking her head back as he licked and bit at her neck, imagining that long, creamy expanse of skin belonging to someone else. Closing his eyes as he surged into her, Jack imagined dark hair and dark eyes staring up at him. And as he ran his hand down her chest and gripped her thigh, pulling it up high over his hip as he spent himself into her body, he bit his lip so he wouldn't say her name.

Samantha.

September—The next morning

Oak Park, Illinois

JACK

"WHO WANTS PANCAKES?"

"Uncle Jack?" Maddie's little head popped out of the tent on her bedroom floor, a mess of dark curls and a hanging-in-there-for-dear-life red ribbon.

"Yeah, *micina cara*[1]—unless you've got an uncle you love more than me?" he asked, plopping down beside her as she shuffled back into her tent.

"I don't have any uncles 'sides you," she replied sassily, tossing out a stuffed rabbit, a pillow, a coloring book, and a toy stethoscope. Jack easily caught each item, used to her routine. Her head popped back out. "I need those," she told him solemnly.

Maddie was the Princess of Preparedness. Even before her mother passed away, she was constantly getting ready for something, whether it was dragging her blocks around or carrying ten different coloring books in case she had the urge to sit down and doodle for the next two hours. She jerked out a surprisingly large giraffe from the tent as she stood. What she needed that for Jack wasn't entirely sure, but he knew better than to argue.

"I want pancakes the shapes of stars," she told him, dragging the giraffe behind her tiny, five-year-old body. "And strawberries. And a turtle."

"For breakfast?" Jack asked, following her dutifully with all her stuff, the doting uncle.

"No. For a pet," she answered, annoyed he wasn't catching on. "Dad said I had to think really hard about it, and I did, Uncle Jack. I want a turtle."

"Okay, *micinia cara*. We'll see what we can do," Jack promised, pausing outside of Jaime's room, listening for movement. It was early still, and Jaime wasn't accustomed to late nights out anymore. Jack figured he'd let his brother enjoy a rare sleep-in while he entertained Maddie.

He watched in amusement as Maddie dragged the giraffe down the stairs by its head. She situated the giraffe next to her in the kitchen as she climbed up a short bar stool so she could watch Jack while he worked.

"Star-shaped pancakes coming up," he smiled, prepping the batter as he took a sip of the coffee he'd made when he let himself in.

Jack saw his brother and Maddie as often as possible—whether it

---

[1] Italian endearment meaning "dear kitty"

was making breakfast or dinner together, going sailing, watching a game, whatever. He'd been busy the past couple weeks, and he'd missed out on their usual time together. But after leaving Rebecca's hotel early this morning, he'd gone home and showered, catching a couple hours of sleep before waking with the sun and heading over to make them breakfast.

"What are you working on, *cara?*" Jack asked as he cooked pancakes on the griddle.

Maddie hunched over her coloring book, focused on it like she was cracking a nuclear missile code. "I'm drawing a house for my turtle, Uncle Jack. I want us to build it," she explained, coloring furiously in purple.

"You got it," he told her, proud his penchant for building things seemed to rub off onto her. "You want a boy turtle or a girl turtle?"

Her little brow knit. "How do you tell the difference?"

Jack thought about it. He had no idea, but he bet his nerdy brother would know.

"Not sure, cutie. Let's ask your daddy when he wakes up. Do you have any names picked out?" He sliced strawberries, placing a little plate of them in front of her.

"Bob."

Jack bit back a smile as he leaned against the kitchen counter. "And if it's a girl?"

"Bob, Uncle Jack. Just Bob," Maddie insisted, sticking her little tongue out in concentration as she continued designing Bob's dream home.

"Alrighty then." He nodded sagely, returning to the pancakes.

"Oh my God, where is the coffee?" Jaime groaned, stumbling into the kitchen. He scooped Maddie up, blowing a raspberry on her little tummy while she squirmed and squealed.

Jack poured Jaime a cup, sliding it toward him.

"Thanks, bro," Jaime sighed in pleasure as he sipped, taking a seat on the barstool next to Maddie. "You're here early," he commented, popping one of Maddie's strawberries into his mouth.

Jack shrugged, flipping the pancakes.

"Daddy, how can you tell a boy turtle from a girl turtle?"

As Jaime explained, Jack fixed Maddie's plate, sliding it in front of her.

Delighted, her mouth formed a perfect O.

"This what you wanted, *micinia cara*?"

"You made me stars, Uncle Jack."

"You're my little star, Maddie." He smiled, ruffling her hair.

"And what am I?" Jaime prompted, looking longingly at the bacon on the stove.

"You're a pain in my—"

"Don't say bad words, Uncle Jack," Maddie chided, wagging her finger.

"Yeah, Jack," Jaime grinned. "Be nice to your baby brother and fix him a plate."

"Say please, Daddy," Maddie directed as she jabbed at her pancakes.

"Please, Daddy," Jaime parroted, winking. Jack rolled his eyes, fixing him a plate while Jaime turned on his tablet, fiddling around with some developer code.

Jaime had always been a bit of a closet geek, messing around with computers and developing software. When he'd decided to start his own software company, Jaime would get lost for hours coding, and Cassie had been grounding for him, reminding him to eat, to stop and pay attention to the world around him. Jack's biggest worry when Cassie died was that Jaime would retreat into himself and cope by withdrawing into a world of binary code and sequences where things could be predicted and carefully controlled. But their daughter had kept him engaged and focused on the present; the day in and day out of taking care of her becoming the new grounding.

Jack slid a plate toward Jaime and sat down across from Maddie with his own. "Papers and tablets down," he commanded, sipping his coffee. Call it an Italian family tradition, but Jack insisted on human interaction at meal times. Used to the drill, they dropped what they were doing, and Maddie reiterated again, for her father's benefit, that she wanted a turtle for a pet, that she had given it serious thought, and that the name of her turtle would be Bob, regardless of the sex.

Jack and Jaime listened attentively, asking questions where appropriate, and nodding as she explained why it was important to build Bob a dream house. In purple. Immediately.

"Okay, Maddie," her dad said, kissing the top of her head. "After breakfast. Let Uncle Jack and me finish while you watch your cartoons, okay?"

"Alright, Daddy. But we need to build Bob a home. Soon." She swept up her coloring book and crayons, flouncing into the family room.

"Swear to God, she's more like Ma every day," Jaime laughed, echoing Jack's earlier thoughts.

"A girl on a mission," Jack agreed.

"A girl who will have a turtle named Bob in a purple popsicle house come hell or high water. What a little nut," he chuckled, getting up to get more coffee. Jaime poured more coffee for both of them before sitting back down and leaning forward conspiratorially. "So…your hot neighbor."

Jack's brows lifted. "We raised thirty million last night, and that's the first thing you ask about?"

"Man, you always beat last year's numbers." Jaime rolled his eyes. "I knew the take was good just by looking at Mitch. He looked like he was high half the night. Let's just cut to the juicy shit—I had no idea you sold the place. And you scored a ridiculously hot neighbor. How does that even happen?" Jaime asked. "Look at my neighbor." Jaime pointed outside the kitchen window at the chubby middle-aged man scratching his belly as he picked up the morning paper. "That's what they usually look like."

Jack shrugged, smiling into his cup. "Got a good offer. You seem okay, so no sense in holding on to it. Besides, I was just waiting for the right buyer. Specifically a 'ridiculously hot' woman."

"Really?"

"Nope." Jack shook his head. "I actually thought Samantha was a man when she made the offer." He chuckled into his coffee cup. "She shocked the hell out of me when she came out of the pool in a swimsuit."

Jaime groaned. "Dear God."

"When are you gonna learn? God loves me." Jack smirked.

Jaime sighed, looking a little jealous. "When did she move in?"

"Recently."

"Is she single?"

Jack leveled him a look. "You saw her date last night." He didn't mention the other man he'd met. *Carey.* He tamped down on a flash of irrational irritation.

"Evan wasn't her date. They work together. I have a meeting with them this week," Jaime informed him archly.

"Really? What about?"

Jaime took a swallow of coffee before answering. "Sam wants to develop a tracking app proprietary to Lennox Chase and its clients. We've both got a window Friday morning."

Jack nodded, saying nothing.

Jaime peered at him. "And I thought I'd ask her out."

Jack put his coffee down so fast that it sloshed over the sides. He cursed, wiping it up.

"I knew it! I knew you were into her!" Jaime crowed, pointing at him across the bar.

Jack rolled his eyes, huffing.

"You two generate enough static electricity to run a biomass heating system," Jaime teased.

"How the hell are you such a geek and related to me?" Jack responded mildly. "Besides, I thought we were going to take the boat out for the last time before we store it for winter?"

"That's why I wanted to ask Sam out," Jaime nodded. "Thought she could join us. You two could get a little better acquainted." He wagged his brows, clearly delighted with himself.

"You get your meddling genes from Ma," Jack murmured into his coffee, though he liked the idea. A lot. The idea of enjoying the boat on a pretty fall day with his family and Sam had him smiling. "You want me to pick up Maddie and take her to the boat first?"

"That'd be perfect."

Jack picked up his fork.

"Oh, and Jack?"

He glanced up.

"You're welcome," Jaime grinned.

CHAPTER 5

September—A week later

Sam's office in the Loop, Chicago

SAMANTHA

IT WAS A beautiful Friday morning, and the sun slanted in warmly, making Sam daydream about taking an uncharacteristic afternoon off to enjoy the end of summertime in Chicago. Perhaps she'd go for a drive in the Corvette. Let the wind whip through her hair.

"You asked how we can leverage more mobile technology for tracking clients? We can set up a special trigger number that when dialed from any phone will automatically download the software like a Trojan and act as a GPS," Jaime was explaining to her, Carey, and Rush in the seating area of her office. "Each client can be assigned their own number, so you know who might be triggering the emergency GPS, particularly if their own phone is lost or stolen." He was drafting his thoughts on the tablet as he spoke.

Jaime Roman was the younger, greyhound-lean version of Jack. He had the same dark hair and light eyes, though his features were narrower and more refined. And though he put on a good approximation of an outgoing personality, she suspected he was an introvert by nature. Where his brother was sex appeal, dynamic confidence, and in-your-face masculinity, Jaime was hyper-intellectual, amusingly endearing, and jumped from idea to idea with the hyperactive zing of a young man.

"It would be more helpful if we had the ability to enhance that functionality of a locater app with a tracking device," Carey pointed out.

Jaime smiled. "So you want to be able to put an electronic leash on your clients in the field?" he asked, making more notes.

"Christ Almighty," Rush chuckled. "Carey here would put tags on all of us if he could."

"So you'd want to have a mobile app you and your team can access from anywhere to locate a client that's not a SIM card?" Jaime thought about it for a moment. "The military makes high-grade chips you can inject under the skin, but I can't imagine many of your clients would agree to that." Jaime paused again, taking notes on his tablet before looking up at them. "The software is a non-issue. We can come up with some really good interfaces for you. We just need to think through the actual tracking devices and how to make them difficult to manipulate, remove, and detect."

"They'd also need to be able to be tracked over long distances," Carey interjected. "Maybe leveraging wireless and mobile networks?"

"Give me a couple weeks. I'll come back with some initial ideas I think you'll like," Jaime replied.

"You'll have very happy clients if you can make this happen," Sam remarked, glancing at her watch. "And look at that—you still have the rest of the day to enjoy the weather," she smiled, indicating the stretch of sunlit windows.

Jaime nodded, slipping his tablet into his bag. "My brother and I were going to take the boat out for the afternoon with my daughter, Maddie. We haven't gotten to enjoy it nearly as much as we wanted this summer. You guys are more than welcome to join us," he told them, light eyes sparkling.

Sam got the distinct feeling he was up to something, though the idea was incredibly appealing. It was the perfect day to be out on the water.

"Do you fish?" Carey asked. "We were talking about heading up the coast, seeing if we could try our luck at some salmon or trout this weekend."

Jaime smiled. "Caught a twenty-pound rainbow trout last time we went out. My daughter made me throw it back, but I got a picture first." He scrolled through his phone briefly before handing it over. A windswept and sunburnt Jaime and an adorable little girl in a life jacket and a pink fishing hat held up their trophy.

"Throw it back?" Rush groaned dramatically. "Now that's a crime. I haven't gotten to go fishing since I moved up here," he sighed wistfully.

Sam narrowly restrained herself from rolling her eyes. Carey and Rush were getting ready to talk tackle, lures, and technique for the next two hours.

Talon chose that exact moment to knock on her door and pop his head in. "Gentlemen." He nodded at them before looking at her pointedly with pitch black eyes.

Her brows lifted in question as he looked at her. "Please tell me you came to save me. Or did you hear this conversation from miles away and decide you couldn't be left out?" she asked, nodding toward the other men.

Intrigued, Talon stepped into her office. "Well, I was going to give you guys an update, but it sounds like you're in need of saving."

Rush snorted. "Hardly. She's just trying to figure out how to extract herself from a fishing expedition gracefully."

Talon's dark eyes brightened. "Fishing? You going with, Boss?"

Before she could shake her head, Jaime stood up, extending his hand to Talon. "Jaime Roman, and I've just invited these guys out on my boat this afternoon. Caught a beauty last time I was out."

"Lee Talon," he responded, clasping the other man's hand. "Yeah, we were talking about going up the coast to try our luck. What kind of boat?"

"A forty-five-foot ketch," Jaime answered. "Perfect for a day like today. Good breeze and an easy sail. If all goes to plan, I'll be sipping a beer and throwing a cast out in about two hours. You guys should join us," he said again, glancing around. His pale eyes landed on Sam.

All her guys wore the same dreamy expression at the mere mention of a fishing trip. Carey would be waiting on her to say the word before he'd agree. She thought about begging off politely and urging them to go without her, but she knew Carey wouldn't feel entirely comfortable with that scenario since the connection to Jaime was through her. She hated to deny her guys the rare pleasure of a leisurely afternoon.

"Well, hell," she smiled ruefully. "Jaime, you've officially ruined my team for work. Anything in particular you'd like us to bring?"

Jaime smiled. "We keep her docked at Monroe Harbor in the summer. She's fully stocked, but if you have a preferred beer, just bring that and your fishing gear. We pull out about noon. Look for the *Evangelina*."

September—That afternoon

Monroe Harbor, Lake Michigan

JACK

"YOU'LL LIKE THEM. They're cool guys," Jaime commented as they watched three men approaching portside.

"At least Maddie will grow up knowing how to fish, pitch a fastball, and punch the lights out of someone with all the testosterone she'll be used to having around," Jack replied, sarcastic. He was not thrilled with the change in plans, but he recognized a package deal when he saw one. He recognized Carey and Evan, but the third guy was new. He was tall and sinewy, distinctly Native American, his long, black hair pulled back at the neck. All three were dressed casually in shorts and boat shoes, carrying coolers and fishing gear.

"What's tessoserone, Uncle Jack?" Maddie asked, coming up behind him to slip her little hand in his. She looked adorably ridiculous in her tiny pink life jacket, pink hat, flippers, and Hello Kitty arm floaties.

"Nothing you need to worry about for many, many years, Maddie," Jack answered before redirecting his overly curious niece's attention. "Why are you wearing your flippers and floaties, *micina cara*? We aren't swimming yet," he teased, poking one of the inflatables around her arm.

"Cause I want to be ready," she responded seriously.

"I promise we'll go swimming," Jack told her, lifting her up in his arms and removing her flippers to toss them into a storage bin on the deck. "But no walking around in those on the deck. You'll trip and hurt yourself," he chided, softening the reprimand with a kiss to her cheek.

"Here's her sunblock," Jaime said, fishing into her bag. "She'll wiggle around, but make sure she gets plenty on." He turned to greet the guys on the deck. "Hey! Welcome aboard. I see you guys came pre-pared," Jaime said with a laugh, helping take the coolers and gear before making introductions.

Maddie was alternately mesmerized by Carey's size and Talon's hair as Jaime introduced her. Her little head bobbed back and forth between the two men as they smiled down at her and shook her hand in greeting.

"Miss Maddie, I have the perfect lure to add to that hat," Evan de-clared when he met her. He opened a tackle box and pulled out a bright yellow lure. Maddie, not easily won over, inspected the lure before nodding at Evan, giving him silent permission to attach it to her hat. He laughed, threaded it in, and stuck some clay on the ends so she wouldn't prick herself if she touched it.

"Where's Sam?" Jaime asked while helping the guys get their gear situated on the deck.

"Probably thinking of ways to get out of fishing," Carey joked, carry-ing one of the coolers down into the galley. "Great boat. If I had this, I'd be hard-pressed to leave it."

"I feel the same," he agreed. "It's terrible we have to store her for most of the winter, but when the weather is perfect like this, I could stay out on her for months."

Jack was putting on Maddie's sunblock when he heard a low whistle from the dock. He looked up and saw Samantha wearing a white linen shirt and her cut offs, that thick, dark hair twisted up in a loose knot, aviators perched on her nose. She smiled up at him from the dock. "Figures you have the finest-looking sailboat in all of Chicago," she complimented, running her hand along the navy blue hull. She admired the boat with unabashed pleasure, fingers running gently along the side. "She's a bona fide beauty."

Jack found himself unaccountably happy to see her. A pressure valve released in his chest, as if he'd been holding his breath until she'd arrived. She looked happy and relaxed to be there, and that made him feel… incredible.

"Thank you," Jack acknowledged. "She's been in the family a long time. We had her restored a few years ago, so you can't tell her age, but Jaime and I grew up on her during our summers," he told her, extending his hand to help her aboard.

She thanked him, pulling her hand from his warm clasp as she introduced herself to Maddie.

"You're pretty," Maddie told her shyly.

"Not a pretty as you, sweet thing," Samantha replied with a grin. "Where's your daddy?"

Jaime popped up from the galley at that moment, talking with Carey behind him.

"I think this boat is a good candidate for testing out the tracking software. I volunteer to steal it, and you all can go about trying to find me," Carey was telling him as he scanned the lake's horizon with a smile.

"That ain't far from the truth," Evan piped up, coming up from the stern. "One of these days, Carey'll just up and disappear, and that's how we'll know he retired."

"Well, that and the postcard he sends us from Tahiti," Talon remarked. He glanced at Samantha. "Now that Sam's here, we ready to launch? There are fish waiting to get caught." He laughed, the sun glinting off an even, white smile.

Within minutes, the *Evangelina* was slicing through the dark blue waters of Lake Michigan, her sails picking up the wind so easily, they were able to shut down the engine shortly after leaving the marina.

Samantha sat up at the bow on a bed of navy striped cushions next to Carey, sipping a beer and enjoying the breeze, her dark hair whipping around her. Jaime steered, chatting with Talon while Evan helped with the jibs. Jack explained what Evan was doing to the ever-curious Maddie while they sat on a wide cushioned bench behind the skipper's chair.

As Jaime steered them along the coast, the group was lulled into relaxation by the rhythmic roll of the hull on the water while the sails undulated in the warm, humid wind. Jack took a deep breath, filling his lungs with sun-warmed air and cool mist, closing his eyes behind his sunglasses in pure pleasure.

"It's a near perfect day," Talon sighed as he sat down next to Maddie, handing Jack and the girl bottles of water.

"What's missing?" Jack asked, taking a sip.

"Ask me that after we're done fishing," Talon answered. "I saw you've got a grill on this boat. Let's see if we can catch dinner."

"You eat the fish?" Maddie asked. "I make Daddy throw it back."

"Catch and release is a good thing sometimes," Talon agreed. "But on my reservation, I grew up living on the land, and we only took what we needed for dinner. So I'll make you a deal. If we get lucky fishing today, we'll keep enough to eat and throw back the rest. Okay, little feather?"

Maddie thought about that before nodding, clinking her little water bottle against his beer when he toasted to their deal.

"Which tribe is your family from?" Jack asked.

"Chippewa. In northern Michigan," Talon answered. "You could steer this boat right into the dock near our reservation."

"You're pretty close to home," Jack nodded. "How long have you been living in Chicago?"

"Couple years now. Rush convinced me to move here after I was finished with my service. It was close to home, and I've always liked the city, so…" Talon shrugged.

"Were you guys all in the service together?" Jack asked.

Talon took another sip of his beer and looked out over the water. "You could say that," he answered.

"Jaime and I grew up here in Chicago. We used to spend as much time as we could on Lake Michigan in the summers, but these days…" Jack sighed. "There's just never enough time to come out, it seems."

"Hey, can you help me lower a couple of the sails so we can anchor and have lunch?" Jaime asked.

"I'll do it," Talon offered, moving up to bow with Evan.

Jack picked Maddie up, carrying her down to the galley so he could work on getting the lunch together. He was surprised to find Carey and Samantha already in there, pulling gourmet sandwiches, cheeses, and fruit from the picnic baskets the yacht club at the marina had packed. He watched for a moment as Carey and Samantha moved around the small space easily, movements economical and fluid, as if they were used to working in confined spaces around each other.

"You two are making me look like a bad host." Jack grinned, accepting the plates of food to take up the deck.

"We're just pulling our weight," Carey responded. "Besides, Sam and I are used to mother henning our crew. Old habits die hard."

"Rush and Talon are spoilt brats," Samantha joked, her affection obvious. "That or we're enablers."

"Don't forget to give Talon extra pickles," Carey responded distractedly as he arranged condiments onto a tray.

"Do we have any Dijon? Rush'll want Dijon," Samantha commented, adding napkins to the spread.

"You're definitely enablers," Jack teased, shaking his head as he accepted the tray from Carey.

"It's to make up for all the surf torture I put them through back when they were rookies," Carey chuckled.

Lunch was a laidback affair. Evan entertained the group with funny stories of growing up on a farm in South Carolina. Jaime and Talon teased Maddie with animal sounds as Evan told her about his pet pig, BBQ, and his pet chicken, Micky. Jack wasn't entirely clear on his naming convention for the chicken, but the pig probably had it coming.

Samantha sat between him and Carey, her bare legs tucked underneath her. She sipped on a beer, her orange blossom and jasmine scent driving Jack wild with each gentle breeze.

"She's not with Carey, if that's what you're wondering," Jaime told him when the guys moved to the stern to set up the fishing equipment, and Samantha disappeared below to get into her swimsuit. "They grew up together."

"And how do you know that?" Jack asked.

"Evan told me. They're like siblings."

"He sure as hell nags me like a brother sometimes," Samantha said from behind them. She looked lithe and athletic in a white, one-piece halter. Jack could feel himself staring, thankful for his sunglasses.

"Why do you ask?" she said casually as she slung a towel onto the cushions and proceeded to rub her legs down with suntan lotion. Jack saw Jaime swallow out of the corner of his eye.

"A beautiful woman leading a team that could have inspired *Call of Duty*," Jaime joked. "If that's not the rare stuff of legend and fantasy, I don't know what is," he grinned. "Naturally, we're curious. I'm on the

PTA for Maddie's school in Oak Park. Hanging out with Navy SEALs and their fearless leader isn't something I get to do every day."

"The PTA is full of alpha women, from what I gather," she replied, her brow raised. "I wouldn't want to mess with any of those hellcats, especially on hostage negotiations."

Jaime mock-shuddered. "Now ain't that the truth? Those are not ladies you tangle with," he said over his shoulder as he ducked down into the galley.

"Did you all work together in the Navy?" Jack asked as he pulled the bottle from her hand, moving behind her to rub the lotion into her shoulders. Her skin was hot, smooth and supple. Jack felt goose bumps raise on his arms while he touched her skin.

"No." She shook her head. "Carey's a few years younger than me. By the time he was a SEAL, my tour was over, so we never worked similar deployments. After he was injured on a mission, he ran some of the BUD/s training. That's how he met Rush and Talon."

"What's that?"

"Basic Underwater Demolition and SEAL school. It's one of the first training regimens all those guys have to pass," she explained, watching the guys cast out lines from the stern.

Maddie was standing on the bench beside them, her own toy fishing rod in hand. Jack smiled at the scene. Three ex-special forces guys and a little girl wearing a tiny pink life preserver with her little pink hat. What a picture that made.

"So how did you get them?" Jack asked, admiring the way her back rippled with the muscles of a lifelong swimmer. He was insanely turned on. A powerful woman. Beautiful and soft, yet so incredibly strong.

She shrugged under his hands. "Rush was ready for something new, and he and Talon were inseparable in the service. They're excellent partners. It was just a matter of time before Talon joined him," she remarked, groaning as Jack massaged a knot from her shoulder, clearly taking advantage of the suntan lotion situation. It was a move as old as the invention of the stuff. He wondered about what else he could get away with, considering three men who would readily kill for this woman stood only twenty feet away.

"*Riiiight* there," she murmured as he pressed into her left shoulder. He nearly stopped when he noticed a scar the size of a nickel there. "You've got magic hands, Mr. Roman," she told him.

"One of my talents," he smiled, tracing the indentation of the scar.

"Among many, I'm sure," she replied, moving away before he could ask her about it. "May I return the favor?" she offered, distracting him.

Jack couldn't hide his pleasure at the thought of feeling her slender fingers on his body. He pulled his shirt over his head, tossing it to the side as she poured suntan lotion on her hands. He felt the small calluses on her hands and the strength and efficacy of her movements as she rubbed the lotion into his skin. She didn't touch him shyly, but she didn't touch him sensually either. She finished rubbing him down before handing him back the bottle and settling back onto the cushions, her eyes closed behind her sunglasses.

"What are the other levels?" Jack asked, settling beside her.

"What do you mean?" she asked, not opening her eyes.

"You said BUD/s was the first training regimen SEALs have to pass."

"The guys are the experts. I'm sure they'd love to brag to you about all the shit they have to survive to make it," she replied flippantly.

"I'm asking you," Jack murmured, turning to raise his face to the dazzling heat of the September sun.

She said nothing for a moment. Jack could hear the guys laughing at the back, Maddie's squeal as they reeled in a fish.

"Those guys survive hell," she told him quietly. "They're the most respected and feared combat unit in the world for a reason. Training usually takes at least a year. The physical conditioning, combat diving, land warfare, parachute jumping—it's unbelievable what they go through. And that's before they even get into their individual specialties."

Jack absorbed the information, alternately impressed and humbled. "What are their specialties?"

"Oh, those guys have PhDs in bullshit, flattery, and skirt-chasing," she chuckled softly, lightening the tension.

Jack laughed alongside her before flipping to his side.

"You have a habit of doing that."

"Doing what?"

"Deflecting with humor." He ran a finger along the hand that rested closest to him.

She cocked a brow, though her eyes remained closed.

"Carey's a high threat protective security specialist."

"What's that?" Jack asked.

"He's trained specifically to protect US and foreign heads of state or high value persons of interest."

"And Evan and Talon?"

She lifted a hand to cover her eyes, turning her head toward him. He couldn't see her eyes behind her sunglasses, but he knew she was watching him.

"Evan's a breacher. He does advanced close quarter combat and is particularly talented with barrier penetration and methods of entry. Talon's a scout and a sniper. Best I've ever seen. Makes expert marksmen look like bush leagues past the three hundred meter mark."

"So basically I'm on a boat with the A-Team," Jack joked, putting his hands behind his head as he leaned back, feigning relaxation.

She smiled, mimicking his move. "Let's just say you and your family are being protected by the best right now."

"Remind me to never piss you off."

Her husky laugh was so soft, he barely heard it.

Jack closed his eyes, enjoying the hypnotic rhythm of the boat swaying ever so slightly with the breeze. Jack listened to Samantha's gentle breaths as they evened out, checking on her even as he knew she dozed. He lazed beside her, listening to the waves slap gently against the boat, cooled by the gentle drift of wind over the deck while the sails furled gently. *To and fro, to and fro...*

JACK WOKE ON a jolt, realizing he was alone. He sat up, looking starboard. He saw Samantha and Evan in the water, Maddie swimming furiously between them with her floaties and life preserver, her little flippers slapping noisily in the water as they laughed and cheered, encouraging her.

"I get it, bro," Jaime said as he plopped down beside him, handing him a water.

"Get what?" Jack asked, glancing over Jaime's shoulder. Carey and Talon sat back at the stern, chatting and drinking beers, legs kicked up in a lazy approximation of fishing.

"The fascination. At first I thought it was because she's—well, look at her." He gestured toward the water. "But once you spend a few minutes with her...*whew*." Jaime shook his head. "She's not your usual fare."

"I doubt she's anyone's usual fare," Jack replied, watching her. All his life, Jack had the benefit of women's attention in one form or another. They were pliant, often pleasing, and at times downright demanding of his attentions. But someone like Samantha, so indomitable and self-contained, held a surprising and nearly fetishistic appeal for him. He'd known her a handful of days and she was already burrowing deeply under his skin.

"You planning on doing anything about it?" Jaime asked, as if reading his mind.

"Have you seen the company she keeps?" Jack joked, casting a meaningful glance at the stern.

Jaime laughed. "You were always one for living dangerously."

"I have a feeling she takes that metaphor to an entirely different place," Jack commented drily.

Jaime shrugged, sipping his beer. "*Volar bene*."[2]

He and his brother chatted aimlessly for a while before Jack joined Maddie in the water and Jaime returned to the stern, helping Talon clean a fresh fish he'd caught. Relieved of duty, Evan and Samantha swam a series of breast strokes in a wide arc around the boat, racing each other. When she finally tired, Jack helped her and Maddie up the side of the boat, passing her one of his robes after she'd finished drying Maddie and herself off.

They said little to each other the remainder of the night, distracting

---

[2] Italian for "good luck."

themselves with grilling the fat rainbow trout, trading jokes and stories with the group while sexual tension crackled between them like a magnetic field. Either the guys didn't notice, were very good actors, or they were too relaxed and sun-dazed to care.

When they finally docked, Samantha placed a gentle kiss on Maddie's forehead. The little girl was passed out on Jack's shoulder, snoring softly. Samantha smiled at Jack before stepping back and waving goodbye to the group. By the time he'd tucked Maddie into Jaime's car, she was gone.

CHAPTER 6

September—Monday morning

Sam's office in the Loop, Chicago

SAMANTHA

"HAPPY BIRTHDAY, SAMMY girl," Carey grinned, strolling into her office.

"Did you hit your head over the weekend?" Sam slanted him a look as he sat down across from her for their usual Monday morning meeting. "My birthday's not for a few months."

Carey leaned forward, punching her intercom. "Marvin," he called out to their assistant. "Can you get me and Sammy some coffees? She looks like she's going to tear my arm off and beat me with it."

"I'll make it a double," Marvin's disembodied voice returned over the speaker.

Sam rolled her eyes. "I'm not in a bad mood."

"Baby girl, you're in a bad mood every morning until you're two coffees in. I'm just the only one brave enough to meet you before you're done with your caffeine IV drip."

"So make my grouchy ass happy then." She sat back in her chair. "Why's it my birthday?"

"Simon Michaelson contacted me, asking for a meeting."

Her brows shot up. "From Leviathan Risk? You're finally going to get him?" Carey had an impressive recruiting list. Michaelson had been near the top of his list for nearly two years.

Carey shrugged. "It's been a long courtship. Michaelson didn't give me all the details yet, but word has it that Leviathan sent him in on a couple bad situations with limited reinforcements. He's disillusioned. Wants out."

"And you're gonna open up your loving arms." She smiled slowly.

Carey looked smug. "I can't help it if Leviathan doesn't know how to take care of their men. Besides, he approached me."

"Remind me of his background?" Sam asked.

"Michaelson was a Major with the British SAS Special Ops. He was in charge of the UK Mobility Unit in Afghanistan."

"Mobility Unit?"

"Vehicular Warfare," Carey clarified. "We don't have another specialist in mobility at his level of play. Think of the team he could develop and train up." His eyes twinkled. "It'd be a sound investment."

"Haven't you been trying to recruit him since we started?" Sam asked, leaning forward. "What was the final straw?"

"What I've pieced together is that Michaelson was sent on his own to Chechnya on a hostage situation. No ground support. He used one of his old military contacts to get chopper cover but got winged trying to get his cargo out. This was the second time Leviathan sent him undermanned."

"*Chechnya?* Christ, that's like sending Bambi into east Texas during hunting season," she remarked. "Was it the Russian military or Chechen factions who had the hostage?"

"Chechen. A splinter faction from the Emir, but the Russian military was no help. Michaelson didn't go into details, but I've heard enough to know it was a clusterfuck if there ever was one." Carey shook his head, disgusted.

"Amateur hour," Samantha agreed. "Leviathan has really started to cut corners. What's going on at that shop?" she wondered aloud.

Leviathan Risk, the top dog in private protection and K&R/Asset Retrieval globally, was headquartered in London and had earned its namesake over the years as a Goliath in the security industry. Their CEO, Lucien Lightner, formerly a British Special Air Services Captain himself, was renowned for being a shrewd and cunning businessman. It was surprising to hear how many bad calls they'd been making recently, even for the sake of the almighty dollar—or pound sterling, in their case.

"Whatever's going on, that shit ain't gonna fly," Carey continued. "Guys like Michaelson don't have any patience for getting their asses hung out to dry if it isn't for Queen and country. They're private sector now. If it's happened to him, you can bet there's a line of guys behind him who are getting the same treatment."

"What's Leviathan's market share these days?" she asked.

"At least forty percent of the K&R market. Last I checked, they've got contracts with the top five underwriters for West Asia, Russia, the Middle East, and North Africa. Since we got in the game, they've expanded security and protection services to compete, but they're still the main pony to beat in Asset Retrieval," Carey told her.

"What do we estimate the underwriters billed in premiums last year?"

"I'm thinking somewhere between forty and forty-five million US dollars, but we'd need to check," he replied.

Marvin stuck his long arms in the office after a short knock on the door. "I bring coffee—don't shoot!" he exclaimed, waving the coffee cups playfully as he edged into her office cautiously.

"Enter slowly and keep your hands in front of you," Carey warned. "And whatever you do, don't agitate her."

"Very funny." She rolled her eyes. "I'm not *that* bad."

Marvin and Carey exchanged looks as Marvin handed her the coffee. He backed away slowly.

"Oh for *chrissakes*! Just because I'm not a morning person," she muttered.

"Not a morning person?" Marvin cocked his head, his grin vivid against his black skin. "Sam, Kim Jong Un wouldn't cross you before 9:00 a.m."

"Wusses, both of you," Sam rebutted, taking a sip as Marvin turned to leave. "Hey, Marv, before you go, I need you to do some research for us today."

Marvin nodded. "Who, what, where?" he asked, whipping out his smartphone. She thanked her lucky stars for his organization. Without him, she and Carey would be adrift.

"I want you to pull anything you can on Leviathan Risk International and their top officers. Get me their financials, any recent news, and their client roster. Set up a meeting for me, Carey, and Ian McCall in our London office for this week, and let the pilots know we're flying out first thing tomorrow morning. Have McCall get his ear to the ground. Carey and I will want to know who's unhappy, why they feel that way, and what it will take to get them over to Lennox. Move any non-priority meetings to next week. Anything crucial gets moved up to today or handed to Rush and Talon. Carey and I can teleconference in from London if they need us."

"You got it," Marvin responded, fingers moving deftly over the screen.

"And please respond to the email Simon Michaelson sent me," Carey added. "Set up a dinner meeting asking him to meet Sam and me at the Hawksmoor Seven Dials in Covent Garden on Wednesday night. I've heard he's a fan of a good steak."

"Will do," Marvin nodded, shutting the door behind him.

"You need me at that dinner?" Sam asked.

"Nah, but I think it'll help."

Sam tutted. "You just want me to be your *la Femme Nikita* eye candy."

Carey laughed, eyes bright. "Nothing sexier than a woman who knows how to hurt you."

"That's sick, Bear," she muttered, shaking her head at him in amusement.

He shrugged. "So we'll be declaring war on Leviathan by Wednesday then?"

"Screw birthdays. This is Christmas," Sam murmured into her coffee, eyeing him over the rim. "We've been looking for a way to take down our top competitor. Let's go to London, do a little fact finding, and see if Leviathan can hold on to their top assets..." She sat back, contemplative. "If you could ask Santa for anything at Christmas, Bear, who else would you like wrapped under the tree in a pretty red bow?"

Carey got a glint in his eye. "Depends on if I've been naughty or nice."

"I think you know the answer to that," she answered, lips curving.

"Naughty then," he smiled, leaning toward her. He held up his huge hand, ticking off each finger. "Simon Michaelson, one. Then Julien Henri, a jungle warfare expert from the French Foreign Legion who's supposed to be close to Michaelson." Carey paused, thinking. "There's an ex-Green Beret named Kurt doing special recon out of Leviathan's Dubai office, and a former Israeli Sayeret Matkal officer based in Paris, Avi Oded. He's one of the best guys in counter terrorism. I want him bad, Santa. *Bad.*"

"Nice list." Sam chuckled, finishing her coffee. "I'll see what I can do."

September—Wednesday night
Covent Garden, London

SAMANTHA

SIMON MICHAELSON COULD give Carey a run for his money in the size department. *Throw a pelt on him, give him a sword, and he'd be a dead ringer for a Visigoth*, she thought as she handed her trench to the maître d, glancing over at the table where Simon and Carey were seated. It amazed her that a man that size had been a specialist in vehicular warfare when it seemed like he'd be more suited to clubbing any unfortunate opponents. Even across the restaurant she could see he dwarfed the table, his biceps massive under his suit as he leaned on the surface, talking with Carey. Simon glanced up, catching her gaze. Sam smiled, walking through the atmospheric warehouse toward them, her Alexander McQueens clicking on the municipal woodwork designed in the floor.

"You must be the infamous Samantha Wyatt," Simon greeted, standing as she neared, his hazel eyes taking her in appreciatively.

"I'm sure my reputation isn't half as interesting as yours," she returned, guessing he was at least Carey's height. He wore a handsomely crafted Savile Row suit, bespoke Jermyn Street shirt, and a City banker tie. But his hands gave him away as they shook hands. They were calloused and rough from years of use, nails clipped to the quick. He glanced over her indigo piqué dress, his gaze admiring.

"Hope you haven't been talking with my ex-girlfriends?" Simon replied as he leaned in, giving her an appropriately continental kiss on each cheek before pulling back, his eyes alight with good humor.

"We were all just having a drink at the bar," she quipped before turning to Carey, giving him a brief hug in greeting.

"How was your meeting?" Carey asked as he pulled out her seat. He looked equally sharp, his all-American blonde looks offset by a gray suit and a crisp blue shirt.

"Long," Sam replied. "I apologize for being late to the party," she said, looking at Simon.

"No worries," Simon responded. "Gave Carey and me plenty of time to get better acquainted."

"What are we drinking?" she asked as a waiter appeared at her side.

"A 2005 Château Lafite Rothschild," Simon replied.

Sam's brows raised in appreciation. "Excellent vintage. You have good taste, Mr. Michaelson."

"Simon, please. Mr. Michaelson makes me think of my da."

"Then you'll have to call me Sam."

"I'll call you anything you want," he flirted, a handsome smile on his face.

Good-looking, she thought. *For a Visigoth.*

She asked the waiter to bring her a glass. "Have you ordered?" she asked the men.

"We were waiting for you," Carey told her, his blue eyes smiling. Things were going well, then.

She and Carey choreographed her late arrival to give Carey more time to get to know Simon, considering he'd reached out to Carey directly. Though they had gotten helpful information from Marvin's research and their London office contacts, there was nothing like a drink between veterans of two of the world's most selective military fraternities to get to the heart of the matter.

"So Simon," she smiled. "How does a Newcastle boy like yourself get into the British SAS's Mobility Unit?"

He looked slightly taken aback. "You know your British accents."

"I can tell a Geordie when I hear one," she replied slyly.

"I never thought I'd get called to the rug by an American." Simon grinned.

"What's a Geordie?" Carey asked.

"Common name for the coal miners from the catchment area I grew up in," Simon explained. "Most Yanks wouldn't know that. This one's good," he laughed, gesturing toward Sam.

"We're no Yankees, sir," Sam objected, allowing her Southern accent to thicken in mock outrage.

"We're Texans first and Southerners second," Carey elaborated, chuckling as he took a sip of his wine.

"My apologies," Simon replied. "Well, the story of how I got into the Mobility Unit is probably going to offend you more than my calling you a Yank."

Sam's brow quirked.

"I used to twock cars as a lad," Simon explained. "Had a natural talent for getting in and out of places I shouldn't be from a young age."

"Twock? Now that's a term I'm unfamiliar with," Sam admitted, accepting her glass of wine from the waiter.

"Taking without owner's consent," Simon clarified with a wink.

She laughed, surprised and amused while Simon shrugged, unrepentant.

"So you went from street urchin to the military."

"When I finally got snagged, it was that or the clink," Simon explained. "Figured I'd be of more use to Her Majesty in the service than in one of her prisons."

"Fair enough. I'm not in the least offended by the way," Sam told him. "I like a man with a colorful background."

"That's one way of putting it," Simon laughed.

"Simon was telling me he served in Afghanistan," Carey told her.

"Really?" Sam asked, wondering if they'd had any overlap.

Simon nodded, his head tilted as he regarded her. "I'd heard about you, in fact. *The Poppy*," he murmured, watching her reaction.

Sam felt her heart stutter, though her face remained pleasantly curious. *"The Poppy?* Where did that nickname come from?" she asked, taking a casual sip of wine.

Simon's sharp hazel eyes assessed her while he twirled the wine in his glass. "Rumor had it your interrogations were so effective, people would tell you anything," Simon said, leaning forward as his voice dropped, as if he were sharing something in confidence. "Never had to touch them, I heard. Men bent on suicide, unafraid of death—they'd fall under your influence and break down, telling you anything." His heavy brow lifted. "Impressive that."

The air thickened. They watched each other across the table, the noise and motion of the restaurant dimming. She was certain she'd never seen him before in the field—or as a civilian. Simon Michaelson wasn't the type of man you forgot. So he was either looking for confirmation of a rumor or he had access to intel far above his pay-grade.

"What years were you in Afghanistan?" she asked, running her finger over the rim of her wine glass, her demeanor relaxed.

Carey's eyes bounced between them as the conversation veered.

"2008 to 2011. Iraq before that."

"I'm going to guess your locations and missions in those countries are as classified as my own," she commented. "But your reputation as a top military operative precedes you. It's just a pity we didn't meet before." Sam smiled, redirecting.

Simon watched her for a moment before taking a sip of his wine. *He's a wise enough man to know an insurmountable barrier when he sees one*, she thought.

"Better late than never," Simon responded finally, his voice casual.

"I'll toast to that," she murmured, holding up her wine glass as the tension in her chest dissipated. They toasted, allowing a pause in conversation to listen to that evening's specials and place their orders. Sam couldn't help but wonder how much Simon really knew about her and her past work.

Carey took over the conversation, prompting Simon to discuss what was going on at Leviathan to make him want to leave.

"It's been a right mess the past year," Simon admitted, running a hand through his closely cropped hair. "I've done two extractions back-to-back where I thought I'd lose my fuckin' ass. Beg pardon," he said to Sam.

"Chechnya? I heard," Sam said, tutting. "That would never have happened with us."

"And the one before that?" Carey asked.

"Somali raid on a Greek-owned oil tanker off of the Horn of Africa," Simon muttered, shaking his head in distaste.

"That was you? Shit, I heard about that," Carey told him, leaning forward. "Didn't some of crew get killed in the ransom exchange?"

"Me and my mate, guy by the name of Henri, got sent in with a team as bloody bait," Simon told them, anger making his accent thick. "It was supposed to be a clean exchange. Two million quid for the crew, but we barely got out. One of my team was killed and three of the crew. Found out after the fact that Leviathan was in league with the tanker's top brass to try to trap the pirates. Apparently, that part of Africa's become one of the most expensive production and transport areas in the world."

"Jesus," Carey murmured, his brows sky high.

"Yeah, it gets better," Simon continued. "Leviathan had it rigged up that they'd get bonuses if the pirates were caught and brought in for questioning. Henri and I took down a couple of them down before the rest escaped, and we actually got a talking to for that, as if we should have just zip tied them after they killed my man and the crew. Greedy bastards," Simon spat, disgusted. He downed his wine, giving Sam and Carey a level look. "I didn't survive the bloody Middle East to get my arse hung to dry so some skive can make more money off my blood, sweat, and tears."

"Amen to that," Carey murmured, nodding in agreement.

"What I don't understand," Samantha wondered aloud, "is why a man with Lucien Lightner's reputation for shrewdness would be willing to risk his best talent repeatedly?"

Marvin had pulled their financials. Leviathan remained solvent. In fact, despite losing share to Lennox, they'd continued to post year-over-year growth, particularly due to their strength in Central and Eastern Africa, the Middle East, and the Baltic States—regions she wanted to take a bite out of. Badly.

"How long have you and Henri worked together?" Carey asked as dinner was served.

"We've done a few retrievals together over the past couple years. Met him in Libya."

"I heard he's from the Congo."

"He is. He was in Libya with the French Foreign Legion," he replied, digging into his succulent bone-in sirloin.

"We'd like to meet with him if he's interested," Carey told him, slicing his rib-eye.

Sam enjoyed Brixham crab and whole sea bream with chili and rosemary while she listened to their conversation with one ear, the rest of her attention focused on calculating all the possible permutations for how Simon could have known about her field work in the Navy. The only publicly available information on her military background would have been her years served, the countries and years for her tours of duty, and her rank and file. She sat back, watching Simon as he enjoyed his dinner.

He was clever. Of course he would have done his homework on her. But he didn't push too hard, knowing she wouldn't relent. *It's not information he wants*, she realized. *He's testing his boundaries...and showing me what he can do.* He wanted to impress her and throw her off balance at the same time. Put himself in a position of strength despite the fact that he'd reached out to them.

"Simon, why did you approach us now?" she asked suddenly, interrupting them. "After Carey's been trying to recruit you for two years. Africa was months ago. That would have been enough to make anyone quit. Why did you do the Chechen gig? Knowing it would likely be more of the same."

Simon put his cutlery down, hazel eyes focused on her. He said nothing as he regarded her.

"I can think of three reasons," Samantha continued, steepling her fingers in front of her as she sat back. "How about a little game of process of elimination?"

Carey watched her, his face a question mark.

"The obvious one would be that you're bitter and you want to stick it to Leviathan."

Simon remained unfazed, his face granite as he watched her.

"No?" Sam's brow quirked. "How about you were put up to meeting the 'infamous' Samantha Wyatt and her cohort by the very company who supposedly strung you out and to accomplish what? A little corporate espionage?" she asked instead. She reached for her wine glass, toying with the stem.

A little smirk ghosted over Simon's mouth.

"You British boys and your James Bond ambitions," Sam smiled, picking up her glass.

"Sam—" Carey began, unsure of where she was headed.

She held up a finger. "Or you're here tonight because something is seriously wrong at Leviathan. Something no one knows. You were going to leave, and justifiably so," she acknowledged. "But your timetable became suddenly urgent." Sam sipped her wine, watching him over the rim.

The skin around Simon's hazel eyes tightened, almost imperceptibly.

"Oh?" She smiled, leaning forward. "I like number three too. Now I just need to know why."

"Your lady's downright scary, mate," Simon muttered to Carey.

"You're not telling me anything I don't know," Carey answered, chewing his steak.

"How did you figure it out?" Simon asked after a moment.

Sam cocked her head. "You're a savvy guy. You know how to take care of yourself in sticky situations. You started nicking cars as a youth, after all. Had plenty of practice covering yourself," she pointed out. "So the only reason you stayed at Leviathan so long was that there was something worth your while. And that's changed. Plus, you aren't the bitter type. You're level-headed. Methodical."

"And you know that how?" Simon asked, his brows raised.

"You work with vehicles and engines. You enjoy mechanics. Everything has its place. And everything has a process. That's what made you a good car thief and got you to major with the SAS at a relatively young age. You don't do emotional responses. That also makes you a proper Brit, doesn't it?" she smiled. "Stiff upper lip and all that."

He regarded her, his eyes admiring. "And how do you know I haven't been sent to spy on you?"

"No offense, Simon, but they wouldn't send you." She grinned. "So what is it? What's going on at Leviathan that's brought you to our door?"

Simon sat back, resting his hands on the table. He looked from Sam to Carey and then back to Sam. "Is this an offer?"

"Bring Henri with you, and I'll double your current salary," she answered. She felt Carey tense with excitement.

Simon's head cocked. "Why do you want Henri?"

"He's an expert in jungle warfare, and he has connections we would find useful," Carey answered.

"He's also a right crazy bastard," Simon said, smiling.

"You'd have to be to join the French Foreign Legion," Carey replied.

"I want my own team," Simon added.

"We run dual leader teams," Carey answered. "Our model is different from what you're used to. One leader runs the client-facing interactions and direct protection, the other runs security and preventative action behind the scenes. That's why we want you to bring Henri," he explained.

"Based in London?"

"If you like." Sam inclined her head.

Simon sat back. "I want a contract waiting for us by Friday."

"Consider it done," Carey responded.

Sam sipped her wine, waiting.

"You're as good as reputation makes you out to be," Simon commented, his eyes full of admiration.

"Flattery will get you everywhere," Sam replied.

Simon rested his elbows on the table, his demeanor completely serious. "Understand I got into this business because I'm good at what I do and because I wanted to stay in the action. The money was worth it after a military pension. Protecting or extracting high-value individuals, businessmen, officials, whatever. They're not all good men. I don't have the luxury of choosing, and I'm usually not bothered by that, but now…" Simon shifted forward. "I won't risk my life for it, and I sure as hell won't get on the watch list of every major government for it."

"You don't seem the type to rattle easily," Sam commented.

"I'm not. But this? Not havin' it." Simon knocked back his wine before leveling her a pointed look. "Leviathan's protecting Ibrahim Nazar."

Carey's eyes widened. "Shit."

Sam leaned forward. "You mean to tell me Leviathan's in league with one of the biggest opium suppliers and known terrorists in the *world?*" she asked in a low voice.

Simon nodded. "I was asked to ship out to Afghanistan this week."

"You know where he is?"

Simon shook his head. "Closely guarded since the American-Russian joint raid on one of his production facilities in Farah. But my initial meeting point was meant to be Kandahar. Last I heard, he was in Pakistan, but the majority of his production is still in Afghanistan."

Carey thought about it. "Makes sense. Easy to get to Helmand, Uruzgan, or Zabal from there—the most likely places he'd be to keep an eye on the rest of his opium if he's not hiding out in Pakistan anymore."

"I wouldn't be surprised, mate." Simon nodded. "Whatever the case, there isn't enough money in the world to get me involved in that bollocks. If Leviathan's doing business with the likes of him—no telling who else Lightner's in bed with these days."

"How many people know about this?"

"I'm not certain." Simon shook his head. "But the team they've got on him is understandably secret. I only know a couple others who've been assigned. They're top-in-class. Don't know if they've agreed to it, though."

Carey looked at Sam.

"Anybody besides you and Henri looking to jump ship?" he asked Simon.

Simon nodded. "I can get back to you."

"Looks like it's Christmas morning after all," Carey smiled.

More like war, she thought. *And where there is war, there is always the residual burn for retribution.* They all had scalps on their belts, but Carey didn't know how she'd gotten her nickname. Or how it haunted her. *The Poppy.* A name given to her by the man she'd killed. Heir to the largest opium source in the world.

And Ibrahim Nazar's eldest son.

CHAPTER 7

September—Friday night
The Whitney, Chicago

J A C K

JACK HADN'T SEEN her in week, not since they'd gone out on the boat.

Her Corvette remained parked in her bay, the lights in the penthouse dark as if she'd never been there. Jack found himself vacillating between irritated and relieved, his attitude increasingly brusque the farther he went into the week with little to no sleep.

He could feel the tension behind his eyes building, the hyperactive firing of his synapses in overdrive as he became more and more wired from the insomnia. Mitch recognized the signs, leaving him alone at work as the week progressed, knowing Jack would hit a state of exhaustion and fall into a deep sleep that would likely take him out for a couple days. Jaime called to check on him, asking if he and Maddie should swing by and stay over. Jack begged off, knowing he'd be fine.

As he watched the hours tick past to midnight, Jack contemplated his options. Self-medicating was obviously out. He hated getting drunk to sleep, and besides that, it rarely worked. He'd simply wake up within a couple hours, groggy and dehydrated. He'd exercised enough this week to drain his muscles, leaving him aching. Sex would just wire him for sound.

Besides, he was avoiding a confrontation with Rebecca, knowing she wanted to have the "Where are we going?" talk since the benefit. He liked her. Obviously. But the idea of a long-distance relationship was both unappealing and potentially maddening for the both of them. Besides which, it would only delay the inevitability of their end, tacking on a tedious and drawn-out drama where one wasn't necessary.

Now, Jack longed for the sweet relief of sleep. So much so that he wondered about what he'd be willing to give up for that relief. As he watched the clock over his mantle strike 1:00 a.m., Jack contemplated his options dazedly. He pulled on a t-shirt over his lounge pants before wandering out to the terrace, seeking respite in the fresh, dark night air. He startled at the rhythmic slap of someone swimming laps in the pool.

She's back.

The tension drained from his body as he saw her through the soft golden lights embedded in the pool. Samantha turned smoothly, arching up and out of the water in the same butterfly stroke he'd seen her do the first night they'd met. Jack watched her for long minutes until she finally slowed, her strokes gentling to a lazy rotation. He was holding out her towel as she walked up the steps, squeezing the water from her hair.

"Hey there, Jack," she breathed, accepting the towel.

Jack's throat worked as he tried to think of something to say other than how relieved he was to see her. He felt unsteady, fought to stay focused through the exhaustion.

"How've you been?" Samantha asked when he said nothing. She peered at him in the low light of the pool, trying to ascertain if something was wrong with him. "You alright, Jack?" she asked, her head cocked.

He nodded once before saying, "Can't sleep," his voice gruff.

"Me neither," she answered, still watching him. "I'm jet-lagged, on London time. I was going to make myself something to eat. Care to join me?" she asked.

Jack nodded again, blinking against bleary eyes. She surprised him by threading her arm through his and strolling to her side of the terrace through the balcony doors. As he came into her home, he glanced dazedly at her spare furnishings, the soft walls and lighting, registering distantly she had Ella Fitzgerald singing softly through hidden speakers. She sat him at her kitchen counter, examining his bloodshot eyes, the hollows beneath from a sleepless week.

"What have you done with yourself, Jack?" she asked, turning toward the stove where she had something cooking gently in a steel pot. "You look like you got dragged to hell and back."

"I think I'm still there," he answered, voice strained. "I have pretty bad insomnia. Most times it's manageable but sometimes…" He trailed off, watching her move around her kitchen. Samantha preheated the oven, pulled a French baguette from a bakery bag, and got butter from the fridge along with a sprig of dill and garlic.

"I find it hardest to sleep when I'm thinking about how badly I want it," she remarked. "Like now. I got into bed at ten and laid there, waiting for it to come. Finally, I figured a good swim and some stew just might be the answer."

"You made stew?" he asked, perking up slightly.

"My housekeeper made stew. I'm fantastic at heating it up," she admitted without hesitation. She minced the dill and garlic before heating the aromatics along with the butter on the stove, tucking the bread into the oven. She added a pinch of flaky sea salt and fresh black pepper to the saucepan.

"Tell me about something to take your mind off it. What sports did you play when you were a kid?" she asked, reaching into a wine fridge she had tucked under her counter.

"Pretty much everything," he admitted. "Basketball, football, track, soccer. I got serious enough about soccer during college."

"Is that how you hurt your knee?" she asked, opening the bottle and pouring them both a glass.

"How did you know I hurt my knee?" Jack replied, surprised she knew about the old injury.

"I noticed it when we were on the boat." She shrugged. "The surgical scar is almost gone, so I figured it happened when you were young." She handed him a goblet of red wine.

They toasted. Jack took a sip, eyes widening at the flavors. "This is excellent," he told her, taking another small sip.

Samantha looked bemused. "Well, if we're going to be stuck awake, we might as well enjoy a good bottle."

She took her wine to the stove, gently stirring the heating butter, checking the stew. He watched her shuffle around in her robe, hair drying with the faint hint of saltwater from their pool. It struck him how laid back she was, barefoot and robed, making no effort to look sexy. But she was lovely, swaying slightly to the music, sipping her wine.

"I'll tell you about my knee if you tell me about your shoulder," Jack murmured, feeling the tension loosening from his shoulders as he relaxed and leaned against the kitchen counter.

She smiled as she put the lid back onto the stew. "You first." Samantha came back the counter, resting on her elbows, hand cradling her glass as she swirled her wine goblet lazily.

"Mitch and I met playing soccer at Northwestern," Jack started. "We instantly disliked each other. I'm not even really sure why. We were both strikers. I had a little more staying power running, so I ended up playing second striker since Mitch is a sneaky, fast bastard," he told her, laughing softly at the memory. "We didn't do well in practice, but during games, we were united. Common enemy and all that."

"I can get behind that," Samantha conceded. "Seen plenty of guys hate each other on dry land and when we get 'em on out on a carrier, you never saw a tighter unit."

"Similar principles minus the fighter jets and nuclear warheads," Jack joked. "So, during a game against U of M, we're up by one and close to the finish. I had the ball and was about to pass to Mitch when the center back and sweeper just came at me like torpedoes. They weren't even really coming after the ball. The sweeper kicked me in the knee so hard I saw stars. I think the center back cleated me as he stepped over. They were already going to get red-carded but Mitch—*Christ*," he laughed softly, wiping a hand down his face, remembering. "I've never seen him so angry. He knocked the sweeper out with a right hook and got the center back in a headlock before the refs could stop him." He took another sip of wine. "The rest of our team joined him. It was like a scene out of *Braveheart*, except in Evanston with college kids and soccer moms shouting and hitting each other with those foam fingers," he chuckled again, shaking his head in humor. "I had to have knee surgery, but we became pretty close after that."

"Did you play again after surgery?" Samantha asked, turning to pull the bread from the oven.

"Yeah, but it just wasn't ever the same. And during recovery, my priorities changed. I think being forced to sit still helped me prioritize."

"And what did you prioritize?" she asked.

Jack thought back, fingers lazily fiddling with the stem of the wine glass. "Up until that, I was just another fraternity jock on the party circuit. I grew up with a lot of opportunities, and I guess it was just a given I'd follow my dad into politics eventually. I never really thought about it until the injury."

"You don't strike me as the follow-the-leader type, Jack. If anything, you seem like the type to expect others to follow," Samantha commented, drizzling hot garlic and dill butter onto the French bread. The scent was so heavenly, Jack's mouth watered.

"You're right," he agreed. "But I didn't have a great deal of drive. Getting stuck in a wheelchair and then crutches was a great motivator. And to be honest, between physical therapy and classes, there wasn't a lot else I had the energy to focus on. I started realizing how much I enjoyed certain things, and how little I cared about others," he conceded.

Jack watched Samantha pulling bowls from the cabinet.

"Can I help?" he asked.

"Sure. Let's keep it casual and eat at the counter. Can you grab those place mats? Napkins and silver in the drawers over there," she nodded.

They moved around quietly, Samantha ladling hot stew into their bowls and Jack setting up their service.

"So what did you find you enjoyed?" she asked, setting steaming bowls in front of them.

"I'm about to enjoy the hell out of this meal. Thank you," he sighed in expectant pleasure, picking up his wine glass. "Cheers."

Samantha chuckled, toasting him. "Everything's always better after a good meal," Samantha said, smiling at him over the rim of her glass.

They dug into their food with gusto, relishing how the tender pot roast fell apart in their mouths, dipping the crusty, buttered bread into their stew.

Jack elicited near-pornographic groans of appreciation. He couldn't remember the last time he'd had such a basic, hearty meal that felt so utterly wholesome and restorative.

"So is this when you decided to become a real estate magnate?" she asked, pouring them both more wine.

"No. That was accidental," Jack admitted, toasting her glass gently. "I discovered how much I enjoyed civil engineering and architecture by proxy. Had this amazing professor who'd take us into the city for field trips, explaining structural development, water systems, bridges. All these places I'd grown up around—I started to see them completely differently. It was like figuring out a Rubik's cube."

"So you're a civil engineer?"

"And an architect," Jack nodded. "Got my master's at Cornell."

"Why don't you design? Or do you, and I just don't realize it?" Sam asked.

Jack shrugged. "I'm not a massively talented architect. I'm good enough to be dangerous. And I also discovered I'm more suited to the business aspects of property development. I'd been around city planning enough through interning with Dad to know how the system worked, and there was a lot I wanted to do. Figured if I wasn't exceptional at designing buildings, I'd improve the skyline in my own way," he said, taking a moment to savor the wine. "What is this? I'm buying a case of it."

She shrugged. "It's a garage wine from a little vineyard a friend of mine owns in Mendocino. Is that why you restored the Whitney?" she asked.

"Among other things," he nodded. "There is such great architectural history in Chicago, but so few firms are interested in funding preservation. Mitch and I do a lot of commercial development outside of downtown Chicago and the Loop, but I like keeping the history of the buildings here intact. The Whitney and a half a dozen other buildings we've restored have shown we can do both profitably. Sometimes it just takes longer and is more of a labor of love than anything."

Samantha glanced through the balcony doors to the dimly lit terrace. The lights of the city twinkled in the distance, the trees of Grant Park swaying gently in the breeze. "I love living here. I told Mitch I used to walk by this building every day when I was in law school. I watched when you bought it, started the restoration. I couldn't wait to see it. When it was featured in *Architectural Digest*, I knew I had to have it." She smiled as she leaned forward. "Tell you a secret?"

Jack nodded.

"This is the first home I've ever bought for myself. Thank you for selling it to me."

Jack grinned. "Yeah, well, I didn't really plan on selling it. Especially after Cassie died. I wanted Jaime and Maddie close, but she's better off in Oak Park, terrorizing the neighbors." Jack laughed. "I remember how much we used to love running around the neighborhood. Would be a shame for her to miss out on that."

"I grew up on a ranch," Samantha told him. "I look back now and realize how lucky I was to have all that land to run around on. At the time, it felt so isolating. No trick or treaters, forty-five minutes of driving the world's most boring road to get to school. Hindsight twenty-twenty, I wouldn't change it for the world."

"Are you telling me you know how to drive a tractor?" Jack teased.

"What?" Samantha looked up, feigning surprise. "You don't?"

Jack just laughed, picking up their bowls and taking them to the sink.

"I'll have you know I may have been daddy's little girl, but daddy had his little girl baling hay, fixing fences, and driving cattle while I was still in grade school," she told him, chuckling at the memory.

"Daddy's self-sufficient princess," Jack smiled.

"He wouldn't have it any other way," she remarked, shooing him away from the sink as he finished cleaning the bowls. "I got a ridiculous-ly huge sectional. Perfect for kicking your feet up," she told him. "Why don't you go sit and finish your wine before I kick you out."

He smiled at that, wandering over to her living room. It was sparse, but comfortable, a beautiful hand-woven silk Persian rug under his feet and her admittedly huge sofa looking soft and inviting. As Jack leaned back on her couch, he felt utterly content. Belly full, a gentle, relaxed feeling from a few mouthfuls of delicious wine, and Ella Fitzgerald crooning in the background. Jack blinked, struggling to keep his eyes open. In a moment, he felt Samantha's hand sift through his hair, her fingernails gently scratching his scalp. His whole body relaxed into the cushions.

"That feels good," he murmured, turning his face into her hand. He pressed a kiss to the inside of her wrist.

Her face seemed to float in front of him, her dark eyes soft and warm.

"Would you do me a kindness?" he asked, already drifting toward sleep.

"Besides feeding you and plying you with good wine?" Samantha teased, fingers still gently scratching his scalp.

"Would you sit next to me?" he murmured, his voice trailing to a husk. He felt her move to sit beside him. She brought him down towards her gently, lowering his head onto her lap. He shifted to his side, sliding an arm around her legs, tucking her closer to him, her terry cloth robe soft on his cheek as her fingers kept sliding through his hair, lulling him.

He wanted to tell her thank you, that it was the best he'd felt all week, that he loved their simple meal and their delicious wine and the easy banter. He couldn't remember the last time he felt so content, so completely relaxed, and he wanted her to keep talking to him, to tell him more about growing up on a ranch, how she knew about garage wines, and how she got that scar on her shoulder.

"Don't let me fall asleep," he murmured. And then he was out.

September—Saturday, late morning

South Side, Chicago

SAMANTHA

SHE WAS DOING alright, considering how little sleep she'd gotten. She'd snapped awake after a couple hours of dozing on the couch with Jack. She must have jerked when she woke because Jack muttered something in his sleep, loosening his arms from around her and shifting, giving her just enough room to slip off the sofa without rousing him. She briefly considered waking him, but decided the charitable thing to do was leave him alone, enjoying the rest that seemed to elude him most of the time. She dragged herself upstairs, collapsing into a deep sleep for a few more hours before her phone's alarm went off.

She and Carey taught a self-defense seminar a couple times a month at a women's shelter in South Loop. She'd suckered Talon and Rush into being her demonstration dummies for today's session after their regular workout in the morning.

Talon showed up to the class with a darkening bruise blossoming across his cheekbone and a cut on the wing of his brow. The cocky bastard was smirking too as he walked into the rec room of the shelter.

"What in the hell happened to you?" Sam asked as he dropped a bag full of pads and gloves.

"Whooped some ass in the Octagon," he said.

Sam eyed his fat lip. "You sure about that?"

"Dumbass got into it with Goro today. He barely got out of there alive," Rush corrected, coming up behind Talon with another bag of pads.

The gym they regularly attended was geared toward professional and trained fighters. Goro was a trained sumo wrestler who had diversified into mixed martial arts and easily had about sixty pounds on Talon. She didn't completely understand their desire to get in the Octagon any chance they got, but she figured their jones for blood sport had a lot to with their natural enjoyment for rough-housing—not to mention the fact that after years in Special Forces, they still missed the adrenaline rush of a hand-to-hand encounter with someone who truly wanted to hurt them. That sentiment was mixed, of course, with plenty of good old-fashioned machismo.

"Psshaaaw." Talon waved off. "I had him."

"You barely got out of that head lock," Carey muttered, joining them with a medical kit. "You're lucky you were able to kick his feet out from under him or he would have done more than he did."

"Chicks dig scars," Talon replied flippantly.

Carey smacked Talon in the back of the head. "Chicks dig guys who aren't morons. You nearly got nailed by Goro back there. You need to work on your Jiu-Jitsu." He proceeded to clean a cut over Talon's brow before slapping on a couple butterfly tapes harder than necessary.

Talon winced and shrugged. "I did fine. Besides, I hate wrestling. I'd rather beat the living daylights out of someone on my feet. More than one way to skin a cat."

Carey rolled his eyes before looking at Sam. "You gotta help this guy get his ground game on. He's too reliant on hand-to-hand and kicks. Can you work with him?"

Sam smiled. "Sharpshooters like their distance. I don't think he'd abide by anyone tugging him down and choking him out, especially me. He'd just lie to St. Peter at the pearly gates and tell him he hit his head in the shower."

"Nah, I'd tell him I died in the arms of a beautiful woman," Talon replied. "No shame in that," he flirted, wagging his brows at Sam.

"No one would have the balls to call Goro a beautiful woman," Sam replied drily. "Now put on your pads. You'll need 'em."

The women who were taking the self-defense course rolled in, greeting Sam and Carey while they checked Talon and Rush out. There were about twenty women, across ages.

"Who're these guys?" one of the women asked, wary.

"Your dream come true," Talon grinned, bowing dramatically in front of the women.

Sam rolled her eyes. "He's right in a way. Carey and I are going to show you how to beat the hell out of these two today," she replied, introducing Rush and Talon by name. "While they're putting on their padding, Carey and I are going to walk you through some great defense moves for an attack from behind and show you how to get out of choke holds."

She and Carey walked the women through several scenarios and defensive strategies before breaking the class up into smaller groups where they could do more interactive demonstrations.

As they were working, Willa Carter, the director for the shelter and a close friend of Sam's, popped her head in, waving Sam over.

"How's it going, girl?" Willa asked, giving her a brief hug.

Sam shrugged. "Good as always. A few new girls, so that's encouraging."

Willa glanced at Talon and Rush swaddled in pads. "I love it when you bring guys they can beat on. Really helps with the therapy, you know?"

Sam chuckled. "I can't speak for Rush, but I think Talon secretly likes it. I never have to ask too much to get him to volunteer."

Willa rolled her pretty blue eyes. "Yeah, that boy's one sick puppy. I asked him to help me get some boxes out of the truck once, and he asked me if I'd repay him with a kiss. I told him he could kiss my ass, and I'm not kidding you, that boy bent right over and did! Right there in the parking lot! Sicko," she laughed, making her long braids rustle.

Sam grinned over at the guys. Carey was showing one group of women how to twist out of a choke hold. Rush showed another group how to use their elbows in an attack, and Talon was demonstrating how to effectively knee someone in the groin. Figured.

"So we still on for tonight?" Willa asked, drawing her attention again. "It's been too goddamn long since we hung out, Ms. *I-live-in-Chicago-just-kidding!*"

"Yup," Sam laughed. "See you at eight, Ms. *I-guilt-trip-my-friends.*"

Willa blew her a kiss and a sassy wink. "You know it! See ya tonight, girl!"

Sam had Rush and Talon simulate attacks on each of the women as she and Carey showed them how to defend themselves with well-placed kicks, punches, elbows, and clutches. Some women remained tentative while others reacted with gusto, working out a few of their anger issues on a hapless Rush and a hyperactive Talon. The guys took the attacks gracefully, though she had a feeling they'd both be sorry for it tomorrow.

"Fuck me, if I take one more hit to the groin—" Talon groaned after a couple hours, laying down on the mat as the last of the women in the class filed out.

"Fuck you, you shouldn't have been teaching them how to knee your boys all lesson," Rush laughed, sitting down beside him to pull off his shin pads. "Besides, if anyone needs to get kicked in the junk, it's you."

Talon reeled up and landed a hard punch in Rush's side. Rush tossed the pads in his hands and jumped on him while Sam and Carey rolled their eyes. Rush, an accomplished wrestler, had Talon flipped over and in an awkward pin within seconds while Talon punched him hard in the shoulder and neck, trying to gain purchase. Rush took the punches, grunting and ducking his head, using his lower body to pin Talon closer to the floor, rendering him ineffective. Carey went back to packing up the gear while Sam watched the guys struggle for a few seconds longer before picking up her gym bag and heading to the door.

"Boss, you coming out with us for drinks later?" Talon called out, shoving Rush off.

"Nah, not tonight, fellas. I got better things to do than watch you guys trying to nail every skirt in sight," she teased, waving over her shoulder. "See you Monday!"

Carey followed her out into the lot. "You sleep last night? You look a little rough."

Sam rolled her eyes. "You always say the sweetest things, Bear."

He shrugged. "I sent you an email but just wanted to confirm that Michaelson and Henri should have the contracts signed by Monday."

She nodded. "That's good news. They give you a bead on anyone else?"

"Yeah. Michaelson will be giving me a list of guys he thinks will want to join us, starting with Cameron Kurt, that ex-Green Beret I told you about."

Sam smiled, unlocking her car. When she sensed Carey still standing behind her, she turned around, head tilted in question.

Carey shifted, looking uncharacteristically uncomfortable. "Saw you chatting with Willa earlier. You two going out tonight?" he asked.

Sam watched him for a moment. "Bear, when are you going to tell that woman you're in love with her?" she asked, leaning against her car. "You just need to suck it up and ask her out, you great big scaredy-cat."

Carey shrugged, looking like a bug pinned under a magnifying glass. A giant, six-foot-six, two-hundred-and-forty pound bug. Squirming nonetheless.

She and Carey rarely discussed their love lives. It was like talking about sex with a sibling, and she could think of about fifty other things she'd rather do than have that discussion, but he'd held a flame for Willa ever since they'd met her at a fundraiser two years ago and started volunteering at the shelter. Sam wasn't sure why he'd never just gone ahead and pursued her, but she was also the last person to meddle in his romantic pursuits.

"Willa's, uh, she's just…" He stopped, at a loss. "You know." A deep blush started crawling up his neck. Sam saw Carey embarrassed so rarely, her eyes actually widened.

"Carrick Nelson, are you telling me you're too shy to ask Willa out?" she asked, astonished.

"She's just—" He faltered, swallowed hard, and rubbed the back of his neck. "She's such a spitfire. She's so damn fiery and mouthy and tough. And she talks a mile-a-minute and—"

"Bear, I have seen you make grown SEALs break down. You wrangle two-thousand-pound cattle like it's nothing—and you find Willa Carter intimidating? You have *got* to be kidding me!" she chortled.

Carey turned around like he was going to walk off and then he stopped, rounding on Sam. "It's different with her. She's different. I just don't really know what to say when I'm around her. Not like she lets you get a word in edgewise anyway," he muttered. "Forget I said anything." He turned back toward his SUV.

"Carey, wait!" Sam said, gathering her breath. "Stop. I just haven't seen you nervous over a girl since…" She looked up. "Well ever. Took me by surprise is all."

The color still high on his cheekbones, Carey glanced at her out of the corner of his eye, waiting for another joke.

Sam should have felt contrite for teasing him, but she was still a bit taken aback to see Carey nervous. Those moments were so rare. Her giant, stalwart Bear had shown nerves only a handful of times in all the years they'd known each other.

"Yeah, I'm having dinner with Willa," she nodded. "We were going to go to Avec, then maybe Buddy Guy's to see some blues. Do a little dancing. You want to meet us?"

"You're not gonna give me shit for this, are you?" he asked, tone foreboding.

"I sure will," she retorted, tossing her bag in the 'vette. "But not in front of her," she winked.

Carey just wagged his head as she started her car up and backed out, waving.

September—Saturday afternoon

The Whitney, Chicago

JACK

JACK WOKE SLOWLY, blinking against the warm light filtering through the windows of the balcony and terrace. The late afternoon sun bathed the living room in a soft, golden hue. He knew immediately he wasn't home, but it took him a moment to gather his wits. He was sprawled out on Samantha's sofa, covered by a soft quilt, a pillow tucked under his head. He could barely recall falling asleep, but he felt more rested than he had in a long time. As he sat up and stretched, glancing around, he could tell from the quiet stillness that he was alone. He saw a note on the coffee table for him that told him to go to the kitchen. In the kitchen, he saw another note folded up in a coffee mug next to an espresso machine.

> *Jack,*
>
> *Welcome back. Turns out I didn't have the heart to kick you out after all. Decided it was better to let you enjoy a little well-deserved rest. Press the button on the machine and you'll get the best coffee you've had in your life. Enjoy.*
>
> *-Sam*

Jack turned on the machine, rubbing his eyes as he waited for the coffee to brew. Glancing at the clock, he realized he'd slept the day away, and he wondered where Samantha was, if she worked on the weekend or was out with friends. He spotted the bottle they drank sitting on the counter, deciding to take it with him so he could order a couple cases. He'd give one of them to her as a thank you for letting him crash at her place.

After the coffee finished brewing, he took a sip, groaning in pleasure. She wasn't kidding. Samantha didn't have much in her home yet, but she had all the essentials down pat. He grabbed the pen she'd left on the counter and flipped over the note.

Samantha,

You're a lifesaver and a saint, and I owe you one. In the meantime, I plan on bribing your housekeeper, stealing your wine, and buying a replica of that sofa. Looks like that's all I need to get a decent night's rest and wake up feeling human again. Well, that and you. Got any plans Sunday afternoon?

-Jack

He smiled, warming at the possibility of seeing her again so soon. He scribbled his number at the bottom of the note before finishing his coffee and rinsing out the mug.

When he got back to his place, he looked more closely at the bottle of wine. The label was rustic, like it had been printed on a simple press. The logo was a scrawled G with a flourish at the end, like a masculine signature. At the corner, under the vintage, the word *appassionata*. Lover. He looked up the vineyard on his phone, leaving a message asking them to call him back so he could make a special order of the vintage.

His phone was ringing by the time he got out of the shower. He picked it up, toweling his hair dry.

"You rang about the wine?" a man's voice asked at the end of the line.

"Yeah, it's delicious. I'd like to get a couple cases of it if possible," Jack replied.

"How did you get it?" the man asked, his voice sharp.

Jack hid his surprise at the gruff response. "A friend of mine turned me onto it," he responded casually. "She said it was a garage wine from

Mendocino. Is that right?"

"Yeah, but that was a small batch. Specially made," the man answered, his brusque voice softening slightly. "Was it Sam?" he asked after a beat.

Jack's eyes widened in surprise. He wasn't sure what to say. He didn't even know who was on the other end of the phone. "Who is this?"

"Grant Gallo. I own the vineyard," the man said. Another long pause. "How is she?" he asked quietly.

Jack squeezed the towel, pieces snicking into place.

"She's good," he answered. "She's happy." The minute he said it, he knew he'd stepped over a line, an invisible boundary into Samantha's past he had no right nosing into. But he couldn't seem to stop himself, realizing who this man had been to her. Who she had been to him.

The man said nothing. Jack got the distinct feeling they were staring each other down over the line.

"That's good," Grant breathed after a minute. "I'm glad for her," he said, seeming to come to a decision. "I have about four cases left of that small batch. I'd be willing to send them all to you if that's what she wants."

Jack thought about it, debating.

"She'd like that," he heard himself answering, not entirely sure she'd like any such thing.

After they'd settled the details on the shipment, Grant said, "Look, I'm sorry if I was a little rude earlier. I just—" He took a breath. "It's been a long time. Tell her I said hi. That I wish her well."

Jack paused a beat, realizing then that she'd probably broken this guy's heart. There was something in his voice. An unsaid longing, a regret. They'd shared something, at least six years ago, going by the vintage. It should have been nothing to him, but it was. It was vitally important to Jack to know that there was someone she might have loved once.

"I will," he responded. "Thank you for the wine."

"Take care of her," Grant said before hanging up.

CHAPTER 8

September—Saturday night

South Loop, Chicago

S A M A N T H A

"OH, *HEEEELL YES*, you're gonna get all up on that!"

Sam nearly choked on her beer mid-draw, quickly covering her mouth with a napkin as she tried vainly to shoosh her friend. But no one shooshes Willa Carter. If anything, that just makes her louder.

"Fuck it, just give me his number. I'm calling him up right now and telling him to meet you at your place in ten minutes. You can book it if you leave now. Why are you waving your hand at my face?! You better put that hand back on your side of the table before I put it back there for you. Oooh *GURL*!" Willa smacked Sam's hand away from her face, using her other hand to grab Sam's phone off the bar table. "I'm calling him. I'm serious!"

"Jesus," Sam muttered, snatching her phone back and shoving it in the back pocket of her jeans. "You are a goddamn menace! Quit yelling my business out in the middle of the bar!" she hissed.

Willa's brow arched and her neck rolled. Sam could almost feel a lecture coming on. "You need to get off your ass and get on top of that man, missy. Listen to Madame Willa."

"You are watching too much psychic network," Sam said, shaking her head at her friend. "I didn't tell you about Jack so you could pimp me out to him. I was just sharing. Now pipe down and drink your margarita."

"And sharing is caring, hunty," Willa declared sagely. "For instance, I care that your *super-ridiculously-hot-sexual-white-chocolate-man-candy* of a neighbor is clearly interested in you and you're tripping like you're not going to do shit-all about it!" She drained her margarita and grabbed their waiter's attention with the swing of one long, bangled arm. "Yeah, I'm gonna need me another one of these!" she called, pointing at her empty glass.

She directed her sharp blue eyes back at Sam, examining her like she was crazy. Willa was a striking woman. Amazonian tall with light brown skin, bright blue eyes, and enough braids to resemble Medusa when she was worked up. Willa was a force to be reckoned with, and that was on a normal day. She was especially striking when she was making a point *and* lit up on the fuel of tequila, like right now.

"I met him a few years ago at a city planning thing involving the shelter, and that man radiates sex. Shit, they can probably track his heat signature from outer space!" Willa leaned forward. "You have had no action since that Mr. *Sensitive-artist-from-Wicker Park* guy, though what the hell you were doing messing around with that kid, I have no idea." She rolled her eyes. "The whole cougar thing is overrated. I hate having to teach these puppies how to stay on the lawn. Oh—thank you! Come to mama!" she cooed at the margarita the waiter slid in front of her. He smiled at her obvious pleasure.

"There's no accounting for enthusiasm," Sam shrugged carelessly. "And I didn't tell you about Jack because I'm not intending to hit that. He's my neighbor. And while we're on the subject of lawns, you don't mess around in your own backyard if you know what I mean. I'm not interested in starting something only to finish it and have to look at him every other day. I don't want weird right next door," she explained before glancing around the bar. "Hell, I can get that here."

"BULLSHIT. I call bullshit," Willa declared. "You are gonna hit that. You two are some of the biggest players I know. The only difference is you're more secretive about it. Your shit's not all over the society pages the next day, but that don't make you any less scandalous, diva. What's the harm? You aren't serious. He's not serious. The only thing that's serious is the amount of sexual chemistry you two could come up with."

Two men picked that exact moment to sidle up to their table. Before one of them could open up with "Well, hello there, ladies," Willa held her hand up and shook her head. "I'm divorced and I run a battered women's shelter. This one is ex-military and can kill you with her purse strap. Keep walking." She jerked her thumb behind her. The guys looked at each other, a little taken aback and a lot relieved before high-tailing it back to where they came from.

"You're such an awesome wing-woman," Sam complained. "If I keep hanging out with you, I'm going to have to sleep with Jack due to lack of options."

Willa shrugged as she licked salt off the rim of her glass. "That's like complaining about getting sent up to the majors. Cry me a river."

"Why do you give a damn about who I get with anyway?" Sam asked. "You need to keep your eyes on your own paper."

Willa rolled said eyes. "You're ridiculous if you think telling me about how this gorgeous, fine-ass man keeps popping up and you're planning on doing nothing about it means I should sit back and say nothing. If you didn't want me to say anything, hunty, you would never have mentioned it. Besides, he asked to see you tomorrow. You want me to hold my tongue? Then don't tell me before a date that you plan on ditching it," she sassed, turning in her chair to check out the band setting up onstage at Buddy Guy's Legends. "Gary Clark Jr.! I *love* that man," Willa sighed, looking uncharacteristically dreamy eyed. The skinny, Texan blues musician smiled beautifully as he and his band opened with "Bright Lights."

They listened for a few minutes before Willa turned back toward Sam, a Cheshire grin on her face. "I know exactly what the problem is," she announced.

Sam's brow arched. "And what, pray tell, is that?"

Willa leaned back in her chair, crossing her long legs. "You dig this cat," she answered, rubbing a finger on her chin. "More than you like. More than you're comfortable with, anyway. Why? What's so different about him?"

Sam resisted down the urge to shift in her chair. Willa was irritatingly on point. Jack was attractive all right, but the more time she spent with him, the more she saw past the highly burnished gloss and the more dangerously close she came to liking his character. Jack was such an engagingly sexy blend of confidence, introspection, and intelligence. She was unprepared for his depth, the devotion with which he loved his family, the earnestness in his face when he talked about his work, his humor.

Sam opened her mouth to deny it when Willa narrowed her eyes, leaning forward. "You better be real careful what you say, hunty. I can see your mind working to come up with BS like a squirrel on a wheel."

Sam laughed. One of the reasons she liked Willa so much was the woman called it exactly like she saw it. While Sam's life was all about dealing with people in a certain way, saying the right thing at the right time, Willa was a *balls-to-the-wall* straight talker. She said exactly what she thought and didn't give a damn if anybody liked it or not, but there was enough genuine care behind her statements that you couldn't dislike her for her lack of tact. You knew Willa was coming from a good place. And you also knew she was too smart to screw around with.

"He's got staying power," Sam admitted, taking a pull of beer, eyes on the band.

"And you ain't looking to have anyone stay or have anyone to hold onto," Willa surmised. "Not your style. Though one of these days you'll have to tell mama about who made you that way."

Sam shrugged. "Nothing you haven't heard before."

Willa's eyes narrowed. "Not from you, I haven't."

Sam took a breath, knowing Willa was planning on digging in and there'd be little she could do to distract her. She didn't want to walk down any memory lanes tonight, so she stuck to the shallow water.

"Jack's unexpected, alright?" she continued. "I thought he'd be this charming, seductive bastard. You know his reputation. And I've made an honest career out of taking on men like that, so I know how they think, how they operate. But Jack—" She shrugged again, feeling uncomfortable. "Jack's not fitting into the box so neatly." She didn't add that she was ninety-five percent certain a fling with him would move from a passing distraction to a full-blown addiction if she picked up the habit.

"Well, damn, girl," Willa murmured. "Sounds like you saw him without all the veneer and you like his brand of human."

Sam blinked. "What?"

"It's simple really," Willa began. "Guys like Jack Roman—they've got it all. Cash, power, purpose, pussy. They're like gods. And they act like gods. But every now and then, you get to see past that version of reality. And you either like what they're made of or you're disappointed by them," Willa explained, chewing on her cocktail straw. "You, my friend—you're beyond turned on by him. Seems like he downright *does* it for you." Willa winked, pointing at her with her straw. "And I'm willing to bet my pathetic paycheck that he feels exactly the same."

"And you're so confident—why?"

Willa rolled her eyes. "Because you, my dear, are a goddess. You've *also* got cash, power, purpose, and what I'm sure is a dynamite pussy. Which means you've got the whip. And powerful, wealthy men might like to act like they rule the world, but we all know they ain't a match for the likes of you," Willa nodded wisely. "You also have a legion of trained killers who would do damn near anything for you, and yet, surprise surprise—" Willa waved her hand casually. "You're self-contained, girlfriend. You don't *need* anybody—much less a damn man. If that doesn't make you catnip for guys like Jack Roman, professional athletes, and well, rulers and shit—then, diva, I don't know what does!" She laughed, eyes delighted before they narrowed, looking over Sam's shoulder. "Wait, is that Carey?" Willa asked, switching gears.

Sam felt relief ease the tension from her body. The last time she'd been so happy to see him, she'd been under heavy fire in Recife.

Carey wove through the tall bar chairs to get to them, dressed in jeans, a blue t-shirt, and a washed black leather jacket. He looked good. Sam noticed Willa notice him looking good. Her relieved smile turned into a smug grin as she watched Willa pop off her bar stool.

"Carey—what are you doing here, you gorgeous man?" Willa asked, giving him a brief hug.

"Hopefully not crashing girls' night out?" he asked, his blue eyes sparkling as he favored Willa with his best smile. He hugged Sam. "What have I missed?"

"Oh, I was just telling Sam why Jack Roman's probably panting after her. She doesn't believe me. I think I'll have to get her drunk as punishment," Willa laughed, wagging her finger at Sam.

"He is," Carey agreed readily, glancing at Sam. "The man's not blind. Most guys would have to be blind not to be blown away by Sammy," he agreed.

Sam rolled her eyes, about to make a smart remark before Willa jumped in.

"And what about you then?" Willa asked, leaning toward him. "You ever had a crush on our girl?"

"I changed his diapers," Sam replied before Carey could answer. "And I taught him how to field dress a deer. He's worshipped me ever since."

Willa's eyes widened. "I knew you two were close but, ewww. Diapers and deer guts? That's... ewww."

Carey barked out a laugh, shaking his head. "I was an infant when she changed my diapers, and I was twelve when she taught me and her little brother how to hunt with our dads. Way to traumatize your friends, Sammy."

"Wait...what?" Willa's eyes bounced back and forth between the two.

"Carey's six year's younger than me. His parents helped raise me and my little brother. We grew up together," Sam explained.

"You have a brother?" Willa asked with a *how-did-I-not-know-this* look.

"Had," Sam corrected succinctly, sliding off her stool. "I'm getting another drink. You two want anything?"

Sam ordered more beers for them as the two got to talking. She lingered at the bar, partly to give them more alone time and partly to avoid any more psych 101 drilling from the far-too-intuitive Madame Willa. When she returned to their table, Willa and Carey were engaged in a lively debate on whether the Bears had any kind of chance this season. Sam sat back, enjoying her beer and listening to the music, involved in their conversation only peripherally.

When Willa finished her margarita, Carey went to the bar to order her another. She grabbed Sam's hand, her expression conspiratorial. "Damn, your boy is hot! I think he's hitting on me!" she shout-whispered.

"No shit, Sherlock," Sam teased. "You good if I bail?"

Willa's eyes narrowed. "You set this up!"

Sam shrugged. "I like you. He likes you. You like him. What's not to like? You two make a cute, super-sized couple."

"Ha ha, very funny, shorty," Willa drawled. "Though it would be nice to date someone I don't have to lean down to kiss in heels," she murmured contemplatively, eyeing him as he headed back toward their table with her drink.

"And if keeping you busy keeps you out of my business, more's the better," Sam grinned. "I'm gonna head out," she declared as Carey set the drink down. She tossed a couple bills on the table before shrugging into her jacket.

"Did you drive?" Carey asked.

She shook her head. "Gonna catch a cab."

"I'll walk you out," Carey said as she hugged Willa goodbye.

"And let another man come chatting up on this one?" Sam teased, gesturing toward Willa. "It's all good. I'll stick close to the front while I wait for a cab. Don't worry," she said, hugging Carey briefly before turning to go.

"You packing?" Carey asked, letting go of her shoulders grudgingly.

"It's Chicago, Bear. Not Caracas. I'll be fine," Sam chuckled. "I'll text you when I get home, 'kay?"

When she made it back to her street, she dutifully texted Carey a thumbs up before getting out of the cab, surprised to see Jack coming down the carpeted stairs of their building as the doorman opened her taxi door.

Jack looked casually elegant in a slim cut gray suit with a dark blue dress shirt open at the neck, and her blatant up-and-down perusal clearly told him so. He smiled at her unspoken compliment, taking her hand in both of his as she got out of the car, his silver eyes twinkling.

"Hey, lady killer," she grinned. "You look like you're up to no good."

"After that much continuous sleep, I have enough energy to light up half the town," he joked.

"Well, damn," she laughed, pulling her hand out of his and sweeping it toward the open door of the cab. "Don't let me stop you. Here, take my cab."

Jack shook his head, helping her shut the door. "I'll walk you up first." He looped her hand under his arm as he escorted her up the steps to the building's front door. It felt easy and surprisingly natural to have her hand tucked in his arm, so she let him lead her to the elevator, wondering where he was heading out to this close to midnight.

"I'm glad I ran into you," he confessed as they neared the elevator bank, his silver eyes earnest. "I wanted to thank you for last night. Best sleep I've had in weeks."

Sam arched a brow, glancing back at the concierge who was giving a decent impression of not eavesdropping.

Jack glanced at him too before guiding her closer to the elevator. He pressed the button. "I was wondering how you feel about craft beer?"

The elevator doors opened and he ushered her in, keying in the code to their floor.

Sam's brow furrowed. *Was he going back upstairs with her?* "I'm generally a fan of alcohol. But I'm not a beer aficionado. I just know what I like," she answered cautiously. "Why?"

He smiled down at her, his attractiveness magnified by the rest and the natural confidence of a man used to getting his way. "I thought we could take a drive up to Milwaukee. They have some of the best microbrews in the Midwest. I used to love to go up there in the fall, but I haven't had the chance in the past couple years. What do you think?" he asked, leaning one shoulder against the elevator as he regarded her.

She caught a heady whiff of his cologne. *Divine.*

What did she think? She thought he could probably talk her into just about anything right now with that *you-know-you-want-to* smile and enough charismatic wattage to blind anyone in the downtown radius. Sam struggled to reconcile this vibrant man with the sexy sleepyhead who had been sitting at her kitchen counter last night. It was amazing how much a little sleep seemed to zap the sizzle right back into him.

She realized he was waiting for her answer. Sam blamed her unchar-acteristic slowness on her buzz. "Hey, sorry." She shook her head, as if to clear it. "You got a helluva lot more sleep than I did, and I think I'm reeling from a just a few drinks. Did we talk about doing something tomorrow and I forgot?" she asked, buying time.

Jack looked surprised before recovering his footing easily. "I left you a note. Thank you again, by the way, for letting me crash. You have no idea how badly I needed it. I was hoping you'd be free tomorrow?"

"Oh, it was no big deal, Jack," she answered casually. "I don't think I could have woken you if I'd tried. You would have slept through heavy artillery fire at that point. Now you can't give me a hard time if I ever come over, eat your food, and pass out on your couch," she teased.

"*Mi casa es su casa*," he replied easily.

The elevator doors slid open. Jack held the doors open as she stepped out.

"Where are you coming from?" he asked, taking in her jeans, knee-high boots, and leather jacket.

"Buddy Guy's," she answered, stopping just outside her door.

"Ah," he nodded in understanding. "You seem like the kind of lady who appreciates the blues." He stood near her, sliding his hands into his pockets.

"I'm not sure if that's a good or bad thing," Sam replied.

They looked at each other for a moment, squared off in their long hallway.

"It's a compliment," Jack replied. "You have to feel intensely to really listen to the blues. You, clearly, are not the kind of woman to go half-measure. Of course it makes sense you'd prefer music that tears straight to the truth of what men are capable of," he reasoned.

She said nothing, the mixture of that perfect amount of alcohol, lassitude, and sexual awareness making her seriously consider laying down her guard for the night. Oh, she knew plenty about what men were capable of, and she wanted badly to know what this man was capable of.

Jack pulled his hands out of his pockets and started toward her.

Sam backed up a step. She had the distinct feeling Jack was doing more than advancing. He was coming for her. He lifted his hand, drawing long fingers down her cheek to run under her jaw, tilting her head up slightly. His head came down just a fraction. She felt her eyelids drop. It would be so easy to take what she needed from this man…

"You never answered me about tomorrow," he murmured, face close to hers. His scent surrounded her. Sam imagined briefly what it would be like to wrap her arms around his broad shoulders, breathe him in, touch the tip of her tongue to his skin…yes…

"Where are you headed tonight?" she heard herself ask, her voice lazy.

Jack didn't move. She watched his pupils dilate, the silver shards of his irises shifting and altering as he thought through his answer. Sam felt the distance between them widen into a chasm. In three hours, probably less, he'd be in someone else's arms. Enjoying the warmth of her body, pressed underneath him in cool sheets somewhere. Probably here, not even thirty yards away. That's what a man like Jack Roman did on a normal night, when he wasn't wracked with exhaustion and laid out on some Good Samaritan's sofa. And Sam would just be an accession—a pleasant addition to his normal range of activities. A nice tee-up to tomorrow evening.

She stepped back; put a hand on her door.

"Jack, I don't want to give you the wrong idea," Sam began, putting a friendly smile on her face as she got ready to deliver the *let's-just-be-friends* speech.

"And what idea would that be?" he asked, regarding her with a sardonic look, like he could see right through her. And he probably could, but she still wasn't going to agree to be added to the good thing that he probably already had going.

"That I'm looking to borrow any sugar," she answered affably. "Consider last night *gratis*. I might need you to do me a good turn one day, but I'm not keeping a ledger. Let's just leave it there, shall we?"

He seemed to consider that, light eyes narrowing momentarily. "You're a negotiator?" he asked, his tone deceptively casual.

"Among other things," she nodded, unlocking her door. As she opened it, she turned back to him, her face pleasantly distant.

Jack stepped forward, and her hand tightened fractionally on the knob. He leaned in, giving her a soft, barely-there kiss.

"So am I," he murmured into her ear.

Sam fought not to react. Her hands itched to run up his arms, loop around his shoulders.

Jack straightened, his eyes smoldering. He ran one long finger ran along her temple, pushing a strand of hair back. "And I'm going to be doing you more than a good turn, Samantha," he told her, studying her face.

"I bet you say that to all the girls, Jack," she replied, notably breathless.

"You're no *girl*, Samantha," he replied with a sexy little smile as he stepped back, releasing her from his gravitational pull. "The offer stands."

Sam made it inside and up to the comfort of her room, a bemused smile on her face. When she undressed, she imagined what his hands might feel like doing it for her. She decided to forgo a shower in favor of a bath. As she ran her hands along slick skin of her belly and her thighs, fingers curling into the wet folds of her sex, she thought of him. She thought of his slow burn smile and the intense light in his eyes. Sam considered his skin, still gold from the summer sun, the way his arms had curled around her waist as he slept, oblivious to everything except his own dreams. She recalled the heady and delicious scent of him. The curve of his spine. The way his hair felt twined in her hand.

Sam came in a luxuriant, supine ripple, imagining his mouth on her under the warmth of the water. And as she lazed in the aftermath, eyes still closed, Sam saw him rising up the slope of her body, trailing the water with kisses, his mouth warm, his tongue luscious.

He moved over her. And in her mind's eye, when she opened her eyes to look up at him, she didn't see bright silver eyes. She saw hazel eyes with striking striations.

"*Shaghayegh*," he whispered in Persian.

Poppy.

Sam startled awake, the water cold around her.

CHAPTER 9

June 2006

Kabul, Afghanistan

SAMANTHA

DAWN ROSE OVER the mountains surrounding the city, its long rays spreading across Eid Gah Square, already bustling with the sunrise prayers, merchants, and commuters. Sam walked into a non-descript building, partially shuttered, the heavy wooden doors closed behind her by US Army guards. They exchanged greetings before she pulled the dark hijab off her head. Sam glanced across the dim, vaulted room to look at a series of makeshift interrogation rooms, which sat still and silent.

"Lieutenant Wyatt."

Sam turned, setting down the bag she was carrying before saluting the man who emerged from the darkness lining the farthest wall. "Good Morning, Lieutenant Colonel Collins."

He eyed the bag. "You bring enough for all of us?"

She smiled in return. "Only if you like chai and *kulcha*, sir," she answered, referring to local tea and biscuits.

He shook his head, muttering, "What I'd give for a good cup of coffee and my wife's chocolate chip cookies," before turning back to the darkened area he'd come from. Collins was a thin man of medium height with steel gray hair and a tidy moustache. He had cool blue eyes and a nice smile when he cared to show it. He was also one of the scariest military interrogators she'd ever met.

Sam followed him down a short hallway into a surveillance room with a long, one-way mirror and observation glass. Computer screens and monitors displayed the inside of the interrogation rooms and makeshift cells. She greeted the four other men in the room, her eyes drawn nearly immediately to the monitor showing a man sprawled on his side on a mattress, his arm covering his face.

"Anything new, sir?" Sam asked, leaning down to touch the joystick on the desk, adjusting the angle of the camera and the zoom.

"No. He's insisting he's a small time *hawala* dealer from Helmand. Still calling himself Mirwais Khan," Collins answered.

"Do you think it's true, sir?"

He shrugged. "Dialect and accent suggests he's from Farah. He's clearly extremely intelligent. Well-educated. And he's endured the advanced interrogation tactics like a stalwart. I'd say he's military trained at least. He won't talk using the usual methods. The CIA is running facial recognition, but we're certain he's high up in Nazar's organization."

"*Hawala* dealer, sir?" she asked. "So he's saying he just moves money for Nazar?"

Collins shook his head. "Not even that. Says he's much lower on the food chain. He insists the photos we have were from the first time he'd ever met Nazar face-to-face."

"May I know his physical condition, sir?"

"Couple cracked ribs, broken nose, two missing teeth, three broken fingers."

Sam nodded, looking again at the man on the screen. He was wearing a tattered tunic and pants, probably still damp with water, blood, and sweat. They'd worked him over pretty well in the past few days. Most men broke under the pain of the beatings, the oxygen deprivation, and the water boarding. Few ordinary men could withstand that level of interrogation.

"Has he received medical attention, sir?" Sam asked, looking at Collins as she straightened.

He favored her with a twitch of his moustache. "I thought you might want to pull a Florence Nightingale act."

Sam gave a brief nod. She twisted on her hijab again, covering her head and the shoulders of her battle dress fatigues. She removed her guns, knives, keys, and pen, laying them out neatly on one of the tables. She picked up the bag she'd brought in.

"I'll station Cartwright and Moon outside the door," Collins told her.

"Thank you, sir."

Sam made her way through the building to the holding room they kept the man in. It was a simple room, small and with enough room for a mattress, toilet, and sink. One half of a wall was a panel of break-proof window, covered in metal fencing. The door, a sliding metal grate. She made her way to the entrance, waiting for one of the guards to release the lock. She stepped in as the guard slid it back, dropping the bag on the floor beside her.

The man on the mattress moved his arm, peering up at her. She was relieved she could still see his eyes under the swollen skin and bruising. He had a heavy beard, though his hair was cropped close. She guessed he was in his late twenties or early thirties, though it was difficult to say with all the damage. He sat up slowly, painfully, clutching his side. Two of the fingers on his left hand were at odd angles. He winced as he let go of his ribs.

"May I help you?" Sam asked him in Persian, gesturing gently at his hand.

"Are you a nurse?" he asked in heavily accented English.

"No," she answered in Persian, smiling gently. "But I think I can help you. If you like."

The man watched her warily for a long moment before giving her a single, abrupt nod. Sam reached into the bag and brought out gauze and tape, some antiseptic cream. She moved toward him slowly, holding her hands in front of her. She sat next to him on the mattress, facing him.

"Will you give me your hand?" she asked.

The man watched her, his body tense. Finally, he extended his hand toward her. Slowly. She noticed the slight tremor, though his face showed no emotion. He placed his hand in hers tentatively. She covered his hand with her other one, looking into his eyes. They were unusual. A startling green hazel with deep cognac-colored striations. He was watching her equally closely, wondering if she was truly there to help him. She saw the question in his eyes. She smiled gently again.

"Does it hurt?" she asked in Persian.

He looked down, his brows drawing together a fraction of a second. He shook his head, lifting his eyes back to her.

A lie.

"Because this will," she said, popping one of his fingers back into place.

He gasped, immediately trying to wrench his arm back, but she held fast to his wrist. "Do you want me to fix the other ones?" she asked gently, not letting go.

He grunted his acquiescence after a long pause, but she was already popping the other one back into place. She held her hand tight over his hand as he jerked and trembled, trying not to make a noise.

She looked at the broken finger on his right hand. "Do you want me to fix this last one?" she asked quietly.

He watched her through pain-addled eyes for a long time. Finally, he nodded slowly. She let go of his left hand and waited for him to place his right in her own. She noticed only slight callouses on both his hands. This man did no field work or farming, nothing mechanical, nothing heavily manual.

"Tell me your name?" she asked.

He looked down again, but his brow didn't knit. His face smoothed infinitesimally. As if he were readying himself. "Mirwais."

Another lie.

She felt along the knuckle of the broken finger for a moment before tugging it into place. He gasped again; this time a choked curse followed. She taped his fingers tightly while he watched her.

When she was done, she asked him to wash his face so she could put antiseptic on his cuts and split lips. He moved slowly but he complied, satisfied she would not hurt him. As he cleaned himself, she pulled out a thermos and two small tin cups along with a small package of biscuits. She poured hot, heavily sweetened chai made the Afghan way before closing the thermos. When he turned around, drying his face on the sleeve of his shirt, he stood stock still.

"Would you like tea?" she asked in Persian. A control question. She watched him closely.

He looked up from the tea to her, his expression surprised, and then a flicker of gratitude. He blinked once as he said yes, his eyes clear. She handed him a small cup. He sipped it, closing his unusual eyes at the small pleasure. She could feel the relief emanate from him. Then he stiffened.

She took a sip from her cup to show him it wasn't poisoned.

She offered him a biscuit.

He took the biscuit, watching her. She also took one, again to show it wasn't poisoned.

They drank their tea in silence. His breathing was labored, his posture stiff from the pain in his body. But he did not complain. He said nothing.

They watched each other.

She offered him another cup of tea. He nodded.

As she refilled his cup, he thanked her quietly this time, touching his hand to his heart.

"Would you like me to put antiseptic on your face?" she asked.

He nodded.

She let him sip his chai while she dabbed the cream gently on his face. Taping his cuts where she could. He placed his tea cup upside down on the floor to indicate he was finished.

"Why are you showing me kindness?" he asked in English.

"Because I need your help," she answered in Persian.

"How can I possibly help you?" He spat out a bitter laugh, following her back into Persian. *Good*, she thought. *It will be easier to get clearer indicators from him in his own language.*

"You met a man named Ibrahim Nazar. Who is he to you?" she asked.

He blinked, his brows gathering slightly. He looked down. Back up. "He's no one to me."

Lie.

"Why did you meet him, then?"

His expression smoothed. "I'm just a *hawala* dealer. He asked me to

COMPLICATED CREATURES 125

send money. That is all."

Lie.

"Do you know where Nazar is?"

Eyes down. Then back up. "No."

Lie.

"Do you know how to find him?"

Brows knit. Blink. Expression impassive. "No."

Lie.

She nodded. Now she knew what his lies looked like. She picked up the cups and the biscuits. When she put everything in the bag, she looked at him again.

"I can't help you with your ribs or your mouth," she told him. "But I can give you something for the pain. Would you like that?"

He watched her momentarily before nodding.

She called out to the guys to come in.

"I'm sorry to have to do it like this, but they won't hurt you while I'm here. They'll just hold you so I can safely inject you," she explained to the man in Persian.

The guards came in. One handed her a small syringe roll.

The man calling himself Mirwais had fear in his eyes as they held him down by his shoulders and arms. But a defiance as well. As if he expected a betrayal.

"Don't be afraid. They won't hurt you while I'm here," she told him again in Persian, looking him in the eyes until he calmed. She turned his arm gently, tapping out a vein.

"Are you sure?" she asked him quietly, again in Persian.

They watched each other for a moment before he finally nodded.

She injected him with number four grade pure heroin. From Ibrahim Nazar's own confiscated shipments to Iran.

She waited as the cloud of euphoria passed over his unusual hazel eyes.

Then she began again.

"What is your name?"

CHAPTER 10

October—Present day

Mogadishu, Somalia

S A M A N T H A

ALL IT GOOD manners. Call it military training. Whatever it was, it was generally Sam and Carey's habit to announce their presence and intentions in a country they were visiting on official business. Just in case. With their names, backgrounds, and current line of business, they'd be flagged anyway. Better to stay friendly, or at the very least, civil.

Sam and Carey liaised with the local CIA field office and the US Embassy in Mogadishu within two hours of touching down to let them know they were in town looking for Cameron Kurt, formerly a Sergeant in the 5th Special Forces Group out of Campbell, Kentucky. They'd tracked Kurt to Somalia, where he was trying to negotiate down a K&R demand for a Dr. Steven Bassett, an employee of Trytium Enterprises, a long-time client of Leviathan Risk. Dr. Bassett had been kidnapped while conducting an evaluation on a uranium ore excavation site his company was considering acquiring. Little had the hapless Dr. Bassett realized the mining operation had been part of a recent takeover by the al-Shabaab, a radical Somalian militia group interested in leveraging his kidnap to fund their more nefarious pursuits.

Kurt had done an admirable job so far, negotiating the radical militia group's initial ransom demand down from twenty million US dollars to three in the forty-odd days he'd been here, if Simon's intel was accurate. The CIA and US Embassy knew the al-Shabaab held Dr. Bassett, also an

American, but no one had provided much more information than that during the debrief, keeping the meeting short and concise.

As Sam and Carey watched Foreign Service officers and CIA field agents file out of the conference room they'd been debriefed in, she chewed her lip. The whole thing reeked of what remained unsaid. The CIA and the US Embassy weren't getting involved for a larger reason. Sam knew it. So did Carey. They exchanged looks before Carey drew aside one of the officers, a former Navy man and a friend from his days at Coronado. Sam remained at the edge of the office, one eye on the office window overlooking the Embassy's cubicle farm.

"What the fuck is going on?" Carey asked quietly.

The man ran a hand through his hair, shaking his head. "We're about ninety-five percent sure they're not giving up Bassett, no matter what Kurt puts on the table to get him back."

"Why?"

"He's a uranium ore mining expert, man. Al-Shabaab thinks they've got buyers in Iran, possibly Pakistan. This isn't about a ransom funding a two-bit militia anymore. The CIA's in on this now," he explained, eyes glancing nervously over Carey's shoulder to the outside window off the conference room. "The Al-Shabaab have graduated from robbing a liquor store to trying to hold up Fort Knox in one leap."

"And?" Carey prompted.

The man's bounced briefly to Sam. She drank her coffee, looking bored, a safe distance away as she kept her eye on the door.

"There's been mining-induced seismic activity spotted by drones patrolling the Northern Maakhir area," he told Carey in a low voice. "It's now an al-Shabaab stronghold. The extraction sites are there. I've seen the pictures from drone surveillance. I'd bet my 401(k) they're keeping Bassett there, running the excavation."

Someone passed the window, looking in on them. Carey patted the guy's shoulder and said in a cordial voice, "You tell your wife I send my best. She makes the best damn lasagna I've ever tasted, and don't tell my mama."

The guy nodded, shaking Carey's hand quickly before leaving the office with a nod to Sam.

"If this shit isn't a recipe for a hot-ass mess, I don't know what is," Carey muttered as they left the Embassy. "Uranium dealing, an expert that may or may not get exchanged for a chunk of untraceable bills, and a highly mobile militia group with the predictability of a squirrel with its ass on fire. I don't like it. Let's get Kurt and get the fuck out."

"If they're sending drones in on regular surveillance, it's a target," Sam murmured in agreement. "Add seismic activity and you're looking at a real possibility of an airstrike within the next twenty-four to thirty-six hours. No one will survive. Bassett's ass is good as grass."

An hour later, they met up with Simon and Henri at the hotel.

"We just missed him," Simon informed them. "Bank confirmed Kurt was in this morning, picking up an undisclosed sum of cash. If he's following protocol, he's underground now. Won't be coming back to the hotel or anywhere anyone can find him with that amount of money."

"Now that Kurt's got the money, the exchange goes down sometime in the next twenty-four hours," Henri added, his expression grave. Julien Henri had a narrow build, supple, ageless midnight skin and a shockingly deep voice tinged with a French lilt. "It gives him enough time to prepare, but he won't want to hold the money for long," Henri told them.

Carey looked up at Samantha. She nodded.

Carey filled them in on what they'd learned at the Embassy.

"Fuuuuck me," Simon groaned. "Bloody airstrikes now? Give a wanker a fuckin' break!"

Henri watched Sam and Carey exchange looks before breaking out into a wide grin as he guessed what they were thinking, his eyes excited.

Simon's head swiveled to Henri. Then Sam.

"We've got the fire power stored in the jet," Sam shrugged. "And we've got the connections to get anything else we need between the four of us."

Carey looked at Simon and Henri. "You boys interested in stirrin' up a little trouble?"

"Like cowboys?" Henri grinned.

"Uh…not quite."

"No, mate," Simon answered. "More like the bloody cavalry. This is so fucking American—I love it!" He shot up. "I need to see a man about a car."

"Henri—See if you can pull some of your remaining strings at Leviathan to get a handle on where the exchange is happening," Sam asked. "If it's somewhere other than the mining area, we need to know that ASAP so we can let our contacts at the Embassy and with the CIA when and where we're doing the extraction," Sam told him. He nodded, pulling out his phone.

They agreed to meet up in an hour in Sam's suite to begin planning.

As Carey followed Sam onto the elevator, he peered down at her. "What was all that about being too damn old to be dragging people out of hot zones a month ago?"

She shrugged, hitting the button to their floor. "What's the point of living without a little risk? And besides, we're already here. What the hell else we got to do?"

"Kurt doesn't even work for us yet," Carey shook his head, smiling in spite of himself.

"Oh, but after this, he will."

October—One day later

Northern Maakhir Region, Somalia

SAMANTHA

"WHAT ARE YOU wearing, love?" Simon Michelson purred.

Sam's lips twitched. *Cheeky bastard.* She touched her earpiece. "You saw me six hours ago. What do you think has changed?"

"You have a gun now," came his reply.

"Careful, Michaelson. I may have just hired you, but I won't hesitate to graze the side of your head with a copper-jacket I polished myself this morning."

"I love it when you talk dirty," he answered, unfazed.

Sam chuckled softly, touching her earpiece to turn off her mic as she adjusted the Leupold scope on her Barrett M95. She scanned the sandy, vermillion cliffs of the mining area they were covering while flat on her belly, her rifle propped on its bipod legs. The whole package fit nicely under her ghillie suit. She couldn't imagine anything less sexy than being covered in burlap netting, sandy dirt, and dried shrub. If Simon Michaelson could use that as a foundation for naughty imaginings, the man was not right in the head.

"Hey, Michaelson," Carey clicked on. "How come you didn't ask what I was wearing?" His amusement was clear even through the comms.

"Don't want to imagine your ugly mug, mate," Simon replied.

"Shut up both of you," Julien Henri chimed in, his voice a hoarse whisper. "You'll give me PTSD."

They were deep in the heart of al-Shabaab territory covered in sand and camo, lying in triangle formation around the encampment, holding rifles that cost as much as a new Kia. Henri was stationed the closest to the site because Simon had called it—he was a right crazy bastard. Over the course of the hours they'd lain in wait, Henri had inched himself closer until he was less than fifty yards out from the encampment they surrounded. Carey was somewhere around a hundred yards out. She was covering both of them at about three hundred yards away. Simon remained hidden among the brush less than a mile away in a modified Humvee kitted out with a machine gun he'd procured from God knew where.

"I've got movement," Henri whispered. "Third tent to the left. Four, no—five tangoes exiting. No sign of the cargo."

Sam narrowed her right eye, staring hard at the tent in the distance through the fine target lines etched into the glass of the scope. She watched a loose tent flap sway in the breeze, noting the wind coming in steady from the east. She made the appropriate adjustments, accounting for the curvature of the projectile, the friction and gravity that would naturally drag the bullet down at that distance. She took deep, even breaths as she watched the men, listening to sounds on the landscape, the breeze, her own heart, her right finger lightly touching the trigger.

"They're just having a smoke," Carey murmured.

"Think they'll let me bum one?" Simon joked after a moment.

"Nah. But I'll be happy to stick a nicotine patch over your mouth," Sam muttered.

"Should have done that years ago," Henri put in. "He would have quit smoking *and* shut up," he whispered.

Sam smirked.

Simon Michaelson and Julien Henri fit right in with the Lennox crew. Between Simon's humor and Henri's taste for risk, they were getting along great with the other guys. Once Simon and Henri had located Cameron Kurt, who was going to their next Leviathan recruit at this rate, she and Carey had decided to take them along for the trip—see if they couldn't help talk the former Green Beret into coming over to their side.

So here they were…six hours lying in the dry heat, waiting for Kurt to arrive as they watched the excavation site. It wasn't clear how he'd be coming in, but it was clear al-Shabaab were guarding only a handful of camouflaged tents surrounding the mining area while the rest of the men drilled and blasted in the open pit. They hadn't seen Bassett yet, but she'd bet her Corvette he was in one of those tents.

A sudden, massive blast ricocheted throughout the site, followed within moments by the ground quaking with aftershocks.

Sam's eyes widened around the scope. *What the fuck had these idiots triggered?*

Dozens of startled men ran from the tents, shouting, swarming the excavation site where the mining blast had been set off. The earth shook again, a slope from the open pit sliding down into the blast area. The men patrolling the encampment took off running for the edge of the site, frantic.

Sam tapped her earpiece. "Move in," she ordered.

Chaos ensued as all three prowled forward amidst the tremors, taking advantage of the crisis. Men poured over the excavation area like ants, hunting for survivors, shouting at each other as all digging and drilling stopped. The ground rippled with another multi-second tremor, causing massive slides of dirt to collapse into the pit. Sam crawled forward, focusing on covering Carey and Henri's positions as they closed in. She could hear the frantic shouting, see the sandy dirt floating above the site and choking the air.

Amid the flurry, a medium-build, white-haired Caucasian man dressed in a tattered khaki shirt and dirty jeans was jerked from the one of tents by two Somalis. His hands came up as they dragged him toward the edge of the site, shouting.

"It's Bassett," Henri confirmed.

"Steady," Sam murmured.

She could see all three men peering down into the blast area, one gesticulating wildly. The ground had finally stopped shaking, but the damage still ricocheted throughout the site. She had no idea how many men were left in the tents, but she doubted more than a handful stayed behind to guard Bassett with the mayhem going on outside.

Sam assessed the two men holding Bassett. They were shouting at him as they pointed at the crater, as if blaming him for the blast effects and the earth's disproportionate response. One Somali was tall with a slight build, carrying an M16 rifle. The other man was heavier set and average height with a semi-automatic gun on his belt. Bassett was shaking his head vigorously in denial. The heavyset one pulled out a knife, jamming it up against Bassett's throat. He continued to shout at Bassett, his words lost in the breeze and the havoc.

"Well, I'll be damned," Simon spoke suddenly over the comms.

Then Sam heard it. The unmistakable bass thump of helicopter blades beating against the arid heat of the desert plains in the distance.

"How the fuck did that git get his hands on a Black Hawk?" Simon said in awe.

Sam smiled in spite of herself. Kurt was clearly a resourceful man, even if he didn't have a hope in hell of getting out of this without their help.

"You sure it's him?" Carey asked.

"Passed right over me," Simon answered.

"Is he alone?" Sam asked.

"Couldn't see anyone else in there with him," Simon replied.

"Let the scene play out," she said as the Black Hawk passed over her position, sending dust and shrub flying around her ghillie suit.

She would have been worried that their cover would be quite literally blown away had the al-Shabaab not been completely distracted with the mining explosion. The Black Hawk was painted a drab khaki color and looked like it had been retrofitted into a utility helicopter rather than the war bird it had been designed to be. No matter. It still had an average speed of 160 mph loaded. She'd take that type of ride out of there any day.

The bird landed about thirty yards from the closest tent. The men holding Bassett were joined by three others. They all turned from the mining area back toward the Black Hawk.

"Simon, get closer," Sam ordered as the chopper blades slowed enough so that she could be heard over the din. "Carey, can you get to the bird?"

"Affirmative," he answered in a low voice.

Kurt didn't power the helicopter down. He was either expecting a quick exchange or hedging his bets on the need for a quick getaway. The rotors continued to sway as he stepped down, wearing an airport mechanic's jumpsuit.

So that's how he got ahold of a Black Hawk, she thought. He'd probably walked right out onto Adden Ade Airfield and stolen it.

Sam began to belly crawl forward again. By the time she'd made it to within a hundred yards, Kurt had already tossed forward a beat up canvas duffel bag. Two men were hunched over it, counting the money, the third holding his rifle loosely, aimed at ground near Kurt. Kurt watched Bassett, still being held by the heavyset guy and the thinner one. The men counting the money looked up, shouting something in Somali to the men holding Bassett. The heavyset man nodded.

All three men drew on Kurt.

"Go," Sam uttered, watching through the scope.

Henri rose up right behind the heavyset man like a ghost from desert ash, silent, covered in dirt and the camouflage of his ghillie suit. He slit the heavyset man's throat so quickly that Bassett wasn't even aware of what had happened until the man's grip on him slackened. By the time Bassett turned to look down at the heavyset man sliding wordlessly to the ground, the second man holding him was clutching his throat, blood spilling through his fingers, flowing down his shirt in thick red rivulets.

Watching intently as the scene played out in front of him, Kurt raised his hands slowly. If he was surprised, he didn't indicate it. Sam watched his mouth moving, distracting the three men who remained unaware of the imminent threat behind them.

Bassett stood stock still, frozen in silent horror as Henri rounded him, his right arm raised, Glock in hand, the suppressor adding another six inches to the barrel. Henri fired at two of the men before the third managed to swing around. Kurt pulled a gun from inside his overalls, nailing the man in the back of the head before he was able to fire on Henri. The shot seemed deafening amid the din. The unmistakable sound of a semiautomatic being fired drew inevitable attention away from the open pit.

Sam immediately scanned the mining zone through her scope, her cheek resting against the stock. Two heads popped up. Three. Four more.

"Shit. Simon get in here! Henri, get Bassett into the bird!" she ordered.

Carey was already climbing into the Black Hawk, starting her back up, the blades whirring back to life.

Kurt swung his head round, gun raised.

Carey waved at him, flashing a smile.

Henri pushed past Kurt, gripping Bassett's lax arm. Kurt got over his astonishment quickly as he snatched up the bag from the bodies, following Henri to the chopper. They pushed Bassett in just as several Somalis ran from the site, shouting, drawing the attention of others, rifles raised.

Sam breathed out, willing her heartbeat to even and slow.

She fired.

One.

Her heart thumped.

She fired.

Two.

She exhaled another breath.

Fire.

Three.

Fire.

Breathe.

Fire.

Methodically, she picked men off like ducks at a carnie booth.

The Black Hawk lifted into the air.

Sam managed to take down six others before the rest got wise, crouching down behind tents, attempting to guess her position while aiming at the chopper.

She heard Simon roaring forward. Now *her* cavalry had arrived. She thanked her stars again that Kurt had stolen the bird.

The chopper ascended rapidly, veering strongly to the left. She couldn't tell whether it was Kurt or Carey flying, but they were all inside, and the Black Hawk was getting too far out of range to be an opportune target.

Simon stopped the Humvee less than fifty yards to her left. Sam collapsed the bipod legs on the rifle, sliding backward in a fluid motion.

Then she saw it.

A Somali emerged from one of the tents, lifting a shoulder-fired Stinger rocket launcher, aimed straight for the Black Hawk.

Sam sat up, holding the butt of the rifle against her shoulder as she aimed…

And fired.

She missed.

Barely.

The man turned, looking her direction, launcher firmly on his shoulder, rocket pointed right at her.

Sam wasn't certain he could see her, but with that kind of firepower, it didn't really matter. In the second and half it took her to draw another breath, she weighed the risk of shooting again and exposing her exact position.

Four lives in the air to her one.

No contest.

She exhaled, firing.

An inch-wide hole bloomed blood, bone, and brain matter, the body dropping, rocket launcher tilting and falling uselessly from the man's hand.

And her cover was blown. Completely.

A hailstorm of bullets rained in her direction.

She heard Simon gun the engine, swerving toward her in a swirl of dirt and track.

I'm a goner, she thought, dropping flat to the ground, shrouded in only her ghillie suit. She didn't have time to set up the bipod, so she used her arm to steady the stock.

Sam fired again and again, her sole focus on taking as many men with her as possible. They were becoming more confident, rising up in ever-increasing numbers, uniting behind the deaths of their brothers.

Simon spun the Humvee to a halt in front of her, letting loose a rain of heavy artillery from the machine gun he'd welded to the hood the night before.

Sam rolled, glancing at the horizon, the Black Hawk now a distant figure against the open plain. She stayed low, climbing into the Humvee as Simon continued to fire, cartridge cases flying out and hitting the hood and ground pinging like fat brass coins.

"Get us the fuck out of here!" she shouted, dropping her rifle so she could take over the machine gun.

Simon shoved himself back into the driver's seat, gunning the engine.

A glancing shot cracked the windshield. Another shattered it. She felt a slicing burn graze her arm, tearing through the fatigue jacket. Sam opened fire, sweeping the tight cluster of men hunched into the ground near the tents.

And then it happened.

The low whistle of a bomb being dropped, followed by a sonic boom, ripples of air pressure beating against the Hummer, deafening all other sound.

Sam was thrown back into the seat.

She looked up at Simon. She could see his mouth moving, could see him frantically spinning the wheel of the Humvee, sand and debris pounding the vehicle from the force of the explosions.

Her ears rung. She hadn't heard that sound since Afghanistan.

But once you know that sound, you never forget it.

Predator drones.

Airstrike.

The real Cavalry.

How American.

CHAPTER 11

October—One week later

Lincoln Park, Chicago

JACK

J
ACK STEPPED INTO the ultra-modern, bi-level dining room of Alinea, following the maître d' to his table. As he strolled across the room, he saw Jaime standing nearby, speaking with Carey and two other men seated at a corner table.

"Carey," Jack acknowledged, coming to stand by Jaime. "Nice to see you. How's it going?"

The men shook hands, and Carey introduced the other men at the table. "Jack, meet Cameron Kurt and Simon Michaelson, two of our most recent recruits," Carey beamed. "We're havin' ourselves a little welcome to the company and a 'thank God we survived last week' dinner."

"Apparently, they barely got out of Somalia a few days ago," Jaime explained, catching Jack up.

"Helluva start," Jack commented, his brows raised. "You guys should be drinking champagne."

"Can't stand the stuff," the one named Simon answered in a thick British accent.

"I'm just so damn happy to be on American soil, I'd have been good with Potbelly's sandwiches and a Coors," Cameron Kurt grinned.

"Now that's the kind of talk that'll get you kicked right outta here," Mitch commented, appearing at Jack's side.

While Carey introduced the men to Mitch, Jack took a minute to observe them. Both Simon and Cameron had the controlled, alert look of military men. Though both were impeccably dressed in fine wool suits, neither looked like the kind of men to be trifled with.

"What are you all up to tonight?" Carey asked.

"Trying to do a little recruiting of our own," Mitch confided. "We're opening up a new restaurant in one of our buildings, and we're here to talk to one of the chefs about it."

"And I'm just along for the ride," Jaime laughed. "I'll never turn down a meal at Michelin-rated restaurant."

"Don't let Jaime's scrawniness fool you," Jack added, slapping his brother's back. "This one can eat his weight and probably yours too."

Carey's brows rose as he glanced over Jaime's lanky frame.

And because he couldn't help himself, Jack heard himself asking, "Samantha joining you all?"

Carey nodded. "She'll be around soon, once she's done getting her stitches out."

Jack stiffened. "Stitches?"

Carey nodded again, expression unconcerned. "Got a little nick while we were pulling Kurt out."

"Jesus, is she okay?" Jaime asked before Jack could say anything.

"Grazed her arm. She'll be fine," Carey told them. "Didn't even notice until she went to get out of her camo."

Jack thought he looked…proud.

"It's my fault, I'm afraid," Simon spoke up. "I should've gotten us out faster."

Cameron shook his head. "Are you kidding? You wouldn't have been there at all if you hadn't been saving my ass. I'm just so glad she was covering for us when they pulled out that Stinger missile."

Somalia. Simon. Stitches. Covering Kurt's ass. Stinger missile? Jack's mind ping-ponged around the implications as he was bombarded with so many thoughts and reactions that he wasn't sure which to address first. Anger was the strongest and at the forefront; so he went with that.

"She was protecting you guys?" he asked, his voice hard. "Shouldn't it be the other way around?"

Carey and Simon exchanged looks before laughing, the sound rippling across the dining room, turning heads.

"He's having me on, right?" Simon asked Carey. "Us protect Sam? Don't know how well you know her, mate." Simon turned to Jack. "I can't think of anyone less in need of protection than that bird."

Jack felt his fists tighten.

"Jack, she's fine. Honestly," Carey told him, noticing his tense expression. "She'll be here soon. You'll see for yourself."

"Sorry to interrupt, gentlemen, but should I seat you together at a larger table?" the maître d' asked, glancing uncertainly at the two groups.

"That won't be necessary," Mitch responded, patting Jack on the back. "Wouldn't want to interrupt the rest of your business dinner."

"Let's have a drink afterward," Jaime suggested before nudging Jack to follow the maître d' to their table. "You guys have a good dinner."

Jack just nodded curtly as they turned to leave.

"What's with your new, scary-looking friends?" Mitch asked as they were seated. "And why do you look like you want to maim men you've only just met?" he added, glancing back across the restaurant.

"Don't know the other guys, but Carey is Sam's business partner at Lennox," Jaime supplied. "We all went fishing on the boat after the fundraiser. He's good people."

"So he's another negotiator?" Mitch asked.

"No," Jaime shook his head. "Carey heads up security."

"What the hell kind of head of security lets his partner get into trouble?" Jack replied, glaring at Carey across the room. "And who the fuck is this guy Samantha let herself get shot at for? And who is this other guy who doesn't think she needs protecting?" He snapped open his menu. Words floated meaninglessly. "Jesus," he muttered, slapping the menu down on the table as the waiter arrived. "I need a scotch and soda." Jack informed the waiter—who heard the secondary message in his tone: *I need it now.* The waiter promptly spun around to get it.

Mitch and Jaime appraised Jack over their menus.

"Starting a little early, aren't we?" Mitch murmured.

"And Somalia?" Jack continued. "*Motherfucking* Somalia? Is she nuts?" He stared hard at Carey and Kurt. "Are *they* nuts?"

Mitch and Jaime exchanged looks.

"Sounds like she's okay," Mitch replied, laying the menu down calmly. "Besides," he continued, "Sam's the kind of woman who can more than hold her own."

Jaime glanced at Carey's table again. "Wonder what military outfits they come from."

"If you have to ask, you probably don't want to know," Mitch drawled. "The inscrutable Ms. Wyatt keeps some deadly company."

"Mitch, man, sounds like Sam *is* the deadly company," Jaime replied, bemused.

The waiter returned with his drink. Jack took a deep swallow, feeling the burn heat up his mouth and esophagus on the way down.

"We'll be having the eighteen-course tasting menu," Mitch told the waiter. "And please send over the sommelier." Once the waiter was gone, he leveled a look at Jack. "Alright, what's going on?"

"What is she doing in goddamn *Somalia?* And what is she doing getting shot at?" Jack snapped. "I haven't seen this woman since she turned me down flat after a night of one of the best sleeps I've had in ages, and *this* is what she's been doing?" Jack took another swallow of his scotch.

"Okay, that'll do for now." Jaime deftly moved the scotch to his side of the table, replacing it with a glass of water. "She turned you down?"

"You've already slept together?" Mitch's eyes danced. "Bravo."

"No, asshole," Jack shook his head. "It wasn't like that."

"But you said—"

"Remember when I had a bad time of it a couple weeks ago?" Jack prompted.

Mitch thought about it. "Yeah."

"What happened?" Jaime piped up, worried. "Did you use?"

"No." Jack shook his head. "I thought about it. God, I felt half crazy, but then she was there. And she stayed up with me. We talked. Ate stew. Next thing I know—I'm waking up on her couch, and I feel like a million bucks."

"And this is all good... right?" Jaime asked, looking confused.

Jack shrugged. He eyed the scotch glass across the table. If he punched Jaime's arm hard enough, he'd be able to reach around him, no problem. He took a breath. "I asked her out. As a thank you. She turned me down flat."

Mitch grinned.

Jaime's brows went up. "So keep asking. What's the problem?"

"Your brother's in a unique position, Jaime. One that is very new to him," Mitch replied sagely.

"And what's that?"

"He's not the one in the position of power." Mitch smirked as the sommelier approached the table.

As Mitch discussed the wine selection, Jaime turned to Jack. "Why are you so worked up?"

Jack brooded before deciding to come clean. "Because I like her. A lot. A lot more than I want to. And I can't stand the idea that she could have been seriously hurt. And I would have known nothing about it."

Jaime considered him. "You're still irrationally hyped up about this though. What gives?"

"*Madre di Dio*, I barely know her, and she's already drives me nuts," Jack groaned, dropping his head back in frustration. "You know I called her ex-lover and bought all the wine he made for her when they were together?"

Jaime's brows rose. "That's not weirdly obsessive or anything."

Jack scowled. "Give me my scotch back."

Jaime took a good look at his expression and then shook his head. "Man, you've got it bad," he told him, sliding his glass back over. "This is your one tonight, so don't hammer it. I'm only giving it back 'cause I feel sorry for you."

"Why do you feel sorry for him?" Mitch asked, returning to the conversation after he'd selected the wine pairings. "He's met his match. He's about to have the ride of his life. Lucky fucker."

Jack took a sip of the scotch, calming down. He didn't bother to contest Mitch because he strongly suspected the man was right.

Jaime and Mitch gave him a reprieve, shifting the conversation away from Sam as Jack calmed down. Mitch was right in one sense. Jack couldn't honestly remember the last time he'd been turned down. And he certainly never anticipated feeling so disappointed about it. He spent the past couple weeks trying and failing not to think about her, losing himself in work, at the gym, inside Rebecca, who'd finally stopped hounding him for the *where-are-we-going* conversation, replacing it with the *oh-yeah-baby-right-there* smutty talk. But at night, late at night when the rest of Chicago was asleep, Jack wondered if he'd run into her again or see her in the pool, slicing through the water. He caught himself listening for her. Watching her door. Glancing at her parked car like it was a sign.

And she was halfway across the world. Getting shot at.

Jack could shake her for that. He wanted to run his hands down her arms, see for himself she was alright, examine her stitches. Kiss her. Then he wanted to spank her. Hard. In the middle of his brooding, Jack caught sight of Samantha entering the dining room.

She was striking in a bold red shift dress. She moved toward Carey's table with a small smile on her face. The men stood, and Carey kissed her gently on the cheek. She shook Cameron's hand, looking pleased to see him. Simon kissed her hand, making a production of it while she laughed it off. Jack felt his hand tense around his glass.

Each time he saw her, Samantha was another version of herself. Last time he'd run into her, she'd looked so damn good in that biker jacket and boots, her hair tousled and wild. Tonight, she looked every inch the sophisticated, urbane business woman, the dark skein of her hair in an elegant twist, diamonds in her ears and on an elegant rope around her neck. Samantha had the polish of money, education, and class. She had the confidence that came with personal power. But she didn't just have power, she had control. And she knew how to wield it. He'd never seen anything sexier in his life. And Jack had known some of the sexiest women in the world.

"Jack?" Mitch asked, trying to get his attention. "What do you think?"

He blinked, his gaze shifting to Mitch. "Sorry, wasn't listening. What was that?"

Mitch and Jaime turned to find the object of Jack's attention.

"Ah, I see. That is cause for distraction," Mitch murmured, his gaze admiring.

"She looks fine. Her arms are covered, but she looks fine," Jaime pointed out.

"She's better than fine. She's a stick of dynamite," Mitch comment-ed admiringly, sipping his wine. "Pure and unadulterated TNT."

"More like a heat-seeking missile," Jack muttered into his drink.

As if she could feel their eyes on her across a dining room full of people, Samantha looked up. Directly at him. She'd been smiling at something Kurt was saying when she caught his eyes. They stared at each other for a few seconds before Jack lifted his glass, saluting her. Samantha nodded in return before allowing Kurt to draw away her attention.

"Hey, it's the point guard for the Bulls," Jaime announced as he noticed the basketball player stepping into the restaurant with his wife. The conversation immediately transitioned to their upcoming season, starting in late October.

Jack listened with one ear while Jaime and Mitch debated the Bulls' roster. He glanced over at her table again. She was leaning forward, listening to Carey. Her hand touched her neck, fingertips toying with the diamond rope around her neck. Jack thought about how those fingers felt sifting through his hair. His imaginings immediately evolved toward the more erotic. He shifted in his seat, looking away. *Enough*, he thought. *Enough of this strange yearning.*

Jack tracked back into the conversation in an attempt to distract himself, speculating on the NBA preseason conference standings while the waiter began bringing out courses. As they dined on king crab with passion fruit and hearts of palm, sweetbreads served with bread and toasted hay, green beans perched on pillows of nutmeg-scented air, and lamb flavored with black truffle, they caught up on life, business, and of course, continued speculations as to Simon and Cameron's military background.

Chef Achatz came out to greet them, accepting their praise for the procession of bold and exquisite tastes for the evening's fare. Though only a small portion of their commercial properties included bars and restaurants, Mitch cultivated relationships with top restaurateurs, chefs, and mixologists as carefully as he selected art. As he and Jack developed properties, particularly historical restoration projects, Mitch approached the culinary masterminds he was most impressed with to develop new concepts. Dinners like this one were a regular "scouting" ritual.

Jaime, who cycled daily and had the metabolism of a jack rabbit, was always happy to be included on tasting dinners. "I need a break from spaghetti and Lunchables," he joked. "And my daughter can't appreciate a five-hundred-dollar bottle of wine."

"Yet," Mitch replied. "God help you when she learns to."

As Chef turned to greet another table, the next course was served. While the waiter began describing the Anjou pear served with onion, brie, and smoking cinnamon, Jack took the opportunity to glance across the room at Samantha again. Her pose was casual, but he could see her resting her arm against the table, cradling it gently as she toyed with the stem of her wine glass. Jack wondered again at what had happened to her in Somalia while he was thousands of miles away, jogging along the lake or sitting in his office reviewing land development deals, oblivious.

"How many more courses?" Jack asked the waiter suddenly.

"Four, sir," the waiter answered, refilling their water glasses.

"Wonderful. In the meantime, please send over a bottle of Macallan 24 to that table," Jack replied.

"Very good, sir," the waiter nodded.

When they finally made their way over to Carey and Samantha's table after finishing their meal, Jack could see the group had already made it through to their second round of the single malt. The waiters helped them arrange additional seats. He sat next to Samantha, Simon on her other side.

"Hey there, Jack," she greeted him, a relaxed smile on her lips. Jack felt the tension melt from his shoulders, her nearness soothing.

"Miss me?" he asked, feeling a little buzzed off the scent of her— her heady fragrance rapidly becoming his drug of choice.

"Desperately," she drawled with a smile. "Did you get introduced to Simon earlier?" she asked, gesturing toward the man at her side.

Jack nodded. "How'd you like the meal?" Jack asked him.

Simon grinned. "Even better than our dinner in London, right, love?" he said, leaning toward her.

She smiled. "Even better now that we're celebrating the both of you joining us."

"Victory tastes sweeter?" Simon murmured in a low voice, his expression teasingly intimate.

"Doesn't it always?" Jack asked, interrupting the moment. *Who the hell was this guy?* Simon glanced up at him, his gaze sharpening. Jack ignored him, watching Samantha. "What is this I'm hearing about you getting shot at?" he asked, touching the arm she was unconsciously cradling.

Her brows drew together momentarily before she relaxed under his touch. "Just a scratch."

"Told ya, mate," Simon smirked, his eyes smug.

Jack gave him a hard look. "It was your fault she was hurt, correct?"

Simon straightened in his seat, expression darkening. "It was my responsibility to get us out, yes."

"So you're new on the job, and you've already failed?" Jack asked pointedly.

"Whoa, whoa, okay," Samantha intervened, holding her hands up. "Nobody failed at anything. We were outnumbered by a hundred men, and we got lucky getting out intact at all. Jack—" She put her hand on his arm, looking at him. "I'm fine. I promise. Look," she said, wiggling the fingers on the hand of her injured arm. She was wearing a blood red ruby the size of a nickel.

"Fuck me, that's a ridiculously huge ring," Simon commented.

"More proof my arm is okay." She grinned as Simon snatched up her hand, examining the ring. "I can carry this sucker around just fine."

"Your bloke buy that for you?" Simon asked, glancing at Jack.

Samantha laughed, her eyes twinkling. "I'm the kind of lady who can buy her own baubles, thank you."

Jack scowled at Simon as he grinned at Samantha. Noticing the look, she withdrew her hand, using it to pick up her whisky glass. "You're not drinking?" she asked Jack.

He shook his head. "No. Had one with dinner, but that's it. I'm driving."

"Well, thanks then. I love a good whisky."

"Nothing sexier than a bird who can hold her drink," Simon commented over the rim of his own glass.

"Call me a bird again, and I'll stab your hand with my fork," she replied lightly.

"Right. Boss. I meant boss," Simon amended with a crooked grin.

Jack would have been happy to stab him with the fork, or the butter knife, dessert spoon…whatever he had at his disposal.

Mitch turned to Simon, asking him where he was from in the UK, and Jack took the opportunity to lean closer to Samantha. "What would I have done if something happened to you?" he asked her softly so no one else could hear.

Samantha's eyes shuttered as she watched him. Jack could feel the air around her tighten though her demeanor remained deceptively relaxed.

"I'd put money on you strong-arming Jaime into the penthouse," she replied.

"I'm being serious," he chided. "I've been thinking about you almost constantly." He traced the angles and lines of her face with his eyes. "You just—disappeared. Come to find out you were in Somalia, of all places. So let me ask you again, what would I have done if something happened to you?"

"Jack—"

"Well, folks, that's all she wrote," Cameron declared, tossing his napkin onto the table. "If y'all don't mind excusing me, I've got an early flight to catch back home to Tennessee and some long-overdue vacation."

They all stood, and Cameron rounded the table to shake Samantha's hand. "I owe you. Big time."

"You're one of us now," she smiled. "We've got your back."

"*Sine pari*,"[3] Cameron said with a responding grin, squeezing her hand.

Jack strongly suspected from his expression that she'd garnered another loyal follower for life.

"We'll see you at the office after Thanksgiving?" Carey asked, clasping Cameron's hand.

---

[3] An Army Ranger motto meaning "without equal."

"Absolutely. I'll have a word with Avi Oded," he promised. "Heard he's next on your list."

"We'd appreciate that," Carey smiled.

"My pleasure," Cameron replied.

"I've got to get home to the kiddo," Jaime chimed in. "I'll head out with Cameron."

And just like that, people began to peel off.

Simon turned to Samantha. "You want to split a cab?" he asked.

"She can go back with me," Jack answered before Samantha could reply. She glanced at him, her brow raised. "I drove," he explained.

"Normally I'd insist on you letting me take that Aston out for a spin, but I've had a couple drinks," she told him mournfully.

"Another time," Jack promised. "If you let me take out your 'vette."

"You have an Aston Martin?" Simon asked.

"A Vanquish. You a fan?"

"You could say I have an appreciation for any kind of fine motor," Simon answered, a glint of humor in his eye. Samantha bit back a laugh. Simon winked at her.

Jack watched their private joke exchange silently while he imagined punching Simon hard in the face. Multiple times. Simon was saved by a fine margin when the waiter delivered their bills at just the right moment.

As they left Alinea, Simon kissed Samantha's cheeks, lingering for a second too long as he glanced at Jack over her shoulder. Jack felt his fists curl, but he kept his hands safely hidden in his coat. Samantha stepped back from Simon, distracting Jack by slipping her arm through his with the familiarity of a lover. He smiled down at her, enjoying standing in the chilly fall night with her, doing something as mundane as waiting for his car.

Jack drove them home in companionable silence, navigating the quiet night streets of Lincoln Park. When he hit Lakeshore Drive, he looked over at her, still and silent as she leaned back in the seat, her eyes closed. Street lamps illuminated her face intermittently, like a measured tempo.

"How many times have you been at risk?" he heard himself ask.

Samantha opened her eyes, her gaze lazy and amused. "You asking how many lives I have left?"

Jack took his hand off the gear shift, grasping her hand. He kissed her palm, breathing in the scent from her wrist. "Do you know or have you lost count?" he asked, watching the road.

He could feel her wondering why he'd ask such a thing. "Including being in this car with you right now?" she asked as he curled their hands into his lap.

"I'm being serious."

He heard her soft, husky laugh. "Clearly. But you're being too serious." She squeezed her fingers around his reassuringly. "I'm fine, Jack."

He pulled into the Whitney, parked in his space next to hers. "Let me get your door," he told her.

"Jack—"

He shook his head, interrupting her before leaning across the console to rub a thumb across her cheek. "I'm not ready to say goodnight to you," he admitted. "Have a drink with me. Please."

He could feel her thinking through her easy-let-down answers, trying to decide which one to use. "Samantha," he breathed in the quiet of the car, their eyes locked. "I want to talk to you, look at you…touch you. Let me. Just for a couple hours. Otherwise I'll just be awake anyway, thinking about it."

Samantha took a deep breath, closing her eyes momentarily before giving him a single, brief nod. "Give me fifteen minutes."

October—That night

The Whitney, Chicago

SAMANTHA

SHE DIDN'T GIVE herself time to dissect it, debate it, or cancel it. He'd been on her mind too, despite how much she'd thrown herself into work the past couple weeks.

"Oh, what the hell," she said to no one, changing into her favorite cut offs and a soft, loose t-shirt, struggling a little with her tender arm. Sam wondered briefly if he thought she'd show up at his door in some sort of see-through negligee, ready to play out a seduction scene. She laughed softly at that image.

Sam walked down their hall, took a deep breath, and lifted her hand to knock. Before her fist connected with the door, Jack swung it open, looking relaxed in lounge pants and a snug black tee. His eyes seemed even lighter silver than usual, dark hair tousled and damp from a shower, the shadow of the day's stubble lining his jaw. He took her in from tip-to-toe, a small smile turning up one side of his mouth, as if he were unexpectedly pleased to see her.

"You thought I'd bail," she accused, poking his chest when she caught his expression.

He grabbed her hand, pulling her into his place. Their layout was nearly identical, with a wide, open living room, two levels of floor-to-ceiling windows in leaded glass, and a sprawling chef's kitchen next to the dining room. Where she had a gently curved steps in polished mahogany, he had a beautiful wrought-iron spiral staircase leading to his second floor. His home was appointed in dark, rich colors with glowing parquet floors and large cognac leather sofas surrounding a modern copper-backed fireplace. Sam whistled.

"I like your version of my house," she admired, taking in the bookshelves, art, and sculptures dotting his home. "It looks like a sanctuary. I'll be lucky if I ever achieve that feel," she conceded.

"If that's what you're going for, you'll need more than a couch, a table, and a bed," Jack teased, watching her look around.

Sam laughed, conceding his point. "But you forgot I've also got coffee, wine, and an excellent stereo. You learn to live with the basics when you're constantly on the road."

"What's your pleasure?" he asked, walking into the kitchen.

"I'll have whatever the Insomniac is having," Sam replied, running her fingers down a modern sculpture of a torso. "I'd like to know what a typical night in the life of Jack Roman looks like. That is, when you're not stalking me at the pool," she teased, turning to look at him.

Jack grinned. "In that case, I'll make tea. Do you drink Valerian, Chamomile?"

"Either is fine." She took a seat at his dining table, a gorgeous, rough-edged redwood that had been polished and sealed to a soft shine. The legs were made of stainless steel branches artfully and individually welded. She loved how he blended traditional and modern pieces, how lived in and warm his place felt despite the grandiosity of the space. Sam spread her hands on the wood, touching the grooves, dipping her fingertips into the whorl of a knot.

He'd left the *Tribune* and the *New York Times* open at the head of the table. She could see he'd been working on the crossword puzzle, though he hadn't quite finished. A worn hardcover peeped out from under the newspapers. She slid her finger under the papers to pull it out gently, watching him from the corner of her eye as he took down mugs, preparing the tea. She probably shouldn't pry, but it was nearly right in front of her, and she was curious about his taste and preferences.

He was reading Nabokov's *Pale Fire*. Jack turned, catching her looking at the book. "Have you read it?"

Sam shook her head, sliding the book back under his papers. "The only Nabokov I ever read was *Lolita*. Beautifully written, if not incredibly sad and more than a little depraved. Why are you reading it?"

Jack carried a small tray over to the dining table. "As an author, Nabokov was almost exclusively defined by that single piece. As much as I was disturbed by *Lolita*, I also thought his writing was beautiful. Here's a man who was a refugee twice, taught at some of the most prestigious schools in the US, and he could write like that in a language that wasn't his mother tongue or even his second language." Jack paused, looking up at her. "I figured I should at least read another piece of his. Try not to judge a body of work by one book I didn't connect with."

Sam accepted the mug he offered her, staring at him. Jack continued to surprise her. By day, this man sported the ultra-glossy veneer of a high-powered and charismatic philistine as effortlessly as he donned his hand-tailored suits. But on nights like these, with his long legs stretched out and his fingers pushing the damp waves of his hair off his forehead, he reminded her that was just one aspect of him—and maybe not even the dominant one at that. What Sam hadn't expected was the intelligent, playful, and introspective side of Jack Roman. She had the distinct notion this would be the beginning of many nights where they would carefully unfold truths about one another like pieces of elaborate origami. And she liked that notion. She liked it a lot.

"You're…complicated," she murmured, watching him over the rim of her mug. "Far more complicated and astute than I gave you credit for when we first met."

His brow arched. "Are you telling me you thought I was vapid?"

"I thought you were a *what-you-see-is-what-you-get* profligate with a penchant for the fast life," she answered readily. "I'll freely admit I wouldn't have imagined you had an architectural passion for historical restorations, read Nabokov, and worked on the Times crossword puzzle." Sam sipped her tea. "It's 'Lafayette,' by the way."

"Lafayette?" Jack asked.

"Nine-letter word for 'The Hero of the Two Worlds.'"

He reached backward to a small console table, picking up a pair of chic black-framed glasses as he looked at the paper. "How did you know that?" he asked, glancing up.

"My father and granddaddy were war buffs. Couldn't tutor for a damn when it came to calculus or physics, but anything to do with history or politics and they were savants," she laughed softly.

Jack looked down at the paper again, his tongue touching his upper lip just so. *Goddamn, this man is irrationally attractive.* Sam smiled her into tea.

"Eight-letter word for 'guarded'? Has an A in it."

Sam thought for a minute. "Vigilant."

"Okay, now you know I only invited you over to help me finish this," he joked, filling in the word.

"So you plan on using me for my mind," Sam quipped.

"Would you prefer I use you for your body?" Jack asked with a brazen smile, his eyes bright behind his glasses.

"I prefer you not use me at all," Sam replied, taking another sip of her tea. "How many do you have left?"

"Two," he said, looking back down at the newspaper. "But I know this one."

"What is it?"

"Thirteen-letter word for 'absorbed to the exclusion of other things.'"

She poured them both more tea, watching the steam rise. "That's not in there."

"Yes, it is," he defended, holding the paper to his chest.

"No, it's not. You're a crap bluffer. You'd never survive playing poker with me and my guys," Sam returned.

"I would do better than survive, I'd wipe the floor with you and your guys," he replied, his brow raised mockingly. "Now quit hemming and hawing. What's the word?"

"Preoccupation," she answered. She sipped her tea. "Stop lying to me."

"I am *not* lying," he insisted.

"Then why aren't you writing anything down?"

He looked down at the paper, made a show of writing something down and then tossed the pen down, crossing his arms. "How did you know?"

"You have a tell," she murmured into her mug.

"No, I don't," he replied. "Wait, what is it?" he asked immediately, his forehead creasing.

She lifted a brow. "If I told you, you wouldn't do it anymore," she drawled. "Now what are you so preoccupied with, Jack Roman?"

"You."

Sam sat back, wrapping her hands around her mug. She'd walked right into that one.

Jack leaned forward, taking off his glasses. "You're an unexpected distraction, Ms. Wyatt."

"You're just bored, Mr. Roman," she replied. "What with all the hours you spend not sleeping. I'm just the latest interesting thing within a thirty-foot vicinity."

"So you admit you're interesting," he pointed out.

Sam shrugged. "I'm a reclusive neighbor with odd hours and an unusual occupation. I don't know if it's really all that interesting, but it's something." She got up, walking across his living room toward the shelves of vinyl records. "What's all this?" she asked, thumbing through a few of them.

"My dad was a traditionalist when it came to music," he explained, following her. "I grew up listening to records. I began collecting, and when Dad moved to D.C., I absorbed his collection as well. Just became a thing." Jack turned on a sleek, modern turntable.

"How are they organized?" Sam asked.

"Genre, Artist, Year."

"Christ, you really are an insomniac," she said, amazed. He had thousands of records, neatly organized on seven-foot shelves.

Jack scoffed, slanting her a look.

"Pick one," she told him. "And tell me why you like it."

He flipped through a few, pulling an album out of its sleeve. "The first record I ever bought with my allowance. I was eight." He placed the needle gently on the vinyl.

Huey Lewis and the News's "Heart & Soul" came pouring out of the speakers.

"Get out of town!" she exclaimed. "I loved this song!"

Jack smiled, showing her the cover. "I knew I liked this song from the radio, and the album was called *Sports,* and I knew I liked sports, so I figured I'd be getting the best of both worlds." He laughed. "I didn't get then that it was just a name."

They listened for a bit. Sam hummed along, thumbing through more records, smiling when she found familiar ones or singers she'd listened to growing up. She pulled out Men at Work.

"Would you play 'Overkill'?" she asked. "I'm dedicating the lyrics to you."

Jack laughed, taking the record from her and deftly switching out the albums. As the song came on, she smiled. She hadn't heard it in years. She lay down on her back, sprawled on Jack's Kilim rug, her uninjured arm behind her head. Jack hummed along, flipping through his other records. When the song finished, he played The Rolling Stones' "Moonlight Mile." Jack leaned over her, offering his hand. Sam smiled quizzically before slipping her hand into his. He pulled her up, interlacing their fingers as he danced her around his living room.

Jack was a fantastic dancer, his movements fluid and easy to follow. Relaxing into him felt instinctive. At the end of the song, he surprised her into laughter with a dramatic dip. He smiled down at her before ducking his face into her neck.

"God, I love your scent. What is it?" he asked, tilting her back up.

"Just a little something I have Hove Parfumeur in New Orleans make for me."

"Elusive." Jack considered her. "Unforgettable," he murmured, the shards of his silver eyes expanding slowly like a languid kaleidoscope. "And *maddening*. It's perfect."

"It's just the scent of a woman, Jack." She smiled. "I have a feeling you like them all," she teased, directing the little jag into the intimacy of the moment.

He released her, guiding her to one of the sofas. "I think you make me out to be more of a womanizer than I really am."

"Really? Because if I were an insomniac, I'd be filling those hours with a ridiculous amount of orgasms." She smirked. "I'd be incredibly disappointed to hear you waste all those useful hours with Dewey Decimal Systeming your records and reading important, dead authors."

"First of all, that's not the Dewey," Jack replied, grinning. "And I may have had my fair share of sex—" He paused when she snorted. "Well, all right, more than fair," he admitted, a touch unrepentant. "But I think you like to come back to that so you can remind yourself not to like me so much," he continued, pulling her feet into his lap. Jack rubbed his thumb into the arch of her foot. She hummed her pleasure, nestling into his sofa.

"The problem isn't liking you, Jack. I like you just fine." She groaned as he worked the ball of her foot, tired from a night of looking pretty in killer heels. She closed her eyes in unabashed pleasure as he kneaded.

"Then what is the problem?"

"You've already got a woman on the stringer, Jack. How many you looking to add to the line?"

His deft fingers worked her toes. She was beginning to feel her muscles slackening as she sank deeper into the soft leather cushions.

"Rebecca and I aren't serious."

"Does she know that?" Sam asked. "Don't answer that," she corrected herself, opening her eyes. "It's none of my business. And I'm hardly looking to get into anything serious myself, but I'm old enough to know better when it comes to guys like you, Jack."

"Guys like me?" he asked, kneading her heel. "And what kind of guy am I?"

"The very best kind," she answered, closing her eyes. "And the worst. The kind you never forget."

"Isn't that something to revel in?" he asked, pulling her closer. "What if I don't want you to forget me?" he asked, running his hands up her bare shins as he hooked her legs over his lap.

"Don't revel in much anymore, I'm afraid," she replied lightly, stretching an arm behind her head.

"That's a shame," he told her, bending to kiss her knee. "I'd be excellent for you, then."

"You'd be something," she agreed with a languid smile. "Not sure what."

"You should take a chance on me, Samantha. I'd be good for you."

Sam scoffed. "You're quoting ABBA to get me in the sack? Does that actually work?"

Jack grinned. "Do you want me to put it on? Get you in the 'Dancing Queen' mood?"

"Only if you want me to respond with an 'S.O.S,'" she teased. "I'm imagining you dancing around to that at three in the morning when the rest of the building sleeps. Do you do that, Jack?" she asked. "Play vintage seventies and dance about in reckless abandon?"

"At three in the morning, I prefer to do something else with reckless abandon," he answered, his smile utterly disarming.

She'd just bet he did. His hands smoothed up and down her calves. His touch was light and thrilling. At this time of night, feeling a little languid and a lot turned on, she was finding very few reasons not to take this man on. Sam began to push up so she could shift away and clear her head. The sleeve of her t-shirt lifted. Jack stared at the bandage on her arm, his mouth compressed in a thin line.

"You gonna tell me about that?" he asked after a moment of tense silence.

Sam fought the instinct to cover her arm, shrugging it off. "Told you—just a scratch."

"A scratch that required stitches?" Jack asked. He lifted his hand to run a gentle finger over her arm. Her skin raised in goose bumps, the pain of her wound sharpening in anticipation. She watched as he traced his finger up to touch the edge of the gauze. Jack edged the tape off, staring at the gash that had been stitched closed with precision so that now it was just an angry red welt. The fresh marks from the stiches crisscrossed the raised skin.

Jack raised his eyes to hers slowly. Silver darkened to a charcoal. "One inch over and it would have shattered the bone."

Sam slid the bandage back on. "It hurt a lot less than some of my other wounds. It's no big deal, Jack."

"Will you tell me what happened?" he asked after a moment.

Sam watched him for a minute, debating. "We went in to get Kurt out of a bad situation in Somalia. When we were trying to pull out, I got winged. I was so pumped up on adrenaline I didn't really realize it until we got back to Mogadishu."

"I think there's more to it than that."

She watched him silently for a moment before she began to laugh.

"Why are you laughing?" Jack asked, squeezing her foot.

"Because you're endlessly curious about my scars. What kind of gentleman are you that you press a woman on her imperfections?"

A lock of hair fell across his eyes as he glanced down at her, a smile tugging his lips. "I guess not much of one at all." He looked back at her arm. "Do you blame me? The women I usually date consider a bad day missing a manicure. You see getting shot in the arm as an annoyance."

Sam's brow popped up, her expression mocking. "We're dating?"

Jack pulled her foot up and nipped her arch. "I'm trying. My quarry's proving elusive."

"I'm rarely the quarry," she replied, trying to pull her foot back.

Jack wouldn't release her. Instead, he dragged her closer, his arms circling her shoulders. He touched his lips to her neck, breathing in again. Sam struggled not to shudder. She could easily escape his grasp, but she didn't want to. She liked this—the easy intimacy, the warmth and comfort of him. They sat like that for a while, listening to the music, her legs draped over his, her back curved into his arm. She couldn't remember the last time she'd let anyone just hold her like this. She began to drowse in her unexpected relaxation.

"Samantha."

She stirred.

"You're falling asleep, baby."

Sam murmured something, tucking her face into his shoulder.

Jack leaned in closer. "Say it again?"

But she was already out.

October—7:00 a.m., the next morning

The Whitney, Chicago

SAMANTHA

SAM FLOATED INTO wakefulness, groaning as she stretched her arms above her head. She felt well-rested, the pain in her arm reduced to a dull ache. As she sat up, tucked under layers of down and crisp linen, she realized she was in a strange room. It looked like one of her guest rooms, facing the wrong direction. As she glanced around, confused, there was a soft knock on the door.

"Come in," she called out.

Jack stepped into the room, holding a cup of coffee. He was wearing dark slacks and a partially open dress shirt, his feet still bare, and he looked more awake and energetic than he had a right to, smiling at her with a sparkle in his eyes.

"I considered giving you a little more sleep, but I don't know what time you like to get into the office," he said as he handed her the coffee, sitting beside her on the bed.

Sam sipped it gratefully, glancing at his wristwatch.

"I usually get up about this time. Thank you for this," she smiled sheepishly, indicating the coffee. "Sorry I fell asleep, but thanks for carrying me in here. This bed is marvelous."

"No problem," he answered. "It was the least I could do after you saved me from falling face first into the floor last weekend."

"Did you get any sleep?"

He sighed happily. "Not long after you. Slept like a baby. Apparently, you're my four-hour sleep cure."

"That's not much, Jack," she chided.

He leaned forward, kissing her cheek and nudging her jaw with his nose. "That's a lot for me," he murmured into the shell of her ear, his breath soft.

Sam shivered, nearly spilling the coffee. His hand clasped around the mug as he pressed another kiss to her temple before leaning back. She felt a little intoxicated from his proximity and the delicious, freshly showered scent of him.

"You're lovely in the morning," he told her, his silver eyes soft. "All sleepy and disheveled. As much as I'd like to tumble you back into bed and keep you trapped in my penthouse all day, I have a breakfast meeting with the mayor, and he's particularly irritable in the mornings." He grinned.

Sam felt the flush in her cheeks as she responded to a vivid mental image of her and Jack, tangled underneath cool linen sheets. "Don't let me keep you," she replied, taking a quick gulp of coffee to hide her sudden diffidence.

Jack grinned at her, as if he could read her mind. As if he hadn't put exactly what she was thinking in there. "You up for a little fun Saturday?"

Sam watched him. "I don't recall applying for any vacancies, Jack."

He smiled at her. "Maybe I'm applying for one."

She looked down, hiding between sips of coffee. "And if I don't have anything open?"

"Then I'll take whatever I can get." Jack placed a quick kiss on her shoulder. "Let me take that little red Corvette of yours out for a drive.

No strings. Just the pleasure of each other's company."

"Well I can't very well allow you to take my car without me in it," she responded.

"And it'd be no fun to drive without you in it. Saturday—whaddya say?" he asked, full of charm.

Sam thought about it briefly. "I should be free after about two o'clock."

"That works. Mitch and I were going to try this gym Carey was telling us about in the morning."

Sam nodded. "Yeah, it's a converted warehouse over in West Loop. I'll actually be there working out with the guys."

"It's a fighters' gym?" Jack asked, his brow furrowing.

"Yeah. They have a lot of fighters, martial artists, ex-military, some cops. The owner is a friend of ours. He's one of the coaches for the US Olympic Judo team."

"Am I gonna get my ass kicked?" he asked, only half-joking.

Sam shrugged, hiding her grin in the mug. "Depends on what you like."

Jack leaned forward and kissed her lips before she could react, the firm pressure of his mouth sending a galvanic zing through her system. He stood up, buttoning his shirt. "I like you. And I'd like to see you in action now that I know you'll be there. We can enjoy the day afterward."

"Jack," Sam said as he moved to leave the room. He paused at the door, turning toward her. "I like you too," she finished softly. "Even if I don't have any vacancies at the moment."

October—That evening

Michigan Avenue, Chicago

JACK

REBECCA PUSHED UP to her tip-toes to kiss his mouth. Jack turned his face so her lips touched his cheek. She dropped back, momentarily surprised.

"How was the day?" he transitioned smoothly, pulling out her seat. They had a corner table in the Signature Room on the 95th floor of the Hancock building. The sun had already set, leaving them with the glimmering lights of the Magnificent Mile on a perfectly cloudless night. She sat down, smiling when she saw the drink he'd already ordered for her.

"Thanks, darling," she said, slipping her hand over his. "After the day I've had, I needed one of these." She sipped her margarita. Rebecca glanced at him. "You're not drinking?"

Jack shook his head. "Not tonight."

"Why not?"

He shrugged. "How's the filming going?"

"Good," she nodded. "I think we should be done in a couple weeks. Today was a nightmare though. The director was in one of his moods..." she set her drink down. "But that's not why you asked me here, is it?" She squared him with a direct look.

Jack sipped his water, sitting back. "One of the many things I really like about you. You're in a bullshit industry, but when you feel like it, you cut right to the chase."

"Can't bullshit a bullshitter," she shrugged. "Especially one from Hollywood. So why are we here tonight, Jack?"

He reached for her hand. "You wanted to know where we were heading a few weeks back?"

Rebecca tensed before waving her free hand airily. "It was an emotional moment. Let's just chalk it up to that, hmm?"

Jack brought her hand to his lips. "You're a stunning woman, Rebecca," he told her sincerely.

After a moment, her blue eyes welled before she blinked the emotion back. The consummate actress.

"But you're not cut out for long-distance relationships," she finished for him, squeezing her small hand around his.

Jack nodded after a moment, setting her hand down on the table. He kept it loosely clasped in his.

"Well, I'll have to make the most of the last two weeks then," she answered, her light voice not quite covering the tremor behind it.

Jack squeezed her hand before releasing it. "Why prolong the inevitable, Rebecca?"

She blinked, took a breath. "So…this is a breakup dinner?"

He leaned forward, pushing her beautiful strawberry hair behind her shoulder. "No. This is a dinner between two friends who shared a wonderful summer together."

"I'm more than your friend, Jack," Rebecca answered readily. "I'm in love with you."

Jack shook his head, his gaze steady. "No, beautiful. You're not. When you leave Chicago, get back home, and start working on your next project, you'll realize it."

"You can't tell me how I feel, Jack," Rebecca replied, a lone tear slipping down her cheek.

He rubbed it away with his thumb. "You're so passionate. So in the moment. It's why you're such a great actress. When you win an Oscar one day, I'll be cheering from the bleachers."

Rebecca tucked her cheek into his hand. "I'm not pretending with you, Jack."

"I know, sweetheart."

They sat like that for a minute before Rebecca pulled back. "Shit," she blinked, dabbing under her eyes. "You've gone and screwed up my mascara."

Jack chuckled. "You're still gorgeous," he assured her.

She drank her margarita. "I'm gonna need like, five more of these."

He smiled at her. "You get whatever you want, beautiful."

"But I don't get you," she pointed out.

Jack slanted her a smile. "Okay, you get almost everything you want."

Rebecca finished her drink. Ordered another. She watched him for a while. "Are you already seeing someone else?" she asked quietly.

Jack shook his head.

"Let me rephrase that," she said. "Are you already seeing her?"

"You'll have to be more specific than that."

Rebecca rolled her eyes. "The woman you were staring at the night of the benefit. The woman in the blue dress."

Jack shrugged. "Nothing's happened."

"But you like her."

"I admire her," Jack amended.

"Why?"

Jack thought about it. "She's completely unlike anyone I've ever met. She doesn't fit into any molds. And she's fierce. She's utterly fierce under all that cool demeanor."

"Oh my God." Rebecca downed her second drink.

"Okay, you're going to have to slow down," he told her. "You're a buck twenty soaking wet. I don't want to have to hold your hair back later."

"You're *in love* with her!" Rebecca accused, pointing at him.

Jack laughed. "No, I'm not."

"Then you're a blind idiot. Because a man who talks about a woman like that more than admires her," she informed him with the arch of her brow.

"You asked."

"I did," Rebecca replied, fiddling with the glass. "I just didn't expect it to hurt so damn much," she admitted, pressing her hand to her heart. "Jack—"

"Yes?"

"Would you mind if I skipped dinner? I don't think I can sit here and pretend. I want to go hurt by myself."

Jack curled a hand on her arm. "Rebecca—"

"Jack, please. Just…please." She pulled away, standing. "I would slap you and flounce away dramatically, but I don't think that'll help." Her smile was tremulous.

Jack leaned down, brushing a kiss to her cheek. "You're lovely, Rebecca." He pressed a gentle kiss to her lips. "I'll miss you," he whispered, pulling back.

Rebecca closed her eyes. "No, you won't." She picked up her clutch, turned to go. Then she said, "But thanks for saying it."

Jack watched her leave.

"Excuse my asking, sir, but was that Rebecca Holland?" the waiter asked when Jack asked for the bill.

He nodded, looking out the window. "The one and only."

"You're a lucky man," the waiter complimented.

And not for the reasons you think, Jack thought, signing the bill with flourish.

CHAPTER 12

October—Saturday morning

West Loop, Chicago

JACK

THE GYM SAM and her team went to was a massive refurbished warehouse in a revival area near downtown and Mitch's loft in the West Loop. One side of the gym held boxing rings and an octagonal MMA cage, and the center of the warehouse was dedicated to huge canvas mats for various martial arts. Free weights, professional gym equipment, rowers, and ellipticals lined the other half of the gym. Nearly ninety percent of the people there were men—and tough-looking bastards at that.

Mitch whistled softly beside him. "I don't know whether to be turned on or scared for my life."

"A little of both," Jack commented, watching men grappling on the mat while Talon and Rush looked intent on killing each other in one of the Octagons. "Either way, I'd say you need to keep your cock covered. Everyone in here looks like they're training for *Game of Thrones.*"

"You made it!" Carey called out, walking toward them in a stiff, white gi cinched with a black belt.

"Yeah. That looks like the easy part," Mitch murmured, glancing at the Octagon again. "It's the surviving part I'm not so certain about."

Carey followed his gaze, "Oh, this is normal for them. They're always pretty entertaining to watch," he told them with a wide grin.

As they neared the Octagon, Talon executed a nearly perfect stomach kick on Rush, knocking him back against the cage so hard that Rush probably saw birdies if he could even breathe. Rush doubled over with a grunt. As Talon advanced with a strong right cross, Rush slipped down to his knees, taking advantage of Talon's momentum to grab his legs, tipping him back and knocking him down to the ground. Rush tried to pin him with a leg bar. Talon slipped out in the last moment, but not before Rush got a solid elbow into the inside of his thigh. Talon howled, punching Rush hard in the side of the head.

"Who's better?" Mitch asked.

Carey shrugged. "Depends. Talon is a classic brawler with a heavy emphasis on kicking. Rush was a wrestler growing up, so he's more a ground-and-pound kind of guy."

"How often do you guys train?" Jack asked.

"Six days a week."

Mitch whistled.

"And Sam?" Jack asked.

Carey shrugged. "Depends on her travel. She teaches a lot now, but she still trains."

"What does she teach?" Mitch asked.

"Judo. She's been a Judo player since she could walk. Her father taught us," Carey told them.

"Who's better? You or her?" Mitch asked brazenly.

"Her." Carey laughed. "Hands down. She can throw me across the room like I'm a Raggedy Anne doll. She's mean too. Zero mercy."

Jack and Mitch's brows raised. Carey was a behemoth. If he had no shame in admitting a woman nearly half his size could level him, she must be damn good.

They watched the guys fight for a little while longer before Carey showed them around, introducing them to some of the professional fighters as well as the amateurs. The owner of the gym was a barrel-chested Asian whose biceps rivaled Carey's despite the fact that he was nearly two feet shorter. He radiated a peaceful, happy aura, though Jack had no doubt he could dismantle a man with the effort he put into making a cappuccino.

"Kim Sensei, these are the friends I was telling you about." Carey introduced them, "Mitch Gartner and Jack Roman. They're business partners and friends of ours. Looking to try out a little unconventional training," he said, humor coloring his tone.

"Nice meeting you two." Kim Sensei smiled as they shook hands. "You ever tried a martial art competitively or are you just interested in training?"

"Collegiate soccer is about as aggressive a sport as I've tried," Mitch admitted.

"Don't let this one fool you," Jack interjected drily. "I've seen him kicking in places no red card will ever justify. And I think I've taken an elbow or two in the face. He's a menace, this one."

Mitch tried and failed to look wry before the facade collapsed into a crooked grin. "Says the guy who used to train with the best amateur boxing prospects in the Chicagoland area," Mitch replied.

Kim Sensei chuckled, leading them to toward the boxing rings. "When was the last time you boxed, Jack?"

Jack shrugged. "On and off now but seriously training? It's been a while. The training was just too intense, with work and other obligations," he admitted.

"How long you do it?" Carey asked.

"Since I was a kid. Italian American leagues, that sort of thing," he responded, watching the guys training on speed bags and punching bags hanging from heavy chains. He hadn't realized how much he'd missed it. Even the smell of a fighter's gym—hard-earned sweat with the slight coppery tinge of blood and the leather scent of the bags. Jack realized how much he'd missed it.

"We offer the more traditional fight training like boxing, Judo, Tae Kwon Do, and Muay Thai where you can join group classes, or we can tailor more specific training regimens for you based on your goals," Kim Sensei explained. "Carey and Sam like their teams to focus on aspects unique to each individual, so each training session combines a variety of techniques. We assess them every week to see how they're progressing, figure out what we might need to tweak or which instructors or training partners they might need to aid in their progress."

"Submit, you sonofabitch!" Rush shouted in the cage, interrupting Kim Sensei.

Everyone turned toward the Octagon, watching Rush hold Talon down in a cradle pin, one arm wrapped around his right leg, the other pinning Talon's left arm.

"I will rip your off arm first and use it to beat *you* into submission," Talon spat out through his mouth guard, struggling.

"Now, boys," Samantha drawled, strolling around the Octagon from the back of the gym wearing a heavyweight gi with a weathered red and white belt. "Finish up this match. Talon, I want you showered and in your gi in ten minutes. Eat a protein bar to get your energy back up. You're wrestling with Simon. We're working on your Jiu-Jitsu today," she informed him, tying her hair back in a tight knot.

Rush eased back, and Talon pushed him off, disgusted. "You're lucky she saved your ass," Rush sniggered.

"Bullshit," Talon muttered, pulling off his half gloves.

"Rush, you're with Carey working on throws and sweeps," Samantha told him before spotting Jack standing with Mitch and Kim Sensei. Her face broke into a grin and she strode over.

"You came," she said warmly, giving Mitch their customary cheek-kiss greeting and Jack a quick side hug. "What'll you two be working on?"

"I'll be working on not getting my ass handed to me," Mitch answered readily.

"I've heard from Jack you're quite the sneaky bastard, Mitch," Samantha laughed. "I'm sure you've got a few very bad tricks up your sleeve."

Mitch peered at Jack. "You really need to stop spreading rumors about me."

"I speak the truth," Jack retorted, holding his right hand up in Scout's Honor.

"Jack, why don't you get back into the ring today?" Kim Sensei suggested. "See how it feels. It's as good a place as any to start."

"You box?" Samantha asked, her brows up.

Jack nodded. "Rusty, but yeah."

"That's fantastic. It's a great sport, and that explains the shoulders," she observed, running her eyes briefly across his torso. Jack suddenly wanted to box a title fight to keep her eyes on him like that.

"Mitch, since you're new to this, why don't you try martial arts? It's more structured and focused on technique. Kim Sensei, are you teaching next?" she asked.

"Good call," he agreed, a smile on his kind face. "Why don't we get you fitted for a gi and then you can try Judo? I'm teaching an all-levels class next. I'll show you guys the locker room and you can get your gear sorted out before you begin training."

As Jack and Mitch moved to follow Kim Sensei toward the back of the warehouse, he caught Samantha's eye while she leaned toward Carey to discuss something. She grinned at him.

"Good luck," she mouthed.

Jack had a feeling he'd need it.

October—Two hours later

West Loop, Chicago

JACK

THERE WAS SOMETHING so utterly satisfying and cleansing about throwing a well-placed, well-executed punch. The perfect, controlled extension of the arm, the power being pulled up from the core through the shoulders, that alignment of wrist and fist, the connection and impact to skin, muscle, and bone.

Jack was exhilarated, on fire, brimming with energy. The adrenaline rush reminded him of his youth, his father training him on one of his rare off-days, the endorphin high of winning a match, all coming together in a smattering of memories that made him feel damn near giddy.

He squared off with one of the boxing instructors, Manny, who was about his height and weight.

"You're rusty but good," Manny complimented, nodding. "The footwork's unmistakable. Let's see what you've got on combos. Focus on speed and hits to the torso."

Jack faked left and struck out with a strong right uppercut, switching to a series of swift jabs and crosses before stepping sideways, just catching the graze of Manny's responding right hook. He bounced on the balls of his feet, keyed up, going back in for another series of combo hits.

They worked in the ring for a good stint until Jack's arms felt like jelly and he was breathing like he'd finished a marathon. He showered and changed into jeans and a dark sweater, feeling pleasantly enervated and sore but replete.

"You did good today," Manny commented, high-fiving him as he came out of the locker room. "You coming back next week?"

"Definitely," Jack answered. "That was the best workout I've had in years. Thanks, man." He caught sight of Samantha coaching Talon on the mats while he grappled with Simon, the burly Brit from the night before. Carey was working with Rush nearby, moving through an intricate set of sweeps and throws.

"You work with those guys?" Manny asked, following his line of sight.

"Nah," Jack answered. "They're friends."

"Those guys are serious," Manny commented. "I'm a professional fighter, and I wouldn't want to meet any of them in a dark alley," he said. "Never seen that guy before though."

Jack followed Manny's line of sight to see Simon bowing across from Talon, shaking his hand as they finished their set. He had on a blue gi and a black belt and was smiling cockily at Samantha, his chest puffed up as he followed her out onto the mat.

Jack thought about turning around and getting his gloves back on.

"Yeah, he's new. Only a *pinche pendejo* would challenge Sam to a match," Manny commented, shaking his head.

"Why?" Jack asked, watching as they came to a stop in the center of a circle, bowing to each other.

Manny barked out a laugh. "That *mami* will fuck you up, bro. When she fights, she fights like she's got nothing to lose. That makes her a real fucking problem, you know?"

Jack absorbed that, fitting in another piece to her puzzle. Her casual dismissal of her injury made more sense. It was nothing to her. She was getting a job done.

"Screw fierce, man, that one's *ferocious*," Jack muttered.

Manny nodded. "Yeah. And protective. She puts all her guys through the paces with training, but *mirar*, she takes care of them," he told him, his admiration clear. "Watches over them all—training regimen, health, nutrition. They're lucky. I never had a boss like that before." Manny's attention was diverted as someone called over to him. Manny waved in acknowledgement. "I've got another training session. I'll catch up with you Monday, yeah?"

Jack nodded. "Thanks for today." he said, shaking Manny's hand before making his way over toward Carey and Rush, both of whom were watching Samantha and Simon as they rounded on each other within the circle on the mat.

Mitch wandered over, freshly showered. "What's going on here?"

"Sammy's gonna exorcise Simon of some demons," Carey answered in a low tone.

"What do you mean?" Jack asked, his brow knit.

"He feels bad about Somalia," Carey explained. "Blames himself because she got hurt. She's going to work him over." He smiled. "Show him she can take care of herself."

"He's twice her size. You're not at least a little worried?" Mitch asked, concern all over his face.

"Just watch," Rush responded, looking giddy.

"It was his fault," Jack grumbled, though no one paid attention because they were all watching Simon advance quickly, striking out in a rapid series of punches and kicks. Samantha backed up with each advance as Simon moved with remarkable speed. He nearly caught her with a right-handed strike to her upper body. Simon came so close to her, Jack sucked in a tight breath. Samantha smoothly blocked Simon's hit across her body, her fingers catching the sleeve of his gi. She used his momentum to jerk him forward. He lost his balance and tipped, recovering quickly.

"Bloody hell, you're fit," Simon admired.

Samantha didn't respond as she watched him circle her. He lunged again. He came close to picking her up, but she struck him hard in the neck and upper chest, drawing a grunt. In the half second he stood stunned by the blows, she grabbed the collar of his gi and jerked him forward again, sweeping her foot out to catch his leg, sending Simon flying head first. Jack nearly cheered, but Simon tucked in a commando roll, popping to his feet quickly. His demeanor was more serious now that he had a glimpse of what he was up against. He moved with more caution, strategizing.

"Don't take this personally, but I won't go easy on you, love," he told her in a low voice.

"Didn't ask you to," she replied before he lit into her with two startling frontal strikes, looking like he was holding nothing back. His arms came back as fast as they'd advanced, careful not to get caught by her hands again as she swiftly pivoted and blocked in spare, efficient movements. But still, she allowed him to get close. Too close. Jack felt like he was going insane as he watched from the sidelines. He knew she didn't need the help—and the last thing she wanted was for him to get involved—but he wanted to do damage to Simon for threatening her. *God, how he wanted to do damage.*

Simon took a step forward and came down with a vicious hammer strike. Jack and Mitch flinched, certain she was about to be crushed. Samantha dropped to her knee, narrowly avoiding brunt of the blow while hooking her elbow around Simon's leg and twisting him to the ground with vicious efficiency. He grunted again as she applied alarming pressure to his knee.

"He's a dead man," Rush commented.

"Why?" Jack asked, not taking his eyes off the mat.

"She gets you to the ground, and you're done," Rush answered cryptically.

Simon attempted to shake her off with no luck. She was behind him in a fraction of a second, pinching something in his neck, forcing him to collapse. She pinned him to the ground with a swift knee behind his shoulder blades. Simon gasped in pain as she continued to exert pressure on his neck and shoulders.

"*Waza ari!*" Carey called out.

Samantha leaned forward to whisper something into Simon's ear before releasing him and stepping back. Simon grunted, rolling back up, determined.

"What did Carey say?" Jack asked Rush.

"Half-point," Rush answered. "A full point and she wins the match," he explained.

Samantha and Simon squared off again. Their size differences were almost comical. Simon looked equal parts mean and turned on now. He moved forward again, feinting a punch while he delivered a stunning side kick that grazed her hip even as she dodged.

Anxiety and protectiveness clawed its way up Jack's esophagus. "Jesus," he muttered.

"Simon'll be praying shortly," Rush commented.

Simon executed a powerful roundhouse, and Samantha bent into the momentum of the kick. Jack was certain it was a death blow, winning Simon the match, but Samantha used the momentum to curl and dive into a fast somersault. Jack's eyes widened. She used Simon's incredible height advantage to dive underneath and behind him, her hand wrapped tightly around the bottom of his gi pants. She jerked his leg behind him, hurling him forward. He put his hands out to break his fall, landing with a grunt. Simon quickly tried to roll away from her, but she was already wrapped around his back, cinching her legs tightly around his lower waist, her hands around the collar of his gi.

As Simon struggled, clawing at her hands and legs around his waist, Samantha twisted her hand around the neck of his gi, making the collar a tourniquet. Simon jabbed her hard with his elbow. She expelled a harsh breath, but she responded by viciously jerking his collar tighter, cutting off his windpipe as she executed the choke hold. Simon swiped at her head. She ducked most of his hits, catching a couple in the jaw and cheek, digging her heels into his diaphragm in retaliation. He gasped, sputtering as she used her feet and hands to squeeze out all his air. One of her hands slipped to his belt. She jerked at the loosened knot.

"What the hell is she doing?" Mitch worried.

"Oh shit," Rush breathed. "That's fucking cold."

"The fucking coldest," Carey grinned. "Submit, Michaelson!" he taunted.

Simon just grunted and sputtered, trying vainly to roll away. Like a Boa Constrictor, the harder he struggled, the tighter she twisted. Samantha stretched back, forcing Simon to arch backward with her. With a quick movement, she had his black belt wrapped around his neck, her other hand still squeezing his collar, cutting off his air supply. Everyone stood transfixed as what little breath Simon had left came out in a pant. With one last massive effort, Simon grabbed at her arms, delivering a vicious elbow to her ribs. Samantha made no sound, though her face blanched. Jack very nearly jumped on the mat, adrenaline and anger surging. Rush stuck out an arm to stop him.

"Just wait," Rush told him, watching Samantha.

"Fuck, he probably cracked her rib," Jack muttered, wiping a distressed hand down his face.

"Simon needs this," Carey responded. "He needs to understand what she's capable of."

"And the poor bastard's about to pass out anyway," Rush smirked.

Simon's eyes rolled in the back of his head. His struggling grew sluggish as Samantha continued to choke him. She was whispering something into his ear. Jack wondered alternately what she was saying and if she was going to kill her own employee with everyone watching.

"Tap out!" Rush shouted. "Tap out, ya stubborn bastard!"

"Holy shit, is she going to murder him right here?" Mitch breathed.

As Simon's body eventually slackened, Carey called, "*Ippon!*"[4]

Simon didn't move as Samantha released him, sliding from under his massive body. Jack stared, stunned to realize she'd choked him into unconsciousness. And with his own goddamn black belt.

Rush clapped enthusiastically. "See, what did I tell you?" he said to Jack and Mitch.

Carey stepped onto the mat and leaned over Simon, slapping his face a couple times as he came to.

"What day is today?" Carey asked.

---

[4] Japanese for "Full Point" in Judo, as in the winner takes the match.

COMPLICATED CREATURES   175

"Saturday," Simon groaned.

"What's five times forty?"

"One hundred thirty."

"Who am I?"

"You're an arsehole," Simon answered, sitting up and rubbing his neck, looking aggrieved.

"You're fine," Carey replied, helping him up. He swayed dizzily for a moment.

"I take it back," Mitch said, turning to Jack, his eyes wide. "You turn and run. This woman's more than your match. She'll be the death of you."

Jack shook his head, bemused. If it was possible, he was even more certain this woman was perfect for him. Carey was right. Samantha was mean, and she had absolutely no mercy. And he liked it. *Oh, yes, he liked it.*

Samantha and Simon bowed to each other. She handed him his neatly coiled black belt.

"I always wanted to see what the hype around you was, Poppy," Simon told her, his hand coming up to rub his reddened neck gingerly. "Never had a woman strangle me with my own belt before."

"Oh?" she said, brow raised. "That's astonishing."

Simon eyed her. "Would it be weird to say you scare the absolute shit out of me and I think I'm half in love with you?"

"You'll have to get to the back of the line then," Jack muttered, coming to stand next to her. He touched her rib where Simon had struck her. "Are you okay, *tesoro?*"[5]

Simon looked from Jack to Samantha.

"Nothing a hot bath and shot of bourbon won't cure," she answered, smiling up to him before turning to Simon. "Carey will draw up an adjusted training regimen for you. I'd like you to pick up some proficiency in other defensive techniques. You're too reliant on your brute strength."

"I thought I was pretty good," Simon told her, sheepish. "Until I

---

[5] Italian endearment meaning "treasure."

met you."

Welcome to the club, Jack thought. *We all thought we were pretty good until she came and knocked us on our asses.*

Samantha conferred with Simon and Carey for a moment longer before turning to Jack, a smile softening her face.

"How'd it go?" she asked.

"Watching you fight a guy nearly twice your size? Yeah, I think I'd rather watch a car accident," Jack replied drily. "Less nerve wracking."

Her lips twitched. "How do you imagine I've made my way, Jack? By asking nicely?"

"You *are* a negotiator," he pointed out.

"Sometimes people need to be made aware of the risks before they can be persuaded," she replied.

"I'm realizing I wasn't really aware of the risks."

"You still aren't," she told him, crossing her arms. "You want to call off that drive now?"

"Not a chance," Jack answered, adamant. "I'm certain you're worth the jeopardy," he replied, tucking a loose strand of hair behind her ear.

Samantha looked pleased and a little relieved, as if she'd suspected he'd just hightail it and run. "Alright then. Let's do this," she said with a smile.

CHAPTER 13

October—An hour later

Somewhere on I-94, headed north

SAMANTHA

"How do you like to be touched, beautiful?" Jack asked, his voice a low thrum. "Like this?" He shifted down, shooting onto the freeway, gunning the Corvette's engine. "Or like this?" Jack shifted back up, maneuvering around slower cars like a seasoned rally racer. The 'vette responded with an aggressive throttle, the throaty rumble characteristic to the 1962 model while she held low and tight to the ground with the acceleration.

Sam watched Jack through dark Wayfarers, bemused. Jack looked like a kid at Christmas, caressing the leather steering wheel, a brash smile on his face as he pushed the car to over ninety miles per hour. The wind ruffled his hair. He looked happy and relaxed in sunglasses and a dark cashmere sweater, sleeves pushed up on tan forearms, the fall sun burnishing the streaks in his hair. She fought the urge to run her fingers through it, leaning forward to fiddle with the stereo instead.

"Three forty horsepower?" he asked.

"Three sixty," she corrected. "V8, fuel injection, three fifty two torque."

"She's amazing," he sighed happily. "I love her. Can I have her?" he asked hopefully.

Sam chuckled, shaking her head. "Uh, no. But you can borrow her on occasion. Impress all the girls," she teased.

Jack leveled a look at her over his sunglasses. "I only want to impress one girl. Any idea how I do that?" he asked, taking his hand off the gear shift to run his fingers along her jaw.

"Good men are hard to find," she answered airily. "Be a good man. She may come around."

"But she's surrounded by good men," Jack pointed out.

"So she has impeccable taste," she replied, pushing her hair back as the wind whipped around them. "You'll have to do something to stand out. You're creative. You'll come up with something."

Sam closed her eyes, leaning her head back to soak up the sun, hiding the unexpected churn she felt over the thought of what a man as wildly sexy and as damnably intelligent as Jack might do to stand out. He was just the kind of guy to give chase. Looking at him now, switching lanes like a speed demon, wind ruffling his hair, light eyes hidden behind sunglasses… she bet he gave *very good* chase.

Jack caught her looking, lifting her hand to his mouth and kissing her knuckles before resting their hands against his thigh. "Do you know how I pick my building projects?" he asked her.

Sam tilted her head, considering him. "I'd put money on you looking for a challenge."

"That's one aspect, yes," he agreed. "I like projects that are complicated but have immense potential. Buildings with history and intricacy that others don't have the patience, skill, or financial wherewithal to take on."

"Your more modern and commercial projects are selected to fund your passion for renovation, aren't they? They're a means to an end," she surmised. "You use them to accumulate power."

"That's empire building." Jack smiled. "Helps the city, creates political capital, makes money—everyone's happy. But what I'm about, what I really love, is the rare jewel. The Whitneys." He squeezed her hand. "And they're not always apparent. You have to look at all their angles to understand what's really there."

"Are you comparing me to a dilapidated building, Jack?" Sam asked, sardonic.

"Not at all, I'm still figuring out what I'm looking at," he grinned. "And I definitely don't know all the angles, but…" Jack glanced over at her. "I know enough to know I want you, Samantha. Now I'll just have to figure out what I can get."

Milwaukee, Wisconsin

SAMANTHA

JACK DROVE THEM into downtown Milwaukee, a smaller city about an hour-and-a-half's drive north of Chicago. They toured the Lakefront Brewery, housed in what had once been Milwaukee's Electric Railway and Light Company's coal-fired power plant, where they tasted ales and seasonal brews. They argued amicably over the best flavors, whether Belgian white ales were as good as American wheat, what paired best with what. They ended up taking their debate to the Milwaukee Brewing Company, where they tried beers with names like "Louie's Demise," "Booyah," and "Love Rock," debating beer names and coming up with a few creative variations of their own, aided, of course, by continued consumption.

They strolled around the waterfront, walking off the beer buzz and enjoying the fall weather. Jack tucked her hand into the crook of his arm, and Sam felt warm from more than just the alcohol.

After a visit to Captain Frederick's Pabst Mansion, the beer baron's restored showcase home, they ended up at the Hinterland Erie Street Gastropub, sitting outside of the renovated Third Ward Warehouse, munching on cheeses and charcuteries, sampling succulent duck rillettes and pan-seared sable fish.

"I gotta get Mitch up here," Jack groaned as he leaned back in his chair and patted his belly. "He would love this place. Forget the James Beard nominations."

"We should get all the guys up here. Beer tours and great food— they'd have died and gone to heaven," Sam suggested while she sipped a saison, savoring the lemony taste.

"That's a really good idea. We should do it before it gets snowy," Jack remarked. "What do you drive when it gets bad out?" he asked.

"I have an old Land Cruiser and an all-wheel Jag if you can't stand the sight of a banged-up old beater sitting next to your pretty little Aston," Sam teased. "What about you? Does that sexy-ass car ever see the snow?"

Jack shook his head. "I drive a Range Rover in the winter," he answered. "I'm a British car nut. What kind of Jag is it?"

"An XJ," she said. "My dad collected cars, so I've always enjoyed them." She laughed suddenly, remembering something. "My granddaddy used to say to Dad, *'Son, what you need with all these cars? You ain't got but one ass,'*" she said in a thick Texan drawl.

Jack chuckled, sipping his beer. "Did you keep his collection?" he asked.

She nodded. "Sitting in a converted barn on the ranch in Texas. I have a guy who keeps them in working order. He worked for my dad. I think it's more a labor of love for him than anything."

"Christ, I bet that's worth a fortune. What all did your dad have?"

She rattled off some of the models and vintages that came to mind, noting Jack's appreciative noises.

"Why did you keep the 'vette with you out of all of them?" he asked after a time.

She thumbed the condensation off her glass, looking away. "Sentimental, I guess," she admitted. "We worked on that one together," she explained after a moment. "I'm no mechanic, but I've got the basics down pat. Dad was always worried I'd be one of those damsel-in-distress types and didn't want me to get taken advantage of."

"You'd kick someone in the pants before you let anyone take advantage of you," Jack murmured, shaking his head. "I pity the asshole who tries to pull one over on you."

Sam smiled at the gruff compliment, glancing across the table at him. Jack looked utterly relaxed, legs crossed casually, his arm hooked over the back of a chair as he watched passersby strolling and window-shopping.

"What?" he asked, catching her watching him.

"Just thinking how much I'm enjoying this," she told him honestly.

And how you just may be the perfectly proportioned antidote to my particular brand of loneliness.

Her business, more than any other, proved how much vulnerability could cost you. And she'd paid for every good thing she had, again and again, until the pain of exposure had made her choose her vulnerabilities sparingly. Pleasure, tenderness, intimacy…these were all luxuries Sam stole where she could find them, cutting off attachment before the potential became too painful to hold onto, knowing separation was an inevitability. She understood that involvement was a weakness she couldn't afford to indulge; she had come to terms with that years ago.

But Jack might be all right. They didn't need each other, after all. An affair would roll seamlessly past him—a pleasant experience in a long line of many. He was so confident, so self-aware and ambitious. He was a man who knew exactly his place in the world; he could control and steer his own destiny. Perhaps they could enjoy each other, wile away a few careless hours, coming together briefly before bouncing back to their respective positions, separate and whole. Sam suspected that they suited each other far more than either realized.

"Why did you join the Navy?" he asked, interrupting her reverie.

Surprised at the question, she took a moment to answer. "Family tradition. My father and granddaddy were both in the Navy. I grew up on their stories, their patriotism. And they didn't really treat me any differently growing up," she reflected. "Maybe because they didn't know any better, but I never felt like I couldn't do something I wanted to if I worked hard and wanted it badly enough."

"What was your mother like?"

Sam sipped her beer, watching a young couple walk by, heads close together as they laughed and smiled at each other.

Young love, she thought. *Nothing ages you faster.*

"From what I remember, she was lovely," Sam finally answered. "She was quiet, artistic. She painted, spoke to me in Japanese. Haikus, I think," she paused, trying to remember. Every year, it became more difficult to recall the details.

"You're half Japanese?" Jack asked, clearly surprised.

"My mother was Japanese. My father was half-Cherokee, half-white. My granddaddy was full Cherokee," she explained.

"Now I get it," Jack said, looking at her intently. "You're so unique. It's difficult to put a finger on it. Your eyes look Asian, but not completely. Your cheekbones remind me of paintings of beautiful Native American women you find in museums, but all the pieces convert into something entirely different when it's pulled together." He continued to gaze at her, seeming to catalog her features individually, as if fitting together the jigsaws of a puzzle.

Sam felt her face heat a little with the beer and the scrutiny. "I do well slipping into most environments," she told him with a shrug. "Tan enough and I can pass for South American. Enough eye kohl and the right garb and I can pass for Turkish or Persian. In Asia, most people assume I'm Southeast Asian. In the States, I guess that just makes me as mixed as ninety-eight percent of the nation."

"How did your parents meet?" Jack asked, fascinated.

"My dad was stationed in Japan toward the end of his enlistment. He met my mother in Kyushu and spent the rest of his time convincing her to marry him, as the story goes. She didn't have much family, so moving to the US seemed exciting to her at the time." Sam paused, taking a sip of her saison. "She didn't realize she was signing up for a cattle ranch in Texas. I don't know that she would have agreed, hindsight twenty-twenty," she admitted, feeling the tinge of sadness she always felt considering how little she recalled of her mother. Her recollections were of a shy, beautiful woman who had a certain melancholia about her. Sam remembered watching her mother painting, looking out the window for hours. If she hadn't had children, Sam wasn't certain she would have stayed. Her dad never mentioned it, but she knew, like all children know, when they're the reason their parents made sacrifices.

Jack seemed to sense the darkening of her thoughts and redirected the conversation. "Is that how you picked up Judo?" he asked.

"Yeah," she nodded. "Dad learned in Japan. Became obsessed with it, and he got really good. He taught us when we were kids, though to be honest, I think he wanted to me to use it against the boys who asked me out in school," Sam chuckled. "He used to say he never wanted to have to take a shotgun out when I finally went on a date. That he wanted the boy to be too scared of me to try any fast moves," she grinned. "Guess he got what he wanted."

Jack barked out a laugh, eyes glinting. "I'll just bet. I think that's actually a really great strategy, if not a little lazy," he remarked. "God help Maddie when she tries to date. Between me and Jaime, any attempt will be doomed."

They were briefly interrupted by the waiter, and they debated whether to order another round.

"No way are you driving," Sam told Jack. Her brow knit. "And I don't think I'm in any condition to drive either," she admitted. "I think I've been in a state of perpetual buzz since the Lakefront Brewery."

He shrugged. "So we stay the night in Milwaukee. You got any other place to be?"

Sam paused, recognizing this was make or break time.

Jack leaned forward, putting his hand on hers. "Nothing happens that you don't want. I'm just suggesting we not end a good time to rush back if neither of us need to."

She considered it for a moment before shrugging. "Sure, why not? I can't remember the last time I drove out of town for the sole purpose of drinking."

They ordered another round, listening to a street musician in the distance.

"Do you speak Japanese?" Jack asked after a while.

"Don't you?" Sam teased.

"Italian," Jack told her. "And so-so at that. Enough to get into trouble. Both my parents grew up speaking Italian, but they only speak to each other in the mother tongue when they're fighting or they don't want me and Jaime to know what they're up to," he laughed. "How many languages do you know?" he asked, tucking his hand under his chin as he leaned on the table.

"Japanese, Mandarin, Spanish, Portuguese, Farsi and Arabic, and enough French and Russian to get the job done. Which basically means all the bad words and how to order people around," Sam laughed. "Oh, and a little Cherokee from my Granddaddy."

"Jesus," he muttered. "I'm an idiot."

She shrugged. "Gift of gab."

"How did you learn all that?" Jack asked, reaching across the table to toy with the bracelets on her arm.

"You know the Japanese and Cherokee. Spanish in high school and Portuguese from spending so much time in Brazil for one reason or the other. Mandarin in college and also on the job. Farsi and Arabic through the military. Russian and French through varied and nefarious means," she grinned, her eyes twinkling.

"I think you're the smartest woman I know," Jack murmured, admiring.

"Don't tell your mom that," Sam smiled, unaccountably pleased at the compliment.

"Our secret then," Jack complied. He reached out to touch a finger to a small charm on one of her bracelets. "Does this mean anything? Or is it something pretty?"

She glanced down at the small 'R' he was holding. She sucked in a tight little breath. "My brother, Ryland."

"Of course," Jack murmured. "The picture over your mantle. Is he younger or older?"

"He was younger."

"Was," Jack repeated, letting go of the charm to stroke his thumb along the back of her hand. "You've survived a lot," he observed.

"Haven't we all?" she replied with careless little shrug.

His gaze sharpened and he squeezed her hand gently. Sam flipped her hand over, letting his fingers run over her palm. The waiter arrived with their drinks.

"Some more than others," he murmured, sitting back but not releasing her hand. "I've been lucky. I know it. I grew up with a big extended family. Lots of cousins, uncles, aunties. My Uncle Gianni passing away from cancer was the most awful thing I could imagine until Cassie died, as insane as that sounds. It was such a shock. Such a glaring, unexpected, and unwarranted misfortune." Jack paused a beat. "We almost couldn't understand it. Couldn't metabolize or accept it."

"There's not a lot of preparation for something like that."

He turned to her again after a moment. "You know the worst? I'm Jaime's *fratellone*.[6] I've always taken care of him, and it's a responsibility I never took lightly. There was nothing I could do for him. Nothing I could do or say to change it. There's no making it right again," he paused to take a shaky breath, running his hand through his hair. "It's strange, you know? Being a grown goddamn man and not knowing how to grieve, much less how to help your brother work through it."

"That's why you kept the penthouse vacant for so long," Sam observed.

Jack nodded, a tight, short movement as he looked up at the moon hanging low over a clear night sky. "I stayed with Jaime for the first month, helping with Maddie, but he eventually kicked me out. Afterward, my parents stayed in Chicago for a year. Dad flew back and forth to D.C. I asked Jaime to move in so many times, but he refused." He looked back down. "It's the right thing, though. Maddie should grow in a neighborhood, like we did. The house we grew up in is only a few streets over. It's taken some time, but Jaime's all right."

"Yes, he is," Sam agreed. "And you?" she asked, squeezing his hand back. "Are you alright?"

Jack nodded, looking at her. "It's foolish. Such a spoilt thing to say, but I realized how lucky I was. You grow up with so much, it becomes rote. You assume you'll always have it—the privileges, the little luxuries. It becomes inconceivable to imagine otherwise." He took a breath. "It was a wake-up call," he conceded.

"You're a good uncle, Jack. A good brother." She smiled gently, remembering what she'd said to him in the car. "And a good man."

He watched her for a moment, searching the sincerity in her expression. "Thank you," he told her quietly, threading their fingers together, his thumb stroking hers.

They sat together for a little while longer, not speaking, enjoying their drinks and the clear, starlit sky. She could hear the distant refrain of a familiar song playing in the distance. Her body felt warm, the tingle of awareness passing through her like a steady current of electricity. Sam

---

[6] Italian for "big brother."

wondered again if they could be good for each other. Even if it was just for a night.

"Jack?"

"Yeah?" he asked, turning to look at her.

He really was a beautiful man, with that fall of dark hair and those iridescent silver eyes of his. Sam smiled at him, her heart skipping a little at the prospect of what she wanted to happen.

"Want to try that luck out?" she asked with a little smile.

Jack's answering look was a slow burn up her nerve endings, his eyes darkening to a smolder as he lifted her hand to his mouth.

"More than anything," he replied, pressing hot lips to the racing pulse at her wrist.

The waiter passed.

"Check, please," she called.

October—That night

Milwaukee, Wisconsin

JACK

JACK WALKED THEM to the historic Pfister Hotel, praying they'd have something good available. The lobby was warmly lit with antique crystal chandeliers, the grand old space inviting as jazz drifted in from the hotel bar, giving the atmosphere a hazy, decadent feel.

"They're playing 'Stella by Starlight,'" Samantha noticed, her husky voice a little dreamy.

Jack couldn't resist pulling her into an impromptu twirl, holding her close to his body. She felt extraordinary in his arms. He pressed his hand into the small of her back, tucking his jaw against her temple. She smelled like fall air and citrus from the saison, and as he swayed with her gently in that quiet, golden lobby, she turned her head to press a sweet kiss to the skin of his neck.

"I'm going to run to the ladies room," she told him. "And you're going to find us somewhere we can enjoy the rest of this evening, Jack. You're going to appreciate your insomnia tonight," she teased, her voice low and velvet. She stepped back and cast him an utterly sexy smile as she turned away.

Jack checked them into the last suite they had available, thanking his luck. He held out his hand to her as she stepped back into the lobby. They moved toward the elevator silently, and he couldn't resist pulling her into him again once inside, winding his arms under her shoulders, his hands tangling in the silkiness of her midnight hair.

"Samantha," he breathed, brushing a butterfly's kiss over her lips before settling over them with a gentle, delicious pressure. He was going to take his time with her, enjoy every sound and movement and curvature of this gorgeous, vital woman. Jack coaxed her mouth open, finding that perfect alignment, shifting her closer while her hand gripped his back, her nails pressing crescents into his shoulder blades. Their kiss became wild and succulent quickly, the tangle of tongues decadent and heady. Jack felt like he'd downed several glasses of champagne in rapid succession, the delirious buzz and the effervescent high of Samantha making him light-headed and punchy.

The elevator dinged, doors sliding open. They pulled apart, blinking at the open floor as if they didn't quite know where they were. Jack stepped out first, pulling her with him as he glanced at the room key for their room number. He turned left, stopped, and then turned right, muttering, "You've got me so damn twisted up I don't know where the hell I'm going."

Samantha laughed softly, squeezing his hand as she followed him to the corner suite he'd secured. He slid the key into the door, turning and backing into the room, unable to wait any longer to gather her back into his arms. Samantha felt good to him. Scary good. He groaned, fitting his mouth over hers again, suckling her silky tongue in a languid, articulate swirl. They shared exquisite, erotic kisses for long, drawn out minutes in the darkness of the hotel room, fingers exploring the planes of each other's faces. Jack outlined the gentle curves of her body, caressing the lines of her rib cage, squeezing the contour of her breasts, loving the weight and feel of them. He felt awash in sensation, thrilling with each discovery as he pulled clothes from her, until she was just in jeans, boots, and the jewelry that glinted at her ears, neck, and wrists.

"You're a dream I've been playing in my mind for weeks now," he told her, pulling away to place a fervent line of kisses along her jaw to the delicate skin of her ear. "A dream within a dream," he whispered, biting the lobe and the diamond in it, his hands sliding over the swell of her hips to the dense, lush curve of her ass. Jack tilted her hips up high and tight, pressing her to his pelvis, making her feel him, urging her against the ardent pressure of his erection until she was the one straining, rocking rhythmically against his grind, her breaths a soft pant along his cheek. He turned back to her mouth, absorbing each sound, each catch as her breath tripped. Jack pulled away from her mouth again, breathing in deeply as he rubbed against her in a taunting, delicious circle.

"I'm going to fuck you so good, so thoroughly, you're going to come yourself hoarse," he promised, hitching her up so she wound her legs around him. He caught her mouth again, swollen and damp, groaning as he pushed her into the back of the door, rocking her against the hard line of his cock with galvanic, exacting pressure. Jack slipped a hand between them, popping open the button of her jeans, tugging the zipper down before his fingers unerringly found the center of her, his thumb gliding tenderly along the gentle ridge of her clit, his fingers massaging, flexing, tracing the outline of her before dipping into the heat, making her buck against him.

"Do you know how you feel to me?" Jack asked her urgently, feeling a little crazy with his need. "Do you know how good you feel against me, Samantha?" He licked her lip, lush and red, giving in to the urge to bite her, to suckle and savor her as his thumb worked in insistent circles, adjusting pressures until he was rewarded with her caught breaths and soft keens. She tugged away from his mouth when it became too much, her head falling back against the door with her eyes squeezed shut as she sucked in a tight gasp of air. Jack stared at her, mesmerized as she rode the edge of pleasure, legs tight against his hips, squeezing rhythmically, as if she couldn't decide whether to push harder against him or pull away.

"Don't fight me, Samantha," he told her. "I'm going to do this all night. Make you come and come and come until you can't think, can't breathe, can't stop me—"

"*Fuuuck*," she hissed, arms tightening around his neck, her hands groping his shoulders as she pushed hard against his hand, jerking a little. "Yes," she breathed. "*Yes*, just—" her hips rolled, pressing her clit into his thumb in sinuous little movements, forcing his fingers deeper inside her. "Jack..." She moved again, chasing the pleasure, head falling forward to open her mouth against his neck. "Jack," she panted, teeth grazing as she called out, "Like that, Jack," she urged. "Just... like... *that*..."

Jack pressed his face to her hair, breathing in her scent, murmuring encouragements, giving her the exact right pressure she needed to reach the apex as she gasped and jutted, begging him to touch her, press her *there, there. God, yes. There. Jack—please. Please. Please...* He felt Samantha clench, her body stiffening while arms and legs squeezed around him, tightly impaled against his fingers, those slick inner muscles rippling, clasping...

Jack spun, carrying her across the suite to the king-sized bed, lowering her gently as she shuddered, watching him strip her shoes and jeans with sloe, pleasure-soaked eyes. He stood over her, tearing off his sweater in impatience, unbuttoning his jeans. Samantha sat up slowly on her elbows, one leg bent against the bed. He saw the dark tangle only narrowly hiding her sex glistening from her orgasm. Jack wanted to devour her, consume her totally. He was burning, *burning up* for her. He couldn't remember feeling this urgency, this madness for another person. He was ravenous for her. He had to have her.

"Jack," she called, holding a slender hand out to him. "Come here." He paused, hands stilling on his jeans. He clasped her outstretched hand, letting her pull him to her, settling between the cradle of her thighs. He slid his forearms under her shoulder blades, feeling the pounding of her heart echoing the pounding of his. He laced the line of her collarbone with hot, humid kisses before drawing up, taking her mouth again. Jack couldn't get enough of her. Couldn't drink enough from her mouth.

"Do you have protection?" she asked, pulling back, her expression drowsy with euphoria. She traced the wing of his brow with her finger, the line of his cheekbone.

He nodded, closing his eyes and turning his face into her hand, kissing the plump flesh of her palm. "I'll take care of you," he whispered.

They held onto each other for a moment, enjoying the shape and feel of their meshed limbs, the warmth of skin-on-skin before Jack retreated, dipping his head to place a line of kisses from her throat to her sternum. He dipped low to her belly, his tongue swirling in the indent of her belly button, making her laugh softly. Samantha ran her fingers through his hair, nails grazing ever so lightly, like she had the night she'd let him fall asleep in her lap.

He closed his eyes momentarily, enjoying the sensation before dropping to his knees at the end of the bed, pulling her forward until her knees were resting over his shoulders. He breathed her in, nuzzling the junction of her inner thigh and sex, luxuriating in the musky, wet scent of her. He dipped his nose against her, following with the searching, silky probe of his tongue, lapping at her, listening to the guttural sounds of pleasure she made as she tilted her hips up to him, opening herself to his exploration.

"You're Eden, Samantha," he whispered against her, licking into her softness, spreading her with his fingers. His tongue twirled against her clit, sucking on its silkiness, driving her mad, making her cry out in bliss. When she came again, holding him hard and close to her, Jack grabbed her wrists, manacling them against her own thighs, listening to her incoherent imprecations, feeling the involuntary clutch of her sex against his tongue. Samantha cried out, begging him to *take her, fuck her, make it last, please make it last,* while she came against his mouth like a wanton, making him murmur his delight, whispering praises against the most sensitive and secret part of her. As her tremors subsided, Jack lapped at her gently, shallowly, bringing her back from the pinnacle with honeyed, shameless kisses that drew out her shudders. He delighted in the wetness that flowed for him, because of him, only for him.

Jack released her slowly, raising up from his haunches, smiling down at her as she sighed and groaned her happiness. Her dark eyes shone bright as hellfire. The way Samantha looked at him in that moment made his chest feel full and tight all at once, as if it were being constricted, her pleasure a cataplasm. The longer she stared back at him, the harder he became, until he was nearly in pain, dying for her, to be as close as he could to her, as deep within this woman as he could get.

He kicked his shoes off, pushing down his jeans and pulling a couple condoms out of his wallet. As he began to straighten, Samantha came off the bed, surprising him. She toppled him to the mattress in a single fluid movement. She straddled him, her stunning body defined by the dim light filtering through the windows.

"Magnificent," he breathed, running the tips of his fingers down her sides, over the soft skin of her belly. He thrummed her clit as she leaned to grab the condom he'd dropped on the bedspread. She tore it open and smoothed it over him, her eyes admiring, a pleased smile on her lips as she looked him over.

"You deserve to be worshiped," she murmured, leaning forward to kiss his flat nipples, her pink tongue coaxing them to hardened points. "You please me," she told him as he watched her dip two fingers into herself, scooping up a small dollop of her own cream. "The proof," she whispered, using her liquid-coated fingers to clasp him tightly, stroking up from the base to the corona, making Jack strain against her secure grip, balancing the knife edge of pleasure and *oh-so-delicious* pain.

Samantha raised herself up on her knees, coming down on him slowly…excruciatingly slowly. She eased him a few inches inside her before rising on a powerful clench, making him call her name and grit his teeth, the tendons of his neck standing out in harsh relief as she did it again and again, taking more of him each time. Each and every thrust translated into maddening and deliberate friction. Jack choked out curses and pleasure and praise, urging her to go *harder, faster, more…just give me more,* but Samantha kept his hips pinned down with her thighs, her hands on his stomach and chest, forcing him to accept her pace, making him relax into the hot, tight clasp of her body until he was mindless… just movement and sound and the feel of sex so good he thought he might be hallucinating it.

Samantha drew his hands up, interlacing their fingers and using them as a counter balance as she rode him, rising and falling, circling her hips in a tight, hot grind. Jack lay helpless against the onslaught, issuing reflexive groans as he threw his head back, awash in sensation. Samantha powered against him, milking his cock so exquisitely he saw stars, all the blood collected only to serve her, to keep her impaled to him.

She pulled back suddenly, drawing the heavy, plum head of him against her slick seam, gathering the moisture and rubbing her clit with his cock in fast and sublime swivels. Jack jerked against the pressure, surprised when she suddenly came off him, tearing off the condom to suck him deep into her mouth, tongue flat against the heavy vein, throat working as she sealed him to her. The suction was so intense Jack struggled against the excruciating rise, fought to stave off the climax against the intensity of the pressure.

"*Christ, Samantha!*" he cried, voice strained as she worked him. "*Jesus,* I'm too close…" he struggled, hands trembling as he clenched her hair, trying to drag her back up.

"Shhh," she whispered against his skin, dark eyes pinning him with wicked intent. She licked the broad head, her tongue touching against the slit where his pre-come pearled. "You'll lie back and take it," she told him, holding him still as the tip of her tongue darted out to lick him again. Slowly. Delicately. Taunting him. "You'll take what I give you, Jack," she told him, her voice low. "You'll give me that pleasure." Samantha sucked him in deep, her fingers working his perineum and testes with provocative pressure, squeezing him in tantalizing intervals as she gave him the best head of his life.

Jack gripped her shoulders hard, indenting her skin, unsure if he was trying to push her off or bring her closer. He wanted to come inside of her, he wanted to watch her face, wanted to make her come yet again; he wanted, he wanted… *God, what the fuck did he want??*

"Samantha!" he shouted, his mind blanking as the sudden, incredible pressure of his orgasm burst down his spine. "YES!! *Fuck, YES,*" he came on a keening groan, fragmenting and releasing into her mouth, his spasms rocking him into her throat in prolonged jolts, vivid and dazing.

As Jack finally stilled, his mind and body trapped in the voluptuous undertow while he struggled to catch his breath, he felt her rest against him, her breath searing and soft against his cock as her hand stroked the tender skin on the inside of his thigh. They lay there for long, silent moments, while he listened to her breathe, his fingers curling into the soft tendrils of her hair, attempting to process the experience.

He'd had a great deal of sex in his life, but this was completely unlike anything he'd encountered. He felt…*taken*. Utterly consumed. One minute he was drawing the climaxes out of her, directing the pace, in control. The next moment he was defenseless against the way she took him, incoherent as she drove him into an intense, nearly unendurable orgasm. Yet he'd been locked outside her, forced to experience the sex without truly experiencing her. As amazing as it was, Jack felt strangely… bereft.

"You wreck me," he confessed, kissing her mouth, tasting himself on her. "Utterly." *Kiss.* "Completely." *Kiss.* "Devastatingly…" Jack sighed as her hand closed around him, thumb grazing delicately over the hypersensitive head, drawing another shudder from him as he kissed her mouth again. Samantha smiled against him before slipping off the bed and walking naked to the bathroom.

Jack took a minute to gather himself, trying to clear his head of the post-sex euphoria fog. He could hear her fiddling with the bathtub faucets, pouring a bath, even as she turned on the shower. He wondered at that as he stepped into the bathroom, watching the large tub fill. He followed her into the shower. She was soaping up, her body flushed and slick, her back to him. His eyes were immediately drawn to a slash along her side, long healed. Another smaller one, on her hip. He bit his lip as he reached out to touch it, his eyes gravitating to the bullet wound in her shoulder he'd seen on the boat. Jack pulled her into him, kissing the scar. Samantha tensed, as if waiting for him to ask her about it. He lifted his head.

"You shower before you bathe?" he asked instead, sensing her guard.

"That's for you," she told him over his shoulder. "Why don't you get in there and let me take care of you?" she suggested, turning in his arms. "I'm almost done here. Just give me a minute."

Jack blinked down at her, sluggishly processing. "You've taken care of me, Samantha. Better than I could have imagined," he murmured, pulling her toward him even as she pushed him gently back. He realized suddenly that she was distancing herself without appearing to. He could feel her withdrawal even as she smiled at him, soapy hands caressing his sides as she stepped back under the shower head, rinsing off. Whatever was happening, it unseated him, but he respected her request, retreating and settling into the tub as she'd asked. He leaned back, dousing his hair before coming back up and closing his eyes, trying not to overanalyze as hot water lapped against him, fragrant and soothing against his loose, aching muscles.

Jack heard the shower stop, heard her toweling her hair and body dry, but he kept his eyes closed, willing himself to stay pliant and relaxed. He felt Samantha slip behind him, her legs sliding around his shoulders as she sat at the edge of the tub. She must have found lotion in the bathroom, because she'd slicked her hands up, massaging his shoulders, neck and chest with sure, consistent strokes.

"Dear God," he groaned, dropping his head against her as she rubbed the column of his neck; she seemed to know all the right pressure points, unwinding and soothing him. "Where did you learn how to do this?" he asked on another long groan as she rubbed tension from his shoulder blades, once again making him feel heedless and sybaritic.

Samantha kissed his temple before drawing her thumbs behind his ears, massaging his head with soothing pressure. "Believe it or not, martial arts," she told him, cosseting him with her forearms as she massaged shampoo into his scalp, drawing him back against her stomach. "When you're learning vital strike points, you also learn the balance of the most pleasurable ones as well. Yin and yang philosophy." She found and rubbed a knot from his lats. "You worked out like a fiend today. You're bound to be tight from all that boxing. A cat could rub up against you right now and you'd be happy," she teased.

"If that's what we're calling your pussy, then yeah," he agreed. "You'd be right."

Samantha laughed softly, working his muscles for a while longer before he dunked down into the water, rinsing the shampoo from his hair and the soap from his body. Jack stood from the tub, accepting a heavy, plush towel from her, pleased with the way she admired him as he patted himself dry. When she moved to turn away, Jack stepped forward, tilting her face up for a kiss.

"I want you again," he murmured against her mouth. "Fire for fire, baby. You gave. Now you'll receive." He dropped the towel, slipping his hands around her and bringing her close within the band of his arms.

Samantha looked up at him with those dark, arresting eyes of hers. "What do you want?" she asked, her breath catching.

"I want you under me. Open for me. Will you let me in this time?" he asked, running his thumb slowly along her jawline.

She closed her eyes, fingers trailing along his stomach.

"Will you?" he asked again, tilting her chin up, forcing her to open her eyes and look at him.

They stared at each other for long moments until she slipped her arms around him, rising on her tip-toes to kiss him so thoroughly, Jack could do little else but give himself over to the sweet, piquant taste of her mouth.

CHAPTER 14

October—Early morning

The Pfister Hotel in Milwaukee, Wisconsin

JACK

SAMANTHA LAY ASLEEP on her side, facing him, her injured arm resting in front of her, leaving a space between them. Jack reached up to stroke her brow, touching lightly so he wouldn't wake her. He was exhausted and replete, uncharacteristically fighting sleep. But he stayed awake, wanting to look at her. Examine her beautiful body. Watch her unguarded face in repose.

As the early morning sun began to filter gently into the room, Jack looked his fill, touching her lightly, gently, here and there. Her skin was so soft, so supple, covering the sleek and disguised power of her muscles. He was beginning to doubt whether he'd ever tire of touching her, seeing her relaxed like this. Especially after hours of mutual, mind-blowing hedonistic worship. Samantha had absolute control of her body. She was its master, and it was her tool. She'd shown him again and again her power and her passion, driving him over the ledge as surely as she drove herself, relentless in her pursuit of their pleasure, taking the reins from him more often than not.

Jack was unused to her level of play, the constant give and take. He was accustomed to control, to directing the scenes. Samantha maneuvered their positions as seamlessly as he did, fucking him as much as he fucked her. He understood now what it felt like to be with an equal. A true sexual partner. There was no imbalance between them. She gave as good as she got. And it may have been the most memorable night of his life, joining the handful he'd had with her since they'd met. He marveled at that—how quickly things had changed in the short time he'd become close to her.

The room brightened slowly, and he noticed the bruising on her rib cage for the first time, evidence of her spar with Simon. Jack felt instantly angry and contrite. He recalled gripping her sides hard at the pinnacle, pistoning into her as if his life had depended on it. He wanted to hurt Simon for marking her, for looking at her, for sharing little jokes with her. He didn't care if it was irrational. It felt right to be furious for this damage to her body. He bent down, brushing a kiss against the bruise, his eyes finding the scars on her side and hip again. They were pale from age against the rest of her skin and marled; evidence that she'd been hurt badly, repeatedly. Anger heated him. As he caressed her scars, Samantha stiffened in sleep, murmuring as she shifted, her leg coming up, putting more space between them.

Jack looked up at her face. Her brows knit, eyes moving rapidly in REM. He wondered what she dreamed about as he began to fall asleep. What visions occupied the unconscious mind of a woman like Samantha Wyatt?

July 2006

Kabul, Afghanistan

SAMANTHA

LIEUTENANT COLONEL COLLINS had worked him over again. But it didn't matter. That wasn't why he was hurting. No amount of water boarding and asphyxiation could compare to the pain of withdrawal from four daily grams of the purest heroin in the Middle East. A casual user could manage happily on one gram a day at $150 a pop for the grade she was giving him. But for this man, this man she suspected was integral to Ibrahim Nazar's organization, she'd steadily worked his dosage up to a full-blown and crippling addiction. The kind of addiction that would take a lifetime to break, if he lived through it. Because he was that good. Good enough to relinquish very little truly valuable information even at the highest points of euphoria.

So now, during the week her country celebrated independence, she watched him writhe and shake on the floor of his cell, pressing his face tightly to the floor as he retched and moaned, begging to die to God and no one. He was still in the first twenty-four hours of his withdrawal, in excruciating agony, the stench of vomit and other bodily fluids he'd involuntarily released clogging the cell. She watched as Cartwright and Moon flinched at the smell, hosing him down as he lay on the ground quaking, pleading, even the feel of the water on his skin excruciating to his overwrought nerves. She wound the hijab around her head.

"Nazar is the money behind the Taliban," Collins told her. "This guy has the keys to the kingdom. The CIA believes Nazar is still here in Afghanistan. We need Mirwais to help us find him and shut him down before he can fund any more militants."

She nodded, stepping out of the control room and into one of the interrogation rooms.

Cartwright and Moon led the man calling himself Mirwais in, wet and shivering, forcing him into the chair facing her. She watched impassively as he crumpled over the table, cradling his head in anguish.

"Angel. Angel, you must show me mercy," he whispered in Persian, his body racked with his sobbing. "The pain—it's unbearable. *Unbearable.* I need you—I need you to help me," he pleaded brokenly, reaching a shaking hand across the table toward her.

"Tell me your name," she said softly, remaining just out of reach.

"Mirwais. I told you!" he cried out, convulsing. "Mirwais!"

She regarded him coolly, watching as he hit the side of his head with his palm once, twice, a third time, trying in vain to distract himself from the pain. She nodded to Cartwright and Moon, who came and held him down in his chair so he couldn't hurt himself again. She pulled a small black roll from her lap, placing it on the table beside her.

Like Pavlov, he gulped, his eyes widening. "Please. I'll tell you anything. Please just give it to me—"

"What is your name?" she asked again.

"Mirwais," he whispered brokenly, his green hazel eyes fixed to the bag, the striations more intense in his withdrawal, the skin around them sallow.

"You know," she began. "You have the most unusual eyes." She paused as he broke his longing stare long enough to look at her. "Such a beautiful color. But that's not the most interesting thing about them."

He dropped his eyes back down to the bag, straining toward it while trapped under the sure and steady hands of his captors.

"The striations in your irises are special. Genetic. An inherited trait," she continued in Persian. It was a guess. She'd only seen photos of Nazar from afar. But the one photo she had of this man and Nazar…there was a familiarity. The way they were holding their heads in conversation, close to each other. There were an intimacy there. She wondered… so she said it out loud, looking for a reaction. "Like father, like son."

His eyes snapped back to hers. The pleading desperation was dimmed only by the flash of something—something akin to fear and anger, mated into a single, painful realization. The look of prey when they know the jig is up.

"Who is Ibrahim Nazar to you?" she asked, touching the bag.

His eyes darted to the bag, then to her. His body quivered, as if he'd been left in ice with no clothes, no comfort.

"I have never hurt you," she reminded him. "I've given you something to help the pain every time you've asked."

"Please," he whispered. "Angel, my poppy—*please*. I'm begging you, Poppy," he said desperately. "Please, *please* give it to me."

"I cannot help you any longer if you don't tell me what I need to know," she continued. "What is your name?"

His gaze darted wildly, from her to the bag back to her and then to Cartwright and Moon, as if looking for an escape, a pressure release valve. Something. *Anything*.

"Who is Ibrahim Nazar to you?" she asked again, unrolling the bag. There were no more syringes, but he didn't know that. He was done getting relief. Now there would be only the awful, gnawing, continuous pain.

His eyes came back to hers: broken, angry, pleading.

She didn't move.

He managed to wait it out for another ten minutes before the pain and the anxiety became too much. When he finally broke, she didn't need to ask again.

"I am Arman! I am Arman Nazar!" he screamed, lunging toward her. "*I am his son!*"

October—Sunday morning

Pfister Hotel, Wisconsin

SAMANTHA

SHE CAME AWAKE with a jolt, sound trapped in her throat. Jack mumbled against her, drawing her closer to him, but she was coated in sweat, adrenaline coursing through her. Sam looked around wildly, recalling where she was, taking breaths in deep gulps while she tried to slow her heartbeat. She stared at Jack, still asleep, the morning light soft on his skin, casting shadows beneath his lashes.

"Just a dream," she whispered to herself. "It's just a dream." She moved her hand to touch her hip when she felt Jack's hand there, the warm clasp of his large palm against both scars. She slipped back quietly, trying not to wake him as she slid from the bed. Jack's brows drew together, his hand searching for her briefly before he settled again into sleep. Sam stood by the bed, holding her breath a few moments before padding into the bathroom and turning on the shower.

She stepped under the spray, pressing her palms to her eyes, trying to shake off the cloying apprehension from the nightmare. Her body was pleasantly sore, used and abused in the most delicious ways. As she soaped down, she allowed herself the luxury of remembering, covering the basest of memories with last night's erotic recollections.

"Give yourself to me, Samantha. Tell me you want…" he whispered as he slid over her. *"Take your pleasure,* tesoro…" *She lifted up against him, pushing and*

pulling him back by his hips and waist as he stroked into her with slick, satisfying *thrusts, teeth and tongue and breath against her neck as he panted, "It's amazing...* *you feel amazing... God, Samantha, it's so fucking good..."*

She touched her tender flesh, the water soothing. They'd been rough at first, passionate, the sexual tension of the weeks before driving their urgent, unrestrained mating. The farther they went, the more it morphed, the interplay eventually giving way to something sexier. A connection. A chemistry that went beyond the physical give-and-take of a simple, rough fuck between two strangers outrageously attracted to each other. Sam considered the way Jack watched her, with total absorption, focused on the moment. He'd been so completely and utterly *present*. The expression on his face while they'd made love had filled her with an unexpected and powerful warmth. Jack looked at her with intimacy. And for the first time in a long time...it didn't feel threatening.

Sam felt coolness enter the space as the shower door opened. Sam turned, watching Jack slide in next to her. He looked sleepy and obscene, his eyes hooded, the stubble on his jaw lending his near-prodigal handsomeness a rough edge.

"Am I allowed in this time?" he asked, voice husky with sleep.

She smiled lazily at him. "You were allowed in many, many times, you greedy, rapacious wolf."

"You forgot hedonistic. Greedy, rapacious, hedonistic wolf," he corrected, sliding his arms around her. "*Il tuo lupo.*"[7]

Sam's smile widened as she began soaping his chest, his arms.

"What time is it?" he groaned, his head falling back. "Why are we awake already?"

She glanced at her Cartier. "It's nearly nine thirty. That's a sleep in for me."

"I must not have worked hard enough," he murmured, nipping her neck. "I was aiming to keep you in bed for longer."

"Check out's at noon," she murmured, smiling.

Jack kissed her nose. "Why don't I order us a ridiculous breakfast in

---

[7] Italian for "your wolf."

bed?"

"That sounds perfect," she answered, her hand finding his cock. "But how about a detour on our way back?"

He leaned down to kiss her, smiling against her mouth. "Anywhere you want to go, *tesoro*. Just tell me where." Jack kissed down the curve of her throat.

Sam turned, pressing herself against the shower wall. "You're going to take me to heaven, Jack," she said, looking over her shoulder at him as he intertwined their fingers. "And then I'm going to take you to hell," she grinned.

Jack bit into her shoulder, making her shudder. "If last night was what hell feels like," he whispered into her ear. "I'll gladly go with you."

October—Sunday afternoon

The Whitney, Chicago

JACK

"I AM AN excellent cook," Jack declared as he pulled the groceries from her car, riding high after successfully convincing Sam to have dinner with him on the drive back from Milwaukee.

"How did you come about this skillset?" she asked, smirking like she'd have to see it to believe it.

"Dad," he answered readily. "Mom's pretty great too—they actually make a great team in the kitchen. Her family are from Napoli and his people are—"

"Roman?" Sam guessed, laughter in her eyes.

Jack threw his arm around her shoulders, squeezing her to his side as they walked toward the elevator. "Okay, smartass. Prepare to have your taste buds wowed. You didn't know Little Italy was off of Grant Park, did you?"

"I'm kind of embarrassed about serving you reheated stew now," Sam told him, stepping into the elevator.

Jack kissed her hair. "Don't be. Second best sleep of my life."

"And the first?"

His mouth stretched wide in a lecherous grin.

"Jesus, you're easy to please," Sam chuckled. "I need to check in for a bit. When would you like me darkening your door?"

"How's seven?"

She nodded, giving him a quick kiss before she disappeared inside her apartment.

October—Sometime before 7:00 p.m.

The Whitney, Chicago

JACK

"HMMM...MORE BUTTER and sage," he thought out loud, tasting the veal saltimbocca. Jack added ingredients, checking on the *gnocchi alla sorrentina*, his mother's recipe. He sipped his Barolo, a firm believer that if you were going to cook Italian, you had to drink Italian. And play Sinatra. For inspiration, of course. Just like his parents had taught him. He was flipping the record when his concierge called up.

"Ms. Holland is here for you, sir."

Jack frowned. "I'm busy at the moment. Could you ask her to give me a call tomorrow?"

"I'm sorry, sir. She's already on her way up," the concierge apologized, unused to the sudden change in protocols.

Jack let out a frustrated sigh. "Okay. Just make sure you get the go-ahead from me in the future before you send anyone besides Jaime or Mitch up."

"Got it, sir. Sorry."

Rebecca's knock sounded at the door. Jack hung up the phone before swinging the door open. "Rebecca. What are you doing here?" He glanced at Samantha's door over her shoulder.

Rebecca's brows knit. She tossed her strawberry hair over her shoulder. "Christ, Jack. It's nice to see you too."

He instantly felt contrite. She deserved better than that. "Sorry," he sighed. "I'm just busy at the moment," he told her.

She glanced at the kitchen, sniffing. "No kidding. It smells amazing," she said, slipping her cashmere coat off and handing it to him after setting down a bag. She was wearing a see-through lace turtleneck and skintight jeans. She looked beautiful, but she was not the beautiful woman he wanted in his place right now.

Jack frowned at her back as he shut the door. *Did she think she was staying?*

"Rebecca, what can I do for you?"

She turned, picking up her Louis Vuitton duffel. "I came to get my things. This week will be pretty hectic with shooting. I've asked the director to wrap my scenes faster so I can get started with my next project," she explained lightly, though her eyes looked sad.

"Rebecca—" Jack started, setting her coat down.

"No," she interrupted, holding her hand up to stop him. "I don't want to hear any platitudes."

"Rebecca, I was going to have your things couriered," Jack said instead.

She shook her head. "I don't want wind of this out before my PR gets ahold of it. I dumped you, by the way," she informed him, moving into the living room.

Jack nodded. "I'm okay with that," he replied, trying to be placating even as he wondered how to get her out. *Just please, please get out of my house now,* he willed her silently.

Rebecca spun on him, her pretty blue eyes hurt. "I just can't believe you're so willing to set aside what we've shared. I know we weren't together very long, but I thought it was amazing, Jack." She pushed her hair back, her expression equal parts smarting and befuddled. "I don't understand how you can drop us like we were nothing."

Jack took a breath, searching for the right thing to say. "Rebecca, I think we're seeing this from different places," he told her gently.

"Clearly," she replied, her brow arched as she transitioned from hurt to *pissed* within seconds. "I'm a goddamn fool." She spun, marching upstairs.

"*Fuck*," Jack groaned, wiping a hand down his face. He glanced at his watch. Samantha would be over in ten minutes if she were on time. He jogged up his stairs.

Rebecca was hastily shoving toiletries into her bag. Jack glanced around, wondering what else she may have left so he could help her get the hell out of his place faster.

"Can I help?" he asked.

She stopped, laughing softly as she peered at him. "I think you've done enough."

"Rebecca," he sighed, watching her from the doorway of the bathroom. "For what it's worth, I'm sorry I hurt you."

She closed her eyes for a moment. "I know, Jack." She strode into his walk-in, pulling down a couple of negligees and opening one of his drawers to remove gorgeous, slinky pieces of La Perla and Agent Provocateur he'd once delighted in pulling off of her like she was a perfectly wrapped present. Rebecca glanced around the drawer. "Where's my corset?"

Jack's brow furrowed. "Corset?"

She rolled her eyes. "The royal blue one you gave me. You don't remember?"

Jack scanned through his recollections of all the sexy lingerie Rebecca had worn in the months they'd dated. He was having trouble filtering out visions of Samantha, memories of Rebecca already fading like wisps in the background. "I'll have my housekeeper look for it. I can have a courier send it over when she finds it."

She nodded sharply, grabbing a couple more things and shoving them hastily into the duffel before sweeping out of his suite. Jack followed her, eyeing his watch again. It would be nearly impossible to avoid a head-on collision with Samantha now. *Not good. Very not good.*

Rebecca's attention snapped to the kitchen as she came down the stairs, her sharp inhalation catching Jack's attention as he nearly ran into her. Samantha sat at his table just as she had the other night, dark hair up in a loose knot, a sweater casually falling off her shoulder, working on his *New York Times* crossword puzzle and sipping from his wine glass as if it were just another Sunday.

Rebecca flipped around to face him, eyes narrowed. "You have a lot of goddamned nerve lying to me like that."

Jack tore his gaze from Samantha, who put down the crossword to watch them calmly. "I didn't lie. I've never lied to you."

Samantha stood, moving toward the door.

"Samantha, don't leave," Jack called to her. "Rebecca was just gathering her things."

"You *asshole*," Rebecca snapped. "You told me you hadn't started things with her. You sat there and lied to my face."

"I didn't lie—" Jack saw Samantha swing open his door. "Samantha, don't leave," he said again, moving past Rebecca to move swiftly down the stairs.

Samantha turned, her expression cool. "You look like you need to get your house in order, Jack. I'll leave you to it."

"Samantha—" He grasped her shoulder. "I ended things with Rebecca before Milwaukee."

"Milwaukee?" Rebecca asked from behind him. "What are you talking about? I *just* saw you."

Samantha looked at him, her gaze assessing. Then she looked at Rebecca, who was seething behind him. "That doesn't change the fact that you need to sort your shit out," she told him calmly, slipping out his door before he had a chance to stop her.

"*Shit!*" Jack whirled on Rebecca, advancing as she stepped back. "All right, let's get a few things straight. First, I *never* committed to you. We were having fun. I thought we were on the same page, and I never tried to mislead you on that score. Secondly, I *did not* lie to you!" he spat out, pointing at her. "I wasn't seeing Samantha while we were together." He walked back to his front door, opening it. "Please leave, Rebecca. You can tell the world you ended it, fine, but no ridiculous slander. We had an adult relationship. Now goddamn act like it!" He swept his hand out the door, waiting for her to walk through it.

Rebecca's mouth opened, closed…opened.

Jack lifted a hand, cutting her off at the pass. "I'll have a courier send you anything else that belongs to you this week," he told her.

"Now, seriously—please just leave."

Rebecca snatched up her coat, shoving her arms through it, massacring him with her eyes. "You don't screw a woman like you did me for *months* and then just turn to the next one, Jack. There's such a thing as karma."

Jack's chin jutted up. "Good thing you're not in charge of it, then."

She picked up her duffel, stepping past him with her shoulders squared. "I'm beginning to wonder what the hell I ever saw in you."

"Likewise," he replied, slamming the door.

CHAPTER 15

October—Wednesday lunch

West Village, New York City

SAMANTHA

"HEY, SAMMY—YOU all right?" Carey asked, setting his papers down on the restaurant table.

Sam was staring out into space, her thoughts drifting back to Sunday evening and Jack's frantic voicemail. *"I'm sorry. That was mortifying. Please, please let me in. Or come over. Just...I need to see you."*

"You've been head-in-the-clouds all morning. You want to review these proposals or what?"

Sam snapped out of it, realizing she'd been staring out over the tables at Sushi Nakazawa toward the front door like she was waiting for Jack to walk in. Her cheeks colored as if she'd been caught watching porn at work. She shook her head, a rueful smile on her face. "Sorry, Bear. Too little sleep. Could you repeat that?" she asked, sipping her tea.

They'd decided to meet over a late lunch after client appointments all morning. Given the mid-afternoon timing, there were only a few idle diners, giving them privacy and the run of the place.

Carey regarded her, shrewd gaze assessing. He crossed his arms after a moment, leaning on the table toward her. "You want to talk about it?" he asked, his voice low.

Sam shrugged. "Nothing to talk about unless you like listening to a woman's worries," she replied, thanking the waiter as he refilled her cup.

"I know we just started this, but Samantha, it's already more than I've experienced with anyone else. Call me. Come see me. Please." She'd listened to his

voicemails a couple times before deleting them. She still hadn't decided what she was going to do with him when she returned to Chicago.

"Give me the request for the proposal?" she asked, pointing at the paperwork sitting next to his elbow.

Carey's brow furrowed. "Sammy, I say this with love, but you're full of shit if you think it isn't perfectly obvious that you're totally distracted and it's not due to lack of sleep."

Sam said nothing, continuing to hold out her hand for the sheaf of papers.

He sighed, handing them to her as he walked through the details. "NBS wants to do a primetime feature on Rio de Janeiro with the World Cup and Olympics coming up. Rick Landiss, the executive producer, wants to walk us through the specifics once they figure out the crew, but it sounds like a four-part feature on the socioeconomic and political situation in Rio before the Games. They have a tentative timeline of two months out."

"Why does he want us?" she murmured, riffling through the contract. "He has basic security on payroll already."

Carey nodded. "Normally, that would be fine, but he wants to hire freelance to work with some established anchors, and he knows those types of photojournalists don't take kindly to the babysitters they normally employ. He also hinted at needing people who could provide translation and assistance with local contacts."

"So NBS wants security who can blend in with journalists, speak Portuguese, and have contacts in Rio they can leverage to get the difficult interviews." Sam thought about it a moment. "I'd say Rush, Talon, and Michaelson for sure. What do you think?"

"Rush is ready to take a lead role now," Carey agreed. "And he's easy to get along with, so it's more likely he'd be a good fit. Talon on background security and sharpshooting makes sense. Why Michaelson?"

She shrugged. "I can think of a couple good reasons. First, he needs to do a hands-on gig without us, see how the guys typically operate. Second, who else would be better for negotiating the nightmare clusterfuck they call a road system in Brazil?" she pointed out. "He'd be perfectly positioned to lead transport and teach some of the guys a few things."

"I like it," Carey agreed, sitting back as the waiter delivered their dishes.

Sam's mouth watered as she looked over the hay-smoked skipjack and the tender sea scallops.

"How many pieces we get here?" Carey asked.

"Twenty-one pieces total, hand selected by Chef Nakazawa," she replied, picking up a piece with her chopsticks.

"Christ," he groaned. "I'll need a burger after this. How can this be enough?" Carey groaned, biting into his nigiri. Then he groaned for another reason. "Forget it. I'll just order three more helpings of this heaven," he sighed in pleasure.

"How many people do they anticipate will be on the ground?" she asked.

"Anywhere between ten and fifteen," Carey answered.

"Okay," she nodded. "Build the proposal around those three guys running point. When does Landiss want to meet?"

"Mid-November."

"Who else is bidding?" Sam asked.

Carey scooped up a wad of ginger, tossing it in his mouth. "Lord, this is good," he sighed. The waiter hastily cleared their dishes, setting down succulent pieces of medium-fatty tuna touched with Japanese mustard over cloud puffs of white rice. "Leviathan was approached peripherally, like us, but nothing definitive. I think it'll be a two-horse race."

"They're going to love that we're stealing their people *and* their clients," Sam smirked.

"By the way, Kurt made good. Avi Oded finally returned my call," Carey informed her, biting into his sushi.

"Really? You two got a meet set?" she asked, knowing how badly Carey had wanted to recruit the ex-Israeli Sayeret Matkal operative.

"Better than that. He's going to be here in New York on Friday, visiting his daughter. I'd like to give him an offer. Take a look," he said, handing her his tablet.

Sam kept half her attention on Carey's chopsticks, preventing him from reaching them over the lip of her plate to snag her tuna while she reviewed the contract. Carey had been stealing food from her plate for as long as she could remember. *Probably one of the reasons he'd grown so damn big*, she thought to herself, eyes skimming through the offer.

"Whoa, that's a big number," she murmured, reading the draft of Oded's financial package. "You want to bring Oded in at Michaelson's level?"

"Well, yeah," Carey shrugged, spearing the mackerel the waiter had set down after clearing the previous dish. "He's one of the top counter-terrorism and hostage rescue guys from the Israeli Defense Force. We don't have another specialist in deep recon at his level. Think of the team he could develop and train up. It'd be another sound investment."

"Why's he interested in jumping ship?" she asked, wondering if Avi Oded was being set up as good-looking bait from Leviathan now that they were losing men to her left and right.

"Kurt said he was asked to go to Afghanistan for the Nazar gig too. Apparently, Oded told them to shove the assignment and took an indefinite vacation to St. Tropez."

Her brows rose. "Nice middle finger."

"Kurt figures he'll be quitting anyway. Might as well get while the getting is good," Carey reasoned.

"How many more are Michaelson and Henri talking into coming over?" she asked, sipping her tea.

"At least four more high profile ex-Special Forces guys from various countries. I feel like I'm reading profiles on one of those dating websites," Carey grinned. "And I want them all."

"Got a lot of experience with that, do you?" she teased, handing him back his tablet.

Carey colored, distracting himself with yet another piece of sushi, this time wild yellowtail from Hokkaido.

"You and Willa still good?" she asked.

He glanced up, a big, happy smile on his mouth.

"Carrick Nelson. Why I do believe you are in love," Sam chuckled. "You've got that doe-eyed look about you."

"Doe, my ass," he looked affronted. "I'm a twelve-point buck, at least."

"Hmm. We'll see what Willa has to say about that," she replied archly.

"Does this mean we get to talk about relationships now? Because if we're going there, I'd like to know how Milwaukee was."

Sam rolled her eyes. "You get to ask me about my sex life never."

"Hey—you started it."

"What are you, five?" she smirked. "Besides, Willa's my girl. You hardly know Jack."

"I know him well enough to know he wanted to kill Simon with his bare hands last Saturday," Carey responded.

"So he's got an over-developed sense of chivalry," she responded, fiddling with her teacup.

"Uh, no. That's not what that was. *Christ*, you're blind," Carey huffed.

"Really? What am I missing then?"

"That guy's gone over you. He's been in deep since the day we went sailing at least."

She thought about Jack's text this morning: *"Where are you, Samantha? I've left you half a dozen messages. Please come over. I want a redo of what we missed out on Sunday. Talk to me. Please."*

"It's casual. Nothing. Hell, it's probably already over," Sam admitted after a moment, wondering where the hell the words were coming from. She never talked about this kind of stuff with Carey.

The waiter brought tiger shrimp on delicate white plates.

"Why?" Carey asked, watching her.

She picked up her sushi. "I'm not exactly Ms. Commitment," she replied, biting into her shrimp. "And he's got women taking numbers to get in line at his door like a deli counter."

"Bullshit," Carey spluttered, laughing.

Sam rolled her eyes. "And what makes you so sure about that?"

Carey lifted his phone, grinning. "Cause he won't stop texting me asking when you're coming back."

She chuckled. "Now you're my dating answering service? My how the mighty have fallen."

Carey downed his tiger shrimp in a single gulp. "Only desperation gets a guy to contact the best friend."

"He had Rebecca Holland at his place on Sunday when he was supposed to be making me dinner. Hardly desperate, I'd say."

Carey's eyes widened. "He's got some balls."

She shrugged. "No big deal. Just a bit of fun."

Carey watched her until she lifted her brows. He held up his hands. "None of my business."

"Exactly," she murmured. "You see Marvin loaded up my meetings in Asia? I think I'll leave Chicago on Friday or Saturday since I'll lose a day traveling."

Carey nodded. "Marvin's got you scheduled for two weeks' worth of meetings now, right? You want me to fly over after I meet with Oded?"

Sam shook her head. "Nah. Hold down the fort in Chicago and keep your eye on London. I'll be meeting with the usual clients in Hong Kong and Singapore. Hopefully picking up a couple new ones in Japan and Korea on the return leg."

Their waiter set down two gorgeous pieces of Alaskan ivory king salmon. Carey issued a little moan of excitement over his favorite sushi. She loved how easily Carey found joy, just like when he'd been a boy. Sam smiled into her tea cup.

"What?" he asked, looking at her with bright, happy eyes, the sushi halfway to his mouth.

"Thank you, Bear," she told him quietly.

"For what?" he asked, his face a question mark as he chewed, his chopsticks inching toward her piece of salmon.

For being you, for being my best friend, my brother, my right-hand...

"For not eating my piece," she smiled, popping the second piece of salmon into her mouth.

October—Thursday night

The Whitney, Chicago

SAMANTHA

SAM WALKED INTO her bedroom, shedding her dress and unwinding her hair from the French twist she'd worn all day. She'd had what felt like a long, endless week of prospective clients to acquire, distressed clients to dispense with, reports on her division's progress, pending promotions, budgets, issues… It was all exhausting, and she had even more ahead of her in Asia tomorrow. She considered bathing and sleeping, but she was too wired and restless to lay down.

You've been avoiding him all week.

Sam admitted to herself that she missed him. Actually missed seeing him, talking to him, his touch… *Dear God, his touch.* She'd always been so good about taking her pleasures while remaining separate; affectionate but uninvolved. But this…*this* was proving too difficult to ignore in the usual way. Sam was craving him, addicted after one evening of the long and luxurious hit that was Jack Roman.

He'd sent her flowers each day this week, according to the concierge. It was a lovely, traditional gesture that both surprised and seduced her when she walked into her penthouse. There was decadently fragrant jasmine interwoven with orange blossoms, stunning, highly cultivated orchids, dramatic and heady magnolias, and ambrosial, blush-tipped peonies that smelled so luscious, she'd closed her eyes as she'd breathed them in.

Each day a new set of flowers… Each day a new note on heavy linen card stock, neatly followed by a bold, scrawling "-*J.*"

Monday: *You're intoxicating.*

Tuesday: *Everywhere, small reminders. How you look, how you taste, your scent. I couldn't stop thinking of you if I tried.*

Wednesday: *I'm waiting for you.*

Thursday: *Come to me.*

Sam glanced at her watch. It was just after eleven. She wanted to go to him, knew he'd be waiting for her, but she was apprehensive, unsure of what it meant to already miss him, to want him this badly when she'd become so good at not wanting anyone or anything too much. Not wanting anything made her good at her job. She always had the upper hand, and having few vulnerabilities kept her calm under the inevitable pressures. But there was something so deliciously alluring about walking the knife's edge with Jack, of allowing herself the pleasure of being near him while trying not to fall into the crucible of his heat.

Sam considered why she was so taken with him, examining the puzzle pieces of what she knew about him in the short time they'd spent together. Jack didn't downplay himself or over amp. He was smart without the pretentiousness; affable and humorous with the right amount of self-deprecation. He was aware of his attractiveness without being shameless about it. But what she liked most, what she was most surprised by, was how thoroughly he lived life without simply languishing on his good fortune and family name. Rather, he enhanced that fortune, working around the conventions that came with his family ties with a slight rebelliousness that was so subtle, one might never see past the high polish he was so good at presenting. In the quiet moments she'd spent getting to know him, she liked that Jack was so unexpectedly grounded despite all the trappings. She could see why women flocked to him, even beyond the physical gratification and the spoils. She couldn't blame Rebecca for her lapse of composure at losing him. Jack Roman was the real deal, the total package. Any woman would be lucky to have him. And she did have him. For now…

Sam took a deep breath, finding her swimsuit and slipping into it, wondering if her regular nighttime swim would be enough to draw him out and if she would be disappointed if it didn't. While she wasn't entirely ready to step up to his door and announce herself, she wasn't going to alter her routines in favor of avoiding him. In fact, if she got very lucky, Jack would save her the effort and come to her. A short, wonderful interlude before she hit the road again in the morning.

The pool was dark and silent, steam rising gently as she turned on the lights. The autumn night air was chilly, making the pool feel warm like bath water. She floated, enjoying it for a moment, before diving underwater, swimming up from the bottom quickly to begin her ritual.

Would he come?

He'll come, her confidence assured her.

But if he doesn't? Her heart asked in kind.

He will.

And if he does?

Sam flipped, kicking out fast, her heart racing.

And if he does…?

Sam breathed deep, launching into a smooth breaststroke, bracing against the cold air before sluicing back into the warm saltwater of the pool. She lost track of the strokes, focusing on form and movement, loosening muscles tight from a day of sitting in endless meetings and the quiet flight home. As she finally slowed, she saw Jack standing at the edge of the pool, watching her with eyes so pale, they reflected the pool lights.

Sam dipped back, pushing her hair over her shoulders before swimming to the edge where he stood, smiling at her with that sexy grin of his. He knelt to his haunches, running a hand down the side of her face as he wiped the wetness off one cheek with his thumb.

"Did you come back to me? Or was it just the allure of a swim?" he asked, tilting her face upward. Jack leaned forward, kissing her gently before drawing back a fraction, waiting for her answer.

"The pool," she answered, turning her face to capture his thumb, giving it quick bite. "I missed the pool," she teased, lowering back down until only her eyes were above water.

He was wearing his late-night uniform of dark lounge pants and a soft tee. Jack gazed at her for a moment before stripping down to dark boxer briefs. She admired his beautiful, athletic body illuminated by the reflections from the pool before he slipped into the water, moving toward her slowly. Jack circled her before ducking underwater. He slid his hands up over her legs first, sliding up her waist and back, his mouth finding hers before he'd even fully emerged from the water. His kiss was hot and dazzling.

She wound her arms around his neck, indulging in the sleek feel of his mouth, the tangle of tongues. *Oh, but could this man kiss.* Sam could feel her limbs grow languid, her body relaxing into him as she relinquished herself to the undercurrent that dragged her closer to him.

"You make me feel edgeless," she murmured into his mouth.

"Likewise," he whispered.

"Being with you…" She slid her hands over the slopes of his shoulders, her legs riding up to hitch over his hips under the water. "Feels so easy, almost visceral," she confessed.

"And you don't like it?" he asked, kissing the hollow of her throat.

"I don't like anything that feels involuntary," she answered, leaning her head back to gaze at the stars over Chicago.

Jack kissed a path down to her breastplate. "You aren't feeling anything I'm not experiencing too, Samantha." His hand slid up between her shoulder blades, drawing up the back of her neck and into her hair. He brought her face back down to his. "I missed you," he whispered against her mouth. "Did you miss me?" he asked with a slow smile, the curve of his mouth sweet and indecent.

Sam didn't respond, and Jack's arms tightened fractionally around her.

"You have a tell too," he whispered, watching her. "When you feel the most, you say the least," he told her.

Jack held her for long, quiet minutes, smoothly circling them round and round in the warm water, gentle drifts of steam rising around them in the dim light. She allowed her muscles to loosen in his arms, enjoying the rare sensation of being held in suspension.

"I've barely slept all week," he confessed. "And when I did, I kept dreaming you were there. I'd be holding you, touching you, and then I'd wake up and realize you were just a dream, a figment. But each time—it felt…" Jack took a quick breath, his eyes lowering to her mouth. "It felt like I'd been robbed of something."

"An orgasm perhaps?" she teased, running her fingers through the wet waves of his hair.

He laughed softly. "That too."

"Tell me about your week," she asked as he swirled them gently in the water, distracting him, distracting herself.

"Mmmm," he groaned, tucking his face into her neck. "Endless meetings on residential and commercial zoning, union contracts, rising prices on steel." He punctuated each statement with a kiss to her neck. "Very little sleep and *a lot* of running and boxing to work out my…*frustration*." He clasped her hips, hands sliding down to her bottom and tilting her up so she could feel his frustration in living color.

"Frustration, huh?" she arched an eyebrow, rocking gently against him, the movement languid and sinuous in the water. "You must be worn out then," she teased. "Overwrought and exhausted from a week of unsatisfying dreams…"

Jack groaned as she bit into this earlobe, tongue teasing the hurt she caused ever so gently. He let her explore him, her fingers slipping over the wet musculature and tensile texture of his body. She didn't linger anywhere, kept her touch light and teasing.

He shuddered, holding her closer. "All week I've felt off. After you left Sunday, I thought it was over, before it even really started—"

Sam cut him off, kissing him with a little pent up frustration of her own. Jack followed her lead, kissing back like he hadn't seen her in weeks, hands tightening to hold her in place as he slanted his mouth over hers. He peeled off her suit in the water and she shivered, her body tense with anticipation. Jack lifted her up in his arms, carrying her from the pool and to his side of the terrace, through the heavy, lead glass doors of his private balcony. His fireplace was on, flickering gently, casting a hazy, golden glow around the room. She wondered dazedly if he planned on laying her out in front of it, but instead he carried her upstairs and into his bedroom, a masculine suite appointed in warm colors.

Jack laid her on a massive bed piled high with quilts and downy pillows. *The bed of a sensualist,* she thought, bemused. Her wet hair spread behind her as she laid back, watching him peel off his soaked briefs before he stretched out on top of her, coming to rest between the cradle of her thighs. He replaced the chill of the air with his hot, smooth skin, touching his tongue to the valley between her breasts, working his way back up to her neck with biting little kisses lined with edge and need.

"I missed you," Jack whispered again, brushing his mouth against the underside of her jawbone, sliding his forearms underneath her shoulder blades, his hands warm and encompassing. "I only had one night with you, and it wasn't nearly enough," he confessed. "What the hell is happening to me?" he seemed to ask himself.

She laughed quietly, nuzzling his face. "Good sex does that to any-one."

Jack pulled up to stare down at her. "I've had good sex, Samantha," he told her seriously. "That was…something else entirely."

She didn't know how to respond to that, so she slid her hands into his hair, thumbs massaging his temples as she brought his head down toward her. Sam suckled his lip, biting him gently before administering a soothing swirl. Jack groaned, seeking to get deeper, searching her mouth slowly with agile swipes of his sweet, delicious tongue. Sam felt saturated with sensation, limbs loose and lethargic. Jack kissed like he was speaking a language to her, some secret, shared communication. Each kiss felt a little reckless and fierce, his mouth hot and demanding. Her fingers tightened and fisted in his hair until he issued a hard growl, nipping her in retaliation. And she loved it. *God, how she loved it.*

Jack muttered something fervent before bending his head to one breast, the pad of his tongue hot as he glided across and flicked the tip, tugging firmly. His teeth grazed over her nipples ever so slightly—a little jagged edge to accompany that soothing wet lash. There was enough pain and pleasure to make her shudder and groan, her abdomen and thighs tightening with each pull and stroke. Sam groaned when he kissed a path down to her belly, gripping his hair tightly again, her hips tilting forward to try to capture him, seeking heat, friction and satisfaction.

When he looked up at her, expression tight with want, she told him in on a rasp, "I need you now, Jack. I need you hard and a little rough."

He pulled back, seated on his haunches, eyes darkening as he slid his hands down her legs and up under her knees. He yanked her down the bed so swiftly she didn't have time to react before he neatly flipped her onto her stomach, pulling her up to her knees as he pressed her down to the bed with a firm hand between her shoulder blades.

Sam felt a trill of excitement rocket down her spine, wondering if he had seen the wetness slip delicately on the inside of her thigh. He had. The next moment, he was licking her, lapping up the tang of her arousal, the bristles on his jaw rasping against the tender skin of her inner thighs. Jack licked her from clit to the tight rosette of her ass, hooking a long finger into her as he rubbed her sweet spot, drawing a long, keening moan from her as she rocked back against him, seeking more pressure, more friction, more of *something…just…more, more…*she chanted, her eyes squeezed shut.

"Fuck, I need this," he gasped against her ass, lashing his tongue against her vulva. "Why do I need you so bad? You're making me crazy," he muttered, kneading and pressing her clit as he tongued her entrance, pulling her hips up higher, nearly lifting her knees off his bed in his urgency.

"Jesus, Jack. Do it," she moaned. "Make me feel it. Make me feel you."

His mouth was so hot, so incredibly urgent as he maneuvered his tongue with his fingers to work her into the first of tight spasms. She was so enveloped in the continuous, unfurling ripples she barely noticed him prepare himself, ripping a foil packet and lubing himself lightly with her wetness. But she felt the low and heavy penetration, the warmth and tingle making her ultra-sensitive tissues undulate around him as he pushed through her channel. Sam felt tight, so tight and swollen from the stimulation, every ridge and vein of him making her edges flutter.

"*Yesss…*" she hissed as Jack rocked into her, tilting his pelvis up at the end of each erotic push to rub her so exactly, so perfectly right that she nearly reared up off the bed, blood thrumming as she felt each surge Jack made with Technicolor brilliance. "Jesus Christ, *yesss, Jack… God, it's perfect. So perfect…*" she groaned while he worked her so thoroughly, pleasured her so completely, Sam was awash in mindless, glorious sensation.

Tonight, Jack was masterful, and oh-so-thoroughly controlled. He didn't pound into her as she'd anticipated, forcing another orgasm from her like a hard and punishing surrender. Instead, he encircled, surrounded, tantalized, sliding and stroking her deep, serving her relentlessly, using his strength and skill to incense her again and again until she was lost, adrift in throb and pulse and breath, crying out her release in soft pants, the spasms of pleasure surrounding, crashing, absorbing.

He withdrew slowly, turning her over to face him, arranging her legs around him, one hitched at his hip and the other braced over the crook of his elbow, plying her open to his perusal, a prurient vision. Her breath hitched as she looked up at him, at the dark flush on his spectacular cheekbones, the silver eyes that stared so intensely back at her.

"Tell me what you want," he whispered, reaching a hand forward to run it down her sensitized and overheated body. "Tell me and I can give it to you. I'll make sure you have what you're thinking of…over and over again. Just say it, Samantha. Tell me what you need," he urged, his thumb strumming her sex, making her writhe again as he nudged within the constriction of her body, tantalizing her, teasing.

Sam knew instinctively that he wanted more than she was offering— a moment's respite, an erotic, self-indulgent foray with a sexy, midnight lover. She considered refusing him, realizing there was something growing powerful and latent between them, something that required negotiation, some kind of compromise... Jack didn't want to take her, to fuck her into mindless acquiescence. He wanted her to say yes to him: to ask, to plead, to tell him she needed him.

Sam pushed up on her elbows, reached up to run fingers down the handsome lines of his face, feeling the scrape of the day's bristle, the intense heat of his skin. Jack pressed his mouth into her palm, eyes fastened on her, hypnotic as he stroked the bell head of his thick cock in and out of her with minute movements, waiting on her, listening for her words. Sam brought his face down to her, kissing him gently before biting his lip hard enough to draw blood. Jack snapped back, startled, a small smear of dark red on his full, wet lip.

She smiled. "I believe I said rough."

Jack's expression darkened as he wrenched her to him with the leg he had curled over his arm, pinning her down with his other as he impaled her with a heavy stroke, the muscle ticking in his jaw. Sam gripped his arms, nails biting into his skin as she groaned, urging him to *do it, take it, take her the way she needed*, but he fastened a firm hand against her, forcing her to follow, refusing her body's harsh demands as he thrust tirelessly, the downward penetration deep, wringing all the sensation from his motion. The low drag of that long cock was maddening against her nerve endings and Sam arched after long minutes of this torture, fracturing on a low cry.

He laughed as she clenched against him, overwhelmed and over-come, trying futilely to clamp her knees to his hips as he held her open, riding out her release as long jolts came through her in jarring shudders, his name an incantation as she flung her head back helplessly again and again.

Jack hoisted her up, pliant and groaning, setting another remarkable rhythm, drawing her down as he came up, every action a controlled counter. He muttered curses and chants with each bias of movement, gripping her to him, touching her again though she couldn't imagine finding the stamina to have another climax. Sam twisted against him, holding his thickly muscled wrist to still him, but he just pushed them down to the bed so his hand was trapped against her as he worked her in fast, hard strokes of his cock and hand.

"Jack, *Christ*, it's too much—*I can't*—" she gasped, trying to stave off the climax, the pleasure nearly excruciating, as he ruthlessly stoked the sensations, staring down at her with glittering eyes.

"You'll come for me again," he promised, teeth gritted as he rooted deep, over and over until she was gasping and desperate, uncertain if this was pain or pleasure, if she wanted him to capture and hold her like this or release and let her go.

"*Jaaack*," she groaned. "*Please just…please…*" she muttered incoherently, moving her hand from his wrist to his fingers, helping him rub her off exactly right, with that perfect amount of pressure, while they both worked furiously toward the rise.

"I'm taking what I want, Samantha," he bit out, as he stared down at her. "Now. *Come now*," he commanded as his self-control splintered and he powered into her, hips snapping forward as his head flung back, lost in the wake of his own ferocious orgasm. Sam was sucked into his undertow, lost in the ebb and flow of their movement, riding that long, delicious wave that rippled from her core. Jack drove deep and held, squeezing her as his shudders began to abate, her name a hoarse recitation. *Samantha—Fuck. Fuck, yes…*

Samantha…

They held onto each other for a long time afterward, bodies cooling as their breaths calmed. Jack said nothing, gave nothing away, but Sam could sense his pensiveness, still cradled inside her warmth, his breath a gentle puff against her collarbone. She pressed her fingers into his head, neck, and shoulders, finding his individual pressure points and kneading through the remaining tension. She felt him gradually relax against her, drowsily shifting to press small, tender kisses to her breast, and she watched as his eyes drift closed, dark lashes heavy, the days of accumulated exhaustion taking over and dragging him into the respite of sleep.

Sam held him for a long time, enjoying his nearness while she was lost in her own thoughts, finally succumbing to the languor enough to doze. As early morning light crept over Chicago's horizon, she opened her eyes to watch the dusty pink and orange rays climb through the still-dark sky before slipping from his loosened arms.

October—Friday morning

The Whitney, Chicago

JACK

JACK'S EYES OPENED slowly, registering the distant sound of his alarm. He groaned, stretching widely, his hands tucked deep under his pillows. He felt…amazing. The sunlight touched the bed, warming him. He sat up on his elbows, quickly aware that he was alone. Knocking back his covers, he turned off his alarm as he swung his legs over. Five or six hours at least, he realized as he glanced at the time. Unheard of.

"Samantha," he called out, rubbing a hand over his face, wincing as he touched his lip. He walked to the bathroom, examining the slight swell in the mirror. Sam's mark. And her resistance. Jack's mood darkened as he realized she'd gone. He splashed water on his face, pulling on some pants before heading downstairs. The pot was on, the waft of hot coffee delicious. Like before, he saw a note folded up in a coffee mug. He plucked it out, wishing she hadn't left.

Jack,

You're breathtaking. Our time was…incredible. I'll never forget it.

-S

He blinked, rereading it. "What the fuck does that mean?" he asked aloud in the emptiness of his apartment. He picked up his phone to call her, but somehow, Jack knew she wouldn't answer.

CHAPTER 16

End of October—Two weeks later

Chicago Midway Airport, Private Jet Terminal

SAMANTHA

"S AM, YOU NEED to get to the gym," Rush told her, his tone urgent. She could hear shouting and whistling behind his voice on the phone.

"Why? What's going on?" she asked, tossing her bag into the passenger seat of the 'vette, tipping the valet at the private jet terminal. She'd just landed from a thirteen-hour flight from Tokyo, where she'd spent the better part of the week in meetings with clients and courting new prospects. The very last thing she wanted to do was watch amateur fighters duke it out at the gym tonight.

"It's Jack," Rush continued, sounding stressed. "He had Manny set up a fight tonight with one of the amateurs in his weight class. Vic Vidal. I've seen this guy fight. Not for nothing, but he's going to annihilate Jack." Sam had never heard the usually laid-back Rush sound truly worried. Now she realized he had every right to be.

"Talk him out of it," Sam answered, her voice sharp.

"I tried. He just asked me where you were, and I told you were still out of town on business. He just said it was going to be fine. Said he had to work off some aggression."

"Why are you calling me then?" Sam asked, gunning the engine as she pulled out of the airport.

"I'm not trying to get in your business, boss, but I figured you'd care that he's going to get his ass kicked." She heard a swell of cheers in the background. "Oh, hell," Rush muttered.

Sam's hand tightened around the wheel. "What happened?"

"He just pushed Vidal off, but he got landed with a combo to the ribs. I'd be surprised if he didn't get a couple of them cracked," he muttered. Sam could barely hear him over the din.

"Where's Mitch?"

"He's here. He tried to talk Jack out of it too, but he just wasn't listening."

Another roar sounded of cheers and jeers.

"How many people are there tonight?" Sam asked.

"At least forty guys. We had to put people at the door. This shit's like white-collar Fight Club."

"Jack won't back down with that many people watching," she reasoned out loud. "He'll have to be KO'd. Shit!" Sam hit the wheel before taking a breath, trying to calm down. "Who's reffing?"

"Manny."

"Where's Kim Sensei?"

"Judo tournament in St. Louis."

"And Carey's out of town this weekend," she murmured to herself, remembering he'd mentioned taking Willa to a lake house on Mackinac Island. "Talon there?"

"Just got here."

"Okay, do this… You and Talon are his corner men. Jack's a politician's son and a stubborn motherfucker to boot, so he won't bow out of this with an audience. He'll want to go hard. You'll both have to advise him on technique and keep his spirits up since Manny's reffing," she paused, thinking about how to handle this as she raced up I-55. "You'll need to be his cut man too. The best we hope for is he gets taken down on a technical knockout before Vidal really does damage."

"You got it, boss—" Rush was interrupted by another rush of cheers and whistles. "Holy shit! I don't fuckin' believe it. Jack knocked Vidal down. He's up again, but that was one hell of a cross—"

"I'm calling Jay," she informed him, hoping their doctor was available at this time on a Friday night. "Get in Jack's corner. I'm fifteen, maybe twenty minutes out. Try to keep him alive until then," she told him before hanging up.

Sam tried to drive calmly as she flew past other drivers, but her temper got the best of her.

"What in the *actual fuck* were you thinking, Jack?!" she shouted into the interior of the car, smacking her palm against the steering wheel again.

Sam had known he would likely be angry with her when she'd dodged him the morning after, but she didn't think he'd go picking a fight because of it. She considered his unanswered calls and texts the past two weeks, hoping he'd back off and recognize their time for what it was—an outstanding, albeit brief, affair. She'd fully expected him to go back to his society queens and starlets and she'd go back to...

What?

She'd go back to...what?

Never mind Jack—what the hell are you doing, Sam?

She took a breath, allowing herself to think about their relationship fully for the first time in two weeks.

The truth was undeniable. She'd run. She'd fucked and run. Because that's what she did. He knew it. She knew it. Hell, even Rush knew it after tonight's spectacle, and Jack had gone looking to beat down or get beaten down because of what was unresolved between them, doing exactly what she hadn't expected him to do. He'd held on, refusing to let it go as she'd expected him to, surprising her yet again. Sam pressed hard on the accelerator, the 'vette shooting forward. She couldn't dwell, couldn't overanalyze. Not right now. It was the path to destruction, and she'd whip herself over this plenty...but later.

Sam palmed her phone. "Jay? Hey, it's Sam. Sorry to bother you on a Friday night, but could you meet me at the gym?"

"Who do I need to patch up this time?" Jay chuckled. "Rush or Talon?"

"Believe it or not, neither of them, but I wouldn't call you if I wasn't worried."

October—Twenty minutes later

West Loop, Chicago

SAMANTHA

THE GYM HAD become so packed in the brief time it took her to arrive that Sam struggled to push in toward the ring. She finally managed to slip through the throng of shouting, cheering men waving cash and yelling a smattering of filthy obscenities, encouragement, and protests at the two men beating the living shit out each other. People filmed the action with their phones. After all, a fight with the darling son of Chicago and an up-and-coming Chicano boxer was big news. This would be sure to hit the *Trib* tomorrow, if not national news. When Sam made it to the edge of the ring and looked up, she was relieved and a little stunned to see Jack still standing—and fighting.

"Oh, *thank God,* she's here!" she heard Rush shout, waving her over to Jack's corner where he stood with Talon. Mitch was on the ground next to them, pounding the boxing mat and shouting encouragements to Jack as he blocked and punched.

When Mitch heard Rush call for her, he wheeled around, eyes a little crazy behind his horn-rimmed glasses. His normally perfectly put together appearance was harried, his blonde hair haphazard, like he'd been clutching at it. Mitch reached through the throng of men shouting at the boxers and dragged her toward him in a tight side hug.

"I don't know if I'm thrilled to see you or if I should rail at you for getting him into this state, but I'm glad you're here either way!" Mitch shouted at her over the noise.

"How's he holding up?"

"This is the seventh round. Jack's exhausted, but he's holding his own. He managed to knock Vidal down once, but I'm worried about the cut over his eye. If Jack bleeds any more, Manny'll probably give him a technical knockout," Mitch told her, head close to her ear so she could hear him over the insanity.

"I've got a doctor on his way. He can check him out between rounds. What the fuck was he thinking?" Sam said, exasperated.

"He wasn't," Mitch answered, eyes on the ring. "He's been ass-backwards the past two weeks. The shortest fuse I've ever seen. I didn't even know he'd scheduled this fight until tonight when Rush called me to try to get help talking Jack out of it. I don't know how I'm going to tell his family he got his ass handed to him brawling. This isn't goddamn undergrad anymore!" he shouted, his eyes following Jack as he parried and shunted one of Vidal's vicious hook and uppercut combos.

Sam watched Jack block or slip the worst of Vidal's punches, goading him into stronger, wider swings, using Vidal's momentum to find openings for his return strikes. At first, she'd wondered if he'd really been looking for a beat down, but he'd lasted this long against an amateur who was easily seven to eight years his junior. If she wasn't so freaked out and angry at him for doing this, she'd actually be fairly impressed.

At the break between rounds, Talon poured water down Jack's throat, coaching him as Rush patted his face dry with a towel, lathering his cuts and his bruised cheekbones with Vaseline as Jack breathed heavily against the padded corner of the ring. Sam swatted the arm Jack had resting against the rope, surprising him. He glanced down at her, astonished, then anger darkened his eyes to gray.

"You choose *now* to come back," he sneered, his voice hoarse.

"I did," she nodded, expression equally dark. "Just in time to see you get your ass handed to you, apparently. What the hell were you thinking, Jack?"

"Hardly getting my ass handed to me," he muttered before pushing away from the ropes and standing. Getting into stance, he tapped his cheeks and forehead to remind himself to keep his guard up as Vidal advanced on him, his expression focused.

The next three minutes of the eighth round had Sam alternately holding her breath, shouting expletives, and howling praise as loudly as any of the men standing beside and behind her. For a guy who had taken up boxing again only recently, Jack had the efficiency and agility of a seasoned fighter. His footwork was light and fluid, following a dance he'd clearly never forgotten.

Vidal fought with the power of youth. He was an aggressive, well-rounded boxer who favored close-range tactics and had a penchant for torso combos polished off with powerful crosses and hooks. She had little doubt he'd managed to crack a couple of Jack's ribs, based on the bruising and welting she could see from a distance. Jack, on the other hand, was a defensive fighter. He had good reflexes and had gotten into a rhythm predicting Vidal's moves about half a second before they happened. Jack was getting better at preventing Vidal's punches from landing with full effect, shifting away at the last moment. Jack was wearing Vidal down with missed hits and maneuvering, steadily chipping away at Vidal's offense with well-placed and masterfully-timed counter punches.

Sam felt a hand grip her elbow and turned, seeing Jay Ross grinning down at her, his baby blues bright with amusement.

"You called for a doctor?" he asked, glancing at the boxers locked in a clinch as Manny tried to break them apart.

"God, am I happy to see you," Sam exclaimed, giving his tall, rangy body a brief hug before pushing him to Jack's corner.

"That's why I joined the Army Medical Corps," he joked. "Women are always happy to see me."

"So are ugly, bruised, and bloody men," Mitch commented, glancing at Jay and his medical bag.

"Don't kid yourself, Jay," Sam muttered. "Women dig the Green Beret, and bloody, beaten men like the morphine. Mitch, this is Jay. He used to be an Army physician. He's stitched up everyone on our team at least once, and he has privileges at a couple hospitals if Jack needs it," she explained.

Jay and Mitch shook hands.

"You fixed Sam's arm?" Mitch asked.

"Yup," Jay nodded. "But that's nothing compared to what I've had to do for those two idiots," he joked, gesturing up at Rush and Talon hanging on the ring. They were busy shouting obscenities as Vidal whaled on Jack. "Shit, your boy's getting pounded pretty good." Jay whistled, watching.

Manny finally called an end to the round.

Mitch groaned in relief, muttering, "Thank you, God!"

Sam grabbed Jay's hand and pulled him forward.

"Jack!" Sam called out, catching his attention.

Jack had just turned back toward his corner when he caught sight of her and Jay. He took one look at their hands and Jay's grin and his expression darkened again, his eyes cold. Jack sat down as Talon poured more water in his mouth, Rush bending to wipe his face down and check his cuts.

"Jack, this is JR," Rush explained. "Sam asked him here to check you out, make sure you're still fit to fight."

"JR?" Jack sneered. "As in '*who shot JR?*'"

Jay chuckled at the *Dallas* reference. "That was an insurgent in Afghany. Long way from South Fork, I'm afraid. How you doing in there, buddy?"

"I'm fine," Jack stated flatly as Rush slathered more Vaseline on his face.

Manny stepped over to their side of the ring. "Jack, you all right? How's the cut?" he asked, checking out the bleeding over his eye. It had been stemmed for the most part, held together by a couple pieces of butterfly tape Rush had smacked on a couple rounds ago.

"I said I'm fine," Jack snapped. "Next round."

Manny looked to Sam. She nodded after a moment, and Manny shrugged, stepping back toward the center of the ring to call a start to the ninth round.

"Your friend is awfully nice," Jay drawled as Jack pushed up, pacing toward the center.

"He's a stupid asshole," Mitch chimed in, watching Jack feint left and come back up with a savage uppercut that left Vidal reeling. "Okay, he's a stupid asshole with a crazy uppercut," Mitch amended.

Sam watched as Jack wore Vidal out psychologically with his defensive strategy. The fewer punches Vidal was able to land, the more he angered, advancing too aggressively, giving Jack openings for ferocious return strikes that left Vidal startled and reeling. At one point, Vidal wavered, seeming to weave on his feet. Manny counted a "standing eight" seconds as he observed Vidal, testing to see if the boxer could go on. Vidal shook it off, laying in on Jack like an enraged bull.

"Knock him down!" men around them shouted, knowing Jack only needed one more knockdown to win a TKO.

Vidal jabbed hard three times before catching Jack solidly in the ribs on a debilitating right hook. Sam could have sworn she heard the bones crack, clutching her own side in a sympathy as Jay and Mitch flinched beside her. Jack grunted from the impact, attempting to duck back, but Vidal was already coming in with another hook. As Vidal lunged forward to land a fatal blow to Jack's kidney, Jack blocked it with a sharp elbow drop, delivering a stunning punch to Vidal's temple. Vidal immediately slumped to the mat. There was a startled silence, then the crowd roared, noise ricocheting and expanding off the warehouse rafters. Sam released the breath she'd been holding in a whoosh, her relief palpable.

"*Holy SHIT!* HE WON!" Mitch shouted as Manny lifted Jack's gloved hand, declaring the victor. Jay jumped up and slid under the ropes with his medical bag, immediately checking on Vidal as he started to come to.

As the crowd hooted and hollered, money exchanging hands, camera phones flashing, Jack and Sam stared each other down, the tension between them nearly tangible. Manny, Talon, and Rush slapped Jack on the back, congratulating him as he glared at her through swollen eyes. Mitch stood beside her, gaze bouncing between them, looking torn between trying to mediate and staying the hell out of it.

"Jay, do you want to check Jack out now or wait until after he cleans up?" she called out, not moving her eyes from him.

"I don't need your boyfriend to check me out," Jack spat out.

"Man, you're definitely concussed," Talon laughed as he helped Jack pull off his gloves. "JR's not her boyfriend. He's our doctor."

"Whatever. I'm fine," Jack retorted, his voice low and angry.

"Jack, you need stiches—" Rush started before Jack turned away, moving across the ring toward the locker rooms. A group of guys helped him down from the ropes, congratulating him with high fives, handshakes, and pats on the back.

Sam turned to Mitch. "Can you make sure he sees Jay? I'm pretty certain he cracked a couple ribs and has a concussion. Jay can also stitch up that gash over his brow," she told him, trying to communicate with her eyes how important it was that he insist on this.

Mitch glanced from her to Jack. "I don't know what the hell is going on between you two, but I think it would be best if you stayed," Mitch told her in a low voice. "I've known him for years, and I've never seen him like this. If you leave now, it's only going to escalate."

Sam remained silent for a moment, debating.

"Fine," she finally agreed, pushing Mitch gently toward the locker rooms where Jack had gone. "Just get him to see Jay."

October—Minutes later

West Loop, Chicago

JACK

"YOU A REGULAR fighter?" JR asked, gently testing Jack's ribs. Jack struggled not to wince. He shook his head mutely, partially because he was too angry to talk to this man that Sam had been clinging to like Jack's life had depended on it and partially because if he opened his mouth to talk, he'd probably just end up wheezing in agony. Better to keep the stoic, stony expression.

"You did good up there," JR continued as he checked Jack's eyes for signs of a concussion. "That hook was something else." He nodded as he finished checking the second eye. "I can stitch you up, or we can get you to one of the medical centers tonight. I know a couple of guys in plastics if you'd prefer—"

"It's fine," Jack interrupted. "Let's just do it now."

JR gave him a local anesthetic, chatting casually to distract him as he stitched up his brow and cleaned up the other cuts on his face. He had an easy-going bedside manner, and he seemed unconcerned with Jack's lack of response. Jack struggled to continue disliking him, trying to conjure the visual of him with Samantha a few minutes ago to fuel his ire.

As the adrenaline ebbed, the fatigue from the fight and the emotional turmoil of the past two weeks took its toll, making him drowsy even as he ached in ways he couldn't have imagined. JR confirmed that he'd cracked two ribs, with bruising on a few others, and that he had a concussion. He recommended painkillers, offering to write up a prescription, but Jack refused, accepting a couple of horse-sized dosages of Tylenol in exchange.

Mitch came in to make sure he was okay before thanking JR. "You want me to stay tonight or call Jaime to come over, you crazy sonofabitch?" Mitch offered, his eyes crinkling with mirth.

Jack shook his head. "He'll freak."

"Yeah, no shit, he'll freak. It'll be all over the papers tomorrow," Mitch informed him. "I've already gotten calls asking for confirmation it was you in all the videos and pictures that made it onto the Internet. You want me to call your family before they find out from the *Tribune*?"

Jack nodded, a little ashamed to be foisting that responsibility onto Mitch, but he was practically a member of the Roman clan. If Jack had been beaten unconscious, the burden of communication would have fallen on Mitch's shoulders anyway. At least he had good news to share.

Jack groaned as Mitch helped him into his track jacket. He was so exhausted and in so much pain that his eyes were swimming. And there was only one person he wanted—*wanted more than anything*—but he was so mad at her for making him feel that way. He loathed feeling raw and hurt and vulnerable. He hated it. He half-wondered if he hated her.

Most of the gym's lights were off by the time he came out of the locker room with Mitch. JR was long gone, as were most of the men who had watched the fight, leaving Manny, Vidal, and a few others standing around, talking.

Jack walked up to Vic Vidal, shaking his hand. "That was the fight of my life, man," he admitted. "I grew up boxing, but this was the toughest match I've ever had. It was an honor."

"Anytime," Vidal replied, a smirk on his cut lips. "Though I plan to kick your ass next time. You're not bad for an old man," he joked, rubbing his swollen jaw.

"You crazy *pendejo*!" Manny exclaimed, clapping Jack on the back. "I couldn't believe it when you asked me to organize this! You keep training, and you can give up that real estate gig and go on the road!"

Jack chuckled, though it pained him. "No fucking way, man. I learned my lesson. I won't be able to breathe without hurting for weeks."

Samantha stepped into one of the spotlights, a few paces away, looking like the Angel of Wrath in the darkened gym, swathed in a fine ivory dress and coat, her dark hair loose around her shoulders. Her eyes were bright with anger, though her face remained impassive. The silence between them hung heavy and static like the ominous atmosphere before a summer storm as they stared each other down.

Manny and Mitch glanced between them, sensing the strain.

"Aww, come on, boss," Talon said, clapping a hand to Jack's shoulder. "Our guy did good. He's been training like a monster—"

"You *knew* about this?" she asked, her voice low and cold.

Talon shrugged, looking uncomfortable. "Not 'til today. I just figured, the way he was working out—" he rubbed the back of his neck, glancing at Jack. "Looked like he was getting ready for something."

Rush came with a gel pack, slapping it into Jack's hand. "For your face. You're gonna look pretty horrifying tomorrow morning."

"Guys," Jack started. "Thanks for being my corner men," he told them sincerely. "I probably wouldn't have lasted that long without your help."

"No sweat," Talon replied, an ornery smile lighting his face as he tied his hair back into a ponytail. "Call me anytime you have a death wish."

"We're just glad you didn't get killed on our watch," Rush joked. "Well, we're gonna go out and celebrate for ya," he said, glancing at Samantha's face. "Good luck with that," he murmured, patting Jack's shoulder as he and Talon turned to go.

Manny excused himself as well, with a caution to Jack to take care of himself over the weekend, leaving him alone with Mitch and Samantha. Jack struggled alternately with wanting to take her into his bruised and battered arms or tell her off for finally showing up and inserting herself where he didn't want her.

"You got this?" Mitch asked Samantha.

"Yeah," she confirmed. "Jack, I didn't see your car outside. Did you drive?"

He shook his head. "Mitch can take me."

"Don't be an asshole," she snapped, a fissure appearing in her cool composure. "I'm heading home now anyway."

"Really? I wouldn't know it the way you're never there," he snarked. "Besides, I don't need you—"

"Jack," she interrupted. "I talked to Jay. He confirmed that you have a concussion. I'll also be checking on you a few times tonight, so let's get that argument out of your system now if that's going to be a problem."

Samantha had the *don't-fuck-with-me-while-I'm-issuing-orders* voice she used with her men. It made Jack want to toss her over his shoulder and spank her while he manhandled her into the bedroom. He suspected he wouldn't have the physical wherewithal to pull that fantasy off any time in the near future. But he was agitated and turned on by the mental image nonetheless.

"I'll swing by tomorrow. Call me if you need anything," Mitch told him as they walked outside. "I'll let your parents and Jaime know what's going on tonight."

Jack nodded stiffly as he folded himself gingerly into the passenger side of the 'vette.

Mitch shut the door for him and leaned in, winking at Samantha. "Have fun playing nurse."

She rolled her eyes, turning the engine over.

The drive back to the Whitney was thick with what remained unsaid between them. Samantha made no effort to break the silence, and he sank back in the bucket seat, closing his eyes against the pounding headache and the burning pain in his ribs, pressing the gel pack to his face.

It had been years since he'd fought rounds in earnest, but the adage was true…getting back into the ring was like riding a bike, so to speak. His dad had started him boxing at a young age at the neighborhood gym and in the Italian American youth leagues, conditioning him to take his knocks and teaching him the mental and emotional endurance to make it through round after round.

"You were born into luck, Gianni, but life is hard. It won't always be easy for you. You need to learn now how to make it through with discipline and fortitude. Get up when you don't think you can; take a beating and still come out on top. My father taught me this. Now I'm teaching you."

He remembered his dad's coaching like it was yesterday. His father, Sandro, had become a senator by the time Jaime was old enough to box, and he hadn't been around as frequently to teach him, so Jack had taken his little brother under his wing, showing him the basics. But Jaime had never loved it the way Jack did—that raw, visceral exchange of power in the ring. Jack had learned young it wasn't just about how fit you were or how hard you could throw a punch. It was the mental stamina, the strategy, and your ability to read others. It was the internal drive that made you push yourself beyond anything you thought possible. Jack leaned his bruised cheek against the cold glass, grateful for the momentary numbness.

Samantha pulled into the garage and parked. They sat in silence for a moment, the engine still rumbling. She turned off the lights and sat back.

"You need help getting out?" she asked, her voice cool.

He shook his head.

"Alright." She turned off the car and slid out quickly, leaving a waft of jasmine and orange blossoms behind her. Her scent triggered memories of her skin sliding against his, blooming with perspiration. Jack squeezed his eyes closed before following her to the elevator bank slowly, his body blazing with pain. Samantha keyed in their floor code, staring at the illuminated numbers as they rode up.

He, in turn, stared at her.

She walked with him to his door, waiting silently as he opened it before sauntering into his kitchen like she owned the place. Samantha checked out the contents of his subzero before handing him a Gatorade. She lifted out the large ice container and a couple gel packs, carrying it all upstairs to his suite. Jack followed, gulping down the drink. She was already pouring a cold bath when he got to her.

"Strip," she told him, her voice brisk and businesslike. Jack pulled a face at her tone and the idea of an ice bath, but he knew his body would thank him for it later. He shivered and sucked in a breath as he sank into the cold water of his Jacuzzi. She tossed the ice into the water over him as the water lapped his stomach and his bruised ribs before slapping the fresh gel packs into his hands.

"Put these on your face and try to relax. I'm going to fix you an electrolyte protein shake," she told him, turning to leave.

Jack grabbed her hand. He slid his fingers through hers, not speaking as he lay back, his body adjusting to the numbing sting of the cold water. He watched her face as she looked at him, all the micro expressions that crossed her mouth and eyes. She was struggling. Her expression was cold, but her eyes flared with emotion. Jack thought he could begin to see past anger in her eyes to the worry, the flash of fear. After long seconds, she slid her fingers from his, stepping out of his bathroom and leaving him alone.

He wasn't sure how long she was gone. He lazed in the cold bath as the dull ache of his muscles numbed, his body sinking like stone, deeper into the water while his mind drifted. Jack thought about waking to find her gone. The vague note. The calls she didn't answer. The unanswered voicemails and texts that had made him feel like an exposed, raw nerve. He thought about how he'd never felt this way about anyone. How he'd never been tied up in knots of anticipation, trigger-hair angry at the merest of slights, bitter at a rejection he'd never experienced. He'd avoided nearly everyone, wondering if he was crazy to be feeling like this, why he couldn't let it go. He'd rewound their time together in his mind until his head had become such a disaster that the only and best way out of it had been to fight.

Jack didn't hear her walk back into his bathroom until she lifted his hand and put a shake in it. He pulled a gel pack off his face to look at her. She'd changed into her favorite cut-offs and an old Texas A&M tee, hair up in a messy knot. She sat on the edge of the bath, watching him.

"You look like a student again," he murmured, his voice sluggish with exhaustion. "Didn't know you were an Aggie."

She snorted quietly. "Yeah, not in years. Drink your shake. It'll help," she told him, pushing the glass up to his mouth.

Jack wasn't sure if it was because he felt hungry and hadn't realized it or if he was just starved for nutrients, but the thick shake she'd made him was up there with some of the most delicious things he'd ever tasted. He groaned, gulping it down. "What's in this? It's heaven."

"Coconut, bananas, strawberries, lemon, salt, orange, and honey."

"Thank you," he gasped between gulps.

"Come on out. I'll rub you down with some arnica."

She hadn't lost her *get-down-to-business* voice despite the dressed down appearance. Jack was too tired and lethargic to do more than help her dry himself off. He followed her naked to his bedroom, sprawling out on his stomach, the room blissfully dark with the exception of a single reading lamp. She crawled up over him, knees bracketing his ass as she rested on the backs of his legs.

"Jay said you wouldn't take any painkillers," she murmured, rubbing arnica cream into his shoulders and back, her fingers smooth and efficient.

"Can't," he muttered into the bedspread.

"Why not?" she asked, spreading the cream along one of his arms, finding and rubbing out the knots.

"I got addicted to pills a while back because of the insomnia. I can't take the chance again," he admitted quietly, shame tinging his cheeks. No one outside of his family and Mitch knew about his struggle, but he felt somehow that her knowing everything about him was an inevitability. It seemed every time he saw her, he laid himself barer, stripping himself down to the quick in slow, inexorable degrees. Maybe that's why it hurt so goddamn much that she didn't care enough to stick around for the rest. And if that were the case, admitting one more thing wouldn't matter.

"I'll give you more Tylenol before you pass out," she told him, her voice softening. "Thank you for telling me," she added quietly, her hands working the strained muscles in his arm.

Samantha stroked and kneaded for long, interminable minutes, and Jack relaxed completely under her silent, thorough care. She gave him more Tylenol before he turned over to lie on his back, groaning as he jostled his ribs. She propped him up on his pillows, rubbing more arnica gently on his chest, ribs and stomach before pulling the sheets up over him, tucking him in.

"Get some sleep. I'll come back to check on you in the morning," she told him, reaching for the light on his night stand.

"Samantha, wait," he said, stilling her hand.

She paused, standing by his bed.

"I was angry with you," he admitted. "I was angry with myself. I needed to do this. To work it all out," he admitted in the quiet dimness of the room.

She nodded once, her eyes on the lamp.

"Will you look at me?" he asked quietly, stroking his thumb across the back of her hand as he drew it down from the lamp and to his chest, cradling it.

At one point during these long, hellish weeks, he'd convinced himself that he was alone in this. That he'd finally been on the receiving end of what he'd been accused of more than once—drawing someone out only to leave them alone, heart in hand, feeling foolish. He'd never really understood it, considered those accusations an overreaction to the natural end of a liaison. And though he tried to avoid doing it by playing on the level, being open about what he wanted with his lovers, now— now he got it. He suddenly, painfully grasped how inexplicably bewildering it was when the one you wanted so badly didn't want you back. He understood. But this—this wasn't it. He felt the current of attraction between them like a live wire as Samantha turned her gaze on him.

"I don't want to fight with you tonight, Jack," she finally said, her voice a little hoarse.

"Thank God," he answered, dropping his head back on the pillow. "Because I'm all fought out. Come here," he said, drawing her down by him. She didn't struggle as he gathered her into the crook of his aching arm.

Jack pressed a kiss to her brow. "Thank you for taking care of me," he murmured, squeezing the hand on his chest. "I know you didn't have to do any of it, but I appreciate it. And I know I have no right to ask, but please stay with me. It's been an awful couple of weeks, and I just want to hold you now," he told her, closing his eyes in exhaustion. "Please, *tesoro*. Tonight, let me…"

Samantha held still against him for a long time, and as he drifted off, he felt her press a gentle kiss to his chest.

Then…nothing.

Just peace.

CHAPTER 17

October—The next morning
The Whitney, Chicago

JACK

JACK SWAM AWAKE to the sound of his phone ringing, his whole body screaming in protest. Samantha was holding the mobile out to him as he blinked blearily up at her.

"I protected you as long as I could. Now it's ringing every five minutes," she told him wryly. "I have a feeling you'd better answer or Jaime will be beating down your door," she said as he saw Maddie's face on his phone's screen.

"Christ," he groaned, struggling to sit up. He felt like he'd been hit by a Mack truck, backed over, and then hit again. Every muscle in his body felt abused.

"Jaime?" he croaked into the phone.

"What. The FUCK. Were you thinking?" Jaime shouted. "Ma is having conniptions! I think she's debating getting on a plane today. I could strangle you. I've been freaking out since Mitch called. *What the fuck were you thinking?*!" Jaime switched abruptly to his soothing "daddy" voice. "Sorry, Maddie. Uncle Jack just made Daddy really mad. Everything's fine, baby. Watch your cartoons in the den. I'll bring you some pancakes soon."

"Jaime—" Jack began painfully as he palmed his cracked ribs, trying to sit up. Samantha left his room, presumably so he could speak with his brother in private.

"The paper is calling you *Jack the Ripper*, didya know that, *che cazzo?*[8] How quaint," Jaime huffed. "Are you fucking kidding me with this shit? This Vidal guy could have massacred you! He's like…eight years younger than you! Man, you're fucking lucky you knocked him out!"

"I've been training. It felt right. I know it was a risk—"

"You've been training for less than a month, you stupid asshole!" Jaime corrected.

"And I boxed for over a dozen years growing up. I knew what I was doing," Jack answered. "Is Mom coming? Really?"

"You'd better call her," Jaime grumbled. "When she hasn't been calling you last night and this morning, she's been on the phone with Mitch and me. I think the only comfort she's taken is that Dad is giddy with pride that you nailed that guy, and we told her Sam's taking care of you. Considering your neighbor's background, she figures you're in good hands."

"You told mom about Samantha?" Jack asked.

"Of course," Jaime sounded surprised. "After Mitch called her and told her she had you see a doctor—"

"You meddling sonofabitch," Jack groaned.

"Hey, don't talk about Ma like that—"

"I'm fine. I've got a couple cracked ribs, and I won't be doing any photos anytime soon, but other than that, I'm okay. *Non mi rompere i coglioni.*[9] Kiss Maddie for me," Jack interrupted before he hung up.

His conversation with his mother was in half-Italian, half *I-am-disappointed-in-your-decisions* English. He'd learned from a young age to just sit and listen. His mother's flare for a good diatribe wasn't lost on anyone. At some point, in the middle of her lecture, Samantha came in with two mugs of coffee. Jack smiled gratefully, putting the phone on mute as he thanked her. When she turned to leave, he snagged her wrist, eyes pleading with her to stay. She climbed on the bed, sitting cross-legged as he tried in vain to interrupt his mother and end the call.

"Jack, the doctor is here to check on you," Samantha called out after

---

[8] Italian for "you dick."
[9] Italian for "stop busting my balls."

a couple minutes, loud enough to be heard by his mother.

"Ma, I've got to go. I'm sorry I upset you. That really wasn't my intention—" Jack started before his mother launched into another string of pissed off Italian. "Right. Right. I love you. *Mi dispiace. Perdonami.*[10] Say hi to Dad for me. Tell him I still have the check hook. It's rusty, but it's still there. Love you, Ma. Gotta go. *Ciao, ciao, ciao!*"

Jack's hasty ending had Samantha chuckling into her mug as he tossed the phone away. She was still wearing her clothes from last night, though she looked as if she'd been awake for a while. Despite the physical agony he was in, he was so relieved and happy to see her still there, his bruised face stretched with a smile.

"You stayed," he murmured, reaching out to rub her leg.

"I didn't want to risk you getting into another altercation if I didn't," she answered drily.

Jack snorted at that, glancing out the windows. He guessed it was mid-morning. He must have slept at least ten hours. If he'd known that was all it took to get a full night of sleep the last couple weeks, he would have taken the beat down earlier.

"Breakfast?" she asked. "You hungry enough to eat real food, or do you want to stick with another shake?"

His stomach growled at the thought of food. Jack leveled a lopsided smile at her.

"Put some clothes on," she suggested. "I know you don't want to, but you need to try to move around a little today, maybe take a swim. It'll work out some of the soreness. I'll be down in the kitchen."

Who would have thought getting dressed could be so excruciating? Jack was exhausted and aching by the time he pulled a shirt and pants on. The bruises on his ribs and his face had fully developed overnight, leaving a smattering of interesting, if somewhat revolting, colors. He didn't bother with shaving after washing his face and brushing his teeth. He'd be working from home this week for certain.

Samantha had whipped up some steel cut oatmeal and honeyed dates, more coffee, and another shake for him. He sat down at the table

---

[10] Italian for "I'm sorry. Forgive me."

slowly, gingerly, thanking her for the layout as he dug in, groaning at how good it was. He was relieved it was all food his aching stomach would be able to digest with relatively little work.

"Everyone's pissed off with me," he muttered, spooning another mouthful.

"Well, yeah," Samantha shrugged, sliding into the seat across from him with her coffee. "You behaved like a jack ass and left everyone to find out after it was too late to talk you out of that insanity."

"If you'd talked to me in the first place instead of leaving the city to avoid me, I might not have done it," he retorted, feeling a little belligerent.

"So…" Samantha began, putting down her coffee, her expression hardening. "We're gonna do this now?" She fixed him with her obsidian stare.

"I told you I was angry," he pointed out.

Samantha watched him, her face morphing into the unflappable mask she donned when she was getting ready to negotiate. Jack had come to not only recognize that mask, but to hate it. It made him want to go head-to-head with her to chip it back. He looked for the flare in her eyes he'd seen last night. This morning, the fury had cooled to an ember.

"What do I owe you, Jack?" she asked idly.

Jack stiffened as if he'd been slapped. He put down his spoon slowly. "Are you implying what I think you're implying?" His voice sounded low even to him. He felt a little dangerous.

Her brow cocked. "Depends on what you think I'm implying."

"That we had some sort of transaction, and I feel slighted." Anger heated his face. "Like a whore."

"Well," she began slowly. "You clearly feel slighted. What am I missing?" she asked, her demeanor relaxed. "Hence the question… What do I owe you?"

Anger beat against his ribcage, singeing his vocal chords. "You owe me honesty, decency, and some kind of communication, Samantha," he responded, glaring at her. "You act like we were just fucking like two nameless strangers. You know more about me than I've told anyone in years," he pointed out. "And you let me inside you, Samantha. It wasn't just sex. I know the difference. I got to you, and you thanked me by running."

Samantha laughed softly. "You're over-dramatizing, Jack. Sure we connected, but so what? We're not in a relationship. We have no rights to each other," she replied, her tone casual.

Jack's hand smacked down on the table, jarring the silver. "It's *not* that I'm upset over rights or exclusivity or things we haven't discussed," he stated vehemently. "It's that you handled me carelessly. Shut me out and shut me down before I even realized what was happening. You surprised me, Samantha," he confessed bitterly. "And I can't believe I'm going to say this out loud, but since I'm already black and blue and this whole conversation already stings, I'll just come out with it," he paused, closing his eyes before staring at her again. "You *hurt* me, Samantha. You fucking hurt me."

Silence.

The silence was so dense, it was nearly palpable.

"We barely know each other—" she began.

"That's a bullshit evasion, and you know it," he countered angrily. "You brushed me off. And I started to consider why. Was it because you felt nothing?" he asked.

Samantha shrugged.

"No. I don't believe that," Jack sneered. "So was it because you felt more than you wanted to? Is it because you know with me it will be bigger than something you can contain and control and relegate to the side when it inconveniences you?"

Samantha's jaw ticked. He was certain she didn't like the exposure or the accuracy of his assessment. He watched her think through ways to get out of this, to detach. He wouldn't allow it. He was already bruised and raw, so he figured he'd go for broke. What else did he have to lose?

Jack leaned across the table. "I see you want to protect yourself from me, but I've also done nothing to wrong you, Samantha. So I'm struggling with something I can't see, some hidden layer or experience I can't know," he continued. "But you're here, and I can't help but think you want me to shove past something. And maybe we're at odds, but I don't want to force your hand. Give me *something*, Samantha," his voice softened. "Christ, I'll take almost anything. But I've fought with this for two weeks, fought last night—"

"You didn't do that for me—"

"I did it because of you, you *infuriating, maddening* woman," Jack nearly shouted, exasperated. "Because you make me feel like something's been torn loose." He stopped, taking a breath as he shoved a hand through his hair. "Do you have any idea how angry I feel? How badly I wanted to hurt someone—hurt myself—to work through it? Because you didn't give me the chance to work it through with you?" he asked, looking at her.

"I owe you nothing, Jack," she murmured.

"Quit making this about paying some unpaid debt," he snapped, cutting off her escape routes. "This is about something far more important. This is about the fact that you feel something for me and you won't give yourself a chance to acknowledge it. So you slice me to distract yourself."

Samantha sat back, regarding him, her expression impassive. "I suspect this won't end well for you, Jack," she said after a moment.

"Maybe not," he shrugged, standing. "But I've never not gone after what I've wanted. And now that we've had the conversation I wanted to have over the last couple weeks the painful, circuitous way, let me be clear," he told her, rounding the table to stand in front of her. He pulled her up, though it cost him, his bruised body aching.

"I won't be nothing to you, Samantha."

"You weren't nothing to me, Jack," she replied, looking into his eyes. "And here I thought I was getting one of the most lauded Casanovas in all of Chicago. You were a lover, Jack. A *great* lover. But that was all it ever was."

"You don't want a lover, Samantha," Jack replied. "You want an opponent." Even as he said it, he was acutely and painfully aware that he was on the receiving end of one of the very conversations he'd perfected over the years. "And you're not going to *'Dear John'* me out of your life."

"I live a complicated life, Jack. I've learned not to create long-term attachments," she countered, a flash of remorse on her face.

"I can name three attachments that I know of. I'm guessing there are more," he finally replied.

"What?"

"Carey," he ticked off his fingers, "Talon, and Rush. You can't tell me you're not attached."

Samantha shook her head. "That's different. We work together. We have each other's backs."

"So now you have someone who has your back in your personal life," he reasoned. "How is that a bad thing?"

"Jack—" she began, her voice a warning.

"No," he interrupted. Jack tugged her toward him again. "I'm not going to listen to you justify why you can't be close to me. I don't know exactly what this is," he gestured between them. "It's not like I went looking for it. But there's something between us that I never anticipated. And I'm not going to let it slide by like so many of the meaningless flings I struggle to remember." Jack took a breath and leaned down, kissing her shoulder. "I want you to be with me in every way that matters," he told her, nuzzling the soft skin of her nape. "And if this doesn't work out, if there's nothing else, then I want to be able to say we had as much of each other as we could." Jack lifted his head to look at her. "Can you do that, Samantha?"

"That's my point, Jack," she murmured. "I don't stay. In my line of work, I'm hardly around."

"You're offering up excuses."

"I'm not," she insisted. "I'm trying to be honest."

"Then I wait," he replied, squeezing her closer. It felt so good to be near her. He'd been so off kilter, missing something he hadn't fully owned up to and didn't completely understand. Now that she was here, it all seemed so clear. So inevitable. "We're together when you're here, and we take it from there. For you, I can do that. For you, I *want* to do that."

"I'm not the girl you wait for, Jack."

"Why not?"

"Because the way I live, there's an exponentially higher chance that I don't make it back," she told him quietly, glancing away.

"So you're not actually against this," Jack murmured, rubbing his thumb against her cheek. "You're just trying to protect me from some imaginary outcome by deciding for me that you're not a safe bet."

"No one's a safe bet," she replied. "But I'm the kind of bet that should come with hazard pay."

"Ain't that the truth?" he smirked.

She switched tactics. "Has it occurred to you that the only reason you're so invested is because I'm not joining the line of women trying to get a piece of you? Perhaps I just present something of a challenge, Jack," she said, pushing him back carefully. "Perhaps you just don't like hearing the word 'no.'"

Jack laughed a little at her accusation. "I have been lucky in that department, yes, but I wouldn't say there's a line." Samantha slanted him a disbelieving look. "Has it occurred to you, Samantha, that even though I don't know everything about you, I want to? That I've been a little bit crazy about you since we met? Has it occurred to you that there's just something about you that works for me on every level?"

"I can think of a few levels you're not going to like," she replied. Her fingers ghosted over his cut brow, the swollen ridges of his cheekbones, and the bruise on his jaw. "Don't do this again," she told him, switching topics. "You don't let someone hurt you so you can name the pain."

"I would have let *you* hurt me some more, if I could have figured out where the hell you were," he replied, only half-joking.

"I'm serious, Jack," Samantha argued. "Vidal could have done terrible damage. You're fit, but don't go looking for trouble. It's irresponsible. You scared the shit out of people who love you."

"People?" he responded, watching her.

"Jaime, your mother, Mitch—"

"You?" he cut to the chase.

"You just managed to piss me off." The thumb that had traced over his brow now pressed hard against the stitches.

Jack winced. "Fuck, I can tell."

"I'll make you a deal," Samantha offered, soothing over the cut.

"Shoot," he replied, pulling her hand from his brow. "I'm in a deal-making mood."

"I won't...avoid you. But the next time you feel like a fight, you call one of my guys if I'm not around. I trust them to put you through the paces without really hurting you."

Jack frowned at her, affronted. "I don't exactly get put down easy."

"I'm not suggesting that," she replied. "But I also don't trust that you won't let your temper get the best of you after last night. If it goes there, so be it. But no more fight clubs with guys who are hungry to make a name for themselves off of powerful men with nicknames like 'Jack the Ripper.'"

"You heard about that, huh?"

Samantha grabbed the paper she'd tossed on the table earlier. Somebody had sold a picture of him standing over Vidal after the knockout, sweat and blood rolling down his chest, his face darkened by a combination of the lighting and his mood, the nickname in a bold headline.

"Do we have a deal?" she asked.

"Are you going to stay with me?" he countered, pushing the paper back.

"I think the deal was that I wasn't going to avoid you."

"But that's not the same as trying," he pointed out.

"Jack..." she began, mounting another blockade. Jack bit her lobe in retaliation.

"I want you, Samantha. Like nothing else," he whispered into her ear.

"I'm no good for you, Jack."

"Samantha, if anyone's going to do terrible damage, it's probably you," he acknowledged. "But it's a risk I'll take. I want every part of you. And maybe, someday, you'll give it to me." He tilted her chin up. "In the meantime, I'll take everything I can get. So do we have a deal?" he asked, looking into her eyes, her mouth just a breath away.

She stared back at him for long moments.

"Do we have a deal?" he asked again.

Her lashes dropped as she looked at his mouth.

"Deal," she whispered, covering his mouth with her own.

Mid-November—Two weeks later

Chicago Midway Airport, Private Jet Terminal

JACK

IT PROBABLY HAPPENED on the boat. Or when he saw her at the elevator before the gala. No, that wasn't it. It happened the first night he saw her swimming, though he hadn't realized it then. Regardless of when it began, he understood what it was now. And though anyone in their right mind would be terrified to free-fall into the depths of Samantha Wyatt, Jack felt a sort of acquiescence, a certain rightness to the surrender, because there was no struggle when he realized he loved her. He simply did. Samantha was the woman he wanted with absolute, crystal clarity. And though he had real doubts as to whether she felt as strongly about him as he did about her, he was certain about one thing: she had him. There could be others, certainly, but not like this. Not like her.

Jack looked up into the chilly Chicago night as he heard the plane approaching. He watched the private jet land on the airstrip in front of him. There was just enough nip in the late fall air for Jack to see his breath puff in front of him as the plane taxied. He was too wired and eager to see Samantha to wait inside his Range Rover.

They'd only had a week together before she'd had to hit the road again. As painful as that recovery week had been, it had also been the best he'd had in as long as he could remember. Samantha had returned to him each night, and they'd done wonderfully mundane things: trading stories, listening to music, making dinner. His body was so exhausted from healing that he'd slept peacefully nearly every night, waking to her, his new normal. The night before she'd left for a business trip to Dubai, they'd made love slowly, a quiet discovery of whisper-soft touches and languorous movement, their joining nearly aching in its reunion. The way they were together now was intimate on another level. But since that night, his body had healed significantly, and Jack had about a hundred different things he wanted to do to her over the next few days.

As the jet door opened, Jack pushed off his car to greet her. The minute he saw her appear, he breathed a sigh of relief. She dressed casually in tight jeans and a dark sweater, her glossy, raven hair down. God, but was she sexy. Samantha shrugged into a camel hair coat as soon as she felt the cold, stepping down the stairs of the jet. Jack scooped her up in his arms, smiling into her hair as she laughed against him.

"Jack—darlin', your face is freezing! Why were you waiting outside?" Samantha exclaimed, clasping his cheeks in her warm hands.

"Missed you," he muttered, pressing a hot kiss to the side of her neck as he squeezed her.

He held her close for a few seconds longer before he noticed the flight attendant waiting patiently a few steps away. Jack pulled back slowly, clasping her hand.

"Your bags, Ms. Wyatt," the flight attendant said, inclining his head as he indicated her garment bag and duffel. "Shall I carry them to your car?"

"Thanks, Harris," Samantha murmured, giving him a soft smile. "Where's the Aston?" she asked Jack, glancing around.

"I wasn't sure how much you packed," Jack answered easily. "Some girls pack a serious set of luggage for just one week," he teased. "So I brought the Rover."

Samantha laughed, the sound throaty and warm, like a sip of his favorite whisky. "Nope. Not me. Just my clothes and grenade launcher."

Jack smiled at her. "Don't joke. I'm liable to believe you," he told her as he led her to his car, helping her in. Jack leaned in to kiss her before shutting the door, thanking Harris for stowing the bags in his trunk. He couldn't resist kissing her again after he got in. He felt a little woozy with happiness, his grin stretching his face as he sped off.

"Whoa there, Cowboy. I don't think we can reach g-force on I-55," she teased.

"Can't be helped," Jack shrugged, casting her a sidelong glance. "Gotta get my girl out on a date."

"Oh?" Her brows popped up. "You gonna take me to dinner before you get lucky?"

Jack's smile was smug. "That's for me to know and you to sit back and enjoy…several times."

Jack took her to Bavette's Bar & Boeuf, a warm, wood- and brick-walled restaurant in River North that felt a little bit like a Jazz Era speakeasy.

"I like it," Samantha murmured, glancing around as he pulled her chair out for her.

"It's the kind of steak joint I figured the cattle rancher in you would surely appreciate," he grinned, reveling in her delighted smile. "They have amazing Chicago-cut rib-eyes."

Jack ordered them a finely-aged Burgundy, brushing her hand with his thumb, unable to stop touching her.

"You're looking at me like you've never seen me before," she laughed, catching him staring.

"I missed you," Jack confessed. "I got used to having you around that week."

Samantha hid her answering smile in her wine glass.

"Good God, did I manage to embarrass the unflappable Samantha Wyatt?" he teased.

She ignored the comment, touching his jaw. "Your face has healed. You look good."

"Thank you." He inclined his head. "It's nice to be out in public without scaring children," he joked.

Samantha drew a finger down to the small scar on his chin. "Tell me how you got this little scar?"

Jack chuckled. "It's kind of ridiculous."

"The best stories usually are."

He sat back, remembering. "I was fifteen. I convinced Carly Esposito to come to my house and relieve me of my virginity. Right after the messy and embarrassingly fast act, my mom surprised us by coming home early from court. I flipped out while I was trying to pull my pants back on and tripped, hitting my chin on my nightstand. *That* was fun to explain." He grimaced.

"How fast?" Samantha teased.

"*Fast,*" Jack emphasized, sipping his wine. "She was an older, more experienced *bellezza*. Looking back, I'm not entirely sure who seduced whom."

"Still got a thing for her?" Samantha asked, her brow raised teasingly.

"Don't be jealous, *tesoro*." Jack raised her hand to his mouth. "Last I heard, she's got four kids and is happily married to the local fire inspector. To be honest, after the two minutes it took, me bleeding all over her dress, and my mother chasing her out of the house with my brother pointing and laughing in tow, Carly really didn't want anything to do me." He tried and failed to look forlorn.

"Oh, God, I bet Jaime never shut up about it."

"Too right. He called me 'Smack-That Jack' all through high school whenever he caught me around girls. I considered tying him to a chair and leaving him in the basement, but that would have upset my parents," he laughed. "How about you? How did you lose your V-card? Let me guess—in the back of a pick-up truck to the high school quarterback?"

Samantha shrugged, slipping into an easy smile. A little too easy. Jack's eyes narrowed.

"I was a late bloomer," she told him. "Didn't help that I scared the shit out of the boys I went to school with and that my dad regularly brandished a gun at anyone who looked at me sideways," she joked.

"So who was he?" Jack asked, pushing for casual though his gut clenched a little. *What bothered him so much?* This was eons ago. Before he knew she existed.

"Just some guy I met in college," she dismissed lightly as the waiter set down hors d'oeuvres of peppered duck and goat cheese terrine accompanied by a dozen Misty Point oysters. "Divine," she sighed.

"Thought you'd like it," Jack winked, serving her first.

Samantha thanked him, trilling with pleasure at the tastes.

"So was this guy your first love?" Jack asked, picking up the thread again after a few succulent bites.

"Was who my first love?"

Jack felt his shoulders tense. "So he was."

Samantha glanced at him. "Who? V-card guy?"

"This guy you don't feel comfortable talking about after all these years."

Samantha sipped her wine, tucking into another oyster. Jack had started to learn to decipher her moods though she communicated so little with her face. He felt the wall again. He wanted to push against it, test its edges.

"I can see why you're a good poker player," he told her. "But I bet I'm a better guesser than you are a bluffer."

Samantha chewed her duck, her expression pleasantly inscrutable.

Jack continued, feeling a little reckless. "V-card guy broke your heart. It took you years to recover. Maybe you still love him a little," he guessed, his own heart squeezing harder at the thought that she was in love with someone else once, now, or ever.

"He was just a guy, Jack," Samantha responded. "And it was a hundred years ago. Why do you care? I'm with you now," she pointed out.

The waiter poured more wine into her glass. She took the moment to sit back from him, observing.

"Because I've become a jealous, love-sick asshole apparently," Jack answered, reaching forward to take her hand. "The very idea of you with someone else, loving someone else…makes me—"

"He was a photographer," she interrupted, her mask slipping a little. She gifted him with a small, rueful smile. "It's sort of the ridiculous adage, I suppose—the artist falling in love with his muse. And I bought it." Her fingers fiddled with the stem of her wine glass. "I was fooled. And I don't like remembering that, I guess." She glanced away, taking a sip.

"At least you didn't get a nick on your chin," Jack joked, trying to lighten the mood after he'd been the one to darken it.

"No," Samantha agreed. "I suppose in that sense, I got away unscathed."

But she hadn't.

He knew it. But he didn't want to pursue it. Because as much as he wanted to know, Jack suddenly didn't want to look over the hedge. He knew intrinsically that whatever he found there, he wouldn't like it any more than he could protect her from it. So he opened the escape hatch.

"Did I tell you about Mitch's latest purchase?" he diverted, digging into his duck.

She picked up the switch in topic readily. "What ludicrous amount of money did he spend this time?"

"You know the British graffiti artist, Banksy? He bought a life-sized photo of one of his New York ambush tags showing two British bobbies making out next to a wooden pallet. He's thrilled with it. He wants to stick it in the lobby at the office," he laughed. "He's being unbearable."

"Seriously?" She shook her head in wonderment. "I don't know what would be more shocking to your business partners—two guys in a passionate embrace next to the elevator banks or the fact that it's British officers."

Jack rolled his eyes. "I was actually more shocked that he was willing to cough up a few thousand for the photo and the frame. It's graffiti, for chrissakes! Isn't the whole idea that it's meant to be free to look at? Isn't it the most democratic kind of art?"

"I love that you're such a businessman," Samantha smirked. "The first two shockers probably didn't really cross your mind."

"Eh," Jack shrugged. "Whatever goes on between two consenting adults is their business. Speaking of which, we're going to plow through the rib-eyes when they arrive because I'm going to take you home and show you exactly what two consenting adults do in private." He wagged his brows, making her laugh.

God, how he'd become addicted to that sound in such a brief time.

CHAPTER 18

November—Saturday night, a week later

The Whitney, Chicago

S A M A N T H A

"YOU LYING LIAR. I know he's here! Where is he? Where are you keeping that beautiful man? Is he strapped to the bed?" Willa asked as she pushed past Sam and into her penthouse like she owned the place. "Wait, is Jack into that? Cause I'm down to watch. For real," Willa declared, spinning around, hand on hip, waiting for Sam to answer.

"Well, hello, Sam! So nice to see you even though it's been a month and I'm so busy with my hands down Carey's pants that I can't see my friends," Sam quipped. She swept past Willa into the kitchen. She'd just opened a bottle of pinot noir before Willa's characteristically dramatic arrival.

"Diva, please. If you knew what that boy had in those pants, you wouldn't blame me one bit," she replied, plopping down on one of her bar stools with a smug smile.

Sam had to admit, Willa looked better than good. She looked happier than Sam had ever seen her. Willa had always had sass. Now she had a sparkle in her eyes that was verging on contagious.

"I grew up with him, and he had this disconcerting period where he wanted to be naked all the time. Drove his parents' nuts," Sam told her. "I know exactly what's going on down there. So where the hell have you been?" Sam asked, handing Willa the glass. "Cheers."

"Mmmm," Willa savored the wine. "That's some good shit, gurl. I love drinking with you. You're like a high-end alcoholic. The people I'm used to drinking with have a hard time paying for Boone's. Now where was I?" she pressed one long finger to her chin. "Oh my God! Carey has some ridiculous moves in bed. I mean, I haven't come like that since— well, let me think, EVER. And he does this thing with his cock—"

"ENOUGH!" Sam stopped her, holding up her hand. "I can't handle it. Seriously," she insisted as Willa opened her mouth to retort. "I cannot discuss sex acts and Carey in the same sentence. You'll send me into counseling for life. Stop."

Willa rolled her eyes. "You're a goddamn prude, Sam. But if we can't discuss my sex life—now that I have one worth discussing—then we'll just have to dissect yours. What's going on with Sir Makes-Me-Hot?"

Sam laughed, hiding her smile behind her wine glass. Just the thought of Jack made her feel disconcertingly happy. She shifted back and forth between enjoying her bliss and not trusting it, depending on the day.

"Disturbingly well," she admitted. "He's crazy for putting up with my schedule, but the times we are together, it's been pretty good so far."

"Where is he tonight?"

"Bulls game with his brother and niece. They're religious sports fanatics."

"Oh! Man after my own heart. Let's turn it on while we chat. When did you get a television?"

Sam rolled her eyes. "Carey's housewarming present. He put it in while I was in Dubai, the sneaky bastard."

"So does Jack have a suite?" Willa asked, getting up and searching for the remote.

"Floor seats."

Willa's eyes widened. "Dayum. We need to get invited next time. Oh! Maybe we'll see them on the sidelines," she commented while she surfed for the right channel. When she got to it, the game was still in the first quarter, playing Dallas. Willa glanced at her. "Now who do you root for? If you say Dallas, we may have to break up."

"I *am* a Texan," Sam drawled, following her into the living room with the wine.

"Psssffft, bullshit. You haven't lived in Texas in years. You're a Chicagoan now. You better own it, hunty." They sipped their wine, watching the game for a minute, hooting at a close up of Derrick Rose. "Wait—that's him, isn't it?" Willa asked, pointing a finger toward the crowd on the screen.

Sure enough, Jack, Maddie, and Jaime were seated courtside center. Jack was sipping a beer with his arm around the back of Maddie's chair. Her dad was handing her a hot dog.

"Who's the kid? Wait, is hunty's man a baby daddy?" Willa asked, surprised. "And who's Jack's skinny twin? Christ, that guy's friggin' hot too!"

Sam laughed, covering her mouth. "You must have an Italian man fetish. Those are the Roman brothers. Maddie is Jaime's daughter."

"Dear God, to be in between that sandwich," Willa sighed, hand to chest. "Is he single?"

"What?" Sam shook her head. "You're already tossing Carey aside for Jaime?"

"Hey, I am entitled to pursue multiple interests as long as everyone's on the same page," Willa answered, fanning her neck. "Though I won't lie, I am really into Carey right now. He's so great, it kind of freaks me out sometimes. I've had so many shitty relationships with shitty men, I feel like it's my God-given right to finally have a good experience but…" She trailed off, taking another sip of her wine. She fiddled for a moment with the bank of colorful bangles she had on one arm.

"You feel like it's too good, and you can't help but worry it's a delusion?" Sam suggested gently.

Willa slanted her a wry look. "Baby, you know insecurity isn't my jam. That's not how I am. But whenever I feel remotely this good—I can't help but think the other shoe will drop," she admitted. "Carey is such a good man. He's a gentleman, he's open to new things, he's respectful; he tries to put me first. He surprises me with nice things like weekend getaways instead of midnight calls from Cook County lockup or five-digit debts." Willa's mouth twisted. "It's like now that I'm finally getting everything I thought I wanted, I don't know what the hell to do with it."

"Grab it and run," Sam shrugged. "That's what I'm doing anyway. I feel like I'm stealing every time I'm with Jack. He's so passionate and effusive and…so *Italian*." Sam paused, thinking about how different he was from any of the men she'd ever experienced intimacy with. "Jack's just so affectionate all the time, I'm just—I'm guess I'm a little overwhelmed," she admitted.

Willa nodded, sipping her wine. "So how fucked up is this? I counsel women all day long on what healthy relationships look like, and now that I'm in one, Carey says, 'I love you,' and the first thing I think is, '*Are you sure?*'"

Sam's eyes widened. "He dropped the L-bomb?"

Willa looked at her in surprise. "I thought you talked."

Sam shook her head. "Not about this stuff. Chinese wall when it comes to our personal lives."

"You're best friends! How is that even possible? And he knows you're dating Jack," Willa pointed out.

"Like I know Carey's dating you. That's the extent of it. We're more like siblings. We're close, but we don't always have to discuss everything. You forget we got good at this in the military," Sam pointed out. "There was a lot we couldn't talk about for years."

Willa whistled. "So before me, who did you talk to about this stuff?"

Sam shrugged. "Not much to talk about. The longest-running thing I had going was in college. Ever since, it's been short-term, mutually beneficial set-ups. Not much to dissect there."

"So you don't know anything about me and Carey?" Willa asked again.

"Not really," Sam answered. "You can talk to me about it, though. As long as it doesn't involve anything that will traumatize me," she warned, eyes flashing as Willa grinned wickedly. "So… *Love*, huh?"

Willa nodded. "He said I didn't have to say anything. He just wanted me to know. He said he figured life was too short to not own up to what he was feeling."

Sam grinned. "Sounds like him."

"Yeah. He was helping me repaint some of the furniture in the rec room last week. It was just a regular night. We were eating takeout from

Tamale Spaceship, for God's sake. You know, those fire-roasted poblanos with the tomato-jalapeno sauce?"

"Stay on topic," Sam replied, sardonic.

"Right." Willa took a breath. "So we're just painting and eating and arguing over the radio, and he says he'll let me choose because he loves me."

"Awww…" Sam teased before Willa smacked her arm with strength. "Ouch! Bitch, you've gotten stronger with all the self-defense classes."

"I've got a good instructor." Willa grinned. "So I kind of freak, right? Deer-in-headlights moment. And that's when he says what he said."

"And then…"

Willa sighs. "And then I hit him with the paintbrush and we got paint all over each other and then that freak started to—"

"Okay, I think that's enough of the descriptive scenario," Sam interrupted, shaking her head. "So now that you've had some time away from it, what do you think?"

Willa shrugged. "I think I'm not sure. I like him a great deal. More than I've liked anyone in a long time. But I'm…I'm just not there yet," she confessed, pouring more wine. "Is that awful?" she asked.

Sam tucked her legs under her, resting her head against her hand as she considered her friend.

"I think you have every right to be cautious, and you're going to come to your own conclusions on your own time. Carey is pretty intuitive. That's probably why he's not pushing."

Willa nodded but remained quiet. They watched the game for a bit before catching another good look at Jack and Jaime on the sidelines.

"So what's the story? Jack tell you how he feels yet?" Willa asked, gesturing toward the flat screen.

"All the time. Constantly," Sam replied. "He's so damn verbal I want to gag him sometimes." Sam's lips pressed into a straight line. "He thinks he's in deep because he wants to be with someone longer than a few dates. He's not in love—it's just infatuation."

"Why?" Willa questioned, brows raised. "Why wouldn't that hot-ass motherfucker love you? You're so cuddly!" Willa teased, leaning forward to try to pinch her cheek. Sam swatted her hand away, laughing.

"Lady, just because 'cuddly' is my middle name…" Sam joked.

"So why do you think it's just infatuation?" Willa pressed.

Sam thought about it. "Well, for one thing, I don't think he's ever dated a woman who didn't fawn over him. And for another, I don't give a damn about his money, his power, or his connections. So he knows I'm only with him for him."

"Aren't you richer than Croesus?" Willa asked. "Don't you own like half the oil in Texas?"

Sam shrugged. "I'm not sure who's richer than who, largely because it doesn't matter and also because I don't bother keeping track. But I think that's a big thing for him, even though he never mentions it," Sam confided. "I think he just expects people to look at him a certain way or want something from him. The fact that I *don't*…" She paused. "I think he couldn't believe I wasn't after him for something. And then he was frustrated I wasn't after him at all. Now, I guess we're just sort of finding a rhythm."

"So what's the problem, diva?"

"There is *no* problem. Maybe that's the issue," Sam shrugged. "When we're together, whether it's at one of those fancy fundraisers or drinking longnecks and playing cards, it feels easy. Except—" Sam glanced away.

"…except when he wants something more from you than you're willing to give," Willa surmised, unerringly on point.

Sam's eyes snapped back to her. "You're goddamn irritating when you're right."

"So he's letting down barriers, and you aren't," Willa concluded.

Sam shifted, feeling a shard of discomfort. "I think that's the other big reason why I think he's just infatuated. Since he knows I'm not with him for the usual reasons, he's more open. He's experiencing things he probably hasn't felt before because he knows I'm not trying to get something from him." She paused, sipping her wine. "Willa, I honestly don't think he's ever been in love before."

"Psshaw, he's a grown-ass man, babe. I'm sure he's been smacked over the head by cupid before," Willa replied confidently.

"I just worry," Sam confessed. "He's completely into this, you know? The trust level is—"

"Incomprehensible," Willa finished for her. "I was like that when Carey just put it out there like… 'Hey, here's my heart. Can you watch it for a sec? 'kay, thanks.' Seriously. What the fuck is that?"

"Exactly," Sam agreed. "All I can think is…*run for cover, Jack.*"

"I think it's because we think the novelty will eventually wear off. We're not the norm for these guys."

"Shit, Willa, who in the hell are we the norm for?"

Willa threw her head back and laughed. "True that." She sipped her wine. "So Jack may be more willing to expose himself than he has in the past, but he's going to expect a little give-for-get, baby girl. You think he's okay with sticking to your *'you-stay-over-there'* method of loving?"

Sam shrugged. "If he's not, this won't go much farther, I suppose. We'll have to focus on dissecting your love life moving forward," she smiled.

"I don't think I need dissecting as much as a fifth of bourbon and a crash helmet," Willa replied drily.

"You think Carey'll let you down?" Sam asked, surprised.

"Nah," Willa answered. "I think I'll let myself down."

"Willa…"

She knocked back the rest of her wine. "We're fucking depressing for a Saturday night. Let's go out."

"Willa—"

She slapped her hand onto Sam's and mock-glared at her. "I don't want to get drunk on your couch and do therapy while I drool over the Roman brothers at the Bulls game I should be at. Let's go dance to whatever's going on at Wild Hare and flirt with boys that are far too young for us and do shots of something we'll regret tomorrow."

Sam grinned at her. "Let me change into something appropriately slutty."

Willa smiled back at her, her bright blue eyes flashing. "Now you're talking!"

November—An hour later

Lincoln Park, Chicago

SAMANTHA

"ALL RIGHT! ALL right, where you from?" Willa asked, pointing at the first guy in the row of four good-looking twenty-somethings lined up at the bar. She'd just teed up four shots in front of each guy. Sam figured they were either going to have a great night or get so blind drunk, they couldn't remember it. Whatever the case, whenever Willa was serving up, there was rarely anyone turning them down.

"Chicago!" The first one answered. He sported pretty blue eyes, a head full of soft curls, and wicked little smile.

"Good, you stay," Willa declared, pointing to the next. "You?"

"St. Louis," the second guy replied, flashing a sexy smile with his rock-boy look and the sexy bedroom eyes.

"Eh. I'll let you stay one round," Willa shrugged. "Don't disappoint me, St. Louis. How about you, bachelor number three?" she asked.

"Evanston!" the cute Asian guy replied, his dimples deepening.

"Barely counts as Chicago, but what the fuck, I'm in a good mood and you're adorable. And you, lover boy?" she asked, looking at the final guy.

He grinned. "Kingston," he answered with a gorgeous Jamaican accent and a vivid white smile set off by flawless dark chocolate skin.

"Ooooh, a tropical brother, I like it!" Willa grinned, clapping. "Okay, boys! My lovely partner-in-crime Sam and I have served you up shots of Cuervo Gold as a thank you for your participation." Willa paused for dramatic effect, winking at Sam. "We do four rounds of trivia across sports, music, and *whatever-we-feel-like*. Last two standing get to dance with us! You ready?"

"What kind of music?" guy number two asked. He had a mop of dark hair, and Sam was willing to bet he was a musician with the skinny dark jeans and lashes so thick he looked like he was sporting boy-liner.

"Whatever kind we feel like testing you on, St. Louis," Willa answered saucily.

Wild Hare was already packed, people surrounding the bar chatting or dancing to excellent dancehall. With Barrington Levy blaring, it was impossible not to be in a good mood.

"You're not drinking with us?" the Jamaican asked.

Willa smiled. "We'll toast the winners before we dance, Winston."

"My name's not Winston. It's Quince," he answered, looking confused. Albeit hot and confused. Sam grinned behind her hand as she leaned on the bar.

"Not tonight, baby. You're how *Willa Got Her Groove Back* right now. So—first question! What was the last year the Chicago Cubs won the World Series?"

"1908!" Chicago guy and Evanston guy shouted simultaneously.

"You two," Willa pointed at St. Louis and Winston. "Drink!"

Chicago and Evanston high-fived.

"To how bad the Cubs suck? Sure!" St. Louis smirked, knocking his shot back.

Willa glared.

Sam smiled. "How many albums did Bob Marley make in his career?"

"Does that include with the Wailers?" St. Louis asked.

"Yup," she nodded. "Answers?"

"Six."

"Over a hundred."

"Fifty."

"One hundred and ten," Winston/Quince answered confidently.

"That's hardly fair!" Evanston disputed. "Of course the guy from Jamaica knows that!"

"Like you'd know when the Cubs won the World Series?" Sam laughed. "You're in a reggae bar, Evanston. Don't be an asshole. Drink up!"

Three guys took their shots in quick tosses, a couple gasping while Winston/Quince grinned.

"Name the top three scorers for the Bulls this season," Willa asked.

As the guys started naming players, Sam felt her phone vibrate in her pocket. She pulled it out of her jeans—it was Jack.

Dove è il mio tesoro?[11]

Sam smiled.

Wild Hare. Up to no good, she replied.

I'm all about you and no good, he answered. *May I join?*

Sam chuckled as she typed, *Depends. You dance to reggae?*

Definitely. Be there in a few.

"St. Louis, you're an embarrassment!" Willa laughed beside her. "Drink! Drink! Drink!"

"At least I'll get drunk fast tonight," St. Louis grumbled, coughing a little on his third shot.

"Sam, get off the damn phone. Pay attention to our contestants. What's the final question?" Willa asked.

Sam tucked her phone back in her jeans, considering the guys. "All right, this is a Chicago *Blues Brothers* question. What kind of car was the Bluesmobile?"

"A Dodge Monaco," Chicago guy answered.

"A 1974 Dodge Monaco," St. Louis added, looking smug.

"What he said," Evanston laughed.

"Yeah, that's what I was going to say," Winston/Quince answered, looking confused.

"Not enough swagger to save you two cheating cheaters," Willa laughed. "Drink up!"

They shrugged, tossing their shots back.

"So Chicago, you get your pick of which of us you want to dance with," Sam told good-looking guy number one. "We have a lighting round now between Evanston and Winston," she declared.

"I'm Jerry," Evanston answered readily.

"And I'm still Quince," Quince added.

"And I still don't care, Winston," Willa sassed. "Okay. Final round...you ready?"

They nodded.

"Name four famous rappers from Chicago!"

"Common, Kanye West, Twista, and Lupe Fiasco," Evanston an-

---

[11] Italian for "Where is my treasure?"

swered, ticking them off his fingers.

"Common, Kanye, Twista, and J Dilla," Quince said, also looking confident.

Willa's brows shot up. "Figures a cute Asian guy from Evanston knows his rappers. Winston, I'm sorry to say…J Dilla was from Detroit. Console yourself in tequila, Winston!"

Sam and Willa picked up Chicago and Evanston's remaining shots and toasted, knocking them back.

Sam felt the buzz slide down her spine. She was officially ready to party.

"Now come claim your prize!" Willa declared. They made their way out to the dance floor, which was packed with enthusiastic, like-minded revelers. Chicago danced with Sam and was shockingly good. His curly hair fell over his brow as he twirled her around and brought her close, dancing front to back before twisting her around to face him. They danced for several songs before she saw Quince cut in to dance with Willa. Even in her buzzed state, she saw Quince impressing the hell out of her with his moves. Willa was hooting and hollering along with several spectators.

At some point, Sam felt an arm slide around her waist, tightening and pulling her back against a hard body. Sam was getting ready to push away when she caught Jack's scent. She closed her eyes, tilting her head back and smiling.

"Hey there, darlin'," she drawled, relaxing into his arms as they danced.

"She's with me," Chicago protested.

"Sorry, man," Jack replied, tightening his arms around her waist. "But this is my lady. I was at the Bulls game. Thanks for holding my place," he smiled, holding out his hand in thanks.

Chicago's eyebrows popped up. "Who won?" he asked as he shook Jack's hand.

"We did." Jack smiled. "You can see how I'd want to celebrate with my girl."

"Holy shit, it's Jack Roman!" Willa shouted over the music, throwing an arm around Jack's shoulder.

Jack directed a dazzling smile her way as Chicago snuggled up to a different dancer. "And you must be the indelible Willa Carter," he replied.

"That smile should be a registered weapon," Willa accused, clearly buzzed off her ass.

"Only in Cook County," Jack quipped.

"We met at a fundraiser years ago. I don't remember you being this good-looking," Willa flirted.

"I'm not, actually," Jack lied, winking outrageously. "You've just got really good liquor in your system."

Willa chuckled, swirling back to Quince while Jack danced with Sam.

Jack ducked his head to kiss her neck.

"Mmm. You smell good," Sam sighed, drawing her arms up and around to twine in his hair. "Must be the pheromone of your favorite team winning."

Jack laughed into her nape. "*Eau la victoire.* You been having fun, *tesoro?*"

"Just indulging in a few bad decisions and a little regrettable behavior," she murmured, tilting her hips into his pelvis as he groaned into her hair.

"Keep doing that, and I'm going to spread you like butter," Jack said in her ear, his breath hot.

Sam twisted, turning to face him as she slid her arms over his shoulders, her fingers twining into his hair. "Darlin', you say the sweetest things," she replied, her voice a little hoarse from the tequila.

Jack kissed her hard, his mouth hungry. She thrilled at the feeling, pulling him closer as they moved to the music. They made out like teenagers until Sam registered Willa hooting and hollering in the background. She pulled back, flushed from too much liquor, the dopamine coursing through her body, and the heat of the dance floor.

"DAMN, you two! I think I had an orgasm by proxy," Willa teased, fanning her neck. "Let's get drinks!" she said, dragging Quince off the dance floor.

They ordered another round.

"What should we toast to?" Willa asked.

"I'm not drunk!" Sam declared.

"*I'm just drinking!*" she and Willa shouted, laughing at the old Albert Collins blues line as they toasted Jack and Quince.

Jack shook his head, knocking back his shot with a smile. "How long have you two been at it?" he asked.

Willa leaned toward him, poking her finger in his chest. "We saw you on television at the game. Floor seats, Jack-Be-Nimble? Niiiiice. And your baby Jack-Be-Quick brother? So fiiiiiine," she told him in a superior, albeit drunken, voice.

"You watched the game?" Jack asked.

"Only part," Willa admitted. "But really we just talked shit about you two. Damn your fine asses! Right, Sam I Am?"

"She gives you weird nicknames when she's drunk," Sam confided to Jack in a loud voice.

"Hey, I heard that!" Willa argued. "And Winston here—" She reached back, groping the air for the Jamaican.

"It's Quince," he corrected again.

"Right, whatever," Willa replied. "And Winston here loves my nicknames!"

"Actually—" he started.

Jack grinned at Willa as she mock-glared at poor Quince. "As I was saying, Jack, you're friggin' HOT. *H-A-W-T, hot,*" Willa spelled, weaving a little. Jack gripped her elbow to steady her. "And my girl here," she continued as if nothing could stop her. "Digs you. Like…really digs you, get me?"

"I think you need another drink," Sam grumbled, interrupting her.

Jack looked bemused.

Sam signaled the bartender.

"No, you're not hearing me, Jack Daniels," Willa insisted, leaning toward him a little, clearly feeling the effects of the shots piling up. "I've been friends with this one for years, and she has never, never talked about anyone like she talks about you. Ain't that right, Sam-ilicious?"

Sam rolled her eyes, picking up her shot. "Jack, ignore her. And it's your turn to toast."

He looked down at her, his expression gentling. "*Cento di questi gior-*

ni...con me.[12]

Willa looked perplexed. Sam tried to translate through the tequila haze. Quince just shrugged and shot, dragging Willa back out on the dance floor.

"It's unspeakably sexy to hear you bullshit me in Italian," Sam told him, wagging her finger. "I bet you speak *bella Italiana* to all the girls."

Jack smiled, kissing her mouth again. "You taste like tequila and bad decisions, *tesoro*. Now how about a little regrettable behavior?"

"You're a bad man, Jack Roman," she whispered against his lips.

Jack pulled back, eyes twinkling. "As long as I'm your man."

Sam was admittedly pretty lit up, but Jack was a seriously good dancer. And though she would never have guessed it, he was obviously very comfortable in the raucous scene that was typical of the Wild Hare on a weekend. His moves were fluid and teasing, and he made her laugh more than once as he sang along with a pseudo-Islands accent that was more entertaining than it was embarrassing.

"How are you as comfortable at a reggae bar as you are at a gala at the Art Institute?" Sam asked in drunk wonder.

Jack grinned. "Same as you, I suppose. You grow up in both worlds."

"You grew up near the Wild Hare?" Sam asked in bewilderment.

"Close. I went to Northwestern," Jack laughed. "Mitch and I used to go to their old location. And you and I both know no self-respecting college guy doesn't know the bar scene." He grinned, remembering something. "And I snuck into this place when the Fugees played a concert here while I was in high school. God, I had the biggest crush on Lauryn Hill."

Sam laughed in disbelief, eyes wide. "Holy shit, you continually surprise me, Jack."

"Why?" he asked. "Cause I liked Lauryn Hill?"

"No. She's gorgeous. Hell, I *like* Lauryn Hill. I'm just surprised you know who the Fugees are."

He laughed at that, pulling her closer to him as his thighs brushed

---

[12] Italian for "May you live a hundred years...with me."

hers. The secure hold of his arms around her felt so incredibly good. Sam realized with the insight a little too much alcohol can expose that she was in real danger of losing a part of herself to this man. And perhaps more astonishing, she wasn't worried about it. The thought was so surprising that she stilled for a moment, looking up at him dazedly.

"You okay, *tesoro*?" Jack asked, running a thumb across her cheekbone.

Sam nodded mutely, cupping his arms. She fished around for the ensuing dismay that would have her making her excuses before she quickly extracted herself, but it wasn't there. She wondered if the absence of panic was caused by the dancing and the buzz of that elusive, *just-the-right-amount* of alcohol filtering through her system. She felt softly-edged and loose-limbed, but she knew it was more than the alcohol… it was the relaxation that accompanied trust.

They danced together for a few more songs before he edged them toward the bar. "You ready to go, or do you need more feel-good libations?" Jack asked in that teasing, sexy voice of his.

Sam tilted her head back. "I want you to take me home and make me scream your name and see the Holy Trinity."

Jack's smile was immediate and dazzling. "I'll get Willa. We'll drop her off on the way."

"You think of everything."

Jack brushed his thumb over her mouth, dipping it in ever so slightly. "Apparently, I only think about you." He smiled wickedly. "And making you cry out my name. And see God and the Holy Trinity."

"Be careful, Jack," Sam laughed, tilting her head. "I might think you're falling in love with me."

"It's done, *tesoro*," he replied, pressing his lips to her temple. "It's already done."

November—Hours later
The Whitney, Chicago

JACK

THE MOONLIGHT SLIPPED into the room, casting an iridescent glow on the skin of Samantha's back. She lay on her stomach as she slept. Jack pushed a tress of her hair back, admiring the smooth line of her shoulder, the shadowed line of her spine in the moonlit room. He saw her old wound, a luminescent circle in the dimness. Jack traced the circumference gently, leaning forward to press a kiss against the vestige of the scar. They'd lived full and diverse lives before each other, but he had a hard time imagining it now, a time in which she wasn't beside him, a time when someone had harmed her, made her fight for her life. Jack closed his eyes, listening to her breathe, his fingers grazing down her back until they came upon the raised cordons of the other scars on her side and hip.

"So brave," he whispered, opening his eyes to look at the marks he stroked. "So strong."

"No."

Jack lifted his head. Samantha watched him, her eyes black.

"Yes," he argued gently, pressing his lips to her shoulder. "You're one of the strongest people I think I've ever met. A warrior," he told her softly, hand ghosting over her hair.

"Jack—no," she breathed, closing her eyes, her face tight, as if she were in pain. "They're reminders. For bad mistakes I've made." Samantha turned her head away. "I'm not proud of them." She spoke so softly that he almost missed it.

"They're reminders that you've survived." He turned her gently, holding her back to his front. His hand slipped up until he found her steady, assuaging heartbeat. When she said nothing, Jack pressed his face to her hair. "Will you tell me about them?" he asked.

Samantha remained silent for a while, slipping her hand over his, resting on her heart. "I can't," she whispered into the darkness.

"Can't or won't?" he whispered back, lips against her hair.

"Both," she admitted softly. "There are things—I can't tell you. Others…" Samantha took a breath. "Other things, you wouldn't want to know."

Jack pressed his hand flat on her heart. "I find that hard to believe, *tesoro*. I've never wanted to know more about a person."

Samantha squeezed his hand gently. "Don't venerate me, Jack. I'll only disappoint you."

He laughed.

She turned in his arms. "Why are you laughing?"

Jack smiled at her, touching her nose. "Because besides my family, you're the only one who's ever tried to protect me. It's…endearing."

"Mitch protects you."

"He's my Carey equivalent. He's basically family," Jack replied, tracing up to her brow with a fingertip. "Don't you know I can take care of myself, baby?"

"Maybe I'm trying to protect myself."

"No, baby," Jack shook his head. "You take care of everyone. That's why they follow you anywhere—why they are loyal to you through anything."

"That's the job."

Jack laughed again, kissing her forehead. "You're an idiot if you think loyalty's something you can pay men for, *tesoro*. And you're no idiot. You know men are only loyal for three reasons."

"Name them."

"Love, fear, and respect," he answered, punctuating each answer with a brief kiss.

"Not sure about the first but I definitely like the last two," she replied, kissing his throat.

"But the first is the best…"

"No—it's the most fickle and erratic. That makes it the most dangerous," she countered.

"Perhaps," he murmured. "But it's also the most powerful, because you can't command it."

Jack slipped his hand into the tangle of her hair, lifting her up and over him. He looked up at her, his free hand running down her neck through the valley of her breasts, coming to rest on her heart again. Samantha watched him, her eyes warming. "Now that you have me here," he began, tugging her down so he could kiss her again. "How will you command me?"

Samantha drew his hands up, holding his wrists down by his head. Her hair cascaded around them, a veil shielding them from the night and the world beyond it. Jack relaxed in the seclusion with her, reveling in the moment and his body's response. *God, how he loved her.* But he didn't say it. Jack knew she'd push away, create distance when he could feel her drawing closer to him every day. But it wouldn't be long before he'd either let it flow out of him unchecked, or she'd finally open her eyes to it. Either way, he felt the confrontation coming; could taste it like ozone before an electrical storm.

Jack felt Samantha brush up against him, teasing. He slid his hands from her grasp, tilting her hips so he could surge into her, sitting up to kiss her mouth while she groaned into his. He pulled back a little, relishing the delicious friction, before pushing up into her again. "You belong to me," he whispered.

But Samantha shook her head.

"Yes," he insisted, pulling her hair so he could kiss and lick her neck.

"I belong to no one," she gritted out, rolling her hips as she peered down at him, a glint in her eye while she undulated, her skin pearlescent in the moonlight.

Jack twisted her hair in his fist, twining it over her shoulder so he could push up to his elbow and kiss the exposed skin there. Bite it. He met her push for thrust, making her gasp, showing her he wouldn't back down. "We belong with each other, *tesoro*," he insisted, pinching her nipple, making her cry out in pleasure laced with that little edge of pain. "You'll see it, baby." She twisted on him in retaliation, clenching him so hard with slick inner muscles Jack thought he saw stars.

"And what will I see, Jack?" she asked, cinching her legs around his waist while they worked each other.

"Inevitability," Jack answered, teeth clenched with the pleasure. "Certainty," he continued, pressing his cheek against her breast as she rose and fell against him. "*Non pensavo di poter provare un sentimento così profondo prima di incontrarti.*"[13]

---

[13] Italian: "Before meeting you, I didn't think I could experience such depth of feeling."

"I don't understand you," she groaned, her hand finding his, bringing it to her sex, registering their duality and their connection. "Something about experience… Jesus, God that feels good…" she shuddered, pressing his fingers tighter to her clit. "Depth of feeling… Christ, *yessss*…" she hissed, her head falling back as he worked her.

"You understand me, *tesoro*. You just don't want to…"

In the darkness of the room, they took each other, straining toward the climax, even as they tried to stave it off, draw the moment out. At one point, they stopped struggling for power, lacing their fingers together, stoking the sensations within each other as they twined together like an intricate knot.

"Jack—" Samantha cried out as her body shook with long, luxurious spasms.

"Let go, *tesoro*," he breathed, coming deep. "Just let go. I've got you," he promised, following her as he hid himself within her, clasping her tighter than he'd ever held anyone.

CHAPTER 19

"WE'VE SELECTED THE team who will be going to Brazil, and after careful consideration as well as your outstanding recommendations from two of our subsidiaries, we'd like Lennox Chase to insure and lead security for the group of journalists, photographers, and camera crew we've selected."

Sam smiled at Rick Landiss, the Executive Producer of NBS's flagship news program, one of the most esteemed and longest-running broadcasts on US television. They sat in his large corner office in Midtown Manhattan, and she was struck with the brief thought that her dad would have loved to have met him. She'd grown up watching Landiss anchor the *Global Record*, an early pioneer to investigative reporting, long before the era of twenty-four seven news networks.

"Mr. Landiss, I've been watching this show for as long as I can remember. It would be an honor to protect your crew," Sam smiled. "Carey and I have the perfect team in mind to accompany your group, though we can talk through some of the specific locations and types of interviews you're looking to conduct to do a bit of fine-tuning."

Carey nodded, adding, "The men we have in mind for this assignment are all experienced in the region and have the language skills and the contacts to make sure your team has the coverage to conduct their interviews as safely as possible."

Rick sat back at his desk, steepling his fingers as he regarded them.

Though he'd long since stepped away from the camera to produce, he had the steely look and character of a man who'd seen and heard it all in over thirty years of hard-nosed journalism. Sam liked his no-nonsense style and his unwavering blue gaze.

"I'd like you to work directly with the photojournalist we've hired to lead the story," Rick told them. "He's put together the initial storyboards and the type of interviews we'd like to conduct for this four-part series. You should know he's used to running an independent operation with little-to-no interference, so I need to make sure his move to prime time is as seamless as possible without affecting the integrity of the work."

"Of course," Sam replied. "Is he used to reporting in unstable situations or has he had any exposure to combat?"

Rick nodded. "He's done several assignments in the Middle East and Africa. He's actually broken a lot of stories major news networks were either unwilling or unable to investigate. But, like I said, he's been operating either on his own or with two or three other photojournalists, so moving to a more extensive news and production crew with a broader team of journalists will be his introduction to the majors."

"Have we heard of him?" Carey asked.

"If you follow the Associated Press and Reuters, probably," Rick answered. He reached for a file on his desk, handing it to them. "Wesley Elliott. He operates an indie agency out of Austin with his partners Martin Perry and Chris Fields. They rep photojournalists and reporters who work mainly freelance, but Wes has been focused almost entirely on fieldwork. He did a powerful set of stories on Syria before most people even knew where it was."

Sam felt her breath catch though her face remained polite and attentive. She felt Carey look at her, though she didn't acknowledge it, glancing briefly down at Wes's picture as she fought to appear unaffected. Wes looked a little wild with week-old scruff and a keffiyeh tied around his neck, his favorite Nikon in his browned hand. She was surprised to even recognize that camera. But then, he'd carried it with him everywhere, even all those years ago.

Perhaps it's because you didn't want to remember, her mind whispered. *He took so many photos of you with it.*

"Does he have prior experience in Brazil?" she asked, handing the file over to Carey, struggling to keep her voice even.

"Some," Rick acknowledged. "Though he does have contacts through his network," he added. "Wes has already got a lead on who he'd like to interview for the first two segments on *Movimento Passe Livre* as well as the Black Bloc youth demonstrators in Rio and Sao Paulo. You heard about the violence last week with the teachers and trade unionists demonstrating in Rio? We originally had this scheduled to kick off a month from now, but he's itching to get down there and get some initial interviews going while the getting's hot. We're months away from the World Cup, and tensions are high."

"Where is Wes now?" Sam heard herself ask.

"In Austin, prepping," Rick replied. "We'd like the team on the ground within the next few days."

"That's not a problem," Carey answered smoothly when Sam didn't immediately respond. "We'll send our team leaders to Austin tonight to sit down with him first thing tomorrow and start working through the details."

"Team leaders?" Rick asked, his brow knitting in question.

"Yes," Carey responded. "We have one person run point with Mr. Elliott at all times, a second to manage tactical operations in the background, and in this instance, we recommend a third leader to manage transport and logistics. Depending on how large the total crew you send is, we generally have at least eight to ten on guard at all times."

"Can this team be discreet?" Rick asked.

"Very," Carey responded confidently. "The team is comprised predominantly of former Special Forces operatives who are used to working subtly in both surveillance and reconnaissance. They won't be obtrusive or a hindrance in any way. In fact, with their language skills, connections, and knowledge of the city, Mr. Elliott and your crew will likely find them a great resource."

"Good," Rick nodded. "We don't generally outfit our news crews with this level of protection detail, but in this instance, with tensions this high, I don't want to take any chances." He paused, taking a sip of coffee. "But let me be clear: I also expect the quality of this investigative reporting to remain exceptional. You need to enable this team to do their job to the best of their ability," he said, leveling them both with a meaningful stare.

"Of course," Sam assured him, her voice steady even though her throat was cotton dry. "We have a great deal of experience in inconspicuous protection, and with our experience in Brazil, Mr. Elliott will likely find more the team more of a help than a hindrance."

They knocked out the rest of the details in the remaining thirty minutes of their meeting with Sam struggling to remain focused over the barrage of suppressed emotion. She kept seeing flashes of the Wes of her memories combined with the photo she'd glimpsed in the folder, wondering at how she could have forgotten the intensity behind the near-leonine shape of his amber eyes. He'd been a head-turner in his early twenties. But with a little age and maturity? *God help her.*

"We're sending the team down in the jet in two or three days. I can confirm the dates by tomorrow," Rick was saying.

"Our leads can go with Mr. Elliott," Carey answered. "If your assistant could email me his contact information, I'll forward it to my men now."

As Rick called in his assistant, Carey glanced at her, his minute expression asking if she was okay as she answered with the briefest of nods. Carey stood to greet the assistant, pulling out his smartphone as she emailed him the data from her tablet.

Sam proceeded to go over some of the high-level contractual details with Rick, forwarding him and his legal team the actual documents from her tablet as they spoke.

"Will you or Carey be part of the team?" Rick asked her.

Carey glanced at her, waiting for her answer.

Sam's face smoothed into a cool, professional smile. "The team we'll assign you is top notch. But if you require us for any reason to engage in the region, we're happy to oblige where appropriate," she assured him.

Rick stood with her, shaking the hand she extended. "I look forward to working with you, Ms. Wyatt, Mr. Nelson," he nodded. "I hear your team are the some of the best in the business," he said, gifting a rare smile.

She inclined her head in acknowledgment. "We'll do our utmost to ensure the safety of your team while they put together what I'm sure will be a very impressive piece of investigative journalism."

"The ratings will tell," Rick replied.

November—A few hours later
Teterboro Airport, New York

SAMANTHA

IT WAS ALREADY snowing in New York. Sam watched the beginning of gentle flurries in the cold night air. She briefly wondered if it would be snowing in Chicago for Thanksgiving.

"He looks the same," Carey commented. "Just a few years older."

No, Sam thought, still looking out the window of the jet as she sipped the mineral water Harris had given her after she'd gotten seated. *He was different. Seasoned. More intense.*

Carey put down his tablet and flipped open the file folder Rick had given them on Wes. "You want to read this file? It's basically his résumé and a little bit of his portfolio. He's done well for himself."

"He was always talented," she responded, eyes tracking the snow lit by the jet's wing lighting.

"Got a great break with AP and Reuters just after he graduated A&M," Carey told her, reading the file. "He was in Yugoslavia covering the uprising against Milosevic while you were going into the Navy."

"I'm graduating, Sammy. And you've got another year before you're in the service. It's a great opportunity. A dream come true. I can't pass this up..."

The flurries were becoming a little thicker, coming down a little bit harder. She laid her head back against the headrest.

"He was in Gujarat during the Muslim fire-bombing of that train while you were deployed to Afghanistan the first time."

"Yours is the only photograph I carry. You're the last thing I see every night. Anywhere I am. Always..."

The jet began a slow taxi toward the runway.

"He got his first major news spread for his work in Darfur while you were on your second tour."

I feel like I'm walking around without a piece of me... I miss you, Sammy. God, I miss you so much..."

Sam listened to the shuffle of papers.

"Looks like he was in the Sudan for a while before he transitioned to Turkey and Northern Iraq," Carey continued. "He got some good coverage of the Kurdish insurgency into Turkish territory. Looks to be right about when you decided to go to law school."

The blue lights of the runway were soothing. She loved the vibrant color, glowing in the cold, black night as the jet turned, taxiing faster. Harris picked up their glasses, letting them know they were second in line for takeoff.

"He started his agency with a couple photojournalist buddies while you were at that law firm."

"I don't want to hurt you, Sammy. God, never that. But we can't keep doing this. I have to end this before we pull each other apart. Forgive me for not being there for you right now. I can't imagine the pain you're going through, but you'll see your way through it—like everything else. You're the strongest person I know, Sammy. You are the love of my life..."

Sam had read that last letter so many times that it had finally fallen apart in her hands. And then it was—enough. She'd let him go, and if she was honest, she relinquished a big part of herself when she did it.

The jet began the smooth acceleration toward liftoff. She closed her eyes, enjoying the momentum. She loved the sensation of barreling down a runway, headed somewhere far, fast—a new city, a new direction. She relished the exact moment when gravity finally loosened its hold.

"He won a Pulitzer for his photos in the Green Zone when we were setting up shop at Lennox."

The jet lifted seamlessly, the roar of the engines quieting as they began the ascent.

Carey put down the file. "Since they've got about twelve people, I think we should double the team size."

"We still agreed on Talon, Rush, and Michaelson?" Sam asked.

"Yeah. Rush will work great with Wes. Michaelson leads logistics, and Talon will be on overwatch as usual. I want to send Henri with him—they can balance each other." Carey paused, waiting for her to weigh in. When she said nothing, he continued. "We can send Talon and Henri down to Rio to get the rest of the team there prepped and ready while Rush and Simon go to Austin to meet Wes."

The jet leveled out. She heard Harris beside her, pouring her another water.

"Could you pour me a bourbon, Harris?"

Carey looked up from the folder. "Make that two."

"Will you want the usual for dinner?" Harris asked.

"Sure," Sam answered, closing her eyes again.

Carey was silent for a while, but she could feel him watching her.

"You going to be all right with this?"

She said nothing.

"I can make sure you're up to speed while I run interference. We have a few gigs coming up that will be more focused on negotiations anyway. I think this will be ninety-five percent security. They've all worked Brazil, and Rush is ready."

The captain announced their altitude, the weather, and time to Chicago.

"Sammy—"

"Your drinks," Harris announced quietly, setting the bourbons in front of them on the small table.

"Thanks, Harris."

Samantha opened her eyes and looked at Carey.

"I'm fine, Bear."

"Fine as in actually okay or as in fucked up, insecure, neurotic, and emotional?" he asked, leaning toward her.

Sam picked up the glass. "You take the lead," she said, knocking a mouthful back. The singe was welcome. "You're right. There's no reason for me to be involved on this, especially with the other clients we have right now," she agreed. "This will be a cakewalk for the guys. They're ready, and with Michaelson and Henri on board, more's the better."

"You want the folder?" Carey asked, holding it out.

Sam shook her head.

They drank in silence for a while.

"Thinking of joining me for Thanksgiving?"

She looked up from her reverie, surprised at the turn in conversation.

"No. Jack asked me to join his family. Willa asked me to come to the shelter. I haven't decided what I'm doing yet," she admitted.

"Mom keeps asking after you. She wants you to consider coming home this year. If not for Thanksgiving, maybe Christmas?" Carey pressed. "Do you some good to be back at the ranch."

"You just want help with the baling," Sam mocked, though her voice sounded strained and tired, even to her. She closed her eyes again.

"That too," Carey chuckled. "It's no fun working the steers without you."

"You should take Willa," she suggested.

"I might. She's got so much stuff going on with the shelter. I keep offering to help, but she says she's got it covered."

"Willa says that, but she still wants your help," Sam told him.

"How do you know that?"

"Because I do."

"So when you say you're okay, you really mean you're not?" Carey inferred.

"No," Sam answered, opening her eyes again. She looked out at the night sky. She couldn't see any stars. "When I say I'm okay, I mean stop asking."

November—That night

The Whitney, Chicago

JACK

JACK FELT FINGERS sifting through his hair. He shifted, the book he'd been reading slipping off his stomach to land on the floor. The warmth of the fireplace lit his skin. He smiled as he breathed in Samantha's scent, still half-asleep.

"You're crashed out on the couch, darlin'," she murmured, finger-nails scratching his scalp gently. He loved when she did that. Jack stretched, his arm curling around her waist as he tucked his face into her thigh. "Come on up to bed."

"*Tesoro*," he mumbled, trying to pull her closer. "I was dreaming," he murmured, feeling her shift and slide next to him on the sofa. His arm looped around her bare leg, pulling her knee up over his hip.

"Don't you want to sleep in that big, comfortable bed of yours?" she asked, kissing his brow. He felt her smile against his forehead, her fingers continuing to thread through his hair.

"We were in Positano. The water was so blue. We jumped off a cliff..." he trailed off sleepily.

"So we plunged to our deaths?" she chuckled. "Nice dream."

"No," Jack mumbled. "I tried to hold you when we landed, but you slipped away as we were rising up." He nuzzled her. "You're always slipping away, *tesoro*..."

Samantha slid a hand under his arm, thumb rubbing his spine. Jack purred his pleasure. "Why would I want to be away from you, Jack?" she whispered.

He felt himself harden, couldn't resist the pleasure of pressing against her.

"Because you love me," Jack replied, pulling the side of her panties down, kissing her in earnest now. "And you won't admit it," he whispered against her mouth.

Samantha shifted closer as he touched her.

"...and if I love you—" her breath caught as he curled a finger into her, touching that perfect spot. "Why would I leave...?" she breathed. "Mmm, that's good," she told him, hips shifting closer. Jack luxuriated in her gentle panted breaths, feeling her clench around his movements, the humid heat of her body intoxicating.

"Let me have you, Samantha," he whispered, fully awake now, urging her higher, tighter against him.

"God, Jack…" she groaned. She took him into her hands in kind, thick and heavy, and Jack pushed forward, the firm pressure of her fingers so indescribably good.

He took her mouth in erotic, drawn-out kisses, biting her lip and then lapping the hurt as she gripped him, rubbing him against where she needed him most. Jack couldn't think, couldn't speak; the urgency to be inside of her blanked his mind as she fitted him to herself. The feeling was so delicious that Jack closed his eyes as he pushed into her, capturing her sounds in his mouth as he rooted deeper into the hot, wet constriction of her body.

"Jack," she gasped into his ear. "It's good. God, it's so, *so good…*" she shuddered, gripping his back.

"You're mine, *tesoro*," he whispered, stroking deeper into her. He impaled her body with tight, disciplined strokes, his pants and sex words mingling with her sighs and moans as she tried to control the inevitable drop toward mindlessness, where sensation and connection reigned. Jack lifted his head, watching her head fall back, the sinews of her neck in harsh relief as she struggled to stave off the climax, her body mastered with a restraint he couldn't quite coax her out of.

But Jack didn't want to shove past Samantha's extraordinary self-control. He didn't want to conquer her through the sheer force of his will and determination to win her over. He doubted that'd work anyway. Nothing would happen with Samantha that she didn't allow. And Jack adored that about her, even if it drove him crazy in equal measure.

"Tell me, baby," he murmured on a delicious withdraw and push. "Tell me how much you want this. Tell me how you want me," he urged, shifting so she was beneath him, pinned and penetrated, world awash in heat and vivid pleasure.

"I need this… I need you…please…" she gritted out, eyes clenched.

Jack swiveled his hips, momentarily setting a punishing pace, pushing them both toward the rise before he slowed, shifting down to a sizzling grind that had her groaning. He held deep, pulsing against the stretch and the rub, tripping their senses, igniting nerve endings and sharpening the arousal. Sam writhed under him, calling his name as she tried to push even closer, her hands gripping his shoulders.

"Say it," he insisted on a low drag and a deep return. "Tell me again."

"The way you feel, Jack…" she shuddered. "The way you move… Make me forget, you make me forget…"

Jack leaned in to take her mouth as he stroked deep into the soft hot heat of her, listening to her cries, watching her heartbeat pulsing at her slender neck. He rocked, ground, circled, and withdrew, surging back with maddening alterations to their tempo, adjusting the friction as each counteraction wore down her self-restraint. When he sensed her edging the brink, he bit her ear, tonguing the sting.

"Give yourself to me," he commanded, need making his voice raw. "Give it to me. I want you, *tesoro*, I want you to…"

Samantha's movement stuttered as she fought, then released, coming in long, voluptuous spasms, crying out to him, her nails indenting the skin on his shoulders and back. Jack reveled in the win—sucking in her breaths as if he could taste the endorphins, relishing her loss of control, enjoying the way she surrendered the vigilance she wore like armor. He rode out the jolts and ripples, pulling her leg up to his shoulder as he chased his pleasure, tasting her cries while he buried himself again and again, over and over until all he couldn't withstand the tidal wave of pleasure cascading over him, the voltage of their shared electricity amazing him as his climax curved and manipulated his spine. Jack moved in and out of her until he'd milked the moment for everything it was worth.

"Jack?" Samantha murmured after long minutes, the silken skin on the inside of her thighs rubbing him as she shifted.

He lifted his face from her neck to look at her, his heart still thudding from their sex, his senses saturated.

Her expression was uncharacteristically vulnerable and a little dazed, eyes backlit with the flicker of something raw. She threaded her fingers through the hair at his temples.

"You're closer than anyone's been in a long time," she admitted, her voice a little hoarse from their love making.

Jack absorbed that morsel, shifting to adjust their bodies sideways.

His hands scooped at her bottom to keep them knit together. He'd live inside her if he could.

As Samantha watched him, her gaze seemed to intensify, as if she were trying to communicate more, giving him another piece to her puzzle.

"I'm in love with you," Jack confessed, looking into her eyes. He knew he was lobbing what could become a hand grenade into the aftermath, but it seemed as obvious to him as it must be to her.

Samantha drew back infinitesimally. Slowly, so slowly she gifted him with a small, sweet smile, as if she were savoring and memorizing the moment. She seemed almost shy, a look so foreign to her that Jack was disarmed by it.

"Is this the first time you've ever said that?" she asked, her voice soft, nearly a whisper.

"It's the first time I've ever felt it *or* said it," he admitted, kissing her. "I don't know what the hell I was doing before, but this is completely different." He kissed her again, breathing her in. "*Senza di te la mia vita non ha senso,*"[14] he whispered.

"Jack…"

He could feel her mind zigzagging even as she traced the column of his throat gently, playing with the hollow there, touching his pulse.

She took a breath. "I'm not—"

"Don't," Jack interrupted, putting a finger to her mouth to stop her. "Don't respond. I know you. I know you'll go there when you're good and ready and not a minute before. I didn't tell you to pressure you into a response. I told you because I need you to know. I want you to know me." He drew his finger down the side of her face.

Samantha nodded after a moment before kissing his throat, breathing against him as they remained in each other's arms, not speaking for a long time. Jack was aware of the atmospheric shift and he wondered what she'd do with the knowledge—but he also didn't care. *He was hers,* he realized. *Hers to possess and consume.*

"One day, you're going to trust me," he told her, tracing the line

---

[14] Italian for "without you my life makes no sense."

from her shoulder to her arm.

She looked into his eyes, startled. "I do trust you, Jack—"

"No, *tesoro*," he whispered, touching the blade of her cheekbone. "You don't. Not yet. But one day you will," he replied, confident.

Samantha dropped her eyes to his chest as she ran her fingers across his clavicle. She chuckled suddenly.

"What?" he asked.

She shook her head, a bemused smile on her face.

"Tell me," he urged.

"It's silly. Just a memory."

"Then definitely tell me," Jack responded.

"I was never a fan of patience. Too bull-headed, I guess. I'd get so pissed off, I could kick something." Samantha admitted. "My granddaddy used to tell me patience was just a form of despair, disguised as a virtue."

Jack grinned, "I'd agree to that."

"And then he'd tell me sleep on it, pray on it, and when I was old enough, if neither of those worked, I could drink on it," she laughed, her eyes twinkling. "I miss that old coot."

Jack laughed with her, smiling at the way nostalgia softened her face. He couldn't resist nipping her lip. "I asked you to Thanksgiving dinner with my family last week. Will you join us?" he asked, pulling back.

Her mouth curved into a lazy smile. "Do I have to cook?"

Jack shook his head. "My parents are insane in the kitchen. I always told them if politics and the law doesn't work out, they should start their own restaurant. Jaime and I are just the lowly sous chefs."

"They sound like quite the pair."

"They are," he laughed. "I think you'll get a kick out of them. I know they'll get a kick out of you."

"Can I bring the wine then?"

"Of course. They'd love that. Particularly if it's a Barolo."

Samantha smiled, absently drawing figure eights on his arm. Jack tugged on a lock of her silky dark hair, drawing her attention back toward him.

"So that's a yes?"

She stopped, looking at him while the firelight danced across her skin. "I'm beginning to suspect you could talk me into just about anything," she admitted.

Jack smiled. "In that case, *vieni qui e baciami.*"[15]

---

[15] Italian for "come here and kiss me."

CHAPTER 20

November—Thanksgiving Day

Oak Park, Illinois

S A M A N T H A

"YOU REMEMBER WHEN Ry and I got cast as turkeys in grade school? And you and Mom made our tail feathers so big, we couldn't get into the truck's cab? Had to ride in the flatbed," Carey chuckled into the phone.

Sam laughed at the memory, recalling the way Ry and Carey rolled around the truck bed on the way to the school, hooting and hollering. "If anyone was gonna get cast as turkeys, it was gonna be you two," she laughed softly. "Your mom and I just wanted to make sure you experienced it in its full glory."

"Depends on how you define 'glory,' I suppose. My butt was so heavy with feathers, I couldn't keep my balance. Didn't I fall off the stage at one point?" he drawled, his Texas twang definitely stronger after a couple days home.

"Bear, honey, I can't help you got two left feet."

Sam glanced up as she heard Jaime laughing next to his mother at the kitchen counter. Sam had been in the kitchen pass-through to the dining room picking out another bottle of wine when Carey had called.

"How're your parents?" she asked as she watched the Roman clan from the dining room.

"Good. They miss you."

Sam ran her finger along the wine rack, swallowing back a lump in her throat. It had been years since she'd gone home, much less for

Thanksgiving. "You know what I miss?" she started, clearing her throat a little. "Your mama's Granny Smith apple pie. You been helping her cook?"

"Nah," Carey answered. "All she does is slap my hands and shoo me out anyhow. I've been awake since the ass crack of dawn with Dad, ass and elbows up in steer," he complained. "God, I missed this," he admitted then, sounding happy.

"Tell them I love them," Sam said as Jack slipped into the dining room, his hands sliding over her shoulders, kneading gently. He'd been chatting with his dad in his study when Carey had called her. She smiled reassuringly at him and held up a finger, mouthing "one minute."

"Tell them yourself," Carey replied. "Seriously, Sammy. They'll be happy to hear your voice."

Sam leaned back against Jack. "I know it. I'll give them a buzz later on, okay?"

"Okey doke, Sammy girl. I'll catch up with you tomorrow, alright?"

"Yeah, Bear. Happy Thanksgiving."

"You too," Carey said, signing off.

"Everything all right?" Jack asked, kissing her temple. His scent wafted around her, and she closed her eyes, enjoying the brief moment of intimacy.

"Yeah. Carey just called to wish Happy Thanksgiving," she explained.

"Is he in Texas?"

She nodded. "At the ranch."

Jack remained silent, waiting for her to say more. Sam strolled toward the built-in wine rack. "So…another bottle of vino?"

"Will you go back?" Jack asked instead. "For Christmas, maybe?"

Sam shrugged, noncommittal. "We'll see. I'm not sure where I'll be in December yet."

"With me," Jack responded decisively as he reached around her for a specific bottle. "Mom's favorite," he confided, gesturing at the Vietti Barolo Rocche.

Sam smiled her thanks.

"If you'd like to be back home in Texas, I'd like to go with you, if that's all right," he told her, tucking a loose tendril behind her ear.

"You know how to bale hay?" she asked.

"I can learn," he replied, a cocky gleam in his silver eyes.

Jaime poked his head through the pass. "We sent you for more wine ages ago, Sam! You look like you know your way around a wine rack. What's the holdup?" he chided, wagging his brows teasingly.

Sam laughed, picking up the wine key to open the bottle. "Here you go, you impatient lush. Next you're going to tell me you can't cook without alcoholic inspiration," she teased. "You guys have already gone through the two bottles I brought, and I suspect we're now actually farther away from sitting down to dinner!" She followed him back into the kitchen, Jack close behind.

"*Un buon vino, un buon uomo, e una bella donna dura poco,*"[16] their mother, Lena, lilted, pulling open the oven door to check on the turkey.

Evangelina Roman was a classic Italian beauty, with a sharp mind and a rapier wit. Jack and Jaime inherited their dark hair and quick tongues from her. She had vivid blue eyes and classic, refined features. It was easy to see where the Roman brothers got their spectacular good looks. The way she was cursing at the turkey, Sam could also see where Jack got his hot-flash temperament.

"Uh oh, better pour more wine, *immediatamente!*" Jaime laughed. "It not only helps with the creative process, it has also been scientifically proven to enhance patience. Doesn't it, Ma?"

"If I wasn't as patient as a saint, I would have asked where we are with the antipasti," Lena declared, holding out her glass as Jaime poured. "Samantha, thank God for you! I understand you know how to manhandle men quite efficiently. I'll need you to hog-tie this one later," she declared, eyeing Jaime's progress.

"I suspect he may enjoy that," Sam replied drily. "It'll only encourage him."

Lena tossed her head back, laughing. "Oh, you're a keeper," she declared. "Jack, this one—I like her," she told her eldest, wagging a

---

[16] Italian for "a good wine, a good man, and a beautiful woman does not last long."

finger in Sam's general direction.

"Me too. I try to show her frequently how much I like her." Jack's grin bordered on nefarious while Jaime smacked him upside the head.

"What am I missing? What's so funny?" Sandro Roman asked, carrying Maddie into the kitchen on his shoulders. Maddie was wearing a pilgrim hat and pink heart sunglasses. She was tapping her grandfather's head with a rainbow wand, to her great amusement. Sandro patiently allowed it, accepting the glass of wine Jaime extended to him.

"Mom's just asking Samantha to hog-tie Jaime," Jack explained, plucking Maddie off his father's shoulders.

Standing side by side like that, Sam suspected she was looking at a tear in the space-time continuum. Sandro was what Jack would look like in another twenty-to-thirty years. Sandro's midnight hair was shot with silver, his handsome face creased at the eyes and forehead with character and good humor. Jack favored his father more heavily than his brother, their silver eyes nearly identical as well as their broad-shouldered, barrel-chested builds. She could see that Sandro grew up boxing from his stature and comportment. She could also see he was a sly old fox if she ever saw one.

Sam knew from his reputation on the Hill that Sandro Roman was capable of charming you into compromise after compromise until you unwittingly realized you were under his control. He'd earned his reputation for being devious and intelligent. She'd bet her right hand that if he hadn't become a politician, he'd be a conman or a mob boss. Perhaps as a career Chicago politician and attorney, he was a little of both.

Sandro's brows lifted as he regarded her. "Oh? Is that like an early Christmas gift?" he inquired idly, toasting Sam lightly with a clink of his wine glass.

Sam chuckled. "It's just a basic skill my dad taught me growin' up, but it did come in useful for handsy boys at dances," she responded as she popped an olive from Jaime's antipasti into her mouth.

"Now that's good parenting," Sandro replied, silver eyes twinkling. "We'll have to teach Maddie that trick."

"You would really tie me up?" Jaime theatrically lamented.

"Nah," Sam answered. "You haven't finished our mobile apps yet. Carey would be devastated."

"Heartless," he answered on a groan. "But we're close. I'll have some protos for you guys next week. You'll be able to test them out."

"Good, because we have a new client traveling to Brazil I want to try them out on," she replied, thinking of Wes and the NBS crew.

"Really? Where? I'll be in Rio meeting with Brasil Telecom in a couple weeks. I could help you with the trialing," Jaime offered.

"Trial? What trial?" Lena asked, hand rolling the gnocchi as Sandro stood at the stove, stirring the acquacotta.

As Jaime explained what they were working on, Sam was struck by the easy domesticity of the moment. Lena and Sandro moved around the kitchen together with the easy familiarity born of years spent together. She noticed Sandro took opportunities to touch her often and with obvious fondness. Sam realized this was where Jack learned his easy affection and tactile playfulness. This is what love looked like to him. It radiated off his parents effortlessly like a pronounced aura. Standing in the kitchen preparing a meal as a family, Sam was acutely aware of how different her upbringing was from Jack's. She glanced to the kitchen table where Maddie was helping Jack sprinkle cocoa powder over a pan of homemade tiramisu.

Jack glanced up, catching her pensive gaze.

Sam immediately smoothed her face into benign placidity as she lifted her glass to him in a silent toast.

Jack's eyes darkened infinitesimally.

"Samantha," Sandro called. "Do you know how to cook *pesce azzurro alla Griglia*?" he asked, pointing at butterflied blue fish fillets in a broiling pan.

"No, sir," she answered. "But I'm pretty sure I can catch it and gut it."

Now it was Sandro's turn to laugh. "I like this one, Gianni. She's a keeper," he told Jack.

"That's what I said," Lena agreed.

Sam's glanced at Jack quizzically. "Your name is Gianni? How did I not know this?"

"Nickname," Jack replied.

"Because of your resemblance to your uncle," Sam recalled. "And you?" Sam asked, pointing to Jaime.

"*Grassoccio*," Sandro answered for him with a big smile. "It means 'chubby.'"

Sam blinked. "That's ironic, right?" she asked, gesturing at Jaime's lean frame even as his ears pinked.

"Dad, stop," Jaime grumbled, slicing thick, freshly baked Italian loaves.

"He was a fat baby," Lena shrugged. "Took me nearly thirty-six hours to squeeze him out. Thought he was going to tear me in half. I was done having kids after that," she confided while Jaime groaned and Jack and his father laughed.

"I will never live that down. I can't help how I came out the womb, Ma!" Jaime cried, slicing the tomatoes for the bruschetta forcefully.

"What's a womb?" Maddie asked suddenly.

"Nothing you need to worry about for many, many years, *micina cara*," Jack answered, rolling his eyes at his brother.

"Come here, Samantha. I'll show you how to cook like an Italian," Sandro urged.

As she helped him slice and prepare the fish with thinly-sliced lemons, parsley, garlic, and bread crumbs, he peppered her with casually-asked questions. Sam was aware he was garnering information on her family and background, but she figured his position on certain Senate committees probably got him access to far more substantial morsels of data than she would provide over a sizzling pan, and Sandro was so damnably charming, she didn't mind the mild and well-meant intrusions. Sam drank Barolo until she was pleasantly giddy, laughing at Sandro's jokes and Jack and Jaime's colorful translations of Lena's occasionally vehement outbursts in Italian.

They nibbled on Jaime's antipasti, opened more bottles of wine, cooked, and listened to an eclectic combination of vintage R&B and Sinatra. Within a couple hours, Thanksgiving dinner was ready. Jack lit the candles, Jaime opened another bottle, and Sam helped Sandro and Lena bring dishes to the table. The feast was stunning, and Sam felt a genuine warmth steal over her body as she observed their handiwork.

"*Pan di sudore, miglior sapore*,"[17] Lena declared.

"*A tavola non si invecchia*,"[18] Sandro responded, seating his wife before rounding the table.

Jack mimicked the motion, dropping a casual kiss to her cheek as Sam sat down.

"Samantha, you are a welcome guest at our table anytime," Lena told her, clasping her hand. "It's been such a pleasure to have you join our family."

Jack slipped his hand around hers under the table, holding it to his thigh as he smiled at her.

She waited for the old uneasiness to emerge, but instead she felt strangely relaxed, perhaps mellow from too much wine and the heat of the kitchen. She didn't analyze her feelings too closely, afraid that if she prodded, she'd lose her contentment as Sandro said a short grace and Lena encouraged Maddie to tell everyone what she was thankful for as they took turns serving her small helpings of nearly everything.

The conversation ebbed and flowed, the meal and wine consumed and enjoyed. Sandro told entertaining stories about the boys growing up, and Lena debated a variety of topics with Jack and Jaime while Sam sat back and watched, entertained by their amicable verbal sparring. Sandro joked and teased while Lena parried and struck. As a couple, they were lovely compliments to each other, and Sam enjoyed deducing which one had greater influences on Jack and Jaime's characters and approach to life. Sam managed to avoid getting drawn too far into the debates, though she didn't try to elude Sandro's continued questioning. She gave simple, straightforward answers that she dressed up with a smile, knowing he was half-curious and half just watching out for the well-being of his eldest son.

Sam liked Jack's parents. They were wealthy, influential, and urbane, but they had a kind of old world anchorage and easygoing air about them that eschewed that kind of affectation. The Romans looked, felt,

---

[17] Italian for "bread that comes out of sweat, tastes better."

[18] Italian for "at the table with good friends and family you do not become old."

and sounded like a family. And watching them together slid another set of colors together in Jack's Rubik's cube. It also explained why he was so good at presenting one side of himself that had very little to do with the other. He'd come by the ability to divide his public persona and personal privacy honestly through years of practice growing up under high-profile parents who kept what happened behind closed doors very real and decidedly unpretentious.

The conversation flowed until long after the dessert and coffee were consumed, and Maddie was passed out on Lena's shoulder. Jack leaned over at some point to ask if she was ready to head home.

"I was hoping we could neck in your childhood room," she whispered, her eyes teasing.

Jack smirked at her, his eyes amused. "I'm pretty certain they converted it to a guest bedroom years ago."

"Liar," Sam accused. "You just don't want me to see band posters and your high school porn collection."

Jack rolled his eyes, shaking his head.

"What's Gianni rolling his eyes about?" Sandro asked.

"Oh, he won't tell me what he was like as a disgruntled youth," Sam replied, a glint in her eye.

Sandro guffawed. "Disgruntled? Hardly. We had to kick him out of the house to go to Northwestern. He kept coming back on the weekends. And then he brought Mitch. Sometimes we wondered if he'd ever left," Sandro confided, laughter lighting his eyes.

"It's true," Lena nodded. "When he wasn't playing sports or at school, he was lounging around, reading, listening to records, and eating all the food in the middle of the night."

"Sounds familiar," she replied as she glanced at Jack.

Jack rolled his eyes. "The town car will be here in fifteen minutes."

"Nice save," Jaime teased, picking Maddie up from his mother. "I'll get her ready for bed. Do you want her here tonight?"

"Yeah," Sandro answered. "Go ahead and put her down. We're taking her out to the Lincoln Park Zoo tomorrow."

"Great—I need some time in the office to get ready for the Brazil trip."

"When are you going again?" Jack asked.

"A couple weeks. Brasil Telecom is looking at expanding the 4G service throughout the country, and they're asking a few companies to come in and pitch apps they want to standardize on their new smartphone operating systems," Jaime explained as Maddie snored gently on his shoulder.

"Who all is going?" Samantha asked.

"Me, Carter Robbison from Movicom, Talvin Gupta from Sentient, and Chen Lei from Babel, that I know of," Jaime told them, rounding the table.

"Those are some heavy hitters," she remarked.

"Bunch of tech geeks, you mean," Jaime chuckled. "Sam, it was really good that you could join us," he said, leaning forward to kiss her on the cheek. "I'll swing by with the test app sometime this week, and we'll figure out some sort of trialing for that client you have in Rio."

Sam nodded, smiling at him and petting a hand down Maddie's sleeping head.

"Bro, you and me, the old boxing club with Dad on Sunday?" Jaime asked. "Be prepared to get your ass handed to you," he told Jack with a wink.

"Better bring Maddie's blanket because you're going to be crying into it," Jack responded, clasping a hand around his brother's shoulder affectionately as he leaned in to kiss Maddie's soft, plump cheek.

"Tell Mitch to come too, if he's back from Indiana by then," Sandro added, smiling. "I'll school all of you."

"*Dal frutto si conosce l'albero*,"[19] Lena sighed.

Lena and Sandro insisted on packing leftovers for them, patting their cheeks and kissing them both as they saw them out. The fall air had become downright cold, especially at that late hour, and Sam could see her breath as they walked toward the waiting town car.

Jack tucked her into his side as they settled in the car, laying his cheek on her head as she leaned into him, enjoying the feel of his fine cashmere coat against her cheek and his long fingers delving into her

---

[19] Italian for "the apple doesn't fall far from the tree."

hair as he stroked her gently.

"I'm glad you came with me," he murmured.

"I liked them," she mumbled sleepily, breathing in his scent. "That's the first family dinner I've been to since..." She distantly heard herself trail off.

"Since what, *tesoro?*"

Sam shifted against him, closing her eyes and drowsing.

"Since Dad and Ryland died," she mumbled, slipping into a food-and drink-induced doze.

Jack didn't say anything, but she thought she felt his arm tighten around her.

November—Later that night

The Whitney, Chicago

JACK

"I'VE NEVER HEARD you talk about anyone like this before, Gianni. I thought her name sounded familiar, and then it struck me. I knew her father..."

Jack guided a relaxed and sleepy Samantha from the car up to his apartment. She'd gone through the mechanics of getting ready for bed in a lethargic daze, crawling between the blankets and sighing happily before promptly passing out.

What he'd give to be able to sleep like her. It seemed she could sleep anytime and anywhere and wake up rejuvenated, even if it was only for a twenty-minute power nap. Jack padded downstairs to pick up his coat. He pulled out the manila envelope, taking it into his study.

"I pulled some of her files. I can't share a great deal with you. A lot of her work in the Navy is redacted, but what details I could share are here..."

Jack eyed the file sitting on his desk warily. It was one thing to do a background check on someone buying one of his properties. It was another thing entirely to read highly confidential and undoubtedly personal information about the woman he'd fallen for without her knowledge or consent.

Jack knew his father meant well. He also knew this was standard operating procedure for a man who garnered favors and clout through information gathering and select, opportunistic sharing of that knowledge. There was so much Jack wanted to know about Samantha, and there was so much she glossed over or didn't share. He knew that her past impacted how she operated and made decisions, and so he'd accepted the file, slipping it into this coat when he knew he shouldn't have.

"I met Robert Wyatt during my first term on the finance committee. He was one of the largest private oil owners in the United States at the time—a real heavy hitter and very savvy. It was terrible the way he and his son died. And the boy was so young…"

Samantha rarely discussed her past, much less her father and brother. Jack knew they'd passed away, but she'd never disclosed the specifics. She seldom talked about her time in the military, though most of her closest bonds were with the men she'd trained and fought with on her tours. She didn't discuss her past relationships, though he knew she'd been loved by at least a couple of other men—and one in particular, who had hurt her to the point that Jack was the one paying for it.

Everything he knew about Samantha was related to what she liked in bed and how she ran her current day-to-day life. Jack felt an irrational and aberrant jealousy of anyone who knew anything about her as he gathered the pieces and shards from the little she was willing to disclose on rare occasions. And now he had a thick file and several cases of her ex-lover's wine hidden in his wine storage, mocking his obsession and tempting him to violate the fragile trust she had in him.

"I can see you love her, Gianni. And I want you to be happy. But I don't want you to be blind. She is complex. Così fan tutte.[20] " His father nodded in understanding. "But her background is labyrinthine. There are things in here you should be aware of if you are serious about her. Things she may not even be aware of…"

Jack reached out, his hand hovering over the manila envelope. He

---

[20] Italian for "that is the way of all women."

snatched it up after a moment, standing and crossing over to his wall safe, tucking it under other documents, obscuring it from his vision. He left the study, taking the wrought iron staircase two at a time, slipping into the bedroom to sidle next to her on the bed.

Samantha smiled in her sleep, murmuring as she slipped her hand toward him, seeking him even as she drifted back into her dreams. This was new. When she'd first stayed with him, she'd remained so still, her sleeping form compact and angled away from him, toward the door, as if in preparation. Now, she seemed to gravitate toward him, reaching for him in the barely-morning hours, her fingers tracing cool sheets until they found him.

"It's normal to love a dangerous woman," his father told him with serious eyes. "They know how to wield their power, and they are not afraid of yours. They make you work for everything you get and it's all the sweeter once you get it. Makes you feel coraggioso[21] *to be able to hold her. I know this, Gianni. Look at your mother." He smiled. "A lioness. But Samantha is dark. She's dark for a reason…"*

Jack looked down at her now, body relaxed in repose, her dark hair a silky skein across his pillow. Samantha was endlessly fascinating, exhilarating him, prompting him to become disconcertingly fanatical. Jack suspected there wasn't much he wouldn't do for her, and yet there was so much about her he didn't understand. It was a massive gamble. Samantha was high-stakes risk personified.

Jack slid off the bed, relieved he hadn't read the file, hadn't broken an unspoken confidence with her, as fragile and imperfect as it was. She would disclose what she could in time, and he had to give her the space to do it. He had to have faith that she would do it. Give back to him what he so willingly gave to her. As Jack undressed, preparing for bed, his resolve solidified, hardened, as everything clarified. He would wait for her. She would be worth the risk.

---

[21] Italian for "brave; strong."

CHAPTER 21

November—A week later

Sam's office in the Loop, Chicago

SAMANTHA

JAIME'S APP WAS nearly flawless. The interface was seamless and easy to use, and it could pinpoint the location of the objects being tracked within a few feet. It also couldn't be disabled unless the user took the SIM card out of the phone or if the locater chip on the object was destroyed. Jaime held up the locater chip, the size of an eraser head.

Sam loved it. "Okay, I won't hog tie you," she grinned, looking down at the app on her tablet as Jaime walked around her large office, watching the dot move on the screen. She noticed another dot farther off screen. She pulled up a separate map. The dot was about eight blocks away from her office. "What is this other dot? Do you have another locater chip?"

"That's Jack," he answered, laughing at her astonished expression. "I programmed his phone's SIM into that prototype to prove it wasn't just a proximity reading," Jaime informed her, looking mischievous and proud of himself.

Sam rolled her eyes. "Somehow, I don't think he's going to like that. God knows I wouldn't."

"What makes you think he's not tracking you?"

She glanced up, expression darkening.

Jaime chortled, shaking his head. "Kidding! I'm kidding. I know you'd do far worse than hog tie me if I did that. That's just a simple locater all phones with SIM cards have, so you can choose to use that as a double-back on clients you're guarding provided they're all right with it. We can test another locater chip by putting it on an object if you like, or we can have one of your team put it on for the day. Anyone you want to annoy?" Jaime asked benignly as he sat down next to her, opening his laptop.

"You're asking who I want to tag besides the man I'm seeing?" Sam asked, bemused.

"Well, yeah. We need a test before we get to Rio, right?"

She thought about it and then buzzed her assistant in.

"Marvin, get me the nearest terrified intern," she said succinctly.

Marvin nodded, unfazed, before stepping out of the office and shutting the door.

Jaime smiled. "You're mean."

"Well, yeah," Sam answered, opening the second app. "Try growing up on a ranch with a bunch of guys and then going to the military. If that doesn't make you a little mean, I don't know what does." She pointed to the screen. "I'm guessing these aren't effective after a certain distance or depth or in extreme heat or cold?"

"I've got a meeting with a chip maker in Taiwan who's been developing this technology. We're looking at ways to waterproof it as well as improve the range through adjustments to the silicone casing. Right now, the silicone makes it lightweight and easy to place on clothes, but short of injecting a chip into your clients, this is a great way of keeping track of them or whatever they're trying to insure." Jaime held up the locater device, showing it to her. "It doesn't require a battery, but it does require wireless or network signals to work, so it can be picked up regardless of the distance as long as they're not being jammed or in one helluva dead zone. As for depth, let's say they place the object in a vault, yes, you'd lose the signal, but the minute it's out, you'd see it pop back up on your app. You can set up a trigger so that it alerts you if it gets out of proximity of that vault or secure location within a certain number of feet," he explained.

"How do you activate it?"

"They're all activated already. But you need to input the login IDs to see them. You just have to look at the ID on the chip to see it on your app." He leaned over and tapped out a number. Jack's dot blinked off the screen. "See? Now you see him." He turned the dot back on. Then off again. "Now you don't."

"You'd better take that off my tablet. He finds out, I have a feeling he'll skin your ass." Sam smiled, shaking her head. "But seriously, you're making me really happy right now," she told him. "I always said my job was like herding cats amongst rocking chairs. This will make it so much easier keeping track of clients on missions. Wait 'til the other partners see what it can do for some of the high-dollar art and jewelry we insure."

Marvin knocked, ushering a young, anxious-looking college intern into her office.

Sam stood, smiling at the intern. "Hi, I'm Sam Wyatt," she said, extending her hand.

"I—I know who you are, Ms. Wyatt," the terrified intern replied, accepting her hand.

"And you are?" Sam prompted. Marvin nudged the kid forward.

"Sorry! I'm uh, I'm Billy Denton, from University of Chicago."

"Great school," Sam nodded. "I went there."

"I know, ma'am," Billy nodded, looking flustered. "Um, how can I—how can I help you?"

"Billy, I need you to pick up some important documents for me. Can you do that?"

"Yes! Yes, ma'am," Billy answered eagerly.

Sam smiled indulgently. "Great. High tail it to O'Hare now, and Marvin will send you the details of your flight and the pick-up."

Billy blinked. "Wait. Sorry. What?"

"You're going to pick up some documents for me, right?" Sam prompted.

"Well, yes, but—"

"Great," she smiled brightly as she patted him on the back, slipping the locater chip under the back of his shirt collar as she turned him toward the door. She thought she heard Jaime snicker. "Marvin will email you your flight information and the address so you know where you're going. Keep your receipts and make sure to submit an expense report this week so you can be reimbursed for meals or whatever.

Good? Okay," she said, her tone friendly. She winked at Marvin, whose expression revealed nothing out of the ordinary as he whisked a disoriented Billy away.

"Oh, Christ!" Jaime gasped as the door closed. He rolled back, laughing. "Where are sending that poor kid, you heartless hell cat?"

Sam shrugged. "How far do you want to test the locater?"

Jaime blinked. "Are you shitting me?"

She crossed her arms, lifting a brow.

Jaime chuckled, shaking his head. "Send the kid to Seattle."

"I'll do you one better," she responded as Marvin knocked again. "Marv, send Billy to Anchorage. Have someone meet him at the airport and hand him an envelope. Make sure Billy texts you when he lands and let me know."

Marvin nodded. "What do you want in the envelope?" he asked, as if he was used to hijinks as a matter of course.

"I don't care. You think of something good. I'm testing out the locater chip we just planted on him. Ask him to come straight back to the office when he returns. No deviations. I slipped it under his collar. Find a way to get it back without him noticing."

Marvin shrugged. "No problem, boss."

Jaime cackled into his fist as Marvin shut the door again. "You are so goddamn mean."

Sam shrugged. "Nah. That's just a little jaunt. Mean would be sending him to Abu Dhabi. You oughta stick one of these on Maddie," she suggested.

"Who do you think was my test case?" Jaime said, an unrepentant grin on his face. "She's the whole reason I developed the app in the first place. I kept turning around and she'd be up to no good somewhere. Keeping track of a five-year-old is no joke!"

"Just to warn you, she's not going to like that when she's sixteen," Sam warned. She sat down next to him again, picking up her tablet. "What's the ID on that locater I just stuck on him?"

Jaime helped her turn it on. The intern was already headed toward the blue line. Looked like he was going to hoof it to O'Hare on the "L".

She smiled again, zooming the screen in.

"So who's taking care of Maddie while you're in Brazil?" Sam asked casually.

"Mom's got her for a few days, but Jack will take over after she heads back to D.C. I've got a nanny who comes in during the day to help out, but she's only part time," Jaime explained. "Ma likes you, by the way," he added.

"What's not to like?" Sam replied with grin.

"She called you *ingambatissima*," he informed her archly.

"Does that mean 'bad-ass?' Because if it does, then she'd be right," Sam teased, though she felt unaccountably pleased that their mother had liked her. Lena was a wickedly intelligent woman and a tough customer, not prone to easy approval.

"Close. It means *really* on the ball," Jaime answered with an approving nod. "She likes that you have your shit together."

Sam glanced at him, expression casual. "I'm glad. She's impressive. It was kind of your parents to let me crash your Thanksgiving like that."

"You didn't crash—"

"I meant to talk to you about what you mentioned after dinner, by the way," she interrupted, leading the back to the more comfortable topic of business.

Jaime's brow creased in question.

"You mentioned Talvin Gupta will be with you on this trip," she continued.

"Yeah?" he asked, perplexed. "He's the CEO of Sentient Applications. Why wouldn't he go?"

"I can't disclose how I know this, but he's been involved with some, shall we say, less than scrupulous characters. May I suggest you limit the time you spend with him in person?" she asked. "And may I also suggest you take my guys with you?"

Jaime looked doubtful. "What do you mean 'less than scrupulous?'"

"Terrorists, Jaime. He's been linked to terrorists," Sam told him flatly. "How are you getting down to Brazil? You're not traveling with him, are you?"

"No." Jaime shook his head, looking dubious. "I was going to go out with Carter on his jet. We're old friends. What do you mean 'terrorists?'"

"His company has been linked to terrorists in Pakistan. I can't tell you more than that, but I'd like you to consider bringing a couple of my guys with you for security on the flight, and I'll have more down there to meet you for coverage," Sam offered.

"You don't think I need K&R, do you?" he sputtered. "I'm just a tech developer."

"Who happens to own a multi-million dollar company that produces locater apps that would be incredibly useful to any number of individuals and organizations who'd rather not pay for them outright," Sam finished.

"Sam, I really don't think that'll be necessary—" Jaime started.

"Jaime, with all due respect, you're wealthy, you come from a big-name family, and you have a great deal to offer and to lose. You're traveling with men who are also wealthy and well-known and have a great deal to offer and to lose. You'll be in a country you are both unfamiliar with and have no real power in. One of your colleagues is known to associate with some highly corrupt and remorseless individuals who are on the watch list of multiple governments. I'd say security is not simply necessary. In fact, I'm saying it'd be *insane* for you not to consider being prepared for any possible outcome."

Jaime was quiet for a moment, absorbing the information.

"Look at it this way," Sam said, changing tact. "You need to meet up with my people anyway to test the locaters on the network crew. You could try it out yourself with the guys I assign to you the first few days—work through some of the kinks. It wouldn't be a massive security detail. Just enough to ensure you've got coverage, and I'm offering this pro-bono."

Jaime chewed on his lip. She could sense him coming down on the right side of the decision.

"Are you thinking of Rush and Talon?" he asked.

Sam shook her head. "They're already assigned to the network client down there, but you'll see them. All my guys are great. Best of the best. You don't need to worry," she assured him, covering his hand with her own. "Think about it, Jaime. Wouldn't your family feel better?"

He looked up at her, his light eyes, so like Jack's, flashing with concern.

She patted his hand, standing. "I'll email you the details tomorrow. You can meet the guys I'd like to fly down with you if you like."

Jaime looked a little bemused. "I never really had a choice in this, did I?"

Sam grinned.

November—Same week

Rio de Janeiro, Brazil

WESLEY

IT WAS ALREADY 1:00 a.m.

Wes eyed the digital clock on the bed as he adjusted the laptop on his legs. He looked back at the screen. A frozen still of Vicki Hendricks interviewing one of the leaders of today's teachers' protests was paused mid-frame. He pressed play again.

"Maria Melo represents just one of over ten thousand teachers who took to the streets in Rio today in peaceful protests for educator wages and the limited resources Brazil has allocated toward nationwide schools while it spends billions to fund marketing and infrastructure for the upcoming World Cup and Olympics—"

Wes fast forwarded the footage to an interview with a teacher from Sao Paulo who was talking about how difficult it was to regulate drug use at schools now that dealers were targeting kids as young as nine or ten with crack and other cocaine byproducts. It was awful, just shocking, and some of his stories were so saddening that they made Wes cringe to hear them, imagining children chasing their dealers like they would an ice cream truck down the streets in favelas. Let CNN and BBC cover the misallocation of funding and resources…this was the gritty reality Wes wanted to focus his lens on.

He had an editor on the crew who was pretty good, but he always liked to review all the raw footage himself first, culling through the best parts right after the interviews, sifting down to the most substantial pieces while everything was fresh. He'd go through it again and again over the next weeks, cutting, editing, refining, consumed with getting it just right, just so until go-time. But tonight, in the peace of the silent hotel suite, he went through the film like he used to go through his negatives on a makeshift light box somewhere west of whatever hell he'd gotten himself to in order to nail the shot.

They'd already been on the ground a week, systematically working through the segments, lucky enough to hit the ground right when the teachers' protests were starting to gain momentum near Candelaria, in downtown Rio. He'd figured out early on that sometimes you needed to be not only in the right location but in the most uncomfortable areas you could imagine to get to the heart of the most eviscerating stories. Although he'd been uncomfortable with it early on, preferring to remain an observer, he'd forced himself to get right in the mix, getting closer to the truth of the moment, no matter how badly he'd wanted to step back, remaining aloof and unmoved while he filmed or photographed silently in the background.

He had interviews with some of the Black Bloc anarchists tomorrow, but he could sense something brewing. In the middle of the crowds, he could feel peaceful protests shifting to something darker, the intentions and motivations morphing into something more violent and chaotic.

Vicki would be up for it. She'd gone prime time a few years ago, but she wasn't so far gone into the corporate network bullshit that she couldn't still roll her sleeves up and get in there. She'd want to keep her street cred alive as a frontline journalist.

"And miss the chance to work with you again, asshole?" Vicki had joked after she'd arrived with the crew on the NBS jet. "Never. How the hell have you been?" Wes liked that about her. She was as beautiful as some of the all-American cheerleaders you grew up fantasizing about during high school, but she had grit, and she could flip the switch on cool professional anchor to beer-guzzling roughneck in seconds flat. He'd watched her do it as she'd switched back to polite professional when he'd introduced her to Evan Rush and Simon Michaelson. Wes also didn't miss the glint in her eye as she checked out Simon when he turned away to speak to one of his men. Wes shook his head in amusement at the memory, shifting his laptop onto the bed and rubbing his eyes. Some things didn't change. Vicki was like a guy in that regard. She enjoyed herself, didn't get too entangled, and then moved on to the next.

They'd had a brief thing in Gujurat, what seemed like eons ago now. He could barely remember anything about the affair past the tumble of sheets and falling off the bed one of the few times they had access to a hotel. He remembered laughing with her, almost as excited about the hot shower as he was the sex. He recalled fighting over the shampoo with her. It had been easy and fun—and apparently forgettable, since he could barely recall what she felt like. He'd resigned himself to that reality after Sammy. Once you got close enough to fire that hot, everything else sort of seemed…lukewarm.

Wes stood, stretching as he pushed his shoulder length hair back. He'd been editing for a couple hours. He'd picked at dinner, distracted over the footage from the demonstration, talking to the team about the Black Bloc, mulling over the rumors they might evolve the demonstration into an anti-government orgy tomorrow. Now Wes wondered briefly if it would be too late to call for room service. His stomach grumbled at the thought.

He could hear Evan and Simon in the living room area separating their rooms. Wes hadn't been in love with the idea of sharing a two-room suite with Evan when they'd discussed logistics, thinking it would feel like he was under constant surveillance, but it hadn't been bad. Evan watched him like a hawk, yes, but he was respectful and surprisingly helpful to the process. He'd been with Wes every step of the way since they'd started, making suggestions and providing alternatives if the locations or shots got too risky, but he didn't actually hamper or hinder the process in any way. Evan also had a better-than-passable grasp of Portuguese that had come in handy daily. And Wes was relieved that Evan just looked like another journalist, though he toted serious firepower in the camera case rather than an actual DSLR. He suspected

Evan had more heat on him than Wes wanted to know about.

"How was check in?" Simon was asking Evan as Wes wandered out.

"Good," Evan answered. "Carey says Sam is sending down some more guys with Jaime Roman. She wants us to meet to try out the tech he's been helping us develop." Evan glanced up when Wes stepped out of his bedroom. "Hey. Couldn't sleep?"

Wes looked down at the coffee table in front of Evan. He had one of his hand guns disassembled the way Wes would have one of his cameras taken apart to clean the lens and the body. Wes shook his head in a mock-grimace. "You routinely stay up polishing your guns in the middle of the night?"

Evan shrugged. "Beats counting sheep."

"You guys hungry? I'm calling room service. See if I can wrangle us up something," Wes said, reaching for the phone.

"I'm always hungry, mate," Simon answered, knocking back a bottle of water.

"Yeah, whatever you're getting is fine," Evan agreed, going back to his weapon.

Wes ordered and then wandered over to the sitting area, kicking back on one of the arm chairs.

"You two ever sleep?" he asked, watching Evan clean his gun as Simon messed around on his tablet, one eye on the television.

Simon shrugged. "Game's on. Try not to miss a chance to see Newcastle beat Manchester City if I can help it," he replied with a smirk, turning the volume up slightly. "And I love the Portuguese and Spanish sports casters—they make more noise than the bloody fans."

Wes chuckled. "True. That's pure entertainment value alone." He watched the game for a few minutes before saying, "I feel like I've watched more soccer in the last fifteen years, but I'm still a diehard football fan."

Evan high-fived him while Simon scoffed. "This *is* football. Not that helmet, padded shite."

"Whatever," Evan replied, grinning at Wes. "You see South Carolina beat Clemson last week? Fifth straight win, baby!"

Wes shrugged. "Mizzou beat A&M to reach SEC. I'm pretty much out now," he admitted, a little forlorn. He didn't get to watch many games, but he always tried to stay on top of his alma mater's scores. Made him feel a little closer to Texas no matter where he was in the world.

"Yeah, that's a shame," Evan sympathized. "My boss would agree with you. I can hear her now, cussing up a storm. She's still pissed A&M didn't break Top Ten this year."

"Is this the Carrie chick you talk to everyday?" Wes asked, getting up to get a beer from the mini bar. "You guys want one?"

"Nah. We're dry on the job, remember?" Simon said, watching the tube.

"At," Wes looked at his watch, "two in the morning?" He turned away from them, looking for a bottle opener in the wet bar area.

"Old habits die hard." Evan shrugged. "Nah. Carey Nelson is a guy. He runs the security side of Lennox Chase. Sam Wyatt runs the Human Asset Protection division; she's more the negotiations and client-partner side. She's the one who's the A&M grad."

Wes's whole body stiffened in shock. He fought not to choke on the beer he'd been knocking back. Thankfully he was still facing away from the guys so they couldn't see the apoplectic expression of surprise that had taken over his face.

"I thought she was Naval Academy like you," Simon remarked.

"Nah. She was Naval ROTC at A&M," Evan clarified. "She and Carey are both Texan, but hell, I like 'em anyway. We Southerners gotta stick together, right?"

Wes closed his eyes for a moment, trying to pull it together. "Damn straight," he replied, swinging around to lean back at the bar. His skin felt hot and tight.

"Well, they don't make them like that in the British military," Simon commented, still watching the game.

Evan chuckled, "They don't make them like that *anywhere*. She's a one of a kind."

Wes ran a trembling hand in his hair, hiding his response by gripping the back of his neck. Evan was right. *She was.* No one knew that better than him. She was the summit you dreamed about after falling off the rock wall. The high you try to chase after that first hit. Sammy was the girl you spend the rest of your life measuring other women against. All guys have them. All guys know.

"Bring me another bottle of water, would ya?" Simon asked.

Wes grabbed a bottle from the bar, tossing it to him as he found his motor functions again, attempting to school his expression. Simon caught the bottle without looking.

Sammy was the boss. Of course she was. And she knew he was on the NBS team. If she worked with the clients, she'd know that. Of course she did. Wes reeled at the implications, trying to absorb the reality, think through the facts. He needed more information. It was clear neither Evan nor Simon realized Wes and Sam knew each other. That they had a history so dense, it hurt to even remember the outermost edges of it.

"Who's this now? Your boss?" Wes asked casually, sitting down again and propping a foot up on the table.

"Yeah," Evan answered, blowing off a brush he'd been using to clean the gun chamber. "Been working for her for almost three years now. I didn't serve with her in the Navy, but she had a reputation as one of the best interrogators in the Middle East."

"No shit?" Wes said, trying to control his heart rate and appear nonchalant.

"He's not kidding. We even knew about her in the SAS," Simon affirmed, eyes still on the game. He groaned when his team lost a shot. "Sodding bastards, how could you miss that goal?"

"What made her so good?" Wes asked Evan over Simon's tirade. He wondered briefly if either men heard the hitch in his voice.

Evan shook his head, a small grin on his mouth. "She's ruthless when she wants to be. Creative. She'll get what she's looking for, come hell or high water. I think the interrogations were more psychological than anything. She's got a way about her."

No kidding. She can tear the heart out of you with just a look, Wes thought. He was saved from his rumination by a knock at the door. Evan gestured him down as he went to do the door, pulling out a 9mm from his holster while Simon moved silently to the wall adjoining, eyes on the door.

"It's room service, guys," Wes sighed. "Not Hezbollah."

"At this hour, I don't care if it's your mum," Simon muttered, holding his own gun up as Evan answered the door.

A nervous-looking man attempted to wheel the food in before Evan stopped him, taking the check off the tray and signing with flourish before politely kicking him out with some cash and an *obrigado e boa noite.*[22]

Wes avoided asking more questions about Sam, trying not to be too obvious. "How did you guys get into this anyway? Is this kind of stuff a typical field for guys getting out of the special forces?" Wes asked, tucking into his sandwich.

"Not necessarily," Evan replied. "I got into it because Carey trained me at BUD/s and recruited me when he heard I was thinking of getting out after my last tour."

"How many tours did you do?"

"Two," Evan replied.

"I'd ask but I don't suppose you'd tell me where," Wes said.

Evan shrugged noncommittally.

"And you?" Wes asked Simon.

"I took some shrapnel and ended up being honorably discharged," Simon answered, popping an empanada into his mouth. "But the thought of going back to merry old England and doing a nine-to-five bored me to tears. Went private with a different group that handled more hostage and rescue situations. Got tired of getting my ass hung out to dry, so voilà! I'm here now."

"It's so much better here, man," Evan stated between bites of a *bauru* sandwich. "Carey and Sam check on the status of all their teams first thing every day. They don't take any other meetings until everyone's accounted for," Evan told him. "They put the team first before anything."

"Isn't that typical?" Wes asked.

Simon snorted into his food, still watching the television.

---

[22] Portuguese for "thank you and good night."

Evan looked at him, amused. "No, man. You get used to being expendable. You're trained to give it all and leave it on the table, but everyone knows that if you don't make it out, that's the cost. When you go private, it's harder to justify without God and country, ya know?"

Wes nodded. "So what's different about your company?" he asked.

Evan polished off his sandwich. "Because to Sam and Carey, we're as much the assets as the clients are to them. They know all of us, and in some cases, we fought together, so we have that bond, and in all cases, we're handpicked."

"How many people work for them?"

"In our division?" Evan asked.

Wes nodded.

Evan thought for a moment. "About a hundred globally. Not bad for almost three years old."

"So she started it," Wes clarified.

"You have a lot of questions all of the sudden," Simon stated, shifting his eyes from the match on the television to Wes. His gaze was steady and watchful.

Wes struggled not to fidget. He feigned casual instead. "I'm a journalist. Goes with the job. Besides, I've been in the field for over a dozen years, and I've never had the luxury of a security task force. Sue me if I'm a little curious about how this all works. This whole thing is about as normal to me as pterodactyls flying down from Sugarloaf Mountain."

That got a chuckle out of both of them.

Evan, by far the friendlier of the two, answered his earlier question. "This business was originally centered on kidnap and ransom, which started getting really lucrative in certain parts of the world in the early nineties."

"Like Latin America," Simon added.

"Like Latin America," Evan agreed. "But it also became a way for rebel factions, militias, and terrorists to raise cash in Eastern Europe, the Russian satellite states, and parts of Southeast Asia really quickly. Nab a well-to-do somebody and get money for delivering them back to safety."

"And you can imagine the kinds of places and the kinds of training it requires to deal with groups like this on their home turf," Simon interjected.

"The perfect gig for ex-special-forces types who don't want to go back to a job in the City?" Wes surmised.

"Fuck yeah, it is," Simon answered. "Only this time, you get paid really well to do it."

"So there are several groups out there that specialize in this skillset and work closely with insurance underwriters," Evan continued.

"But I thought Lennox Chase was an insurance company?"

"Exactly," Evan stated, finishing his meal. "That's the genius of it. Sam became an attorney after leaving the Navy. She was negotiating mergers and deals with high-level executives. Carey was running a security company protecting these high-level executives. They decided to join forces and pitch the idea of providing preventative insurance *before* K&R became necessary, cutting down payouts for premiums. That's why the division is called Human Asset Protection. Lennox Chase just happened to be the first takers."

"I should do a story on you guys," Wes murmured.

"Nah, not us," Evan said. "You should see Sam and Carey in action together."

"Really? Why?" Wes asked, feeling his heart speed up again. He remembered Carey as Ryland's friend. Last time he'd seen Carey, he'd just been a kid, barely in high school.

"They're an amazing team," Evan commented, snapping Wes back from his reverie. "Like two halves of a whole brain in the field. I don't think they even need to talk to each other. It's like watching a Vulcan mind meld."

Simon laughed out loud. "The danger twins. I like it."

Wes felt his heart constrict. Were they just business partners? More than that? His head throbbed with the implications.

"I'm glad you're up," Evan said, shifting topics. "I was going to talk to you about this in the morning, but I'm ninety-five percent certain the demonstrations are going to get ugly tomorrow. We need to talk about logistics and how to get what you want accomplished without killing you in the process."

November—End of the month

Sam's office in the Loop, Chicago

SAMANTHA

"HOW WAS CHECK-in with Rush and Michaelson?" Sam asked, reviewing end-of-the-week status reports with Carey in her office, the late Friday afternoon sun filtering through her windows.

"Wes apparently wants to do a story on us." Carey smirked. "He was asking a lot of questions last night, according to Rush. And Simon wanted to know how Wes knows you."

Sam's gaze snapped up. "What?"

"Wes wants to do a story—"

"What in the actual fuck, Bear?" Sam's brow furrowed. "Did he tell Simon he knew me? How did Wes hear about me?"

Carey shrugged. "Dunno. But Simon said his body language gave it away pretty quickly. Said he tensed up tighter than a virgin at the mention of your name."

"Jesus."

"He ain't comin' for ya today, Sammy girl," Carey chuckled. "Why does it matter? It was only a matter of time before he found out you were at the other end of the leash. You want to tell me why you're still so broken up over this guy?"

She blinked, pushing back from her desk to turn and look out her window. It had been a crystalline, sunny day and now the late afternoon sunlight glinted off the buildings of downtown Chicago like hot coals. Sam drew in a slow breath. The pressure she'd felt ever since Wes came back into the picture built behind her eyes. "I'm not broken up, Bear," she countered. "Just figured he'd do his thing, we do ours. I just don't really want to visit Christmas past, you know?"

Carey observed her for a moment. "That's the funny thing about history, Sammy. You can't outrun it. And it's the damndest thing—it often repeats itself."

"What do you know about it?" she snapped, her voice laced with anger. She could taste the bitterness in her mouth, fueled by that awful pressure banding around her temples and making her head throb.

"Not much," Carey admitted. "I was just a kid, but I remember how messed up you were back then. Between your daddy and Ryland, and then Wes. Momma said you'd gotten your heart broken so many times, she didn't think you'd ever be able to put it back together again."

"Your momma's a screaming romantic, and you know it," Sam said flatly. "I'm fine. Stop fucking pushing it," she replied flatly, staring outside. "And getting over what's left of your family dying takes a helluva lot more juice than getting over a lover, let me tell you."

Carey stood. He was behind her before she knew it, wrapping strong arms around her. She stiffened as he drew her back against him. Sam briefly considered throwing him as she forced herself to relax into his grip.

"I take offense to that," he murmured, resting his chin against her head. "You think I don't know you're calculating how to get out of my hold? I'm not Ryland, but I'm just as much your brother. Always have been."

"Bear—"

"Shhh," he whispered. "Just shut up and lean on me for a little while. I don't know what happened, but it fucked you up good, Sammy. You were never the same after that. And it wasn't just your daddy and Ry passing."

She closed her eyes, throat working as she fought off the wave of emotion that his words evoked. *Fuck...* she could feel tears rising up from nowhere. This wasn't like her to react—wasn't what she wanted to revisit. The pressure behind her eyes became overwhelming.

"It's the middle of a freaking work day—" she started, struggling to keep the tremor out of her voice. She held onto the anger with both hands, trying to push it up and out of her. Use it to fight Carey—and the emotions he was encouraging—off.

"So we're the bosses, big deal," Carey countered, squeezing her closer. "No one can see us. No one can see this, Sammy. I've got you."

He pressed a gentle kiss to the top of her head. It was such a sweet, kind gesture, Sam couldn't hold back the rush of emotion that accompanied it. She squeezed her eyes shut, tears welling.

Anger. Hold onto the anger...

"Why do you push? Why are you always fucking pushing?" she snarled, elbowing him hard and jerking away.

Carey caught and squeezed her tighter. "Because you've been twisted up around this axle ever since his name came up, and I know you. I can see you're messed up over this."

"I'm *not*—" she denied on a choke, as the tears she hated so much sprang from her clenched eyes, hot and furious. Sam couldn't remember the last time she'd cried. Couldn't remember the last time she'd let anyone see her weak. She hated the sudden need to hold onto Carey, the vulnerability she felt at the accuracy of his assessment. In fact, she hated Carey in that moment, for knowing her so well, for making her acknowledge that she wasn't alright.

"You take care of everyone all day long," Carey said, pressing his cheek against the top of her head. "All day long. You've got your shit and everyone else's all together. I know that. I know what you can do," he murmured. "But you're not alone in anything. Never have been. Let me take care of you, baby girl. It's my job. It's my privilege as your brother," he told her, hugging her tight. "Whatever's happened, I'm here, Sammy. I've got you. I've always got your back."

"I can't," she rasped. "I *can't, Bear!*"

Sam registered distantly that she'd begun shaking like a leaf. The harder she tried to control it, the harder she shook. She could always control it. She could always detach when feeling became too intense, too acute.

"I'm here, Sammy," Carey murmured. "I've got you. Just feel. Just let yourself feel..."

The thick bands of his arms tightened. And somehow, the restraint felt good. It felt stabilizing and necessary. She was shaking so hard now, it felt like she was having convulsions. Thick, painful tears rolled down her face, wetting her blouse. A sob tore out her chest like it had been wrenched from her. Sam struggled, against him, against herself, the sounds tearing, wrenching.

She knew this sound. She'd heard it before. When her mother died. When her granddaddy died. When her father and brother died. When Wes left her with a letter, alone at their funeral. It became a blur of painful recollections. One long, awful loop that brought her to the door of darker memories.

Memories of making men in dark rooms in foreign countries cry out, breaking them down to nothing but grief and pain, because she knew how to do it, knew exactly how it felt to be taken to the brink and dropped. To feel hopeless.

Devoid.

And she became good at it; real good. Samantha was too good at taking fear and wrapping it like a cord around someone's neck, strangling the air out. Because she knew agony. Slept with it close to her. Held onto pain like a weapon.

Now after all these years, she used it like a shield.

No one got in. Because no one got out.

No one got out...

She didn't deserve this, she thought. *She didn't deserve someone to hold her.*

To forgive her.

To love her.

"Yes, you do, Sammy. *You do,*" Carey said against her hair, following her as she collapsed forward, one hand clutching his arm, the other flattened against the glass of the window, so cold against her hand.

"I've—*I've done so many things,* Bear," she sobbed as ragged sounds tore out like they'd been flayed from her. "I've done too many things. I can't go back. *I can't go back,*" she gasped. The noises coming from her made her gasp with their strength—ugly and rearing after so many years being tamped down.

"We all have, baby girl. We all have," he murmured, rocking her now. Mumbling comforting things, soothing things.

She realized distantly she wasn't crying over Wes. She'd done that as a girl, years ago. He was just a trigger. She was crying for everything that was, that had been—that tender, innocent time when she'd spend hours riding the ranch with her father, playing cards with her brother at the kitchen table, making love to Wes on lazy sunlit afternoons. She mourned the person she'd been before life had warped and shaped her... before it had given her the weapons and the will to use them. The hurt vibrated in her chest—only more painful this time because the scar tissue was thick and subcutaneous. That final awful ending with Wes had been the gateway. And he'd pushed her through it when she thought he'd be her lifeline; the one thing God had left for her when he took everyone else...

"I'm here. I'm here," Carey promised, his murmured reassurances accompanying the gentle pressure of his hand wiping tears from her face.

She registered Carey picking her up and carrying her the short distance to her couch, cradling her in his arms the way he would a child. Her head throbbed. As the crying jag slowed, Sam was left with the hollowed out dullness of emotional exertion. Her body was wracked with exhaustion, quaking with occasional tremors as she quieted against Carey. He was so gentle, so careful with her; it ached all the more.

Sam tucked her damp, flushed face against his neck, a mixture of shame and relief soaking up what was left of her grief. They were both silent for a long time. She watched the sun set, casting long, distorted shadows against her walls.

"You're the toughest person I know," Carey told her in the cool quiet, his voice a rumble under her cheek. "But there's no reproach in needing somebody every now and then."

Sam spread the fingers she'd wrapped around his dress shirt, her fingers sore from clasping at him like her life had depended on it. She smoothed the wrinkles in his dress shirt absently. Her face stung a little from the salt of her dried tears.

Carey rubbed her cheek with the rough pad of his thumb. "We've done and seen terrible things, baby girl. That changes you," he continued. "But you've chosen to protect people for a living. You can say whatever you want, but that's the bare truth. And you may have had many reasons to do what you did in the military, but fact is, you saved countless lives with the intel you got. I don't know what you did to think of yourself this way, but I know you aren't evil. I know evil. You're just hurt." He sighed. "Hell, honey. We all are. You just happen to hide it better than most."

"Apparently, not well enough," she whispered.

"Don't you know, Sammy girl?" he whispered back with a gentle smile. "I know all your tells."

Carey held her for a long time, both of them lost in thought and memories. And as nightfall blanketed her office, Sam felt safe enough to tell him; to tell him what had happened to her all those years ago after her dad and Ryland died; what made her so good at her job in the military.

And how she'd come by the nickname *Poppy*...

CHAPTER 22

December—Saturday afternoon
Jaime's house in Oak Park, Illinois

JACK

"YOU'RE NOT DOING it right, Uncle Jack," Maddie huffed, squirming on the bar stool.

Jack concentrated, tying the ribbon around her pigtail like he was looking for the right wire to diffuse a bomb. "I'm trying, *micina cara*. Quit moving around."

Jaime walked into the kitchen, took one look at the lopsided pigtail and sighed. "You're doing it wrong."

"Well, *Madre de Dio*, Jaime," Jack said, exasperated. "I didn't know there was a right and wrong way to tie a ribbon!" Maddie and Jaime twisted around and glared at him in such an identical fashion he nearly laughed aloud.

Jaime put Maddie's suitcase and backpack down by the kitchen door and swung back around, slapping Jack out of the way. "Here," he stated calmly. "I'll show you how to do her hair. You might want to video this, you idiot. Little girls take their hair *very* seriously," he informed his brother archly.

Jack sighed, stepping back. He fumbled with his phone. That actually wasn't a bad idea, though he wondered if he could get Samantha to help him. He smiled. He could easily imagine Samantha helping Maddie get dressed in the mornings while explaining the proper way to field strip a pistol.

"Are you videoing this?" Jaime asked, pulling Maddie's silky fine hair out of the ridiculous knot Jack had managed.

"Yeah, *il stronzo*,"[23] Jack muttered. "Just show me."

"Okay, step one, make sure you've brushed all the tangles out. Step two, make an even part in her hair like this…"

Jack zoned out while Jaime went on and on about ribbons and plaits and getting the rubber band tight but not too tight. He adored his niece, but he had a strong feeling she'd be learning to do her own hair while she was staying with him this week.

"Callie will pick her up from Montessori and take her out until you get home. I've asked her to pick up the groceries and bring them over the first night so you have all the food you need for Maddie."

Jack looked affronted. "I have food, and you know I cook better than you do."

Jaime rolled his eyes. "I mean her kid stuff like bologna and fish sticks."

Jack recoiled. "*Madonne*—fish sticks?"

"She likes them." Jaime nodded. "Make her dinner, but those are for snacks and stuff."

Jack shuddered. "She's eating like we ate growing up. Fresh fish, homemade pasta, and if she wants crap, I'll throw a couple hot dogs on the grill, but that's it."

"I like it when you grill, Uncle Jack," Maddie offered, flipping through one of her coloring books at the kitchen counter.

"I know you do, baby," Jack told her tenderly as he lifted a triumphant brow at his brother.

"Can we grill the fish sticks?" she asked.

Jaime snort-laughed while Jack rolled his eyes.

"Maddie, baby, go to your room and look for anything you might want to bring to Uncle Jack's that Daddy might have missed, okay?" Jaime urged, helping her off the stool. She ran off to her room in a flash of little limbs and pink tulle.

"Is she wearing a tutu?" Jack asked, feeling a little unsure.

"Yeah. Ever since we started her in dance class a couple months

---

[23] Italian for "asshole."

ago, she'll wear it after class for a couple hours until she gets tired of it," Jaime explained as he left the kitchen. Jack trailed after him, typing into his phone. "What are you doing?"

"Taking notes," Jack muttered.

Jaime smirked, shaking his head at his brother. "You'll figure it out. I know it's been a little while since she's stayed with you for more than a couple nights, but you'll do well."

"I feel like every time she stays with me, she has totally different needs," Jack confessed, his brow creasing as he typed. "It's diapers and formula, then it's pull-ups and Velcro shoes, now it's hairdos and fish sticks. How the fuck do you learn all this?"

"Stop saying '*fuck*,' first," Jaime scolded. "She's in the repeating-things phase. And it didn't happen overnight. It's been years with Mom and Callie, the PTA, parenting handbooks, and a lot of patience and Advil. You gonna be good with this? I can ask Ma to come back if it's too much."

"No." Jack shook his head. "I got this. Nothing could be scarier than a newborn. At least she can talk now." He smiled grimly at the memory of Maddie's seemingly ceaseless midnight wailings as an infant. It had been a good thing he was already an insomniac. "You ready for the trip?" he asked, glancing at Jaime's open garment bag on the bed.

"Yeah," Jaime shrugged. "Should be good," he answered, stepping into this closet to pick out clothes. "I've been wanting to expand into Latin America. Did you know Brazil is one of the world's biggest mobile markets? They have something like two hundred and sixty-eight million subscribers nationally. That's like a penetration rate of more than one point three lines per person," Jaime stated, holding up ties in the mirror.

"God, you're a geek," Jack teased. "Go with the blue and the yellow ties."

Jaime nodded, rolling the ties and tucking them into the bag. "Did Sam tell you she's sending a couple guys with me?"

Jack looked up, surprised. "No. Why?"

"One of the guys on the trip has some shady connections, I guess. You wouldn't know it, looking at him, but she thinks he could invite some unwanted attention. She says it's just a precaution."

Jack didn't like the sound of this new information one bit. His brother was naturally laidback, but he felt like he wasn't saying something. Jack also wondered why Sam hadn't mentioned anything to him before she left on her business trip. "Define 'shady.'"

Jaime shrugged, wandering back into his closet to pull out shirts. "She didn't say. She just asked me to take a couple guys with me and Carter on the flight and said there'd be a few more there to connect with. Makes sense since I'll be helping Rush and Talon later this week to test the app I've been developing for them."

"Is that it?" Jack asked.

"Well, yeah," Jaime said, pulling open his sock drawer. "I think so. We're testing the locaters on me the first few days anyway, so her guys will have a bead on me pretty much all times. Makes sense." He tossed a few pairs of socks into his bag, looking up at Jack sitting at the edge of the bed. "Stop worrying. It's fine."

"I'm not worried," Jack replied quickly.

Jaime smiled smugly. "Yeah. You are. That's like your side hobby. 'Worry about Jaime,'" he air-quoted. "I'll be with a few tech geeks and armed men who work for your girlfriend and staying at the Palace Hotel. The most trouble I'll get into is ogling girls at Ipanema. What's to worry about?"

"You ogling girls at Ipanema," Jack answered readily. "You're likely to get your face slapped."

"You're just jealous," Jaime joked. "Though with Sam by your side, I can't imagine you really want to look at anyone else. She's *sei figa!*[24] He grinned, narrowly ducking Jack's hand. "Speaking of which, where is she?"

"She had a trip down to Houston come up. She'll be back in a day or so."

"You've got a good one, Jack," Jaime told him as he rooted around his drawers for tees and jeans.

"I know it," he answered, swallowing. The file had continued to weigh on his mind since his dad had given it to him. He thought about

---

[24] Italian for "smoking hot."

shredding it. But it just sat in his safe, secret. He hated the weight of it. The implications. "I could use your advice, actually," he heard himself say. He hadn't been planning on telling Jaime, but this felt too big to hold onto.

Jaime looked up, surprised at Jack's pained expression. "What's up?"

"So, you know how Dad pulled me aside during Thanksgiving?"

Jaime thought about it. "Yeah?"

"He gave me a file he had put together on Samantha."

Jaime's brows rose to his hairline.

Jack ran a hand through his hair. "I know."

"Jack, man, tell me you didn't read it."

Jack shook his head. "He told me I should. He said there's redacted shit in there, but that I should read it if I was getting serious about her. Christ, I know he's trying to help but—"

"Shred it," Jaime interrupted. "Set it on fire. I don't care what you do, but you need to get rid of it. I know Dad meant well, but seriously, you read it and it could have really harmful implications to this relationship, especially where you both are right now." Jaime sat down next to him, putting his hand on Jack's shoulder. "Jack, trust is a huge issue when things are still new like this. If she thinks you're operating behind her back, she won't ever look at you the same. There won't be a way to go back."

"You're right. I know you're right," Jack sighed, rubbing a hand over his face.

Jaime paused a beat. "But you've been holding onto it. Why?"

Jack sighed, pushing up from the bed, pacing. Jaime crossed his arms, waiting patiently while Jack tried to verbalize it.

"She's amazing. She's the most amazing woman I've ever met. Could even imagine," he admitted. "But she's so complicated. Everything's a goddamn mystery, wrapped in an enigma—"

Jaime let out a huff of laugher, his eyes twinkling. "She's a woman, bro."

Jack rolled his eyes, shaking his head. "No, Jaime. It's not just that. I know women," he reminded him. "Sam's a far more complicated creature. She's straightforward, but she's shrouded. She's open in the moment, but opaque about the past and the future. I know she cares about me, but I know I care about her more." He paced across Jaime's room. "I know I'm not seeing the full picture. I know I'm on an uneven playing field. And I need to level it out." He ran frustrated hands through his hair. "I love being with her, but when we're not together, it just becomes painfully clear to me that the only thing I really know about this woman is what she likes in bed."

"Is that bad? I thought that was kind of like your thing?" Jaime teased.

Jack rolled his eyes. "I'm being serious here. I'm one hundred percent into her and she's like…a friggin' black box. I've got a file I know I shouldn't look at, but…*merda!*"[25] He looked up, catching Jaime's grin. "What?"

"You're obsessed, man." Jaime's grin widened. "Welcome to love. Now, when are you going to marry her?"

The thought had crossed Jack's mind on several occasions. That didn't prevent him from punching his brother's arm. "Be serious."

"Owww!" Jaime glared. "Your goddamn boxing is making you mean and aggressive," he griped. "And I *am* being serious. Everyone knows the only way you handle an obsession is to either marry it or get rid of it. Sam has to be the coolest, smartest, not to mention *sexiest*, woman you've ever been with. You'd be a fool to fuck this up. Throw out the fucking file."

"Don't say '*fuck*,'" Jack grumbled, eyeing the doorway. Maddie was playing music in her room down the hall. He could hear her banging away on her little keyboard. God help him, she'd better not bring that infernal thing to his place.

"Love isn't level," Jaime continued. "Whoever sold you that is talking a crock full of shit. There are no accurate measurements. And oftentimes, one person may love the other person more, and sometimes that even switches around. And occasionally, you luck out and you're both in the same place at the same time. But you holding this file over her isn't going to make it an even playing field. It's going to litter it with

---

[25] Italian for "shit."

landmines."

"I'm not holding it over her—"

"Uh, yeah, bro, you are," Jaime interjected. "There's redacted shit in there, dude. There's a reason you don't know some of that. But more importantly, it's none of your business until she chooses to *make* it your business. And she'll do that on her own time, in her own way, and you need to be okay with that. I know you're new to this, but that's a big part of what loving someone is about. Loving all of them, even if you don't understand it all. And trusting them, even when it's incredibly hard to do."

Jack stopped pacing, staring at his brother. Jaime nodded back at him. Jack sighed, knowing his brother was totally right. He knew it to his core. "How'd you get so smart?" Jack asked gruffly, sitting down next to him.

Jaime shrugged. "Cassie taught me a lot. Sometimes I think we got married too young. But then I look at the time we got to share, and I don't regret any of it. But we did a lot of growing up together as a result. We had to learn a lot of this the hard way."

"I don't think there's an easy way," Jack responded.

Jaime grinned at that. "Ain't that the truth?"

The music stopped. They both looked expectantly at the doorway when they heard Maddie's little feet pounding down the hallway. "Daddy, where's my microphone? I need it for Uncle Jack's."

Jaime chuckled, turning to Jack. "Just remember how much you love my kid this week. Especially when you want to mix barbiturates into her milk."

"Dude, *I'd* take those before I gave them to your daughter," he joked. "Maddie, I've already got a microphone at my place," Jack blatantly lied, hoping her little mind wouldn't retain the deception or the desire for the microphone in the first place by the time he got her there.

"And keyboards?" she asked doubtfully.

"And keyboards," he lied smoothly, elbowing Jaime sharply as he opened his mouth.

"I like to karaoke," Maddie told him seriously. "I'm gonna be a big singer, Uncle Jack."

"I'm sure you will, *micina cara*," Jack answered as Jaime gasped, clutching his side. "You can be anything you want."

She nodded as if a decision had been made before turning and running back to her room.

Jaime punched his arm hard in retaliation, parrying back quickly. "You'll regret that. She's going to be hounding you for a microphone all week."

"I'll think of something to distract her," Jack answered. "Now finish packing. Your car will be here in a few minutes."

Jaime nodded, tossing a few things into the bag.

"Jaime?"

His brother looked up.

"Thank you," Jack said quietly.

Jaime grinned and tossed a pair of socks at him. "*Ma non metterla giu' dura!*[26] It's nice to finally be able to help you out for once," he laughed, leaning down to zip up his bag. "I love you, brother. Now take my daughter to your house, make her fish sticks, and burn that file."

November—Saturday afternoon, same time

The Wyatt Ranch, Texas

SAMANTHA

THE TEXAS SKY was turbulent. Clouds hung low and pregnant with what would be a magnificent thunderstorm. The kind of big sky storm that rolled through once every few months, wetting the normally dry plains, making everything lush and verdant for a few days after. But it was hell to get ready for. Grant, Carey's dad, would be working with all the cattle hands to make sure the steer were wrangled together in the fencing, grazing the same pasture instead of enjoying the freedom of being spread out along the range.

---

[26] Italian saying for "don't make such a big deal out of it."

Sam stepped out of the Jeep, her boots making a satisfying crunch on the gravel drive up to the stables. The stable boys were busy pulling the horses in from the corrals. She wondered briefly if she should go to the main house and announce herself or if she should just get on a horse and ride out. The urge to ride out was fierce. She couldn't remember the last time she'd been on the back of a horse—that was a long time for a girl who'd grown up on one.

"Well aren't you a sight for sore old eyes," a gruff voice called out as she neared the stables. Gus, one her father's favorite hands, stood behind her, leaning heavily on a cane. She hadn't seen him in years. Sam tried to reconcile her memory of the black-haired cowboy she'd grown up with to this weathered old man. He had the same bushy eyebrows, the same flashing dark eyes.

She felt a wide smile stretching her face as she clasped the old cowboy in a tight hug. She felt his arthritic hand patting her back.

"Gus, you old bastard, how come you aren't out with the hands?" she asked gently. "Showin' em how it's done?" Sam breathed in the familiar faint scent of hay and tobacco.

"Got old, Sammy," he replied. "All these young bucks think they know better anyhow," Gus joked, his voice just as craggy and gruff as she remembered it.

He'd taught her so much about horses. Just looking at him, she knew he wasn't able to ride anymore. It hurt her to realize it, knowing how much he loved the animals. It struck her then how much time had passed since she'd come home—how much she'd missed. She patted his arm.

"Got a good quarter horse for me?"

"Yeah." He nodded, eyes amused. "Yours. We just pulled her in the stalls, but we can rig her up for you. She'll be happy to see you after all this time."

"She's still alive?" Sam asked, surprised.

"She's only twenty, darlin'." He shrugged. "You know those quarter horses can get up to thirty-five or forty, no problem."

Sam smiled. "Take me to her?"

She held his arm while he hobbled over to Valkyrie's stall. The sleek black mare looked up at her under obscenely-long eyelashes. She was still as beautiful as ever.

"Val," she cooed. "Hey, honey girl. You miss me?" she asked, taking a lump of sugar from Gus's hand to extend it to her mare. The horse nickered gently into her hand, her long tongue accepting the offering. Sam rubbed the horse's velvet nose as she sidled closer. "Yeah, honey girl. You remember me," she breathed, running her hand down her horse's ebony head and mane.

"The boys are busy getting the other horses in from pasture, but we can get her ready," Gus offered.

Sam shook him off, patting his weathered cheek. "I ain't a princess just 'cause I moved to the city," she scolded. "I can saddle her myself."

She chatted with Gus while she got Val ready to ride. He was a grandfather now, he told her proudly, showing her pictures on his phone. The ranch was good. He was still taking Grant to the cleaners on poker night. The town had a new minister, and his favorite diner had changed hands, so the food was different, but they still had the best ham in the county. Sam smiled at the news, laughing when he told her jokes about the younger hands, telling her about teaching one of them how to fix the old tractor Grant refused to get rid of despite the new John Deeres in the tool house.

"Which field are they in?" she asked, pulling on deerskin gloves.

Gus radioed one of the hands, getting their location.

She mounted Val smoothly while Gus led them out past the gated corral. He looked up at the heavy, darkening sky. "Figure you got about an hour at most 'fore all hell breaks loose, kiddo. Here." He tossed her an old cowboy hat. "Just in case."

Sam grinned as she slid it onto her head, tightening the string under her chin. "See ya, Gus!"

Sam wheeled Val around and took off in a gallop, the wind whipping past her, Val's long hair flying in the wind, touching the reins. The feeling of riding like this was unparalleled. She smiled as she raced down the pasture, enjoying the cool air. She felt like a young girl again. Windblown and wild. She realized she hadn't breathed properly since yesterday with Carey, her heart heavy and her mind a tangle of mess and emotion. A huge weight lifted off her the faster she and Val flew down the gentle slopes of her family's land.

When she found Grant and his men rounding the steer, she saw him turn on his horse, his blue eyes narrowing, trying to figure out who was riding Valkyrie into a roundup. She registered the exact moment he figured it out. He broke into a beatific smile. Sam felt immediately warm, followed by the sweet relief of his unspoken welcome home.

Her heart was pounding with exertion and exhilaration as she pulled up next to him. "Heard y'all needed some help," she said casually, lifting a brow in question.

"Heard right," he answered easily, eyes bright with love and happiness. "New guy on the left flank. Show 'em how it's done."

"Sure thing, *jefe*,"[27] she replied, calling her Uncle Grant what all the hands would call him. She could see the other men exchanging glances, wondering who she was. Sam rode up the flank, herding the steer toward the east range, startling the young hand who was struggling to cut some of the calves from the broader herd.

They worked together in tandem, getting most of the herd up to higher land, away from the river that cut through the ranch land and had a tendency to flash flood during thunderstorms.

Before long, Sam felt the fat drops of rain hitting the plain, the darkness of the clouds almost completely blocking the sun as the clap and roll of thunder hit the big Texas sky like an orchestral crescendo. She heard Uncle Grant whistle, a signal to head back. They peeled off from the herd, riding back fast before the storm got too intense and scared the horses. They were all drenched by the time they got back to the stables; the rain coming down in sheets. Gus had the stable boys lined up, ready to take care of the horses.

Uncle Grant stepped behind her as she dismounted, helping her down. He wrapped her in a bear hug, swinging her around before she was fully off the horse. Sam threw her head back, laughing as he twirled her. The rain washed the sweat from her brow as her hat got knocked off by the deluge.

---

[27] Spanish for "boss."

"You came home!" he crowed. "Sammy girl's back!" he hooted and hollered.

"Hey, Uncle Grant," she laughed, squeezing his neck. "I missed Aunt Hannah's cooking."

"Bullshit. You missed my ribs better, and you know it," he joked, setting her down. "Let's get you inside and dried up."

Her Aunt Hannah was on the wide porch of the pristinely painted, sprawling ranch house of her childhood, a warm smile spreading across her face. Carey had his father's height and broad build, but he had his mother's kind face. It'd been so long, she'd forgotten the acuity of the likeness. And seeing Aunt Hannah waiting for her like she had when she was young made her so happy, Sam felt her eyes water, grateful the rain hid the tumult of guilt and emotion she was struggling to hide. But as she neared the house with Uncle Grant and met Aunt Hannah's eyes, she knew she was forgiven for years of absence. Sam knew everything would be fine just as sure as she knew this would always be her home.

Sam walked into her Aunt Hannah's open arms, breathing in the scent of powder and apples. She shut her eyes tight as she melted into her embrace. "I'm getting you all wet," she mumbled into her Aunt's shoulder, wondering if she could hear her small voice over the pounding rain.

"Hush. That's what the dryer's for," Aunt Hannah whispered. "I missed you, Sammy girl," she said as she brushed a tender hand down Sam's wet hair and back. She felt her Uncle Grant pat her shoulder too. Sam squeezed tighter for one more moment before letting go to step back, wiping at her face hastily with the back of her hand.

"It's raining cats and dogs. Let's get you inside," Uncle Grant said, hustling them both into the kitchen.

Sam took in the space in wonder as she pulled off her wet boots in the wide mud area. Carey had mentioned they'd just remodeled, but this was magnificent. The open plan kitchen was equipped with top-of-the-line stainless steel appliances, a massive fridge, a huge six-burner range, a double oven, and a counter top that any chef would want as a work-space. They'd added a sun room that held a massive, rough-hewn table that could easily seat twelve. The windows and skylights made it all the more airy and spacious-feeling.

"My God, Aunt Hannah," she breathed, taking in the terracotta tiles and the stained cabinetry. A large, brick fireplace sent the smell of cedar into the air and warmed her wet, bedraggled body.

"You like it? My dream kitchen?" Aunt Hannah asked.

"Like it? Are you kidding? I think you'll have a hard time getting me out of it," she joked, warming her hands near the fire.

"We have the hands over for dinner so often, it just made sense to expand. The minute I heard you were back, I got your favorite spaghetti on the stove."

"Gus gave me away?" Sam grinned.

"Your duffel is in your room," her aunt replied, patting her shoulder. "Now go get a hot shower and come back down here. Keep me company while I work on dinner and make you a pie."

When Sam came down the stairs twenty minutes later, freshly showered and in a warm flannel shirt and clean jeans, she was greeted with the smell of flour, sugar, and cinnamon. She stilled at the bottom of the staircase, overcome with nostalgia.

Uncle Grant was seated at the counter, drinking a cup of coffee while Aunt Hannah peeled apples. Rockabilly played on the stereo. Aunt Hannah smiled at Sam over her shoulder, her once-long blonde hair was now cut into an attractive, sleek bob.

"I like your hair, Aunt Hannah," Sam told her, coming behind her Aunt to hug her middle.

Aunt Hannah touched her hair self-consciously, a little smile on her mouth. "You do? I still haven't got used to it. Cut it a few months back, and I feel a half-a-head lighter, I swear."

"You're the prettiest woman in three counties," Uncle Grant declared, looking up from the paper.

"And you're the biggest flirt in five," Aunt Hannah countered, wagging her finger at him. He laughed it off, his eyes mischievous before taking another sip of coffee.

Sam poured herself a mug before sliding onto the stool next to him. She sighed, enjoying the coffee, the company, the warmth of the fire, and the soothing, unparalleled feeling of being home.

"You staying for a while, Sammy girl?" Uncle Grant asked.

"I got a couple days," she shrugged. "But I promise not to be a stranger this time," she said quietly, smiling at him.

After breaking down yesterday in her office with Carey, she'd yearned for the safety and comfort of something known. The floodgates had opened, and all the hurt and pain that had scalded her insides, leaving her inert and tender. She'd stayed awake all night, wondering if it hurt so badly because it always had or if everything felt magnified because she'd held it down for so long that a powerful release was inevitable. She'd packed a bag first thing this morning, telling Jack she had last minute meetings in Houston, and found her way home.

"You come back anytime you want," Aunt Hannah told her. "You just better tell me next time, missy, so I can make you a proper pot roast."

"I will, Aunt Hannah," she promised.

"So tell us what you and Carey are getting up to in Chicago," Uncle Grant asked.

"You just saw him for Thanksgiving!" Sam protested teasingly. "Your boy could talk the ears off a chicken. I know for a fact you're all caught up."

"Well not from your point of view, missy," Aunt Hannah argued with a small smile as she sliced the apples. "Now go on. What's the latest and greatest?"

They talked for a long while, laughing and trading stories about what was going on at the ranch and in Chicago. She shared a couple of her and Carey's antics and told them about their business while Uncle Grant told her about the recent rodeo in town and the amount of cattle they were thinking of taking to stock in the spring.

"So Carey tells me you've got a beau," Aunt Hannah said as she slid the pie into the oven.

Sam nearly choked into her coffee mug. Uncle Grant patted her back gently, a smirk on his face. "You know that boy can't keep a secret from his mama."

"Jesus," Sam muttered, shaking her head.

"And an Italian, too? *Oooh-wee*—that man's a looker," Aunt Hannah chuckled while Uncle Grant laughed silently into his coffee.

"Oh my God, did you look him up?" Sam groaned.

"Well, hell, what's the Internet for?" Aunt Hannah laughed. "How else am I gonna find out about you, Sammy girl?"

Sam felt guilt hit her heart hard. Uncle Grant and Aunt Hannah didn't deserve the distance she'd been putting between them these last few years. They shouldn't have to read up on her on the web. They sure as hell shouldn't be hearing about what she was up to from only Carey.

"Hey, hey, you know we're only teasing you," Uncle Grant told her, squeezing her shoulder affectionately.

"We're just happy you're home," Aunt Hannah agreed, pouring her more coffee. "Now, seriously. You tell me about your young man."

"He's in his thirties, Aunt Hannah," Sam answered, sardonic.

Aunt Hannah's brow arched. "Well, he's still half my age, isn't he?"

"Fair enough," Sam chuckled. "Jack's…good. He's a surprisingly good man."

"Why's that so surprising? You date a lot of assholes?" Uncle Grant asked before Aunt Hannah smacked him with a spoon. "Ouch!"

"Language in the house. You're not with the ranch hands, Grant Nelson!" she scolded.

Sam snickered while Uncle Grant rubbed his arm. "No, I haven't dated a bunch of—" She halted while her Aunt eyed her. "Jerks. It's just that Jack's got a reputation for being a bit of a lothario. I guess I wasn't expecting him to be more than some businessman playboy," she admitted. "I thought it was going to be something light. You know, just a casual thing. But it's become…" Sam trailed off, unsure.

"Carey says that man's head-over-heels for you," Aunt Hannah said archly, tearing the lettuce for the salad.

Sam shrugged, hiding her face behind her coffee mug.

"You been in love since that Wesley character?" Uncle Grant asked, watching her.

Sam shook her head, looking down.

"You know there's nothing wrong with falling in love and getting hurt a little, right, missy?" Aunt Hannah said as she arranged the salad. "Teaches you where the ledges are."

Sam took a breath, nodding.

"You were just a girl then," Aunt Hannah continued. "Whatever you've got now with this Jack fellow's different. You're a woman now. Lived a full life thus far, and it won't be the same like before."

Sam rubbed the handle on the mug. "I didn't say I was worried."

Aunt Hannah smiled gently at her. "Sammy, honey, you didn't need to."

"You miss your Aunt's all-seeing eye?" Uncle Grant joked, standing to help Aunt Hannah set the table.

Sam helped take down the china. "She should have been in military intelligence," Sam replied. "Taliban wouldn't have stood a chance."

Uncle Grant chuckled at that. "So how's Wyatt Petroleum holding up these days?" he asked, giving her a much-needed break from the personal life questions.

"Better than ever. You'll be real happy with your dividend check this quarter," Sam replied, helping her Aunt get the food ready while Uncle Grant sorted out drinks. The ranch was a profitable operation, but the real Wyatt fortune came from the black gold lining dense shelves of fine-grained shale throughout West and Central Texas and off the coast of the Sabine Pass and Galveston.

Her granddaddy had been a talented and gutsy wildcatter and her father a savvy businessman, buying up wells and consolidating when many smaller producers were tanking during the oil crisis in the seventies. They'd been early entrants into offshore drilling. Thanks to her granddaddy's keen nose for crude and her father's sharp eye for business potential, she was the largest private owner of offshore rigs in the Gulf and one of the richest private oil owners in the United States. Though she didn't oversee the day-to-day, she chaired the Board of Directors at the company headquarters in Houston.

"Good!" Aunt Hannah declared. "You can finally take me on that cruise in the Mediterranean."

Sam looked at her uncle, noting the sudden scowl. Uncle Grant had been made a millionaire years ago with his portion of the ranch and the shares her father had left him in Wyatt Petroleum. It wasn't a matter of money. If anything, her uncle just hated being away from the ranch for extended periods of time.

"How long's the cruise?" Sam asked.

"Three weeks," her aunt replied dreamily.

Sam glanced at her uncle. "A happy woman is a happy home," Sam said to him under her breath.

Uncle Grant rolled his eyes, shaking his head. "Don't I know it," he muttered, bringing over the hot plates of spaghetti her aunt had ladled. "Who'll watch the ranch?"

"Gus," she shrugged.

Uncle Grant shook his head. "How about you and Carey come back for a couple weeks. See if you can handle it? Help ole' Gus out."

"That's an excellent idea!" Aunt Hannah agreed. "You two back home," she sighed. "Now that'd be a sight to see."

Sam said nothing, though a part of her liked the idea. Perhaps the most surprising thing about coming home was that it had been as easy as slipping into a warm bath. Working the steer, riding the pasture...being inside the home she'd grown up in. It wouldn't be a tremendous hardship. Maybe she could do it again, be here without all the painful memories, find peace surrounded in the place and things she knew like the back of her hand...

Her aunt and uncle left it alone, seeing they'd planted the seed. Sam warmed at every pat and squeeze, feeling comfortable and safe in the heavily scented kitchen, eating a hearty, simple meal of spaghetti with sauce from scratch, a meal she'd loved as a child. She savored the hot, crusty garlic bread, corn on the cob, and salad from Aunt Hannah's garden like a Michelin-rated meal in a top-tier city. They shared Irish coffee with a dollop of Chantilly cream while they waited for the apple pie to cool. At one point, "My Blue Heaven" came on, and Uncle Grant swung Aunt Hannah into his arms for a quick two step on his way to get more coffee.

"What on earth?" her Aunt cried, her laugh a sweet trill as he twirled her around the kitchen. "What has gotten into you?" She playfully smacked her husband's arm.

"I'm just happy, Hannah. Our girl's back home," he smiled, winking at Sam over her shoulder as he maneuvered his wife over the terracotta tiles. A rush of emotion made Sam's eyes well, and she ducked her head into her coffee cup, watching her aunt and her uncle dance around the kitchen over the rim. She blinked furiously, wondering where the hell all of this damn weepiness was coming from. In the space of twenty-four hours, she'd become an emotional Tilt-A-Whirl. Sam cleared her throat gruffly while her Uncle Grant dipped Aunt Hannah dramatically, making her laugh before she pushed away, shooing him off so she could cut slices of hot apple pie.

"More coffee, Sammy girl? Or more whisky?" her Uncle Grant offered, wagging his heavy brows in mischief.

"It's a school night, Uncle Grant," she chuckled. "Don't we have to get up early tomorrow to check on the cattle after the storm?"

His face lit up in a pleased smile. "You helping me tomorrow?"

Sam nodded. "If you'll have a stuck-up city girl," she joked.

"Darlin', you may be stuck-up, but you ain't no city girl," her uncle teased back, his eyes warm. "Eat your pie. It'll be an early mornin' and you'll need the energy," he assured her.

Sam tucked her smile in her shoulder. For the first time in years, she felt so indescribably happy to be home...

July 2006
Kabul, Afghanistan

SAMANTHA

NIGHT HAD DESCENDED over Kabul, the cooling desert air making the warehouse chillier than it already was. Sam could hear the faint, tinny sound of the evening prayers over loudspeakers in the distance. She nodded at Moon and Cartwright. It was time to finish this.

Arman sat in the chair, his head lolled onto his shoulder, passed out from the exhaustion and dehydration of withdrawal. She reached down, slapping him awake. He jerked, looking up at her with his sallow hazel eyes.

"I've told you. I've told you everything," he whispered, his voice hollow. Broken.

"Known associates, locations of his productive yields, dealers: all interesting," she murmured. "But not what I need to know. I want your father. Tell me everywhere you know you can find him."

"I can't," Arman shook his head, his expression pathetic. "I don't know this. He moves constantly."

"But you know how to find him. You are his son. You know exactly how to reach him."

"No, Poppy. I swear. I don't. He finds me. He always finds me."

Her eyes narrowed. "And how do you think he'll react once he finds his son, an addict, prostrate and begging like a parasite?" she asked, her voice dipping dangerously.

Pallor covered his now-gray skin. A thin sheen of sweat covered Arman from fear or withdrawal—perhaps both.

She knew where they found Arman to begin with, knew how his father would find him given enough time. They'd just have to set the trap and wait.

"Please, Poppy," Arman whispered through cracked lips. "Please," he looked up, eyes pleading for mercy.

She smiled. "I know exactly how to make you feel good again, Arman. I'm going to take you back to that brothel. And we're going to give you all your father's opium you can handle."

Arman's eyes lit, feverish with the idea of the high. He licked his dry lips.

"How long do you think it will take him to find you?" Sam asked idly, stepping back.

"A week. No more," Arman whispered.

She knew with absolute certainty he wasn't lying. In fact, she doubted if it would even take that long. Sam nodded at Cartwright and Moon. "We go tonight."

CHAPTER 23

November—Tuesday Afternoon
Rio de Janeiro, Brazil

WESLEY

"SO IS JAIME Roman a raving geek or an ironic, glasses-wearing hipster?" Wes asked Evan while they sat in the hotel bar, waiting for the famous app developer. "And what kind of guy develops locater software and technology anyway? You sure he isn't government? I don't know how I feel about being tagged and tracked like an endangered species," Wes muttered, feeling restless.

"Believe it or not, he swears he developed it to keep track of his five-year-old." Evan grinned. "He's a good guy. Definitely no G-man. You'll like him," Evan assured him. "And you'll have to take your civil rights up with the network. Landiss is the one who agreed to Sam and Carey's request to have you and your team test it out."

Wes's skin tingled at the mention of Sam. He'd done a few searches since he found out that she was heading this operation and gotten basic, salient facts—she was based in Chicago, an attorney, a senior partner at Lennox, but it was all vague, and it only served to make him want more. Pictures were impossible to locate. A nice trick. Even her gender was rarely referenced. Wes had been subtly asking questions the past few days, garnering more information.

He knew from Talon that she was a helluva fighter and the second best sharpshooter in the outfit after to him. He knew from Evan she was a card shark, and the kid Wes remembered as her little brother's best friend was now her closest confidante and business partner. He knew from Michaelson she had great legs, but hell, no one knew that better than him. Wes wondered crassly if any of them had ever had her legs wrapped around them and then felt ridiculous and irrationally jealous for even thinking it. But each time he heard mention of her or Carey, he felt that familiar stomach clench.

The only thing Wes knew with absolute certainty was that he wanted to see her again and that the feeling wasn't mutual. She'd had plenty of opportunities since she clearly knew who she was protecting on behalf of NBS. Wes had debated asking to meet her through her team or reaching out to her directly—at least until the locater chip they wanted him and the team to test out had come up.

At first he'd been resistant to testing the locater chip, mostly on principle. Wes had never been on anyone's leash, and that's how he liked it. But then he realized his obstinacy and her knowledge of him would make the perfect foil for forcing the issue. Sam would know he'd never agree to being tracked, even if it was supposedly for his own safety. She'd also realize he'd figured out who she was. He'd already told Evan and Simon he wanted to do a story on her and Carey. What if he made that a condition for testing the chip? Though NBS had okayed it at the practical level, each individual on the team had to agree to being tracked, considering the massive potential for violation of their civil liberties without their consent. Whether they were in Brazil or not, they were all American citizens. Maybe if Sam agreed to let him interview her for a story, he'd agree to being Jaime Roman's guinea pig.

Simon Michaelson strode into the bar. "They're ten to fifteen minutes out. He's coming from a building on Avenida Almirante Barroso," he told them, clearly agitated. "Fuck, I don't like it."

Evan watched him quizzically. "What's he doing there? That's right in the heart of where the protestors are congregating."

Simon dragged a frustrated hand over his hair. "He was in meetings over at the Brasil Telecom office there. Bollocks, had I known he was coming from there, I would have taken over the convoy."

Evan stood. "Wes, you've got two cameramen out there videoing background footage, right? Kiefer and Smith? Let's call them and see what they're seeing."

Wes nodded, tossing a few Brazilian *reals* onto the bar. Tensions had been high since last night, and the city felt electric with the release of pent-up emotion and fission of the political divide. But the turmoil had already begun to morph into random acts of violence with small lootings and other petty crimes.

"Last time Smith and Kiefer checked in, they thought the protestors had surged to over fifty thousand people," Wes told them as they headed to the large conference room they'd reserved for the production crew and equipment.

The editor, Vicki, and some of the crew were huddled near a make-shift station reviewing last night's footage and discussing the other interviews they had lined up for later in the afternoon.

"Anybody heard from Kiefer or Smith yet?" Wes asked, sidling up to the editor.

"Yeah, just checked in. Said armored police and military just rolled in," Vicki told him. "We were getting ready to come and get you. I say we scrap the interviews and go straight to the action. Feels like all hell's going to break loose if they're bringing in the military."

"Bloody hell," Simon muttered, pulling out his phone.

Evan gestured to Wes for an aside. "Look, I know you want to go out, but give Simon and me a minute to get a bead on the situation. Okay?"

Wes nodded, but he already knew what the situation would likely be. He'd seen this play out before in other countries, under other regimes. If the government wasn't able to tamp down on the dissent by nightfall, all hell would break loose. Evan had to know it would be virtually impossible to keep Wes, Vicki, and the crew cooped up in the hotel away from the action. Even now, Wes could just discern the sound of distant chanting over the usual sounds of the city.

Simon motioned to Evan. They engaged in a close conversation Wes couldn't hear. He moved toward them, fiddling with his camera. Simon caught the approach and immediately lowered his voice before Evan nodded and Simon stepped away, leaving the conference room.

"What's going on?" Wes asked, perplexed by the intense look replacing Evan's generally congenial demeanor.

"Protests have gotten violent in two sectors. People are smashing windows, setting fires, and vandalizing the Council Chamber." Evan paused, taking a breath. "Unfortunately, I'm worried about Jaime. The route his security team took him down has been overtaken by protesters trying to get to the sectors. He's trapped in the vehicle with a couple members of our team. They're trying to figure out how to get him out safely."

"Wait—is he in one of the sectors where it's heating up?" Wes asked.

"No, he wasn't near that section of Pista Central. It's not violent yet, but there are so many protesters overrunning the main street where the Brasil Telecom office is that we can't move him. We're sending Simon in."

"Why?"

"He's a specialist. He can get in and out of places faster," Evan explained.

Wes grabbed his camera bag and a small HD recorder, heading for the doors.

"Where the hell are you going?" Evan's hand landed on his shoulder.

"One of the world's best-known developers is trapped in an internationally-covered protest. If you think I'm not filming that, you're outta your mind," Wes answered, over his shoulder. "You're already uncomfortable that you can't get in there and help. It's all over your body language. He's your friend, right?"

Evan grunted, stopping Wes again as he opened the doors. "I don't need you adding chili to the sauce, Wes."

"Evan, welcome to guarding a photojournalist. This is what we do," Wes replied over his shoulder. "I'm getting the shots of the riots with or without you. You'll want to tell your guys to watch out for the rest of the crew since Vicki looks like she's ready to dive right in there with Kiefer and Smith." Wes watched Evan glance back at her.

"You're a giant pain in my ass, you know that?" Evan muttered, tapping his earpiece and speaking to Talon in a low voice while he followed Wes out. "Talon, have Henri cover Vicki. She's heading out.

Get the other men on the crew. Wes and I are going after Simon and Jaime." He followed Wes out through the lobby and the front doors.

Wes, a lifelong runner, hit the cobblestone streets of Rua da Quitanda, hurling past beautiful colonial buildings and shop fronts, looking for the fastest way to cut across to Avenida Almirante Barroso, where Jaime's car was trapped. The streets were clogged with people shouting, waving political flags, chanting slogans. Evan kept pace with him easily, eyes watchful.

"How's Simon getting to them?" Wes shouted.

Evan tapped his earpiece. "Chariot, position?"

"Who's Chariot?" Wes asked as they ran past a group of students in white and blue uniforms, supporting their professors and decrying the government. They didn't blink at the two gringos pushing past them.

"Simon. He's got a Ducati," Evan answered.

"Where the fuck did he get that?" Wes asked, pushing past more protesters.

"May have borrowed it from the hotel parking lot. We're going left."

Wes swung into an alley as Evan took the lead.

"He's a couple minutes away. If we keep running at this pace, we're probably five minutes away from Jaime's position," Evan shouted over his shoulder.

They broke onto Avenida Almirante Barroso like they were shooting out of water. A human barricade of students, teachers, and trade unionists stood shoulder to shoulder on the roads in a cacophony of shouting, waving, and chanting. Wes had no idea how Simon was navigating through it on a motorcycle. He could barely see more than two feet in front of him, caught among the bodies, being dragged along the current. He felt Evan yank him back toward the edges.

"If you're hell bound and determined to do this, then at least stay close," Evan told him, his eyes deadly serious. Gone was the laidback good ole boy. Wes was looking into the eyes of an operative. He gave Evan a brief nod, holding up his camera and taking shots as he wove through the sidelines and stragglers behind Evan.

"We need a better vantage point," Evan shouted as they struggled past people. He glanced around quickly before jerking his head toward an apartment in a building with a couple of open, latticed balconies. Evan slammed up the stairs of the building, Wes hot on his heels. Evan rounded the bannister and flew to one of the apartment doors. He began pounding on the door, speaking in rapid Portuguese.

The door opened a sliver, a scared boy behind it. Evan crouched, speaking softly to him, holding out money. The boy opened the door, allowing them in. Wes smiled at him. Evan said something gently to the boy, and the boy led them toward the balconies, clutching the cash. Wes leaned out. Visibility was good in both directions. He immediately began filming the scene with the handheld.

"There they are," Evan told Wes, pointing down the road.

They could see the SUV. People were rocking it violently as they pushed through the road, shouting. Wes wondered if they were deliberately trying to turn it over or if there were just too many people for the space. Perhaps it was a bit of both. He could see Simon's massive body pushing through the chaos toward the car. He stepped off the bike, but he didn't open the door, glancing around as if in some kind of anticipation.

"What the fuck is he waiting for?" Wes asked.

"A sharpshooter to get into place. We need coverage just in case shit gets crazy."

Wes watched the crowds chanting and flooding the streets. "I don't know, man, it looks pretty fucking crazy already."

"Uptown One, are you in place?" Evan asked into his earpiece, listening. "Alright, one sharpshooter's in place. That's better than none," Evan told him, his eyes serious. He touched his earpiece again. "Vicki's out with two other cameramen, filming three blocks away. Henri's with her."

Wes nodded, a little relieved. "I know she can handle herself, but fuck, man, I'm glad you guys have our backs."

Evan glanced over at him, his eyes amused. "Aren't you supposed to be some war-hardened photographer like Robert Capa?"

Wes rolled his eyes, looking back through the camera lens as he zoomed in on Jaime's car. He caught Simon wedging the bike perpendicular to the back door of the SUV so they could open the door. A man dressed similarly to Simon and Evan stepped out, ushering another taller, lankier dark-haired guy out behind him.

"Is that Jaime?" Wes asked.

"Yeah," Evan confirmed.

Simon hustled Jaime toward the bike, shoving a helmet in his hands. As soon as they mounted the bike, Simon gunned it and took advantage of the people around them who were startled by the noise to maneuver down the street on the sidewalk.

A sudden commotion distracted Wes as several masked people dressed in black rounded the corner about a block down, closely followed by a phalanx of armed police. Simon stopped the bike as the police managed to completely blockade the road within a matter of seconds amid shouts and hysterical screaming from the peaceful demonstrators. Simon just managed to wheel the bike back around toward the opposite end of the street. He was moving remarkably quickly considering the size of the crowd he was maneuvering around when one of the demonstrators tossed a Molotov toward the police brigade. A shot was fired in return. Wes felt the tumult burst from the crowds in a ripple of violence as all hell broke loose. He filmed two tear gas cylinders thrown up into the air, raining down fumes on the bedlam choking that section of the Avenida. People went berserk, screams filling the air as people tried to scatter, pushing and clambering over each other.

"Uptown One, do you have a visual on the Chariot?" Evan shouted over the mayhem, scrambling to the farthest end of the balcony, trying to see Simon and Jaime through the mayhem.

Wes zoomed the lens, scanning left then right and back again but the smoke from the tear gas was too thick. There was a sudden staccato burst of gunfire as the crowd shrieked and attempted to get down the streets away from the police. Simon emerged from the crowd, riding low and tight to the bike, one hand holding the handle, his second scrambling to grip Jaime's forearm as he slumped forward onto Simon's back, his helmet lolling as Simon struggled to keep the bike balanced and hold onto Jaime simultaneously.

"Shit! *Fucking shit*," Evan muttered, spinning around and shouting something to the boy in Portuguese as he ran for the door. "Wes, keep your ass here. DO NOT MOVE!" he commanded over his shoulder as he slammed out the front door.

Wes saw the boy running into the bathroom. He turned to look over the balcony again, searching for Simon and Jaime through the zoom. When he finally caught sight of them amid the masses, Simon had abandoned the bike. He'd slung Jaime's inert body over his shoulder as he continued down the street with the crowd. Wes caught sight of Evan fighting the deluge toward them, ducking and rushing as several masked demonstrators tossed Molotovs at the advancing police barricade. The tear gas became so dense, it made Wes's eyes water and his throat burn. He pulled a bandanna from his pocket, wrapping it around his nose and mouth as he squinted around the apartment, looking for the boy. He was relieved to see the boy hadn't left the bathroom. Wes swung around, gripping his camera, trying to see through the lens with tearing eyes. He finally caught sight of Evan blocking like a lineman while Simon followed, carrying Jaime over his shoulders as people shoved and poured around them.

Wes backed off the balcony, rushing to close the shutter doors against the fumes. He ran toward the back of the apartment, looking for a bedroom. He ripped a blanket off the bed, dragging it out to the kitchen. Wes knocked everything off the kitchen table, covering it with the blanket, shouting for the boy to come out in broken Portuguese. He grabbed paper towels off the kitchen counter. The boy peeked out, holding what looked to be a makeshift medical kit. Wes smiled encouragingly at him, gesturing him to bring it over. He had gauze, cotton balls, SpongeBob Band-Aids, antiseptic, and tampons. Wes fought off near hysterical laughter just as Evan burst through the door.

"Jaime's been shot," Evan told Wes breathlessly. "I need you to get up to the roof of this place. See if there's enough space for a chopper to land. *GO!*"

Simon moved into the doorway more slowly, careful not to jar Jaime's unconscious body against the door jamb while Evan spoke to the boy, asking for other supplies as Simon laid Jaime down carefully on the blanketed table. Wes spared Jaime a glance. His skin was blanched and damp with perspiration. Blood seeped from his lower left shoulder through the jacket he'd been wearing.

"Wes," Evan barked as Simon laid Jaime onto the table. "*GO*, god-dammit! I need to know if I can get a bird here. Call me from up there."

Wes headed into the hallway, looking for a staircase. Given the age of the building and the lack of an elevator, he doubted it was more than a mid-rise. He leapt up the stairs, two at a time, grabbing the metal banister as he swung around up another flight. When he made it to the top, he glanced up and down the halls, only seeing apartment doors.

"Christ Almighty, *come on!*" Wes panted, running down one hall, then another. He slammed into a window at the end of the hall toward the back of the building, trying to see outside the dingy window. He caught sight of an old fire escape just outside. "Fuck!" He yanked futilely at the window handle. The frame must have been painted shut years ago. He'd have to break it open.

Wes stepped back and leveled a side kick at the lower part of the window. He felt the give, but it didn't shatter. He stepped back again and heaved, sending as much power into his leg as he could, focusing on weakest part of the glass and frame. The window exploded open, shards of glass falling out and around. He withdrew his foot carefully, whipping off his jacket to cover his arm as he knocked the rest of the glass out.

Wes levered himself up and out, clasping the metal brackets of the little fire escape. He climbed quickly, hustling over the railing. The roof was probably large enough for a helicopter to land, but it looked suspiciously soft in the afternoon heat. He could hear the shouts and commotion of the crowd clearly from up here. Wes ran across the roof, confirming his suspicion that it'd be too weak to hold up enough for a landing. He was amazed he'd made it across without falling through the softening tar in the afternoon heat. He palmed his phone.

"Tell me we can do this," Evan answered, still breathless. "It's bad. The bullet's too deep. We think it got his lung. We need to get him to a hospital."

"We have two logistical issues," Wes answered quickly. "The fire escape is a partially enclosed ladder outside the back hallway window. Two men can't fit in the enclosure. The roof is plenty big but it's weak. I could feel parts sinking while I ran across it." He glanced around. "There's a modern office building two buildings to the west. Can you get a bird to land there?"

"It'll have to work. Get back down here," Evan told him.

"On it," Wes replied, already hustling back toward the railing.

When he made it back to the apartment, the blanket was already covered in blood. Jaime's head lay to the side, his bloody jacket and shirt torn off and on the floor. Evan had packed the wound with tobacco from one of Simon's cigarettes and was pushing a tampon into the bullet hole to staunch the bleeding. The little boy was patting Jaime's forehead with a damp towel while Wes murmured calmly to him in Portuguese. Simon stood at the balcony, talking rapidly into his earpiece.

"Help me lift him," Evan told him. Wes stood at Jaime's shoulders at the end of the table, gently picking him up. Evan smeared what looked like Vaseline on a swath of gauze he applied to the wound. He began wrapping the torn strips of a sheet around his shoulder, neck and chest. Jaime was gray, his skin clammy, his dark hair wet with sweat.

"We both need to carry him out," Evan told him as he bundled the blanket back around Jaime, trying to normalize his dropping body temperature. "Simon's clearing the path, okay? I'll have his injured side. You need to hold onto his other shoulder and leg like this." Evan showed Wes what to do.

"The boy?" Wes asked. The little boy was standing in the living room, watching everything with fearful eyes.

"He's a latchkey kid. His mom works at one of the offices downtown. The safest thing for him is to stay locked up here. I gave him money to give his mom for the mess," Evan explained.

"Simon, grab my camera," Wes said as he and Evan lifted Jaime. The walk down the stairwell and out of the building toward the SUV was long and arduous. Wes had never carried dead weight before, and he certainly hadn't done it while trying to avoid people running for their lives. The mass exodus of protesters had fully given way to a clash between police and a mixture of people from masked anarchists to furious unionists, hurling rocks and bottles, setting things on fire. Thankfully, some of the tear gas had dispersed, making it slightly easier

COMPLICATED CREATURES   351

to breathe. Though the crowd had lessened slightly as people ran off or sought shelter, the once charming Avenida Almirante Barroso looked like a scene out of Kandahar. Simon led the charge, blatantly pushing people out of the way as he pressed toward the office building.

Two security guards stood inside the revolving doors, watching the commotion. Simon shouted for them to open the doors they guarded. The guards shook their heads vehemently, gesturing for him to step back. Simon pointed toward Jaime, shouting in Portuguese. The guards looked at each other, unsure of what to do. A worried-looking office worker rushed them from behind, speaking urgently to the guards while gesturing toward Jaime. Another worker followed and another, clearly trying to convince the guard to open the doors. Simon continued to shout through the glass, gesturing toward Jaime.

Wes felt his arms growing heavy from holding Jaime up, but the adrenaline was still surging through his veins. Some combination of the people inside pleading with the guards, Simon's constant shouting or Jaime's bleeding and prone body must have snapped the guards out of their wariness. One leaned down, unlocking the door. Simon pushed in, speaking to the guards in halting Portuguese, clearly asking about the elevators and access to the roof and a helipad. One of the workers pleading their case to the guards pushed toward Jaime, pulling the blanket down. She asked them questions, checking his pulse. Evan answered. Wes looked between the two, trying to figure it out.

"She's a trained nurse," Evan explained. "Simon, do they have a helipad?"

"Yeah, mate. We gotta get our fuckin' asses up there," Simon responded grimly, following one of the guards toward the elevator banks as the second guard locked the door, barring workers trying to leave and other people attempting to get in from outside with an assault rifle. Simon spoke into his earpiece rapidly, exacting their location to someone on the other end. "Talon's got the chopper on its way," he informed them as they followed the guard into the elevator.

The guard eyed them warily, clutching his AK-47 like he might have to use it. The Brazilian nurse called to her colleagues. One ran forward with a large medical kit. She fumbled in it, pulling out some sort of pack.

"What's that?" Wes breathed, watching her tear it open, wrapping and pressing it against Jaime's wound.

"An Olaes bandage," Evan explained. "It's like a tourniquet. It seals the wound temporarily. We use it in the field."

"Rush." Wes heard a weak voice in the tense silence. The hoarse whisper had come from Jaime. Wes glanced down. Jaime was staring blearily up at Evan from his prone position.

"I'm here, buddy. We got you," Evan assured told him.

"Rush. Maddie… *Maddie…*" Jaime babbled incoherently, his eyes glazed.

"She's okay," Evan assured him. "She's okay," he said again and again, trying to reassure him.

The elevator doors slid open. The guard went out first, gesturing toward a large metal door indicating roof access. He unlocked it and Simon ran up, glancing around, looking for the chopper as he spoke into the earpiece again.

The noise from the riots on the street were muted at this height but still discernible. The guard left them to go back downstairs, slamming the door behind him.

"Less than three mikes out," Simon shouted at Evan.

"Maddie," Jaime whispered brokenly before passing out, his head dropping to the side.

"Who's Maddie?" Wes asked Evan as they waited for the unmistakable sounds of helicopter blades slicing through the thick, humid air.

Evan looked up at the sky, his eyes apprehensive. "Maddie's his daughter."

CHAPTER 24

November—Tuesday afternoon

An airfield near the Wyatt Ranch, Texas

SAMANTHA

THE PHONE HAD started going off every ten minutes two hours ago with status reports about what was going down in Rio. Carey had already been in the air, on his way to client meetings in Atlanta when he'd gotten word. They'd fueled up for the trip to South America at Hartsfield-Jackson. Marvin had the Wyatt Petroleum jet sent up from Houston to come get her in record time. She'd showered and changed from her ranch wear, giving her Aunt and Uncle hasty hugs and kisses, promising an imminent return before jumping into the Jeep and gunning for the airstrip.

Sam had waited to call Jack until she knew more, but the truth was that she was dreading the call. He thought she'd been in Houston on a business trip when she'd been revisiting old wounds—and spending time licking those wounds—back home these past few days. Their conversations had been brief, her exhaustion real from working all day on the ranch, her body pleasantly sore from the labor. Jack may have been busy with work and Maddie, but he knew something was off. He was too observant and intuitive not to sense it, but he was also patient enough not to push her.

And now. *Jesus Christ.* Now she had to tell him that his brother was in critical condition in Rio de Janeiro and that she'd been unable to prevent it, though she'd been the one to suggest he have protection in the first place. Logically, Sam knew her men had done everything right.

Hell, Rush and Simon had jumped in as well, dragging Wes into the madness, though she suspected they wouldn't have been able to shake Wes's involvement had they tried. If anyone was going to be front and center of a riot, it'd be Wes. It was Jaime who should never have been caught in the crossfire.

Sam slammed her hand on the steering wheel. The Brasil Telecom building had simply been too damn close to the protests. What had started as a ten-thousand-person, one-day peaceful demonstration had erupted into national mayhem, with over one hundred thousand people taking to the streets over several days, sparking similar debacles in Sao Paulo.

They should have requested a change of meeting locations. They should have kept Jaime in the office for longer. They should have choppered him out of the meeting instead of taking a vehicle.

Countless scenarios and diversions filled her mind while she sped toward the airstrip near the ranch, but she knew it was fruitless and counterproductive. They'd been trapped in a sudden tumult that only anarchists could cook up. It'd been six of her men, including Rush and Simon, against thousands. They'd gotten Jaime to the hospital, but the bullet had entered his back and played pinball with his lung, collapsing it. He was in surgery, but it was too soon to tell. She felt angry, impotent, and scared, the trifecta of the worst possible fucked-up emotions she could be experiencing in a time like this.

Sam pulled up to the airfield. The plane hadn't landed yet, but she knew the ETA had it coming down within the next five minutes. She glanced around, watching the golden fields surrounding the small strip swaying gently in the wind, their wheat color faded against the setting sun. Sam closed her eyes, breathing in the post-storm scent of damp grass and quenched earth, trying to draw peace from her memories of this place. Her heart clenched—for Jaime, Jack, Maddie, their parents...

Distantly, Sam heard the engines of the jet. She focused on her breathing, allowing the calm to sharpen her hearing, her sense of smell, the tensile feel of the steering wheel. She felt the jet touch down on the field, heard the flaps lower to slow it down on the aging air strip. Opening her eyes, Sam re-centered and focused, stepping out of the

Jeep and tucking the keys under the mat, knowing Marvin would have someone figure out the rest. She grabbed her duffel, walking to the plane as the doors opened.

Once she was situated on the plane, she reached for her phone.

"*Tesoro*, I was just thinking about you—" Jack started. She could hear Maddie in the background.

"Where are you?" she asked quickly, cutting him off.

"I'm picking Maddie up from dance class. Why?" he asked, sounding alert.

"I need you to call me when you're in a private place. I need to talk to you about something."

"Samantha—" he started. His breath hitched. "What's going on? Where are you?"

"I'm on a plane in Texas."

"Are you coming home?" he asked simply, as if all she needed to do was return to him.

"Jack, I need to talk to you, but I don't want it to be with Maddie present. Can you call me back when you've got some privacy?" she asked, keeping her voice calm and level.

"Give me thirty minutes."

They were the longest thirty minutes she'd experienced in a long time. She didn't have any updates on Jaime's condition when Jack returned her call.

"Tell me," was the first thing out of his mouth. "Whatever it is, we'll figure it out. Just talk to me."

"Jaime's been shot."

Jack sucked in a sharp breath. She could hear rustling, as if he'd sat down right where he'd been standing.

"He's in surgery. I don't know what the status is, but he was in critical condition when my team choppered him to the hospital," she continued, pausing to see if Jack would respond. When he said nothing, she continued. "There have been demonstrations going on in Rio. He got caught in one on his way out of his meetings with Brasil Telecom. They turned violent as we were trying to get him to safety. He caught a stray bullet in his left shoulder that punctured his lung. There's been a lot of internal bleeding and his lung collapsed. I'm on a jet to Brazil now."

"I'm catching the first flight out or chartering a plane," Jack responded, finding his voice.

"No. Jack, no," Sam replied, adamant. "You need to take care of Maddie. Rush was with him, said he kept calling for his daughter. Jack, you *have* to take care of her. I'm already on the plane. Carey's about an hour ahead of me. We've got this. I promise you we'll do everything in our power to take care of this."

"Like you took care of him? Like you took care of *protecting* him?" Jack erupted, his voice rising. "May I remind you that it was your idea to send a security team with him? He called me last night. Told me it was your idea to keep him separated from the rest of the group because you didn't like one of the men on the trip," he accused. "What's happened to them? Where are they?"

Sam closed her eyes, touching her temple. "I don't know, Jack. They weren't our responsibility."

"*Responsibility?*" Jack asked, incensed. "My little brother was your responsibility, and look at what's happened. *Motherfucking hell*, Samantha, I'm coming down there, and you're not going to stop me."

"Jack, *please*—"

"Maddie has only one parent left in this world. I'll be damned if she loses him too," he said. "Which hospital is he at?"

Sam gave him the information, struggling to keep her voice level and calm, seeming to only agitate him further.

"I'll call you back with my flight details. Mitch will take care of Maddie tonight until my parents can come back here," he informed her acidly.

"Jack, please don't do this. Take a minute to calm down—think rationally. You won't help Jaime by being in Brazil. You've never even been to Rio. You don't speak the language or have connections. Please trust me to handle this. Carey and I are on it. I swear to you. *Please?*" she asked, her tone increasingly urgent.

He said nothing for a moment before he sneered, "Trust you? Samantha, I don't even *know* you. You've been lying to me for the past few days. I don't even know if you're in Texas right now. You think I didn't pick up on that?" he responded, shifting from white-hot furious to icy in seconds. "I've been trusting blindly, hoping you'd come around— hoping you'd open up to me. And this happens, and I realize I'm holding onto smoke. You're smoke and mirrors, Samantha. And now my brother could die on your watch, and you want me to sit still and do nothing but have faith in someone who can't—" Jack took a shaky breath. "*Won't* be honest with me. *Ever.*" She heard Jack slam his hand down in frustration.

"Jack," Samantha replied levelly. "You can be angry with me as a lover, but this is my job. I am telling you everything I know. But you have to understand, nothing is without risk. No one could have predicted how quickly the violence would erupt, nor where it would happen. Nor could they know that Jaime would literally be caught in the crossfire while we were trying to get him to safety. However you feel about me personally, you and I both know that professionally, my team is the top of the field. And I'm telling you we have this. Jaime is in the best hospital. He has a team of surgeons working on him. Let me at least get there first and find out what's going on before you charge down. Please stay with Maddie. At least for tonight," she urged, rubbing a hand to her temple, trying to keep her voice level.

Jack was silent for long, interminable moments. Sam waited him out.

"My family is everything to me," he finally said.

"I know that, Jack," she answered softly. "I know they mean more to you than anything, and that you'd do anything for them. That's why I suggested he have security in the first place. I'm sorry this happened, but I will do everything in my power to get him back to you. I promise you this. I *promise* you."

"When do you land?"

She gave him an estimation, telling him she'd call him intermittently throughout the flight with any salient updates. As she got ready to hang up, she heard him say something. She held the phone back up to her ear.

"Jack? Are you there?" she asked. "I missed what you said."

She heard him release a pent up breath.

"Tell me where you've been," he asked, his voice suddenly quiet. "I need to believe you right now, and I need to have faith you're leveling with me. Just tell me where you've been."

Sam sighed. "I went home. I was at my father's ranch in Texas."

"Why?"

She closed her eyes, leaning her head back. "I've been..." *God, why was this so hard to admit?* "I'd been feeling...off. I needed to re-center. I needed to come back home."

"Why? Why have you been feeling off?" Jack asked, his voice low.

Sam rubbed her temple. "Look, Jack. I don't think it's a good time—"

"Just tell me, Samantha."

"A few reasons," she sighed. "I've just had a lot of triggers hit recently—"

"By me?"

"Including you," Sam amended quietly. "I've been operating a certain way for a long time. It's not right or wrong, Jack. It—it just is. Our relationship, it's brought some things up. Maybe because you're thawing me out, I don't know, but us, combined with the holidays, seeing you together with your family and a couple other things happening—it brought a lot home. And I've been having memories. Things I hadn't thought about in years. It's been—" she took a deep breath. "It's been a painful reawakening. I needed to get grounded." Sam paused, closing her eyes. "I'm sorry, Jack. I'm sorry I couldn't tell you."

"You could have told me," he corrected her. "You just chose not to."

She didn't bother to argue, knowing he needed to vent. When he didn't say anything else for long, tense moments, Sam wondered if he was still there or she'd been talking to dead air. Rather than being agitated by that thought, she felt relieved. If she'd lost him, maybe it was be for the best—

"Tell me why you're sorry."

Sam blinked her eyes open. They were over the Gulf now. She could see the lights of oil platforms and nearby ships dotting the otherwise black surface of the water.

"I'm sorry I couldn't—" she stopped. "That I didn't tell you," she amended. "I'm not used to this. It's new to me, this kind of intimacy, the feelings…associated. I thought I'd just go home for a few days, handle things, then reemerge, and it'd be fine. I'd have it sorted and no one would be the wiser," she admitted quietly. "I wasn't trying to hurt you, Jack."

"Define sorted?" he asked, ignoring her last statement. She tried to imagine his face, but she couldn't tell his emotion from his voice.

"I was trying to figure out how to be all right again."

"Samantha—" Jack's voice gentled. "Tell me why you're not all right. Tell what you need."

"Time," she breathed. "Jack, I just needed some time, but now I need to remain focused on Jaime right now. Let me do that for you and your family. Work is grounding. You know this about me. Please let me just bring him home to you."

Jack fell silent once again. She knew immediately he wouldn't agree to anything when it came to Jaime. "Call me as soon as you get another update."

"I will, Jack. I promise." Sam paused, listening for his breath on the line, but he had already hung up. "I love you, too," she whispered. "I'm sorry I couldn't say it before. But Jack, I love you too…"

She spoke to dead air, the sun setting on the distant horizon beneath the bank of clouds.

November—Tuesday night
Hospital Copa D'Or in Rio de Janeiro, Brazil

WESLEY

"*SAMMY*," WES BREATHED, halting as he saw her. He spilt the coffee he was carrying, he'd stopped so fast. Everything stilled for an indeterminate amount of time as he stared. He'd know her anywhere—the line of her straight nose, the dark wing of her brow, that supple skin over the high slice of her cheekbone. All his knowledge of her slid from the safe shelf of his memories to the forefront of his mind. Memories flooded him as he stared at her profile, his heart squeezing. Sam stood a few yards away, conferring with one of the surgeons, unaware of him. Evan pulled up beside him, holding two coffees.

It was late. Long after visiting hours. They'd come back to the hospital once they'd heard Jaime made it out of surgery. Wes knew Evan was friends with Jaime and that he worried about him, and Wes knew he would have lain awake replaying the day over and over again anyway. He'd figured they might as well remain close, see what news they could find out if they were going to be sleepless regardless.

Evan followed Wes's line of sight. "That's my boss, Sam Wyatt," Evan told him. "She just got here. Come on. I'll introduce you."

Wes nodded mutely, watching Evan walk toward her, handing her the coffee as he came to stand beside her. Sam accepted the cup without looking up, murmuring a thank you as she faced the surgeon. They were speaking in fluid Portuguese. Wes had no idea she spoke the language.

Sam looked up suddenly, sensing she was being watched, her pitch dark eyes clashing with his. He saw her blink once, drawing back slightly, like she was uncertain of what she was seeing. Then the full weight of her gaze honed in on him. Wes faced her, feeling dazed and pinned by her narrowed eyes. Something palpable circled between them. She turned away to finish speaking with the surgeon, shaking his hand. Wes moved forward, unable to look away from her.

"God, Sammy, you look…" he began.

"Wes," she interrupted. "How are you?"

Evan's gaze bounced between them, his brows knitting. "You know each other?" he asked surprised, looking back and forth between them.

Sam favored Wes with a small, professional smile, her eyes cool. He immediately hated that expression, feeling himself bristling as she distanced herself without moving.

"In a manner of speaking." She replied to Evan's question causally. "We went to school together."

"We were also *together* for three years," Wes added, clasping her hand and attempting to pull her toward him. "Let's not forget about that," he murmured.

Sam stiffened her hand, using the tenseness in her forearm to prevent him from drawing her into him. Her casual laugh sounded hollow to him.

"Wes here was a real lady killer at A&M," she remarked, glancing at Evan with an insolent little smirk. "You look well, Wes, given the circumstances. Rush tells me you were integral to getting Jaime Roman to the hospital today." She took a sip of her coffee. "Thank you for that."

Wes felt his throat working, anger crawling up his neck as she continued to regard him coolly, her expression neutral, though her eyes flashed with—something. She shifted back slightly, putting Evan between them.

"I was happy to help," Wes replied when he really wanted to say, *"Why the hell are you acting like we were nothing to each other?"* He decided to make a little chink in that armor; he didn't care who was watching. "Not a day goes by that I haven't missed you, Sammy," he told her quietly, ignoring Evan's brows rising.

Samantha's eyes turned obsidian, her expression shifting from cool to hard in a fraction of a second.

"You want an update on Jaime?" she asked, stepping back again as she shot an aggrieved look toward a transfixed Evan.

Evan nodded mutely, apparently still floored by their interaction while Wes fumed.

"He's still touch-and-go," she began. "The surgeon said they handled the primary hemorrhaging, but they're worried about atelectasis—another minor lung collapse." She ran a frustrated hand through her hair. "Jaime has a postoperative fever, so they're keeping their eye on infection and septicemia. He'll be in the ICU for a while. We'll get another update in a couple of hours," Sam told him, glancing at her watch. "Take Wes and head back," she said without so much as looking at him. "We're gonna need all hands on deck with the news crew now that all hell's broken loose here with the demonstrations."

"Will you keep me and Talon in the loop?" Evan asked. "He kept calling for Maddie." He shook his head, stopping. "We just want to know he's alright."

"Of course," she murmured, patting his arm gently, her eyes softening. "You did good today, Rush. You saved his life," she told him quietly, their exchange marking a certain familiarity that surprised Wes. And made him blind with jealousy as he watched silently.

"What about you, boss? Is Jack flying in?" Evan asked, his tone concerned.

Sam shook her head. "Jack's got Maddie, so I'm trying to keep him in Chicago for now. Carey checked us into the hotel, but he should be around shortly. Just head back with Wes for now, okay? There's nothing more to do tonight," she said, giving Evan a reassuring smile before stepping back. She looked at Wes, professionalism shuttering her expression again. "Thank you again for your role today. We appreciate what you did," she told him, as if he'd done her a solid.

Wes wanted to grab her and shake her. Then kiss her. *Badly.*

"I'll stay," Wes responded obstinately, irritated with her order to leave, however politely packaged. "I'll be up anyway, working through footage on my laptop. I'd prefer to stay until we hear more." He glanced at Evan. "And I know he would too."

Sam regarded him briefly before turning back to Evan, effectively ignoring Wes. "I need to call Jack," she said simply before striding down the corridor.

Evan rounded on him as soon as she was out of earshot.

"You *dated* Sam?" Evan asked suddenly, his tone accusing.

"It was more than that," Wes replied, staring down the corridor. "We were together. I loved her." He'd imagined seeing her again countless times. Never in his wildest imaginings had he thought it would be in a hospital in Rio de Janeiro where she looked at him like a stranger. He willed her to come back down the corridor—to react to seeing him again after so many years with anything other than casual disregard, as if they'd never meant anything to each other. The warmth and open frankness so inherent in her was gone. She'd cooled, hardened into a beautiful and intricate piece of armor. She was another person now.

Evan stared at him, perplexed. "Then why the hell didn't you say anything?" he asked. "Why did you ask those questions about her like you didn't know her?"

"Because I lost sight of her when we were young," Wes admitted quietly. "And I wanted to know her again. I couldn't believe she'd come back into my life again after all these years."

"What the fuck did you do to her? She can barely stand you," Evan pointed out, crossing his arms with a guarded expression of disapproval.

Wes closed his eyes, rubbing his hand down his face. "That's between me and her, but I will tell you this," he opened his eyes again, looking at Evan. "Not a day's gone by that I haven't missed the hell out of her." He glanced down the hall again. "I used to wish I'd find my way back to her…and it's happened." He shook his head. "*Shit*, I almost can't believe it."

Evan appeared torn, shifting. "Look, man, I don't know what the hell happened between you two, but during the short time I've known you, you seem like a decent guy." He looked uncomfortable, but he forged on. "Wes, Sam's not available," he explained. "That's why this shit's so personal to her. Jaime's the brother of the man she's with now."

Wes blinked. "The guy she's calling?"

"Yeah."

Wes fell silent for a moment before looking up at Evan. "I don't care."

Now it was Evan's turn to blink. "What?"

"I said I don't care." Wes replied stubbornly. "That woman's the best thing that ever happened to me, and I don't believe in coincidence." Wes felt like everything was crystallizing. He looked at Evan again. "You know what longing is, Evan?"

Evan watched him for a moment before nodding mutely.

"I've spent more than a dozen years trying to fill a void that wasn't a void. It was a promise. I didn't understand it then, but I do now. I'm not walking away from her twice."

"A promise? You're not making any sense—"

Wes laughed, a short, mirthless bark of laughter. "I am. I absolutely am. I don't give a damn who this guy is. He's not me." He looked down the corridor again. "And she's not his. She's mine. No matter where we've been, no matter what's gone down, that's just the truth. Always has been—it's just clear to me now."

November—A few minutes later
Hospital Copa D'Or in Rio de Janeiro, Brazil

SAMANTHA

"GET IT TOGETHER. Get it together," Sam chanted, pressing a hot palm to her chest, trying slow the sharp beats of her heart as she slumped against the door jamb of the small room she'd shut herself in. Sam glanced around, taking in the small conference table, the soothing pastel walls and bland watercolors, the potted orchid, realizing what it was. This was the place people were told horrible things or given a piece of relief, delivered news or information they shouldn't receive publicly. This was the confessional that witnessed what medicine could and could not do—and what you had or didn't have to work with.

Sam had known that she'd see him again, but goddamn, *nothing* had prepared her for the full effect of Wesley Elliott or her reaction to laying eyes on him again. She felt like she'd gotten singed by that vivid amber gaze, the air between them crackling with latent tension. He looked…arrestingly good. He'd been a head-turner and a rascal when he was young, but now… Sam swallowed, her throat working against the dryness. His once boyishly good-looking features had seasoned into planes and angles so breathtaking her hand had nearly risen of its own accord to trace them. That riotous mess of golden curls she'd run her fingers through as a girl had darkened to a burnish. No, the pictures in his file hadn't done him justice—they couldn't. The distant memories of her once-lover and childhood flame had nothing on the intensely handsome man who stared at her like he'd been given some kind of reprieve.

Sam pressed hot palms to her eyes, groaning. Wes Elliott was the ex of every woman's nightmare—the one you never forgot, never forgave and for damn sure still ached over because everyone had their kryptonite, and that man had been hers since she set eyes on him as a girl. He reminded her with one look why she'd loved him so passionately and with such abandon. Wes had been it. *The Guy*. Her Guy. And long ago, Sam had naively believed they'd last a lifetime, before she'd learned the hard and inevitable truth that nothing lasted lifetimes, even if you thought you had the power and endurance to manufacture the outcome.

Sam's phone rang in her pocket, and she snapped upright, palming it and looking at the screen. *Jack*. She felt her face heat as if he'd just caught her out at something.

"Jack," she answered breathlessly. "I just finished speaking with one of the surgeons. Jaime's out of surgery."

"Tell me what's going on," Jack responded, his voice urgent.

She broke down what she'd found out, answering the questions he peppered her with. "He has a postoperative fever, so he's still in the ICU. I should get another update from the surgeon in a couple of hours," she explained.

"Have you seen him?" Jack asked.

"Not yet. The risk of infection is still too high. They said the soonest I could see him would be sometime tomorrow. How's Maddie?" she asked, her voice softening as she asked about Jaime's daughter.

"She's okay," Jack sighed. "We decided to keep her in the dark for now. Mom and Dad got here a couple hours ago."

"Will you stay with them?" she asked.

Jack remained silent.

"Are you coming here?" she asked instead.

"I don't know."

"Jack…" she breathed.

"*Don't*," Jack bit out. "Don't tell me not to come. He's my baby brother."

"I know. I had one too once. Heaven and Earth couldn't have kept me from him if something like this happened," she reminded him quietly.

"I'm angry," Jack admitted after a moment of tense silence. "And I'm scared for him, Samantha." His voice shook.

"You'd be a stone not to be," Sam assured him. "I know how much he means to you. He knows how much you love him."

Jack stayed silent on the line.

They listened to each other breathe.

"My dad wants to fly down, but the State Department is dead against it. We both think I should fly out instead," he told her after long moments.

"I understand," she answered. "Carey and I are here. I'll call you again with any updates. You tell me what you decide."

"All right," he responded, his voice distant and tired.

"When was the last time you slept, Jack?" she asked gently.

"More than a couple hours? Days. I don't know." Sam imagined him rubbing his brow, a habit of his when he was tired or irritated. "Maybe before you left," he admitted.

"Will you lay down? Please? I know you're wired, but you won't be in any kind of condition to make this trip if you don't try to get at least a couple hours tonight," she urged. "You need to be in operating capacity for your family. Please."

"Samantha, what the hell are we doing?" Jack asked suddenly. "Because you're acting like somebody who loves me, but you lie and avoid and shut me out. I don't know what the hell we're doing. I don't know what the hell to think." The harsh words came out in sudden whoosh, like the words were pressing up and out of him.

"Jack—" she started, her answer catching.

"I just want to be clear, Samantha," he continued. "Because nothing else is clear right now. Are you just acting this way because you feel guilty for lying to me and not being able to protect Jaime?"

Sam felt trapped, wedged between his anger and her conscience. But she didn't want to be forced into emotional declarations. She wouldn't be. Not by him. Not by anyone.

"I care about you, your brother, and your family. I wouldn't be here otherwise," she answered honestly.

"But besides your duty and your guilt, you're removed, aren't you?" he asked pointedly. "You've been distant since you left. Hell, maybe before—just when I thought we were getting somewhere—"

"Jack, you're overwrought and exhausted—" she refuted. "But now is not the time to mix those conversations. What you need to be one hundred percent clear on is that Jaime is my priority right now."

Jack laughed bitterly. "I knew you would do terrible damage. You even warned me—you're so kind," he choked, "...but I thought I wanted you badly enough for the both of us," he murmured, his voice fading.

"Jack, stop it," Sam snapped, her anger uncharacteristically rising to the top, out of her control. "I don't want to argue with you about our relationship over the phone in a hospital waiting room while your brother fights for his life." She closed her eyes, pinching the bridge of her nose. "If you want to come here, okay. If you can find it to trust me to handle this, I'll do it. Either way, please try to get some sleep. I'll have more information for you soon."

He said nothing.

She listened to his silence, imagining his jaw clenching. "Jack?"

"You're right," he said after long moments. "Call me when you hear more."

"You're my first call," she assured him.

He hung up.

Sam sat in the room for a minute, collecting her thoughts, trying to calm down and praying that Wes wasn't standing right outside, waiting for her. Her phone rang again in her hand. Relieved, she saw it was Carey. Sam raised the phone to her ear.

"*Christ*, Bear—where the hell have you been?"

"He's otherwise indisposed, I'm afraid," a man with an elegant, British accent responded.

Sam stiffened. "Who is this?"

"We haven't yet been introduced," the man responded casually. "My name is Lucien Lightner. I presume I'm speaking with Samantha Wyatt?"

"Why are you in possession of Carey Nelson's phone?" she asked instead.

"Oh, we ran into each other at the hotel. Had a nice chat. I've been looking forward to meeting you for some time, Ms. Wyatt. Even before you began trying to take what's mine."

Sam waited a measured beat while everything slowed. "What exactly are you referring to, Mr. Lightner?"

"Now, now, Ms. Wyatt. You aren't going to pretend you haven't poached several of my top operatives and key clients in the past few months, are you?" he replied silkily. "Did you think I wouldn't notice?"

"Can't take what you never really had, Mr. Lightner. Especially if they left you willingly," she answered lightly, her mind racing through all the permutations, trying to figure out where this conversation could go.

"We'll have to disagree on that point, Ms. Wyatt," he answered, his blithe tone hardening. "You came after things that belong to me, so I felt it was more than appropriate to reciprocate, given the circumstances…" Lightner had Carey. He'd either hurt him or kill him to get to her. Any negotiations would be limited at best.

Samantha hardened. "Be careful, Mr. Lightner. You may think you're exacting revenge, but you're walking the fine line of declaring war," she told him in a low voice.

"Oh, I'm not concerned," Lightner replied. "My benefit here is actually more peripheral. You declared war, as you put it, a long time ago."

Sam's fingers tightened on the phone. "Enlighten me."

"You killed someone you shouldn't have, my dear," Lightner purred. "Ibrahim Nazar has waited to meet you for a very long time."

Sam's eyes widened, her fingers tightening on the phone.

"You'll come to me, or Carrick Nelson will see his last sunrise shortly," Lightner informed her. "Wouldn't want that, would we? Didn't you two grow up together?"

"You harm him, and I'll spend the rest of my life dismantling you and everything you care about," she told him in a low voice.

"It may be a short life, Ms. Wyatt. In which case, you'll want to see what you can accomplish. I know how you enjoy a challenge," Lightner taunted. "Meet me at Santos Dumont Airport alone in one hour or you'll find pieces of your partner scattered along Copacabana."

EPILOGUE

The Whitney, Chicago

JACK SAT IN the darkness of his study, staring at the lights twinkling around Grant Park and up the gentle curve of Lake Shore Drive. He nursed a scotch. Maybe the third or fourth, a rare occurrence for him. He hadn't had anything to drink while he had Maddie. The first thing he'd done was make himself a stiff drink when his parents had picked her up to take her to their house in Oak Park. He could hear Mitch banging around in the kitchen, making something for them to eat. Maybe the drinks combined with his general exhaustion would help him find that elusive sleep for a few hours. He felt haggard and stiff with worry.

"You look like shit," Mitch had told him unceremoniously when he'd come over. "I'm making you something to eat and crashing here tonight."

Jack knew what that statement was code for. Mitch was worried he'd relapse. If there were ever a time, now would be it. He didn't have anything in the house besides liquor to put him to bed, but he didn't plan on drinking until he passed out. Jack knew he looked like hell. He'd held it together until his parents had shown up, worry lining his father's face and his mother's eyes red and swollen. Thank God Maddie had been too sleepy to notice as he'd transferred her to his mother's arms.

Jack rubbed his eyes, gritty from exhaustion, before setting the scotch down, the side of his hand touching the file he'd fished out of his safe impulsively before calling Sam. He fingered the edge of the file his father had given him. He was feeling a little reckless, incredibly helpless, and riding the crest of his growing anger.

In some distant, objective part of him, he knew she wasn't to blame for Jaime's situation. If anything, it could have been a lot worse. Jaime could have been caught up in the debacle with no protection at all. He'd watched the news. He saw the mayhem engulfing the streets of Rio. He also knew he could trust her to handle this, but *goddamn it all…*he was furious with her. Furious with her for lying, for keeping him in the dark, for not reciprocating his feelings, for making him feel insane and insecure—emotions that were so foreign to him that he wanted to beat the shit out of something in retaliation. If he had the wherewithal to go to the gym and throw down with Manny, he would have. He wanted to do something. Fight his way out of the uselessness and the ache and the fury. Jack wanted to do something permanent and damaging.

He was already hurting.

Why not set everything else on fire and just watch the blaze?

Jack tossed the drink back, flicking open the file.

The first few pages were general background. He read through details of her schooling, unsurprised by her grades, her choice of sports, the basic facts of her family—or lack thereof. Her military history started early. She was young when she joined NROTC. Only nineteen. A legacy. There were activities, program participation notes, evaluations, recommendations. It was vaguely insightful but unsurprising given what he knew about her already. She was twenty-one her first full-fledged year as a naval officer, based out of the Kennedy Irregular Warfare Center. Her performance reviews were outstanding.

Her medical and psychological evaluations read like Greek. He wished he hadn't opted out of that science, leaning toward engineering instead to satisfy his architectural requirements. He did understand the summary, though. She was described as independent, analytical, highly intelligent, and exceptionally determined when tasked with something she believed in. She valued factual knowledge, shunned incompetency, and strove to either create structure or uphold it. She had extremely high standards for others, but none more than herself. She was motivated by internal purpose rather than external factors. Jack snorted. He knew all of this. He read on.

She had significant trust issues stemming from fear of abandonment.

She was a deep introvert with the ability to perform as an extrovert in appropriate circumstances. An excellent linguist and good at establishing rapport when necessary while maintaining objectivity and a level of disengagement. She had strong control of her own emotional state, followed her own moral compass. She was recommended for Counter Intelligence and something called HUMINT. Jack squinted, looking for the acronym's definition.

Human Intelligence.

Of course.

Another set of papers looked like some kind of internal report. The file was red-stamped **Classified**. The initial coroner's report had proven inaccurate. Her father and brother were not killed by a drunk in driving accident. Trace amounts of barbiturates were in both of their systems, suggesting foul play. The drunk driver was a local townie alcoholic, but one witness stated she saw him climb into a cab leaving the bar, not driving his own vehicle. Designated a possible assassination attempt. No suspects detained, though several candidates proposed based on an offshore drilling gambit in the Gulf of Mexico Robert Wyatt had secured exclusive rights to just before his death. Jack scanned the short list of names. He looked up two of them on his phone. One was a major oil tycoon based in Houston, an old rival. Another was a Sharif with a prominent position within OPEC with disturbing ties to redacted individuals in Iraq, Iran, and Yemen. Investigations inconclusive. Based on what she'd told him about her family, she didn't know about this. This must have been what his father had meant...

Jack began to flip through the next cluster of papers in the folder, noting most were redacted U.S. Naval documents. Through the maze of black boxes, he glimpsed words like *hostile assets, detainment, advanced interrogation techniques, psychological exertion, physical impairment, pharmacologic-induced influencing techniques, long-term effects—*

Mitch knocked on his study door, poking his head in. "Dinner's on. Come eat and tell me what's going on with Jaime."

Jack must have looked shell-shocked.

Mitch pushed open the door, looking at the file Jack held. "What are you reading? You look sick."

Jack snapped the file shut, weaving up to his feet. "Nothing." He shook his head. "I just can't concentrate. You know I haven't slept—" He tried to craft an excuse as Mitch's eyes narrowed.

Jack set the file down, trying to appear casual. He strode to his safe, still open from his earlier foray for the file, just after he'd started drinking. He shoved the file in, swinging it shut, feeling oddly relieved when the telltale snick signaled the automatic lock. Jack turned back to face Mitch, who was still watching him, head crooked and his arms crossed. "You haven't kept much from me. What gives?"

Jack swallowed, shifting uncomfortably. Secrets. A file full of secrets, and he'd just started to peel back the lid of a Pandora's Box he knew he couldn't shut now if he wanted to. And he wasn't sure he wanted to.

But did he really want to know? And what would he do with the information? And Jaime—God, Jaime...

Jack closed his eyes. "I need to go to Brazil," he told Mitch. "I need you to help me get a jet booked to leave first thing in the morning."

ABOUT ALEXI LAWLESS.

It's simple, really. You see that woman sitting to the side at the executive meeting discussing company financials and strategies to increase profitability next quarter? The one who looks like she's struggling not to look bored? Yeah. That was me. And that was my life, day in, day out, for over a dozen years. A successful life, by many standards, and not an unhappy one, but not *the Dream* either. You see, there were two things I wanted for myself. Okay, three if you include champagne. *The Dream* was to write and to travel, sampling life and local cultures with no rush, no agenda. It was not an insurmountable dream by any means, but faced with actually *doing* something about it v. dreaming it might happen one day (like after 65)… well, that was daunting. But risks usually are. And I couldn't help but think it would be so much worse to look back and wonder, *"Why did I wait my whole life to do something I really wanted?"*

So I took the plunge. Quit the gig, packed up and hit the road. This book was written while traveling around islands in Asia, hiking over mountains in South America and driving across deserts and canyons in the United States. I thought I'd start with a simple love story, but it became so much more. An obsession. A fantasy—about complicated characters I hope you enjoyed reading as much as I enjoyed writing them. You've just finished reading the fruits of the new labor… the labor of love. The labor of *the Dream*.

Did you like Complicated Creatures?

If you'd like to share your thoughts and post a review on the website you purchased this book on, I, for one, would be incredibly grateful. You can also post reviews about the book at Goodreads.

Interested in Upcoming Releases?

If you want to be the first to know when New Releases come out, click here to get excerpts, playlists, cover reveals and launch dates: www.alexilawless.com